Prentiss Ingraham, W. F. Cody

Seventy Years on the Frontier
Alexander Major's Memoirs of a Lifetime on the Border

ISBN/EAN: 9783337140960

Printed in Europe, USA, Canada, Australia, Japan

Cover: Foto ©Raphael Reischuk / pixelio.de

More available books at **www.hansebooks.com**

Prentiss Ingraham, W. F. Cody

Seventy Years on the Frontier

Alexander Major's Memoirs of a Lifetime on the Border

SEVENTY YEARS ON THE FRONTIER.

Alexander Majors.

SEVENTY YEARS ON THE FRONTIER

ALEXANDER MAJORS' MEMOIRS

OF A

LIFETIME ON THE BORDER

WITH A PREFACE BY

"BUFFALO BILL" (GENERAL W. F. CODY)

EDITED BY

COLONEL PRENTISS INGRAHAM

CHICAGO AND NEW YORK

RAND, McNALLY & COMPANY, PUBLISHERS

1893

DEDICATION.

Rand, McNally & Co.
CHICAGO.
PRINTERS
AND
PUBLISHERS.

CONTENTS.

		PAGE.
Preface, by Buffalo Bill		9
Note to Reader		13

CHAPTER.

I.	Reminiscences of Youth	15
II.	Missouri in Its Wild and Uncultivated State	25
III.	A Silver Expedition	32
IV.	The Mormons	43
V.	The Mormons' Mecca	63
VI.	My First Venture	71
VII.	Faithful Friends	78
VIII.	Our War with Mexico	85
IX.	Doniphan's Expedition	90
X.	The Pioneer of Frontier Telegraphy	99
XI.	An Overland Outfit	102
XII.	Kit Carson	107
XIII.	Adventures of a Trapper	119
XIV.	Trapping	125
XV.	An Adventure with Indians	128
XVI.	Crossing the Plains	137
XVII.	"The Jayhawkers of 1849"	150
XVIII.	Mirages	157
XIX.	The First Stage into Denver	164
XX.	The Gold Fever	168
XXI.	The Overland Mail	173
XXII.	The Pony Express and Its Brave Riders	182

8 CONTENTS.

CHAPTER.		PAGE.
XXIII.	The Battle of the Buffaloes	194
XXIV.	The Black Bear	201
XXV.	The Beaver	215
XXVI.	A Boy's Trip Overland	221
XXVII.	The Denver of Early Days	228
XXVIII.	The Denver of To-day and Its Environs.	232
XXIX.	Buffalo Bill from Boyhood to Fame	243
XXX.	The Platte Valley	247
XXXI.	Kansas City before the War	253
XXXII.	The Graves of Pioneers	258
XXXIII.	Silver Mining	267
XXXIV.	Wild West Fruits	272
XXXV.	How English Capitalists Got a Foothold.	277
XXXVI.	Montana's Towns and Cities	285
XXXVII.	California's Great Trees	290
XXXVIII.	The Flowers of the Far West	294
XXXIX.	Colorado	304
XL.	The Surgeon Scout	317
	Conclusion	320

W. F. Cody
"Buffalo Bill."

PREFACE.

As there is no man living who is more thoroughly competent to write a book of the Wild West than my life-long friend and benefactor in my boyhood, Alexander Majors, there is no one to whose truthful words I would rather accept the honor of writing a preface.

An introduction to a book of Mountain and Plain by Mr. Majors certainly need hardly be written, unless it be to refer to the author in a way that his extreme modesty will not permit him to speak of himself, for he is not given to sounding his own praise, being a man of action rather than words, and yet whose life has its recollections of seventy years upon the frontier, dating to a period that tried men's souls to the fullest extent, and when daring deeds and thrilling adventures were of every-day occurrence. Remembrance of seventy years of life in the Far West and amid the Rocky Mountains!

What a world of thought this gives rise to, when we recall that a quarter of a century ago there was not a railroad west of the Missouri River, and every pound of freight, every emigrant, every letter, and every message had to be carried by wagon or on horseback, and at the risk of life and hardships untold.

The man who could in the face of all dangers and obstacles originate and carry to success a line of freighter wagons, a mail route from the Atlantic to the Pacific, and a Pony Express, flying at the utmost speed of a hare through the land, was no ordinary individual, as can be well understood.   And such a man Alexander Majors was.   He won success; and to-day, on the verge of four score years, lives over again in his book the thrilling scenes in his own life and in the lives of others.

Family reverses after the killing of my father in the Kansas War, caused me to start out, though a mere boy, in 1855 to seek to aid in the support of my mother and sisters, and it was to Mr. Alexander Majors that I applied for a situation.   He looked me over carefully in his kindly way, and after questioning me closely gave me the place of messenger boy, that was, one to ride with dispatches between the overland freighters—wagon trains going westward into the almost unknown wild dump of prairie and mountain.

That was my first meeting with Alexander Majors, and up to the present time our friendship has never had a break in it, and, I may add, never will through act of mine.

Having thus shown my claim to a thorough knowledge of my distinguished old friend, let me now state that his firm was known the country over as Majors, Russell & Woddell, but it was to Mr. Majors particularly that the heaviest duties of organizing and management fell, and he never shirked a duty or a danger, as I well remember.

Severe in discipline, he was yet never profane or harsh, and a Christian and temperance man through all; he governed his men kindly, and was wont to say that he would have no one under his control who would not promptly obey an order without it was emphasized with an oath. In fact, he had a contract with his men in which they pledged themselves not to use profanity, get drunk, gamble, or be cruel to animals under pain of dismissal, while good behavior was rewarded.   Every man, from wagon-boss and teamster down to rustler and messenger-boy, seemed anxious to gain the good will of Alexander Majors and to hold it, and to-day he has fewer foes than any one I know, in spite of his position as chief of what were certainly a wild and desperate lot of men, where the revolver settled all difficulties.

It was Mr. Majors' firm that originated and put in the Pony Express across the plains and made it the grand success it proved to be.

It was his firm that so long and successfully carried on the business of overland freighting in the face of every obstacle, and also the Overland Stage Drive between the Missouri River and Pacific Ocean, and in his long life on the border he has become known to all classes and conditions of men, so that in writing now his memoirs, no man knows better whereof he speaks than he does.

In each instance where he has written to his old-time comrades for data, he has taken only that which he knew could be verified, and has thrown out material sufficient to double his book in size, where he felt the slightest doubt that it could not be relied upon to the fullest extent.

His work, therefore, is a history of the Wild West, its pages authentic, and though many of its scenes are romantic and thrilling, it is what has hitherto been an unwritten story of facts, figures, and reality; and now, that in his old age he finds his occupation gone, I feel and hope that his memoirs will find a ready sale.

W. F. CODY,
"Buffalo Bill."

TO THE READER.

In preparing the material of my book, I desire here to give justice where justice is due, and express myself as under obligations for valuable data and letters, which I fully appreciate; and publicly thank for their kindness in this direction those whose names follow:

Col. W. F. Cody ("Buffalo Bill") of Nebraska.
Col. John B. Colton, Kansas City, Mo.
Mr. V. DeVinny, Denver, Colo.
Mr. E. L. Gallatin, Denver, Colo.
Judge Simonds, Denver, Colo.
Mr. John T. Rennick, Oak Grove, Mo.
Mr. Geo. W. Bryant, Kansas City, Mo.
Mr. George E. Simpson, Kansas City, Mo.
Mr. John Martin, Denver, Colo.
Mr. David Street, Denver, Colo.
Mrs. Nellie Carlisle, Berkeley, Cal.
Mr. A. Carlisle, Berkeley, Cal.
Mr. Green Majors, San Francisco, Cal.
Mr. Ergo Alex. Majors, Alameda, Cal.
Mr. Seth E. Ward, Westport, Mo.
Robert Ford, Great Falls, Mont.
Doctor Case, Kansas City, Mo.
Benj. C. Majors, May Bell P. O., Colo.
Prof. Robert Casey, Denver, Colo.
John Burroughs, Colorado.
Eugene Munn, Swift, Neb.
Rev. Dr. John R. Shannon, Denver, Colo.
Thos. D. Truett, Leadville, Colo.
Will C. Ferril.

Yours with respect,

ALEXANDER MAJORS.

Seventy Years on the Frontier.

CHAPTER I.

REMINISCENCES OF YOUTH.

My father, Benjamin Majors, was a farmer, born in the State of North Carolina in 1794, and brought when a boy by my grandfather, Alexander Majors, after whom I am named, to Kentucky about the year 1800. My grandfather was also a farmer, and one might say a manufacturer, for in those days nearly all the farmers in America were manufacturers, producing almost everything within their homes or with their own hands, tanning their own leather, making the shoes they wore, as well as clothing of all kinds.

My mother's maiden name was Laurania Kelly; her father, Beil Kelly, was a soldier in the Revolutionary War, and was wounded at the battle of Brandywine.

I was born in 1814, on the 4th day of October, near Franklin, Simpson County, Kentucky, being the eldest of the family, consisting of two boys and a girl. When I was about five years of age my father moved to Missouri, when that State was yet a Territory. I remember well many of the occurrences of the trip; one was that the horses ran away with the wagon in which my father, myself, and younger brothers were riding. My father threw us children out and jumped out himself, though crippled in one foot at the time. One wheel of the wagon was broken to pieces, which caused us a delay of two days.

After crossing the Ohio River, in going through the then Territory of Illinois, the settlements were from ten to twenty miles apart, the squatters living in log cabins, and along one stretch of the road the log cabin settlements were forty miles apart. When we arrived at the Okaw River, in the Territory of Illinois, we found a squatter in his little log cabin whose occupation was ferrying passengers across the river in a small flatboat which was propelled by a cable or large rope tied to a tree on each side of the river, it being a narrow but deep stream. The only thing attracting my special attention, as a boy, at that point was a pet bear chained to a stake just in front of the cabin where the family lived. He was constantly jumping over his chain, as is the habit of pet bears, especially when young.

From this place to St. Louis, a distance of about thirty-five miles, there was not a single settlement of any kind. When we arrived on the east bank of the Mississippi River, opposite the now city of St. Louis, we saw a little French village on the other side. The only means of crossing the river was a small flatboat, manned by three Frenchmen, one on each side about midway of the craft, each with an oar with which to propel the boat. The third one stood in the end with a steering oar, for the purpose of giving it the proper direction when the others propelled it. This ferry would carry four horses or a four-horse wagon with its load at one trip. These men were not engaged half their time in ferrying across the river all the emigrants, with their horses, cattle, sheep, and hogs, who were moving from the East to the West and crossing at St. Louis. Of course the current would carry the boat a considerable distance down the river in spite of the efforts of the boatmen to the contrary. However, when they reached the opposite bank the two who worked the side oars would lay down their oars, go to her bow, where a long rope was attached, take it up, put it over their shoulders, and let it uncoil until it gave them several rods in front of the boat. Then they would start off in a little foot-path made at the water's edge and pull the boat to the place prepared for taking on or unloading, as the case might be. There they loaded what they wanted to ferry to the other side, and the same process would be gone through with as before. Reaching the west bank of the river we found the village of St. Louis, with 4,000 inhabitants, a large portion of whom were French, whose business it was to trade with the numerous tribes of Indians and the few white people who then inhabited that region of country, for furs of various kinds, buffalo robes and tongues, as this was the only traffic out of which money could be made at that time.

The furs bought of the Indians were carried from St. Louis to New Orleans in pirogues or flatboats, which were carried along solely by the current, for at that time steam power had never been applied to the waters of the Mississippi River. Sixty-seven years later, in 1886, I visited St. Louis and went down to the wharf or steamboat landing, and looking across to East St. Louis, which in 1818 was nothing but a wilderness, beheld the river spanned by one of the finest bridges in the world, over which from 100 to 150 locomotives with trains attached were daily passing. Three big steam ferryboats above and three below the bridge were constantly employed in transferring freight of one kind or another. What a change had taken place within the memory of one man! While looking in amazement at the great and mighty change, a nicely dressed and intelligent man passed by; I said to him:

"Sir, I stood on the other bank of this river when a little boy, in the month of October, 1818, when there was no

2

improvement whatever over there" (pointing to the east shore). I also stated to him that a little flatboat, manned by three Frenchmen, was the only means for crossing the river at that time. The gentleman took his pencil and a piece of paper and figured for a few moments, and then turning to me said: "Do you know, sir, those three Frenchmen, with their boat, who did all the work of ferrying, and were not employed half the time, could not, with the facilities you speak of, in 100 years do what is now being done in one day with our present means of transportation."

Since that time, which was six years ago, another bridge has been built to meet the necessities of the increasing business of that city, which shows that progress and increase of wealth and development are still on the rapid march.

The next thing of note, after passing St. Louis, occurred one evening after we camped. My mother stepped on the wagon-tongue to get the cooking utensils, when her foot slipped and she fell, striking her side and receiving injuries which resulted in her death eighteen months later.

On that journey my father traveled westward, crossing the Missouri River at St. Charles, Mo., following up the river from that point to where Glasgow is now situated, and there crossed the river to the south side, and wintered in the big bottoms. In the spring of 1819 he moved to what afterward became La Fayette County, and took up a location near the Big Snye Bear River.

In February, the winter following, my dear mother died from the injuries she received from the accident previously alluded to. The Rev. Simon Cockrell, a baptist preacher, who at that time was over eighty years of age, preached her funeral sermon. He was the first preacher I had ever seen stand up before a congregation with a book in his hand. Although my mother died when I was little more than six years of age, my memory of her is apparently as fresh and endearing as though her death had occurred but a few days ago. Many acts I saw her do, and things I heard her say, impressed me with her courage and goodness, and their memory has been a help to me throughout the whole career of my long life. No mother ever gave birth to a son who loved her more, or whose tender recollections have been more endearing or lasting than mine.

I have never encountered any difficulty so great, no matter how threatening, that I have not been able to overcome fearlessly when the recollection of my dear mother and the spirit by which she was animated came to me. Even to this day, and I am an old man in my eightieth year, I can not dwell long in conversation about her without tears coming to my eyes. There are no words in the English language to express my estimate and appreciation of the dear mother who gave me birth and nourishment. I would that all men loved and held the memories of their mothers more sacred than I think many of them do. One of the greatest safeguards to man throughout the meanderings of his life is the love of a father, mother, brother and sister, children and friends; it is a great solace and anchor to right-thinking men when they may be hundreds and thousands of miles away. Love of family begets true patriotism in his bosom, for, in my opinion, there is no such thing as true patriotism without love of family.

Returning to the events of 1821, we had in the neighborhood of the Snye Bear River a great Indian scare. This happened in the month of August, when I was in my seventh year, after my father had built a log cabin for himself in that part of the country which afterward became Lafayette County, Mo. My mother had died the winter before, leaving myself, the eldest, a brother next, and a sister little more than two years old.

Mrs. Ferrins, a settler who lived on the outskirts of the little settlement of pioneers, was alone, except for a baby a year old. She left the child and went to the spring for water. When she had filled her bucket and rose to the top of the bank, she imagined she saw Indians. She dropped her bucket, ran to the cabin, took the child in her arms, and fled with all her might to Thomas Hopper's, the nearest neighbor. As soon as she came near enough to be heard, she shouted "Indians" at the top of her voice. Polly Hopper, a young girl of seventeen, hearing Mrs. Ferrin shouting "Indians," seized a bridle and ran to a herd of horses that were near by in the shade of some trees, caught a flea-bitten gray bell mare, the leader of the herd, she being gentle and easier to catch than the others, mounted the animal without saddle, riding after the fashion of men, and started to alarm the settlement.

My father was lying in bed taking a sweat to abate a bilious fever. A family living near by were caring for us children, and nursing my father in his sickness. My brother and I were playing a little distance from the cabin when we heard the screams of the woman, shouting "Indians" with every jump the horse made, her hair streaming out behind like a banner in the wind. We were on the very outside boundary of the settlement, and some signs of Indians had been discovered a few days previous by some neighbors who were out hunting for deer. This fact had been made known to the little settlement, and the day this scare took place had been selected for the men to meet at Henry Rennick's to discuss ways and means for building a stockade for the protection of their families in case the Indians should make an attempt of a hostile nature. So the first thoughts of the families at home were to start for

Rennick's, where the men were. This accounts for the young woman going by our house, as she had to pass our cabin to reach that place. My father, sick as he was, jumped out of bed when she passed giving the alarm, took a heavy gun from the rack, hung his shot pouch over his shoulder, took my little sister in his arms, and, like the rest, started for Rennick's, my little brother and I toddling along behind him.

A family living near by, consisting of the mother, Mrs. Turner, two daughters, a son, and a little grandson, also started for Rennick's. They would run for a short distance, and then stop and hide in the high weeds until they could get their breath. The old lady had a small dog she called Ging. He was on hand, of course, and just as much excited as all the rest of the dogs in the neighborhood, and the people themselves. The screams of the girl Polly Hopper, and the ringing of the bell on the animal she was riding, aroused the dogs to the highest pitch of excitement. In those days dogs were a necessity to the frontiersman for his protection, and as much of a necessity on that account as any other animal he possessed, and consequently every settler owned from three to five dogs, and some more. They were the watch-guards against Indians and prowling beasts, both by night and day, and could not have been dispensed with in the settling of the frontier.

To return to our trip to Rennick's: When the old lady and her flock would run into the weeds to hide and regain their breath, this little dog Ging could not be controlled, for bark he would. The old lady when angry would use "cuss words," and she used them on this dog, and would jump out of her hiding-place and start on the trail again. Of course when the dog barked he exposed her hiding-place. They would run a little farther, and when their breath would fail, they would make another hiding in the weeds, but would scarcely get settled when the dog would begin his barking again. The old lady, with another string of "cuss words," would jump out of the weeds and try the trail again a short distance. This was repeated until they reached Rennick's almost prostrate, as the distance was considerably over a mile, and the day an exceedingly hot one about noon. My father, though sick, was more fortunate with his little group of children. When he felt about to faint, he would turn with us into the high weeds and sit there quietly, and, not having any dog with us to report our whereabouts, we were completely hidden by the high weeds, and had a hundred Indians passed they would not have discovered our hiding-place.

In due time we arrived safe at Rennick's, and strange to say, my father was a well man, and did not go to bed again on account of the fever.

When Polly Hopper reached Rennick's and ran into the crowd, she was in a fainting condition. The men took her off the horse, laid her on the ground, and administered cold water and other restoratives. She soon regained consciousness and strength, and of course was regarded as a heroine in the neighborhood after that memorable day. One can well imagine the excitement among the men whose families were at home and exposed, as they thought, to the mercies of the savages. They scattered immediately toward their homes as rapidly as their horses would carry them, fearing they might find their families murdered. For hours after we reached Rennick's there continued to be arrivals of women and children, many times in a fainting condition, and all exhausted from the fright, the heat, and the speed at which they had run.

Mr. Rennick, who was one of the first pioneers, soon had more visitors than he knew what to do with, and more than his log cabin could shelter. These people remained in and around the cabin for two days, and until the men rode the country over and found the alarm had been a false one and there were no Indians in the neighborhood.

One of the first occurrences of note in the early settlement of the West was the visitation of grasshoppers, in September, 1820, an occurrence which had never been known by the oldest inhabitants of the Mississippi Valley. They came in such numbers as to appear when in the heavens as thin clouds of vapor, casting a faint shadow upon the earth. In twenty-four hours after their appearance every green thing, in the nature of farm product, that they could eat or devour was destroyed. It so happened, however, that they came so late in the season that the early corn had ripened, so they could not damage that, otherwise a famine would have resulted. The next appearance of these pests was over forty years later, in Western Missouri, Nebraska, and Kansas, which all well remember, as there were two or three seasons in close proximity to each other in the sixties when Western farmers suffered to a great extent from their ravages.

For five years, from 1821 to 1826, nothing worthy of note occurred, but everything moved along as calmly as a sunny day.

In the month of April, 1826, a terrible cyclone passed through that section of the country, leaving nothing standing in its track. Fortunately the country was but sparsely settled, and no lives were lost. It passed from a southwesterly direction to the northeast, tearing to pieces a belt of timber about half-a-mile wide, in that part of the country which became Jackson County, and near where Independence was afterward located, passing a little to the west of that point.

The next cyclone that visited that country was in 1847; this also passed from the southwest to the northeast, passing across the outskirts of Westport, which is now a suburb of Kansas City. The third and last cyclone that visited that section of the country, about eight years ago, blew down several houses in Kansas City, and killed a number of children who were attending the High School, the building being demolished by the storm.

POLLY'S WARNING.

CHAPTER II.

There was about one-fourth of the entire territory of
Missouri that was covered with timber, and three-fourths
in prairie land, with an annual growth of sage-grass, as it
was called, about one and one-half feet high, and as thick as
it could well grow; in fact the prairie lands in the commencement of its settlement were one vast meadow, where
the farmer could cut good hay suitable for the wintering of
his stock almost without regard to the selection of the
spot; in other words, it was meadow everywhere outside of
the timber lands. This condition of things would apply
also to the States of Illinois, Iowa, and some of the other
Western States, with the exception of Missouri, which had
a greater proportion of timber than either of the others
mentioned. The timber in all these States grew in belts
along the rivers and their tributaries, the prairie covering
the high rolling lands between the streams that made up
the water channels of those States.

Many of the streams in the first settling of these States
were bold, clear running water, and many of them in Missouri were sufficiently strong almost the year round to
afford good water power for running machinery, and it was
the prediction in the commencement of the settlement of
these States by the best-informed people, that the water
would increase, for the reason that the swampy portions in
the bottom lands, and where there were small lakes, would,
by the settlement of the country, become diverted, its force
to run directly into and strengthen the larger streams for

all time to come.   And to show how practical results over-throw theories, the fact proved to be exactly the reverse of their predictions. There has been a continuous slow decline in the natural flow of water-supply from the first settlement of the country.   Many places that I can now remember that were ponds or small lakes, or in other words little res-ervoirs, which held the water for months while it would be slowly passing out and feeding the streams, have now become fields and plowed ground.   Roads and ditches have been made that let the water off at once after a rainfall. The result has been that streams that used to turn ma-chinery have become not much more than outlets for the heavy rainfalls that occur in the rainy season, and if twenty of those streams, each one of which had water enough to run machinery seventy years ago, were all put together now into one stream, there would not be sufficient power to run a good plant of machinery.   The numerous springs that could be found on every forty or eighty acres of land in the beginning, have very many of them entirely failed.

The wells of twenty or thirty feet in depth that used to afford any quantity of water for family uses, many of them in order to get water supplies have to be sunk to a much greater depth.   Little streams that used to afford any quan-tity of water for the stock have dried up, giving no water supply only in times of abundance of rain.   All the first settlers in the State located along the timber belts, without an exception, and cultivated the timber lands to produce their grain and vegetables.   It was many years after the forest lands were settled before prairie lands were cultivated to any extent, and it was found later that the prairie lands were more fertile than they gave them credit for being before real tests in the way of farming were made with them. The sage grass had the tenacity to stand a great deal of grazing and tramping over, and still grow to considerable perfection. It required years of grazing upon the prairie before the wild grass, which was universal in the beginning, gave way, but in the timber portions the vegetation that was found in the first settling of the land gave way almost at once. In two years from the time a farmer moved upon a new spot and turned his stock loose upon it, the original wild herbs that were found there disappeared and other vegetation took its place. The land being exceedingly fertile, never failed to produce a crop of vegetation, and when one variety did appear and cover the entire surface as thick as it could grow for a few years, it seemed to exhaust the quality of the soil that produced that kind, and that variety would give way and something new come up.

The older the country has become, as a rule, the more obnoxious has been the vegetation that the soil has produced of its own accord. But there has been in my recollection, which goes back more than seventy years, a great many changes in the crops of vegetation on those lands, showing to my satisfaction that there is an inherent potency in nature, in rich soil that will cover itself every year with a growth of some kind. If it is not cultivated and made to produce fruit, vegetables, and cereals, it will nevertheless produce a crop of some kind.

The first settlers in the Mississippi Valley were as a rule poor people, who were industrious, economizing, and self-sustaining. From ninety-five to ninety-seven per cent of the entire population manufactured at home almost everything necessary for good living. A great many of them when they were crossing the Ohio and Mississippi to their new homes would barely have money enough to pay their ferriage across the rivers, and one of the points in selling out whatever they had to spare when they made up their minds to emigrate was to be sure to have cash enough with them to pay their ferriage. They generally carried with

C

them a pair of chickens, ducks, geese, and if possible a pair of pigs, their cattle and horses. The wife took her spinning wheel, a bunch of cotton or flax, and was ready to go to spinning as soon as she landed on the premises, often having her cards and wheel at work before her husband could build a log cabin. Going into a land, as it was then, that flowed with milk and honey they were enabled by the use of their own hands and brains to make an independent and good living. There was any quantity of game, bear, elk, deer, wild turkeys, and wild honey to be found in the woods, so that no man with a family, who had pluck and energy enough about him to stir around, ever need to be without a supply of food. At that time nature afforded the finest of pasture, both summer and winter, for his stock.

While the people as a rule were not educated, many of them very illiterate as far as education was concerned, they were thoroughly self-sustaining when it came to the knowledge required to do things that brought about a plentiful supply of the necessities of life. In those times all were on an equality, for each man and his family had to produce what was required to live upon, and when one man was a little better dressed than another there could be no complaint from his neighbor, for each one had the same means in his hands to bring about like results, and he could not say his neighbor was better dressed than he was because he had cheated some other neighbor out of something, and bought the dress; for at that time the goods all had to come to them in the same way—by their own industry. There was but little stealing or cheating among them. There was no money to steal, and if a man stole a piece of jeans or cloth of any kind he would be apprehended at once. Society at that time was homogeneous and simple, and opportunities for vice were very rare. There were very few old bachelors and old maids, for about the only thing a young man could do when he became twenty-one, and his mother quit making his clothes and doing his washing, was to marry one of his neighbor's daughters. The two would then work together, as was the universal custom, and soon produce with their own hands abundance of supplies to live upon.

The country was new, and when a young man got married his father and brothers, and his wife's father and brothers, often would turn out and help him put up a log cabin, which work required only a few days, and he and his spouse would move into it at once. They would go to work in the same way as their fathers had done, and in a few years would be just as independent as the old people. The young ladies most invariably spun and wove, and made their bridal dresses. At that time there were millions of acres of land that a man could go and squat on, build his cabin, and sometimes live for years upon it before the land would come into market, and with the prosperity attending such undertakings, as a general thing would manage in some way, when the land did come into market, to pay $1.25 per acre for as much as he required for the maintenance of his family.

Men in those days who came to Missouri and looked at the land often declined to select a home in the State on account of their having no market for their products, as above stated, everybody producing all that was needed for home consumption and often a surplus, but were so far away from any of the large cities of the country, without transportation of either steamboats or railroads, for it was before the time of steamboats, much less railroads—for neither of them in my early recollections were in existence—to make them channels of business and trade. Men in the

early settlement often wondered if the rich land of the
State would ever be worth $5 per acre.

Missouri at that time was considered the western confines
of civilization, and it was believed then that there never
would be in the future any white settlements of civilized
people existing between the western borders of Missouri
and the Pacific Coast, unless it might be the strip between
the Sierra Nevada Mountains and the Pacific Ocean,
which the people at that time knew but little or nothing
about.

In 1820 and 1830 there were a great many peaceable
tribes of Indians, located by the Government all along the
western boundary of Missouri, in what was then called the
Indian Territory, and has since then become the States of
Kansas, Nebraska, and Oklahoma Territory. I remember
the names of many of the tribes who were our nearest
neighbors across the line, and among them were the
Shawnees, Delawares, Wyandottes, Kickapoos, Miamis,
Sacs, Foxes, Osages, Peorias, and Iowas, all of whom were
perfectly friendly and docile, and lived for a great many
years in close proximity to the white settlers, even coming
among them to trade without any outbreaks or trespassing
upon the rights of the white people in any way or manner
worth mentioning.

There was a long period existing from 1825 to 1860
of perfect harmony between these tribes and the white
people, and in fact even to this day there is no disturbance
between these tribes and their neighbors, the whites. The
Indian troubles have been among the Sioux, Arapahoes,
Cheyennes, Apaches, Utes, and some other minor tribes,
all of which, at the present time, seem to have submitted to
their fate in whatever direction it may lie. There is one
remark that I will venture here, and it is this, that while
the white people were in the power of the Indians and

understood it, we got along with the Indian a great deal better than when the change to the white people took place.   In the early days white men respected the Indian's rights thoroughly, and would not be the aggressors, and often they were at the mercy of the Indians, but as soon as they began to feel that they could do as they pleased, became more aggressive and had less regard for what the Indian considered his rights.   Then in the early days Indians were paid their annuities in an honest way, and there was no feeling among them that they were mistreated by the agent whose duty it was to pay them this annuity.

I was acquainted with one Indian agent by the name of Major Cummings, who for a long time was a citizen of Jackson County, and for a great many years agent for a number of the tribes living along the borders of Missouri. There never was a complaint or even a suspicion, to the best of my knowledge, that he or his clerks ever took one cent of the annuities that belonged to the Indians.   The money was paid to them in silver, either in whole or half dollars, and the head of every family received every cent of his quota.   Therefore we had a long period of quiet and peace with our red brethren.   It is only since the late war that there has been so much complaint from the Indians with reference to the scanty allowances and poor food and blankets.

CHAPTER III.

A SILVER EXPEDITION.

In the summer of 1827 my father, Benjamin Majors, with twenty-four other men, formed a party to go to the Rocky Mountains in search of a silver mine that had been discovered by James Cockrell,* while on a beaver-trapping expedition some four years previous.

At that time, men attempting to cross the plains had no means of carrying food supplies to last more than a week, or ten days at the outside. When their scanty supply of provisions was exhausted, they depended solely upon the game they might chance to kill, invariably eating this without salt. These twenty-five men elected James Cockrell their captain, as he was the only man of the party who had crossed the plains. Being the discoverer of what he claimed was a rich silver mine, they relied solely upon him to pilot them to the spot. The only facilities for transportation were one horse each. Their scant amount of bedding, with the rider, was all the horse could carry. Each man had to be armed with a good gun, and powder and ball enough to last him during the entire trip, for the territory through which they had to pass was inhabited by hostile Indians. No cooking vessels were taken with them, as they depended entirely upon roasting or broiling their meat upon the fire. When they could not find deer, antelope, elk, or buffalo they had to do without food, unless they were driven to kill and eat a wolf they might chance to get. When they reached the buffalo belt, however, 200 miles farther west,

---

* An uncle of Senator Cockrell of Missouri.

there was no scarcity of meat. The country where they roamed was 400 miles across, reaching to the base of the Rocky Mountains, and extending from Texas more than 3,000 miles, very far north of the Canadian line. The buffalo were numbered by the millions. It often occurred in traveling through this district that there would be days together when one would never be out of sight of great herds of these animals. They stayed in the most open portion of the plains they could find, for the country was one vast plain, or level prairie. The grass called buffalo grass did not grow more than one and one-half to two inches high, but grew almost as thick in many places as the hair on a dog's back. Other grasses that were found in this locality grew much taller, but one would invariably find the buffalo grazing upon the short kind, especially so in the winter, as the high winds blew the snow away from where this grass grew. There were millions of acres of this grass. The buffalo's teeth and under jaw were so arranged by nature that he could bite this short grass to the earth; in fact no small animal, such as a sheep, goat, or antelope, could cut the grass more closely than the largest buffalo. Strange to say this short grass of the prairie is rapidly disappearing, as the buffaloes have done. In crossing the plains with our oxen in later years we found it impossible for them to get a living by grazing on the portions of the plains where this grass grew.

The party in question soon reached the Raton Mountains not far from Trinidad, now on the Atchison, Topeka & Santa Fé Railroad. It is proper to state that after leaving their homes in Jackson and Lafayette counties, Mo., they traveled across the prairie, bearing a little south of west, until they reached the Big Bend, or Great Bend, as it is lately called, of the Arkansas River. At this point they found innumerable herds of buffalo, and no trouble in finding grass and water in plenty, as well as meat. They followed the margin of the river until they reached the foothills of the Rocky Mountains; then their captain told them he was in the region where he had discovered the mine. He found some difficulty in locating the spot, and after many days spent in searching, some of the party grew restless and distrustful, doubting as to whether he ever discovered silver ore, or if so, if he was willing to show them the location, and became very threatening in their attitude toward him. He finally found what he and they had supposed was silver ore. This fact pacified the party and perhaps saved his life, as it was a long way for men to travel through peril and hardships only to be disappointed, or, as they expressed it, "to be fooled." They were disappointed, however, when they found nothing but dirty-looking rock, with now and then a bright speck of metal in it. Not one of them had ever seen silver ore, nor did they know anything about manipulating the rock in order to get the silver out of it. Many of them expected to find the silver in metallic form, and thought they could cut it out with their tomahawks and pack home a good portion of wealth upon their horses. They thought they could walk and lead their horses if they could get a load of precious metal to carry, as their captain had done a few years before, when he sold his beaver skins in St. Louis, took his pay in silver dollars, put them in a sack, bought a horse to carry it, and led him 300 miles to his home.

It must be remembered that this was the first prospecting party to look for silver that ever left the western borders of Missouri for the Rocky Mountains. After finding what they supposed was a silver mine, each one selected some of the best specimens and left for their homes. Everything moved along well with them until they arrived at about the point on the Arkansas River where Dodge City now stands. They camped one evening at the close of a day's travel, ate a hearty supper of buffalo meat, put their guard around their horses, and went to bed. Two men at a time guarded the horses, making a change every three hours during the night. This precaution was necessary to keep the Indians, who were in great numbers and hostile, from running off their horses. But on that fatal night the Indians succeeded in crawling on their bellies where the grass was tall enough to conceal them from the guard. It was only along the river bottoms and water courses that the grass grew tall. When they got between the guard and the horses, they suddenly rose, firing their guns, shaking buffalo robes, and with war-whoops and yells succeeded in frightening the horses to an intense degree. Then the Indians who were in reserve, mounted on ponies, ran the horses off where their owners never heard of or saw them afterward. Part of the Indians, at the same time, turned their guns upon the men that were lying upon the bank of the river. They jumped out of their beds, over the bank and into the water knee-deep. The men, by stooping under the bank, which was four feet perpendicular, were protected from the arrows and bullets of the enemy. There they stood for the remainder of that cold October night. One of the party, a man named Mark Foster, when they jumped over the bank, did not stop, but ran as fast as he could go for the other side. The water was shallow, not being more than knee-deep anywhere, and in some places not half that depth. The bottom was sandy, and at that place the river was some 400 yards wide. In running in the dark of the night, with the uneven bottom of the river, Mr. Foster fell several times. Each time it drew a yell from the Indians, who thought they had killed him, for they were shooting at him as he ran. After being three times ducked, he reached the other side and dry land.

His clothes were thoroughly drenched, and his gun, which was a flint-lock and muzzle-loader, entirely useless. Just think of a man in that condition—his gun disabled, apparently a thousand wolves howling around him in all directions, the darkness of the night, the yelling of the Indians on the other side, and 400 miles from home; the only living white man, unless some of his comrades happened not to be killed. He remained there shivering with the cold the rest of the night. When daylight appeared he started to cross the river to the camp to find out whether his comrades were dead or alive. He reached the middle of the river and halted, his object being to see, if possible, whether it was the Indians or his party that he could see through the slight fog that was rising and slowly moving westward and up the river. His comrades, who fortunately were alive, could hear, in the still of the morning, every step he made in the water. After standing a short time he decided that the men he saw moving about were Indians, and he was confirmed in the belief that all his party were killed, so he ran back to where he had spent such a doleful part of the night and there remained until the fog entirely cleared away. He then could see that the men at the camp from where he fled were his comrades. He returned within about sixty yards from where they were, stopped and called to my father, who answered him, after some persuasion from the rest of the party, for they all felt ugly toward him, thinking he had acted the coward in doing as he did. When my father answered his call, he asked if they would allow him to join them. After holding a consultation it was agreed that he might come. He walked firmly up to them and remarked:

"I have something to say to you, gentlemen. It is this: I know you think I have acted the d—d coward, and I do not blame you under the circumstances. When you all jumped over the bank I thought you were going to run to the other side, and I did not know any better until I had got so far out I was in greater danger to return than to go ahead. For, as you know, the Indians were sending volleys of bullets and arrows after me, and really thought they had killed me every time I fell. Now, to end this question, there is one of two things you must do. The first is that you take your guns and kill me now, or if you do not comply with this, that every one of you agree upon your sacred honor that you will never allude, in any way, or throw up to me the unfortunate occurrences of last night. Now, gentlemen, mark what I say. If you do not kill me, but allow me to travel with you to our homes, should one of you ever be so thoughtless or forgetful of the promise you must now make as to throw it up to me, I pledge myself before you all that I will take the life of the man who does it. Now, I have presented the situation fairly, and you must accept one or the other before you leave this spot."

The party with one accord, after hearing his story, agreed never to allude to it in any way in his presence, and gave him a cordial welcome to their midst. They treated him as one of them from that time on, for he was a brave man after all. Think of the awful experience the poor fellow had during the night, and in the morning, to reach an amicable understanding with his party. One can readily see that he was a man of very great courage and physical endurance, or he could not have survived the pressure upon him. It was a sad time for those twenty-five brave men for more reasons than one. Knowing that they were 400 miles from home, late in the fall, without a road or path to follow, no stopping place of any kind between them and their homes on the borders of the Missouri, which was as far as civilization had reached westward. The thought that impressed them most deeply was in reference to one of their comrades by the name of Clark Davis, whom they all loved and honored. He was a man weighing 300 pounds, but not of large frame, his weight consisting more of fat than bone. It was the universal verdict of the party that it would be impossible for him to walk home and carry his gun and ammunition as they all had to do. They would go aside in little groups, so he would not hear them, and deplore the situation. They thought they would have to leave him sitting in the prairie for the wolves to devour, or hazard the lives of all the rest of the party. Some actually wept over the thought of the loss of such a dear comrade and noble-hearted man. Should they chance to reach their own homes, for they were all men with families, the idea of telling his family that they were obliged to leave him was more than they felt their nerves could endure. In my opinion there never was a more brave and heroic group of men thrown together than were those twenty-five frontiersmen. All were fine specimens of manhood, physically speaking, between thirty and forty years of age, and with perfect health and daring to do whatever their convictions dictated.

They went to work and burned their saddles, bridles, blankets, in fact everything they had in camp that they could not carry with them on their backs. This they did to prevent the Indians from getting any more "booty." After all their arrangements were made for leaving their unfortunate camping-place, they started once more for their homes. They traveled at the rate of twenty to twenty-five miles per day. They could have gone farther, but for the fact that they had no trail to walk in. The grass in some places, and the drifting sand in others, made it exceedingly irksome for footmen.

My father was frequently asked after his return:

"Was there no road you could follow?"

He would answer:

"No, from the fact that the drifting sand soon filled every track of a passing caravan and no trace was left of a trail a few hours afterward."

A few years later on this shifting of sand discontinued, and grass and small shrubbery soon began to grow and cover many places that were then perfectly bare. One-half of the distance they had to walk was covered with herds of buffalo, the other half was through desolate prairie country, where game of any kind was seldom seen. It was on this part of their journey that they came near starvation. It only took them a few days after leaving the buffalo belt to consume what meat they had carried on their backs, as men become very hungry and consume a great deal of meat when they have long and tiresome walks to make. In the first week of their march their convictions in regard to Clark Davis were confirmed, as they thought, for his feet blistered in a terrible manner, his fat limbs became exceedingly raw and sore, so he of necessity would lag. Then they would detail of a morning when they started, a guard of five or six men to remain with him for protection from the Indians. The rest of the party would walk on to some point they would designate for camping the next night, and he with his little guard would arrive some three or four hours later. This went on for seven or eight days in succession, each day they expecting the news from the guard that he had given up the hope of going any farther. But in time his feet began to improve, in fact his condition every way, and he would reach camp sooner each day after the arrival of the party. After they had passed the buffalo belt, where meat was abundant, and struck the starvation belt in their travels, Mr. Davis' fat proved a blessing and of great service. When fatigue and want were to be endured at the same time, he began to take the lead instead of the rear of the party. Several days before they reached home they would have perished, but for the fact that he alone had sufficient activity and strength to attempt to hunt for game, for they had seen none after leaving the buffalo. They had reached a place called Council Grove—now a city of that name—in the State of Kansas, about one hundred and thirty miles from their homes. After so many weeks of hard marching they thought they could go no farther, and some dropped on the ground, thinking it useless to make the attempt. At this juncture Clark Davis said:

"Boys, I will go and kill a deer."

My father said the very word was tantalizing to a lot of men who were almost dying of hunger. They did not know there was a deer in the country, or anything else that could be eaten, not even a snake, for cold weather was so near even they had disappeared. Davis, however, determined on his hunt, left his comrades, and had traveled only a few hundred yards until he saw two fine deer standing near. Directly the men in the camp heard the report of his gun, and as soon as he could reload they heard a second report, and then a shout, "Come here, boys! there is meat in plenty." You may imagine it was not long until every one joined him. They drank every drop of blood that was in the two deer, ate the livers without cooking, and saved every particle, even taking the marrow out of their legs. This meat tided them over until they were able to reach other food.

Never before in the history of the past, nor since that time, did 150 pounds of surplus fat—so considered until starvation overtook them—prove to be of such great value, and was worth more to them than all the gold and silver in the Rocky Mountains. When the test came, it was found to be one of nature's reservoirs that could be drawn upon to save the lives of twenty-five brave men when all else failed them. Mr. Davis, as well as the rest of the party, no doubt often wished it could be dispensed with, as after losing his horse he carried it with great suffering and fatigue, before they learned its use, and that it was to be the salvation of the party. We often hear it said that truth is stranger than fiction, and this certainly was one of the cases where it proved to be so.

They finally reached home without losing one of their party; but they all gave the man whom they expected to leave to the wolves in the start the credit of saving their lives. When Mr. Davis reached his family the first thing his wife did was to set him a good meal. When he sat down to the table he said, "Jane, there is to be a new law for the future of our lives at our table." She said, "What is it, Clark?" He answered, "It is this. I never want to hear you or one of my children say bread again." "What then must we call it?" asked his wife. "Call it bready," said he, "for when I was starving on the plains it came to me that the word bread was too short and coarse a name to call such sweet, precious, and good a thing, and whoever eats it should use this pet name and be thankful to God who gives it, for I assure you, wife, the ordeal I have passed through will forever cause me to appreciate life and the good things that uphold it."

The outcome of this trip was drawing the party together, like one family, and they could not be kept long apart. It is a fact that mutual suffering begets an endearment stronger than ties of blood. It was interesting to me as a boy to hear them relate their experiences in reference to their hard trials and forebodings that were undergone, with no beneficial results. Some of them sent their specimens to St. Louis to be tested for silver, but received discouraging accounts of its value. If a very rich mine had been found at that time it would not have been of any practical value, for they were more than thirty years ahead of the time when silver-mining could be carried on, from an American standpoint, with success.   There was no one west of the Alleghanies with capital and skill enough to carry on such an enterprise, and there were no means whatever for transporting machinery to the Rocky Mountains.

CHAPTER IV.

NOTHING of very great note occurred in the county of Jackson, after the cyclone of 1826, until the year 1830, when five Mormon elders made their appearance in the county and commenced preaching, stating to their audiences that they were chosen by the priesthood which had been organized by the prophet Joseph Smith, who had met an angel and received a revelation from God, who had also revealed to him and his adherents the whereabouts of a book written upon golden plates and deposited in the earth. This book was found in a hill called Cumorah, at Manchester, in the State of New York. They selected a place near Independence, Jackson County, Mo., in the early part of the year 1831, which they named Temple Lot, a beautiful spot of ground on a high eminence. They there stuck down their Jacob's staff, as they called it, and said: "This spot is the center of the earth. This is the place where the Garden of Eden, in which Adam and Eve resided, was located, and we are sent here according to the directions of the angel that appeared to our prophet, Joseph Smith, and told him this is the spot of ground on which the New Jerusalem is to be built, and, when finished, Christ Jesus is to make his reappearance and dwell in this city of New Jerusalem with the saints for a thousand years, at the end of which time there will be a new deal with reference to the nations of the earth, and the final wind-up of the career of the human family." They claimed to have all the spiritual gifts and understanding of the works of the Almighty that

D

belonged to the Apostles who were chosen by Christ when on his mission to this earth. They claim the gift of tongues and interpretation of tongues or languages spoken in an unknown tongue. In their silent meetings, the one who had received the gift of an unknown tongue knew nothing of its interpretation whatever, but after some silence some one in the audience would rise and claim to have the gift of interpretation, and would interpret what the brother or sister had previously spoken. They also claimed to have the gift of healing by anointing the sick with oil and lay- ing on of hands, and some claimed that they could raise the dead; in fact, they laid claim to every gift that be- longed to the Apostolic day or age. They established their headquarters at Independence, where some of their lead- ing elders were located. There they set up a printing office, the first that was established within 150 miles of Independence, and commenced printing their church liter- ature, which was very distasteful to the members and lead- ers of other religious denominations, the community being composed of Methodists, Baptists of two different orders, Presbyterians of two different orders, and Catholics, and a denomination calling themselves Christians. In that day and age it was regarded as blasphemous or sacrilegious for any one to claim that they had met angels and received from them new revelations, and the religious portion of the community, especially, was very much incensed and aroused at the audacity of any person claiming such interviews from the invisible world. Of course the Mormon elders de- nounced the elders and preachers of the other denomina- tions above mentioned, and said they were the blind lead- ing the blind, and that they would all go into the ditch together. An elder by the name of Rigdon preached in the court house one Sunday in 1832, in which he said that he had been to the third heaven, and had talked face to face

with God Almighty. The preachers in the community the
next day went en masse to call upon him. He repeated
what he had said the day before, telling them they had not
the truth, and were the blind leading the blind.

The conduct of the Mormons for the three years that
they remained there was that of good citizens, beyond their
tantalizing talks to outsiders. They, of course, were
clannish, traded together, worked together, and carried with
them a melancholy look that one acquainted with them
could tell a Mormon when he met him by the look upon
his face almost as well as if he had been of different color.
They claimed that God had given them that locality, and
whoever joined the Mormons, and helped prepare for the
next coming of the Lord Jesus Christ, would be accepted
and all right; but if they did not go into the fold of the
Latter Day Saints, that it was only a matter of time when
they would be crushed out, for that was the promised land
and they had come to possess it. The Lord had sent them
there and would protect them against any odds in the way
of numbers. Finally the citizens, and particularly the
religious portion of them, made up their minds that it was
wrong to allow them to be printing their literature and
preaching, as it might have a bad effect upon the rising
generation; and on the 4th of July, 1833, there was quite a
gathering of the citizens, and a mob was formed to tear
down their printing office. While the mob was forming,
many of the elders stood and looked on, predicting that the
first man who touched the building would be paralyzed and
fall dead upon the ground. The mob, however, paid no
attention to their predictions and prayers for God to come
and slay them, but with one accord seized hold of the implements necessary to destroy the house, and within the
quickest time imaginable had it torn to the ground, and
scattered their type and literature to the four winds. This,

of course, created an intense feeling of anger on the part of the Mormons against the citizens. At this time there were but a few hundred Mormons in the county against many times their number of other citizens. I presume there was not exceeding 600 Mormons in the county.

Immediately after they tore down the printing office they sent to the store of Elder Partridge and Mr. Allen, who was also an elder in the church, and took them by force to the public square, stripped them to their waists, and poured on them a sufficient amount of tar to cover their bodies well, and then took feathers and rubbed them well into the tar, making the two elders look like a fright. One of their names being Partridge, many began to whistle like a cock partridge, in derision. Now, be it remembered that the people who were doing this were not what is termed " rabble " of a community, but many among them were respectable citizens and law-abiding in every other respect, but who actually thought they were doing God's service to destroy, if possible, and obliterate Mormonism. In all my experience I never saw a more law-abiding people than those who lived where this occurred. There is nothing, however, that they could have done that would have proved more effectual in building up and strengthening the faith of the people so treated as this and similar performances proved to do. For if there is anything under the sun that will strengthen people in their beliefs or faith, no matter whether it is error or truth, if they have adopted it as true, it is to abuse and punish them for their avowed belief in whatever they espouse as religion or politics.

A few months after the tearing down of the building, a dozen or two Mormons made their appearance one day on the county road west of the Big Blue and not far from the premises of Moses G. Wilson. Wilson's boy rode out to drive up the milk cows in the morning, and saw this group of Mormons and had some conversation with them, and they used some very violent language to the boy. He went back and told his father, and it happened that there were several of the neighbors in at the time, as he kept a little county store; and in those days men generally carried their guns with them, in case they should have a chance to shoot a deer or turkey as they went from one neighbor's to another. It so happened that several of them had their guns with them; those who did not picked up a club of some kind, and they all followed the boy, who showed them where they were. When they got in close proximity to where the Mormons were grouped, seeing the men approaching with guns, the Mormons opened fire upon them, and the Gentiles, as they were called by the Mormons, returned the fire. There was a lawyer on the Gentile side by the name of Brazeel, who was shot dead; another man by the name of Lindsay was shot in the jaw and was thought to be fatally wounded, but recovered. Wilson's boy was also shot in the body, but not fatally. There were only one or two Mormons killed. Of course, after this occurrence, it aroused an intense feeling of hate and revenge in the citizens, and the Mormons would not have been so bold had it not been for their elders claiming that under all circumstances and at all times they would be sustained by the Almighty's power, and that a few of them would be able to put their enemies to flight. The available Mormon men then formed themselves into an organization for fighting the battles of the Lord, and started to Independence, about ten miles away, to take possession of the town. On their way, and when they were within about a mile of Independence, they marched with all the faith and fervor imaginable for fanatics to possess, encouraging each other with the words, "God will be with us and deliver our enemies into our hands." At this point they met a gentleman whom I well knew, by the name of Rube Collins, a citizen of the place, who was leaving the town in a gallop to go home and get more help to defend the town from the Mormon invasion. He shouted out as he passed them, "You are a d—d set of fools to go there now; there are armed men enough there to exterminate you in a minute." They were acquainted with Collins, and supposed he had told them the truth; however, at that time they could have taken the town had they pressed on, but his words intimidated them somewhat, and they filed off from the big road and hid themselves in the brush until they could hold a council, and I presume pray for light to be guided by. During this time there were runners going in all directions, notifying the citizens that the Mormons were coming to the town to take it, and every citizen, as soon as he could run bullets and fill his powder horn with powder, gathered his gun and made for the town; and in a few hours men enough had gathered to exterminate them had they approached. In their council that they held they decided not to approach until they sent spies ahead to see whether Collins had told them the truth or not. They supposed he had, from the fact that they found the public square almost covered with men, and others arriving every minute. As quickly as the citizens had organized themselves into companies (my father, Benjamin Majors, being captain of one of them), they then sent a message by two or three citizens to the Mormons, where they were still secreted in the paw-paw brush, and told them that if they did not come and surrender immediately, the whole party that was waiting for them in the town would come out and exterminate them. This message sent terror to their hearts, with all their claims that God would go before them and fight their battles for them. After holding another council they decided the best thing they could do

NATURE'S TABERNACLE.

was to go and surrender themselves to their enemies, which they did. I never saw a more pale-faced, terror-stricken set of men banded together than these seventy-five Mormons, for it was all the officers could do to keep the citizens from shooting them down, even when they were surrendering. However, they succeeded in keeping the men quiet, and no one was hurt. They stacked all their arms around a big white-oak stump that was perhaps four feet in diameter, and at that time was standing in the public square. Afterward the guns were put in the jail house for safe keeping, and were eaten up with rust, and never to my knowledge delivered to them. They then stipulated that every man, woman, and child should leave the county within three weeks. This was a tremendous hardship upon the Mormons, as it was late in the fall, and there were no markets for their crops or anything else that they had. The quickest way to get out of the county was to cross the river into Clay, as the river was the line between the two counties. They had to leave their homes, their crops, and in fact every visible thing they had to live upon. Many of their houses were burned, their fences thrown down, and the neighbors' stock would go in and eat and destroy the crop.

It has been claimed by people who were highly colored in their prejudice against the Mormons that they were bad citizens; that they stole whatever they could get their hands on and were not law-abiding. This is not true with reference to their citizenship in Jackson County, where they got their first kick, and as severe a one as they ever received, if not the most severe. There was not an officer among them, all the offices of the county being in the hands of their enemies, and if one had stolen a chicken he could and would have been brought to grief for doing so; but it is my opinion there is nothing in the county records

4

to show where a Mormon was ever charged with any misdemeanor in the way of violation of the laws for the protection of property. The cause of all this trouble was
solely from the claim that they had a new revelation direct
from the Almighty, making them the chosen instruments to
go forward, let it please or displease whom it might, to
build the New Jerusalem on the spot above referred to,
Temple Lot. And, as above stated, whoever did not join
in this must sooner or later give way to those who would.

I met a Presbyterian preacher, Rev. Mr. McNice, in Salt
Lake City a number of years ago at the dinner table of a
mutual friend, Doctor Douglas. It was on the Sabbath after
hearing him preach a very bitter sermon against the Mormons, denouncing their doctrines and doings in a severe
manner, and while we were at the dinner table, the subject
of the Mormons came up, and I told him that I was
thoroughly versed in their first troubles in Missouri, and he
asked me what the trouble was. I told him frankly that it
grew out of the fact that they claimed to have seen an
angel, and to have received a new revelation from God
which was not in accord with the religious denominations
that existed in the community at that time. He hooted at
the idea and told me he had read the history of their troubles there, and that they were bad citizens with reference to
being outlaws, thieves, etc., who would pick up their neighbors' property and the like. He insisted that he had read
their history, and showed a disposition to discredit my
statements. I then told him *I* was history, and knew as
much about it as any living man could know, and that there
were no charges of that kind against them; they were
industrious, hard-working people, and worked for whatever
they wanted to live upon, obtaining it by their industry, and
not by stealing it from their neighbors. He then scouted
at the idea that people would receive such treatment as

they did merely because they claimed to have seen angels and talked with God and claimed to have a new revelation. I then referred him to the fact that fifty or sixty years previous to that time the public mind in America lacked a great deal of being so tolerant as it was at the time of our conversation; that not more than one hundred years ago some of the American people were so superstitious that they could burn witches at the stake and drag Quakers through the streets of Boston on their backs, with a jack hitched to their heels; that the Mormons to-day could go to Jackson County, Mo., and preach the same doctrines that they did then, and the result would be that they would be laughed at instead of mobbed as they were sixty years ago.

I was sitting in a cabin with my father's miller, a Mr. Newman, a Mormon, at the time of this trouble. Mr. Newman's mother-in-law, who lived with him, was named Bentley; she had a son in the company that surrendered at Independence, and who walked six miles that evening and came home. The young man walked in and looked as sad as death, and when asked what the news was he stood there and related what had taken place that day at the surrender. They all sat in breathless silence and listened to the story, and when he was through with his statement and said the Mormons had agreed to leave the county within three weeks, the old lady, who sat by the table sewing, raised her hand and brought it down upon the table with a tremendous thud, and said:

"So sure as this is a world there *will be* a New Jerusalem built."

I relate this little incident to show that even after they had met with such a galling defeat how zealous even the old women were with reference to their future success. But it is my opinion that the more often a fanatic is kicked and abused, the stronger is his faith in his cause, for then they would take up the Scriptures and read the sentences expressed by Christ:

"But before all these they shall lay their hands on you and persecute you, delivering you up to the synagogues and into prisons, being brought before kings and rulers for my name's sake." "But take heed to yourselves, for they shall deliver you up to councils, and in the synagogues ye shall be beaten; and ye shall be brought before rulers and kings for my sake for a testimony against them."

From such passages they have always drawn the greatest consolation, and one would ask one another, "Where are the people the blessed Lord had reference to?" Another brother, with all the sanctity and confidence imaginable for a fanatic to feel, would answer, "Well, brother, if you do not find them among the Latter Day Saints you can not find them upon the face of this green earth, for we have suffered all the abuses the blessed Lord refers to in the Scripture you have just quoted."

I have said before that the Mormons all crossed the Missouri into Clay County, where they wintered in tents and log cabins hastily thrown together, and lived on mast, corn, and meat that they would procure from the citizens for whom they worked in clearing ground and splitting rails, and other work of a like character.

In the spring they were determined to return to their homes, although they were so badly destroyed, and claimed again as before that God would vindicate them and put to flight their enemies. The people of Jackson County, however, watched for their return, and gathered, at the appointed time, in a large body, on the opposite side of the river to where the Mormons were expected to congregate and cross back into the county. Their spies came to the river, and seeing camps of the citizens, who had gathered to the number of four or five hundred strong (I being one of the number) to prevent their crossing, then changed their purpose and sent some of their leading men to locate in some other part of the State, for the time being, with the full understanding, however, that at the Lord's appointed time they would all be returned to Jackson County, and complete their mission in building the city of the New Jerusalem. The delegation they sent out selected Davis and Colwell counties as the portion of the State where they would make their temporary rally until they became strong enough for the Lord to restore them to their former location.

During that spring the citizens of Jackson County, feeling that there had been, in many cases, great outrages perpetrated upon the Mormons, held a public meeting at Independence and appointed five commissioners, whose duty it was to meet some of the leading elders of the Mormons at Liberty, the seat of Clay County, and make some reparation for the damages that had been done to their property the fall before in Jackson County. They met, but failed to agree, as the elders asked more and perhaps wanted to retain the titles they had to the lands, as they thought it would be sacrilege to part with them, for that was the chosen spot for the New Jerusalem. During the time that elapsed between the commissioners crossing the river in the morning and returning in the evening, the ferryman (Bradbury), whom I have often met, a man with a very large and finely developed physique, a great swimmer, was supposed to be bribed by the Mormons to bore large auger-holes through the gunwales of his flatboat just at the water's edge. The boat having a floor in it some inches above the bottom, there could be no detection of the flow of the water until it was sufficiently deep to cover the inner floor. The commissioners went upon the boat with their horses, and had not proceeded very far from the shore until they found the water coming up in the second floor and the boat rapidly sinking. This, of course, produced great consternation, for the river was very high and turbulent. Bradbury, the owner of the ferry, said to his two men:

"Boys, we will jump off and swim back to the shore."

As above stated, he was a great swimmer, and had been known to swim the Missouri upon his back several times not long before this occurred. When the water rose in the boat so that it was necessary for the commissioners to leave it, three of them caught hold of their horses' tails, after throwing off as much clothing as they could before the boat went down with them. The other two men who could swim attempted to swim alone, but the current was so turbulent that they were overcome and were drowned. Those who hung on to the tails of their horses were brought safely to shore. One of the men drowned was a neighbor of my father's and as fine a gentleman and good fellow as ever lived. His name was David Lynch.

I remember well their names, and was well acquainted with two of the men who were pulled through by their horses, S. Noland and Sam C. Owens, the foremost merchant of the county, a man who stood high in every sense, and of marked ability.

This occurrence put the quietus on any further attempt to try to settle for the damages done the Mormons when driven from the county, for it caused in the whole population the most intense feeling against them, and they never were remunerated.

When Bradbury jumped off the boat he swam for the shore, but was afterward found dead, with one of his hands grasping the root of a cottonwood tree, so there was no opportunity for trying him for the crime, or finding out how it was brought about. It was supposed that he was bribed, as no one knew of any enmity he had against the commissioners.

The town the Mormons started, which they selected for their home in Paris County, they called Far West. This was the first experience that the people of Western Missouri had with the emigrants of the Eastern or New England States. Brigham Young, who afterward became the leader of the Mormons, was from Vermont, and many others composing the early pioneers of the Mormon church were from the New England States; some, however, from Ohio and Illinois, as well as some proselytes from Missouri. Up to the time of their appearance in Western Missouri the entire population was from some one of the four States—Virginia, North Carolina, Tennessee, or Kentucky.

It has been claimed by some that one of the causes of the dissatisfaction was that the Mormons were Abolitionists. This, however, played no part in the bitter feeling that grew up between them and their neighbors, for at the time of their coming to Jackson County there were but very few slaves, the people generally being poor farmers who lived from the labor of their own hands and that of their families. And then, when the Mormons were driven entirely from Missouri to Illinois, which was a free State, they soon got into difficulty with their neighbors there, as they had done in Missouri. It is claimed now, universally, by the people of this country that polygamy, or the plurality-wife system, is the only objection that good citizens can have to Mormonism. This was not the cause of their difficulties or their trouble in Illinois and Missouri, as they had never, up to the time they left Nauvoo, Ill., proclaimed polygamy as being a church institution. And as I have previously stated, it was their clannishness, as is natural for a church to do, more or less, only they carried it to a greater degree than other denominations. Also the new doctrine they were preaching, stating that they were the only and chosen people of God, and that they had the key of St. Peter,

which was lost during the dark ages and was revealed again
to Joseph Smith, their prophet; that the Lord would stand
by them and enable them to prevail in their undertakings
as against any array of opposition, no matter how much
greater the numbers might be than their own.

They built up the city of Far West, of several thousand
people, and while there increased very rapidly, having
missionaries in many parts of the country preaching their
doctrine. As quickly as an individual would accept their
faith, they would at once rally to the headquarters, and in
the course of a few years they had put a great deal of the
prairie lands into cultivation and increased their numbers
until they were so formidable that when they began to be
odious to their neighbors by showing a hostile attitude
toward any power that might interfere with them, they got
into trouble much in the same way as they did in Jackson
County.

A party of Gentiles and Mormons met at a point called
Horn's Mill, and became involved in a quarrel, when there
were some killed on both sides. This created such a feeling in the community that both Mormons and Gentiles felt
insecure, living neighbors to each other as they were, and
the trouble went on until it culminated in the Governor,
Lilburn W. Boggs, calling out a portion of the militia of
the State and ordering them to Far West, the Mormon center. The Mormons were drilling continuously, and increasing their facilities for fighting, when the militia reached the
place designated, and organizing, placed themselves in
battle array. The Mormons were also drawn up in long
lines, and for a short time it looked as if a bloody battle
was unavoidable, but before any engagement occurred the
Mormons again surrendered. They then agreed to leave
the State of Missouri, and in April, 1839, the last of the
band left Far West, moved across the Mississippi into Illi-

nois, where they afterward located and built the city of
Nauvoo, but with no better results with the people in the
free State than they experienced in Missouri. This shows
that slavery had nothing to do with the hard feelings and
prejudice they aroused in every community in which they
lived.

The Mormons' new village was named Nauvoo, which
means Peaceful Rest. While there, having increased to
fifteen thousand souls, they built a temple to the Lord,
which was, perhaps, the finest building that had ever been
erected in the State up to that time. During the year
1844, trouble arose between them and the Gentiles, to sup-
press which the militia was called out, and in June of that
year a writ was sworn out for the arrest of the Mormon
prophet, Joseph Smith. His brother Hiram and Elder
Taylor, who, after Brigham Young's death, became president of the church, accompanied him to Carthage, Ill.,
where he went to give himself up. Arriving at Carthage,
all three were put in jail, where a mob succeeded in killing
the two brothers and seriously wounding Taylor, who carried some of the bullets in his body during the remainder
of his life. On the death of Joseph Smith, Brigham Young
was chosen by the church as its prophet, president, and
leader.

After three severe experiences in establishing settlements in Missouri and Illinois, they determined in their
councils to emigrate farther west and start a colony which
would be composed of Latter Day Saints, where they would
be entirely distinct and separate from any antagonizing
elements. At that time Salt Lake Valley, being under
Spanish dominion and a thousand miles from any white
settlement, was ultimately chosen as the spot best suited
for their purpose.

After leaving Nauvoo, Ill., they went to Council Bluffs,

E

Iowa (called by them Kaneville), traveling through the State of Iowa, and undergoing the greatest hardships and sufferings any people were ever called upon to endure, being without money, some of them without the proper means of transportation, destitute of almost all the necessities of life, and a great many sick on account of exposure to the elements. Arriving at the place above named, on the Missouri River, they went into winter quarters, and the next spring planted and raised crops in that vicinity, the greater number of the emigrants remaining there for the next two years.

In the spring of 1847, at the time war was being carried on between the United States and Mexico, Brigham Young started west with a band of from seventy to seventy-five pioneers, having, I believe, an impression that in Salt Lake Valley might be found the Mecca of their hopes. They arrived in Salt Lake Valley on the 21st day of July of that year. Previous to this, in 1846, at the call of the President for troops for the Mexican War, Brigham Young raised a regiment of a thousand volunteers to go to Mexico, under a stipulation with the United States Government that, when the war was over, the survivors should receive their discharges in California. This agreement was made in view of the fact that they had already resolved to go west into Spanish territory.

The treaty of peace between the United States and Old Mexico, at the close of the war, resulted in the Government of Mexico giving up to the United States all the territory possessed by it lying north of the present boundary line between the two countries, so that, after all the exertions the Mormons had made to effect a settlement on Spanish territory, in less than a year they found themselves still in the United States, where they have ever since remained, having built cities and towns on the colonizing plan in every available portion of the Territory of Utah, and having quite a number of colonies in other Territories, with one at present established in Mexico, as I have lately been informed.

I have met in later years and become familiarly acquainted with many of the leading spirits of the Mormon church, and have had large business transactions with Brigham Young and many other prominent Mormons, among whom were Captain Hooper, General Eldridge, Ferrimore Little, William Jennings, John Sharp, Lew Hills, Gen. Daniel H. Wells, Wilford Woodruff (now president of the Mormon church), Joseph Smith, and George Q. Cannon, and a fairer, more upright set of gentlemen I never met.

I have heard all the leading elders of the Mormon Church preach, including Brigham Young, Heber Kimball, George Q. Cannon, George A. Smith (the historian), John Taylor, Orson Pratt, and Elder Woodruff, who is now president of the church.

Orson Pratt was the ablest expounder of the Scriptures, particularly of the prophecies, in the Mormon church. He was the man chosen by Brigham Young and his counselors to discuss the subject of polygamy, from a Bible standpoint, with the Rev. John P. Newman, who was at that time pastor of one of the Methodist churches in Washington, D. C. I, among many other Gentiles, was present and heard the discussion, which took place in the Mormon Tabernacle.

President Young, as he was invariably called by his own people, was the boldest, most outspoken man I ever saw in the pulpit. I remember hearing him one Sabbath day when he was preaching in the Tabernacle, which seats 13,000 people, and on that day was packed to its full capacity, there being probably one hundred and fifty or

more strangers present—excursionists from the East on
their way to California, who had stopped over Sunday to
visit the Mormon church, and listen to the immense organ
and singers, but whose greatest desire was to hear Brigham
Young expound the Mormon doctrine. These strangers
were given the most prominent seats by the ushers, and
this is the only church in which I remember strangers
having precedent over the regular church members in being
seated. When Brigham Young was well along in his discussion, it occurred to him that the strangers present would
want to know the size of his family, as that was a question
often asked by visitors, so he ceased his discourse and
said: "I suppose the strangers present would like to know
how many wives and children I have," and then proceeded
to say he had sixteen wives and forty-five living children,
having lost eight or ten children, I believe. He then proceeded to finish his discourse.

I was present on another occasion when he was preaching to a very large congregation, and he said to them:

"Brethren, we have thieves, scoundrels, perjurers, and
villains in our church, but the day will come when the tares
will be separated from the wheat and burned up with
unquenchable fire; if this were not so, however, we could
not claim to be the church of Jesus Christ, for he said that
the kingdom of God was like a great net, which, being cast
into the sea, brought all manner of fishes to the shore."
He was the only preacher I ever heard make such remarks
to his own people, and recognize the church as being the
true one because of the tares that grew among the wheat.

The Mormon church taught regeneration through baptism by immersion. In the commencement of their service
a chapter from either the Old or New Testament was generally read, and during the discourse frequent reference
was made to the Book of Mormon and to Joseph Smith,
their prophet.

President Young was one of the smartest men, if not the ablest man, it was ever my fortune to meet. He was a man well posted on all subjects relating to the business interests of the country, and especially to his own people. His bishops and himself settled all manner of difficulties arising out of business or church matters without the assistance of courts, and he always insisted that every difficulty should be settled by arbitration of the members of the community in which the disputants lived.

In the ten years I lived in Salt Lake City, which was from 1869 to 1879, I never heard any talk among the Mormons about the gift of speaking the unknown tongue, or the interpretation thereof, as they claimed to have in Missouri. They, however, claimed to possess all the gifts of the Apostolic age and, as I have stated in another place, the keys of St. Peter. They believed in church authority, as do the Catholics, and in a personal God; they differ widely, however, from their Catholic brethren when they come to the marriage relation, the Mormons believing their bishops and elders should each have many wives, the Catholics, on the other hand, denying marriage to their priests.

Mormon communities, like all others, are made up of those who are reliable and those who are not—in other words, the good and the bad. Polygamy, which was practiced among them for more than a quarter of a century, they claimed upon scriptural authority was practiced in the Apostolic days. Let that be as it may, perhaps there never was a time in the march of civilization when to adopt such a practice would have been in more direct opposition to the moral sense of the civilized world than the present one of the nineteenth century.

In by-gone days, when the people depended upon their own and home productions for their living, the larger a

man's family, with every one a worker, the easier it was
for him to get along. Not so now, however, but it is just
the reverse.

The Mormons believed that church and state should be
one, and that the laws of God should be the laws of the
land; therefore many of them persisted in practicing polygamy after Congress passed laws prohibiting it, preferring,
as they said, to practice the higher law in disobedience to
the laws made by men, and many of them have gone,
singing and dancing, to the penitentiary, consigned there
by the courts for violating the statutes because of their
belief.

CHAPTER V.

THE new Mormon temple marks the history of the Church of Jesus Christ of Latter Day Saints from the day when Brigham Young and his few followers first set foot in the new promised land. It is a work commenced in the wilderness, and completed forty years afterward.

The laying of the cap-stone of the temple recorded the culmination of a work the Mormon people have been eagerly anticipating for nearly two generations. It recalls, too, many chapters of history abounding in interest. It tells a tale of patience, industry, and unswerving devotion to an object and a religious principle.

It is forty years ago since the corner-stones of this temple were laid, and although there have been occasional lapses of time when nothing was done, and often only a few men employed, the work has practically been going on continuously.

Not more than a few days after the arrival of the Mormon pioneers in the Great Salt Lake Basin, the prophet, Brigham Young, was strolling about in the vicinity of his camping-place in company with some of the apostles of his church. The days previous had been employed in exploring the valley to the north and south. These explorations satisfied them that there was no more favorable location to commence the building of a new city in the wilderness than the one on which they had first pitched their tents. The night when Brigham took that stroll was at the end of a perfect day in July. Looking to the south the valley stretched away into magnificent distances and beautiful vistas as lovely as eye ever beheld. Over in the west was the Great Salt Lake, with its huge islands rising from the mirrored surface of its waters, and burying their mountainous heads in the white of the clouds and the blue of the sky. In the east were the cold and rugged ranges of the Wasatch. To the north were the brown hills that guarded the city in that direction. It was a scene to inspire beautiful and poetic thoughts, and Brigham gazed about him, apparently delighted with the sublimity of the glorious prospect.

Turning his eyes to the east he struck his cane into the earth and said, "Here is where the temple of our God shall rise." Not a word of dissent was heard to his proclamation. There were no suggestions that better sites might be had. Brigham had issued his edict, and when he had spoken it was law to his people, so solemn that all indorsed it. From that moment the Temple Square was looked upon as sacred to the purpose to which it had been dedicated.

Remembering with what matchless courage this great Mormon leader had conducted his insignificant army across the desert from the Missouri River, and through the mountain defiles into this then wilderness, it is impossible to still the thought, "Did his imagination's eye peer through the mist of years and see the gray and solemn pile which is now the temple?"

But that July night when Brigham Young struck his cane on the ground was in 1847, and nothing was done toward building the temple until six years afterward. Still it is doubtful if the original intention had ever been abandoned.

At first it was intended to build it of adobe, but when a mountain of granite, fine in its quality and most beautiful in color, was found some miles from the city, that material was substituted. On a panel just above the second-story window of the east end of the temple is this inscription:

HOLINESS TO THE LORD.
THE HOUSE OF THE LORD
BUILT BY
THE CHURCH OF JESUS CHRIST
OF
LATTER DAY SAINTS.
COMMENCED APRIL 6, 1853,
COMPLETED —— ——

Below the word " completed " there is a blank line where, when the last piece of stone has been chiseled and the frescoer has applied the last touch of his brush, a date will be cut into the marble slab. That date may not be inscribed for two or three years yet, for there is still very much to do on the interior.

April 6, 1853, was a bright day in the history of Zion. Not only was the semi-annual conference of the Mormon church in session, but the corner-stone of the great temple was to be laid with imposing ceremonies. The first company of Mormon pioneers to enter the Salt Lake Valley only numbered 143, but six years afterward the city had a population of nearly 6,000 people. It was a city, too, peculiar and unique in its customs and the character of its residents. By that time Utah had many large settlements, and from the most remote of these the saints came to assemble at the center stake of Zion. They came wearing their brightest and best garments and their happiest faces. Presumably their souls were possessed of that sweet peace which passeth all understanding. A grand procession was formed in honor of the ceremony about to be celebrated.

An old program of that parade, and the exercises of the day, is yet in existence, and it is notable that the church dignitaries were the most conspicuous figures in the pageant. There were the presidents, apostles, and bishops, the high priests, the counselors, the elders, and all the lesser degrees of Mormon ecclesiastical authorities.

Flags were flying, bands were playing—there were two bands in Utah, even then. Four corner-stones were laid, four dedicatory prayers offered, in which the Almighty was invoked to bless the building then begun, and four orations were delivered.

There are many conflicting stories in regard to the designer of the temple. A man by the name of Truman C. Angell was the first architect, and he drew the plans, but it was in the fertile genius of Brigham Young that the ideas of form and arrangement were conceived. These he submitted to Angell, who elaborated them. Doubtless Brigham had based his conceptions on the descriptions he had read of Solomon's temple, but however much of the plans he may have cribbed, to him belongs the credit. He claimed the design of the temple, even to the smallest detail, had been given him by a revelation from God.

Angell devoted his life to this building. After him two or three others directed the construction, but for the past four or five years Don Carlos Young, a son of Brigham's, has been the architect.

For many years the progress was exceedingly slow. The foundations were sunk sixteen feet below the surface. There was a great yawning hole to be filled with rock, every one of which had to be pulled by ox teams. Many people remember how slowly the building rose. They say it was several years before the walls could be seen above ground. But there was no hurry and nothing was slighted, for the temple when completed was intended to be as enduring as the mountains from which the stone it was built of was quarried.

No better illustration of the infinite patience, the ceaseless industry, and the religious zeal of the Mormon people could be given than they have manifested in this work. It was a stupendous undertaking. They possessed no modern mechanical appliances; everything had to be done by the crudest methods. Considering these difficulties, and the immense character of the work, it inspires wonder and admiration.

The temple quarries are in a mountain-walled cañon called Little Cottonwood, twenty-two miles from the city. For many years, or until 1872, every stone had to be hauled that distance by ox teams. The wagons were especially constructed for that purpose, and some of the stones were so large that four or five yoke were required to pull the load. How slow and expensive a building of this magnitude must have been, when such methods were employed, can readily be appreciated. But in 1872 a branch railroad was built from the Temple Square to the quarries; since then the construction has been more rapid and less expensive.

Figures only give a suggestion of its gigantic proportions. It is only when seen from a distance that its massiveness manifests itself. Then it towers above the other tall buildings of the city like a mountain above the level plain—it stands out solemn, grand, majestic, and alone. It is 99 feet wide and 200 feet long. The four corner towers are 188 feet high; to the top of the central western tower is 204 feet. The main, or eastern tower, is 211 feet to the top of the great granite globe, and on that the statue of the angel Gabriel stands, the figure itself being 14 feet high. Above all these points are the supplementary spires, on which the electric lights will be fixed. The lights on these sky-piercing spires will be interesting, for they will be so powerful as to penetrate the darkest corner of the valley, and will be like unto a beacon to a watching mariner. That on the main, or eastern spire, will be placed below the statue of the angel, and will be reflected upward, surrounding the figure with a brilliant halo.

In the designing of the temple, no startling architectural innovations seem to have been attempted. The exterior has a poverty of ornamentation, yet perhaps that is the most attractive feature. But the interior is exceedingly interesting. There are all manner of eccentricities and queer unexpected places. In the four corner towers are winding stone staircases reaching to the roof, each having 250 steps. These were all cut by hand at a cost of $100 apiece, and they are anchored in walls of solid masonry. The largest room is in the top story, and is 80 x 120 feet and 36 feet high. This is to be used as an assemby hall, and will have a capacity to seat 1,000 people. The other rooms are much smaller. There is the fount-room, where baptisms are performed, for the Mormons, like the Baptists, believe in immersion. They baptize for the remission of sins, and the living, acting as proxies, are baptized for the dead.

As understood, if a person has some dear friend or relative who has passed into the beyond without having had the saving rite of baptism administered, the living can attend to that little formality so as to insure the dead a peaceful sojourn in the agreeable climate of the hereafter.

The uninitiated do not understand the purposes of Mormon temples. They are not intended to be used for public worship. Services of that character are never held in them. They are designed to be used for the meeting of the priesthood and for the performances of ordinances and ceremonies of marriage, baptisms, etc., and for the administering of ecclesiastical rites—the conferring of priestly degrees.

Thousands of people have seen this great monument which has been built by this peculiar people to their more peculiar religion, and have described the impressions it made on them.   Some, in a too-pronounced enthusiasm, have declared it to be a wonder in architecture—a triumph in its way—as something grand, almost marvelous in its conception.   It is not.   There is little that is exceptionally remarkable about it.   True, there is much to impress one, but it is rather its bigness and general appearance of solemnity than anything else.   Then there is something in its historical associations, the great difficulties overcome, and the great zeal displayed in its construction that inspires admiration.

Rudyard Kipling, who once saw it, in a vein of his keenest satire characterized it as "architecturally atrocious, ugly, villainously discordant, contemptuously correct, altogether inartistic and unpoetical," and other adjectives equally as forcible and uncomplimentary.   But he was probably more severe than just in his criticism.   There is nothing about it to shock the artistic eye, and there are a few things to please.

A word about the statue that is perched on the topmost pinnacle.   Certainly that is pleasing to the artistic soul.   It is the work of a finished sculptor, who is even now not wholly unknown to fame.   He is C. E. Dallin, and was born in Salt Lake City not much over thirty years ago. But the statue: It is not of marble, but of hammered copper, covered with gold.   To the eye it looks as if it were made entirely of that metal.   It is a very fascinating piece of work, and on its high pedestal it glistens in the sunlight as if made of fire.   One prominent Mormon has said the statue is not intended to represent Gabriel, but the angel Moroni proclaiming the gospel to all the world.   It was the angel Moroni, it will be remembered, who showed the golden plates to Joseph Smith from which the Book of Mormon was written.

From Dallin's boyhood he began to display the artistic

bent and temperament of his nature. Before he ever had any instruction, he modeled in clay with such success as to attract attention to his work. Then he went abroad to study, and at the Paris Salon of 1888 he received the medal of "Honorable Merit" for his "Peace Signal," that being a full-sized figure of an Indian brave on horseback holding his lance in such a manner as to be a signal to his fellow warriors at a distance that all was well. He has also done other meritorious work, and is at present engaged on a statue to be built on one of the corners of the Temple Square in honor of Brigham Young and the Mormon pioneers.

There have been many extravagant statements made concerning the cost of this temple. Figures have been placed as high as $6,000,000, which is nearly double its actual cost. As it stands to-day, $3,000,000 have probably been expended, and not more than half a million will be required to complete it.

The laying of this cap-stone practically completes the temple. There is not another stone to be laid, all that remains to be done being confined to the interior, and that is mostly in a decorative way. In its fulfillment there is great rejoicing in the hearts of the Mormon people. It has been a work requiring the toil of years, the manifestation of much self-denial, and the display of religious earnestness and sincerity almost without a parallel.

CHAPTER VI.

MY FIRST VENTURE.

When I grew up and became a married man, with daughters who were to be clothed and educated, I found it impossible to make, with the labor of one man on a farm, sufficient money to meet my growing necessities. I was raised on a farm and had always been a farmer, but with increasing expenses I was compelled to go into business of some kind, where I could accumulate a sufficiency for such purposes.

As I was brought up to handle animals, and had been employed more or less in the teaming business, after looking the situation all over, it occurred to me there was nothing I was so well adapted for by my past experience as the freighting business that was then being conducted between Independence, Mo., and Santa Fé, New Mexico, a distance of 800 miles.

At that time almost the entire distance lay through Indian Territory, where we were likely, on a greater portion of the trail, to meet hostile Indians any moment.

Being a religious man and opposed to all kinds of profanity, and knowing the practice of teamsters, almost without an exception, was to use profane and vulgar language, and to travel upon the Sabbath day, another difficulty presented itself to my mind which had to be overcome.

After due reflection on this subject I resolved in my innermost nature, by the help of God, I would overcome all difficulties that presented themselves to my mind, let the hazard be whatever it might. This resolve I carried out, and it was the keynote to my great success in the management of men and animals.

Having reached this determination, and being ready to embark in my new business, I formulated a code of rules for the behavior of my employes, which read as follows:

"While I am in the employ of A. Majors, I agree not to use profane language, not to get drunk, not to gamble, not to treat animals cruelly, and not to do anything else that is incompatible with the conduct of a gentleman. And I agree, if I violate any of the above conditions, to accept my discharge without any pay for my services."

I do not remember a single instance of a man signing these "iron-clad rules," as they called them, being discharged without his pay. My employes seemed to understand in the beginning of their term of service that their good behavior was part of the recompense they gave me for the money I paid them.

A few years later, when the Civil War had commenced, I bound my employes to pay true allegiance to the Government of the United States, while in my employ, in addition to the above.

I will say to my readers that, had I had the experience of a thousand years, I could not have formulated a better code of rules for the government of my business than those adopted, looking entirely from a moral standpoint. The result proved to be worth more to me in a money point of view than that resulting from any other course I could have pursued, for with the enforcement of these rules, which I had little trouble to do, a few years gave me control of the business of the plains and, of course, a widespread reputation for conducting business on a humane plan.

I can state with truthfulness that never in the history of freighting on the plains did such quiet, gentlemanly, fra-

NEBRASKA CITY IN OVERLAND FREIGHTING DAYS.

ternal feelings exist as among the men who were in my employ and governed by these rules.

It was the prevalent opinion, previous to the time I started across the plains, that none but daring, rough men were fit to contend with the Indians and manage teamsters upon those trips. I soon proved to the entire contrary this was a great mistake, for it was soon observable that both men and animals working under this system were superior, and got along better in every way than those working under the old idea of ruffianism.

It is my firm conviction that where men are born commanders or managers there is no need of the cruelty and punishment so often dealt out by so many in authority. With men who have the key of government in their natures there is little trouble in getting employes to conform strictly to their duty.

I have seen, to my great regret and dislike, such cruelty practiced by army officers in command, and managers upon steamships on the seas and steamboats on the rivers, as well as other places where men were in charge of their fellow beings and had command over them, as should receive the most outspoken protest, and ought not to be tolerated in christendom.

If men in charge would first control themselves and carry out, in their management of others, the true principles of humanity and kindness, pursuing a firm and consistent course of conduct themselves, wearing at the same time an easy and becoming dignity, it would do away with all the cruelties that have so often shocked humanity and caused needless suffering to those who were compelled to endure them. I found that an ounce of dignity on the plains was worth more than a pound at home or in organized society.

With all the thousands of men I had in my employ it was never necessary to do more than give a manly rebuke, if any one committed any misdemeanor, to avoid a repetition of the offense.

In all my vast business on the plains I adhered strictly as possible to keeping the Sabbath day, and avoided traveling or doing any unnecessary work. This fact enabled me to carry out perfectly the "iron-clad rules" with my employes. When they saw I was willing to pay them the same price as that paid for work including the Sabbath day, and let them rest on that day, it made them feel I was consistent in requiring them to conduct themselves as gentlemen.

In later years, when my business had so increased and the firm of Majors & Russell was formed, I insisted on carrying my system of government and management into the business of the new firm, and the same course was pursued by the firm of Russell, Majors & Waddell as I have above narrated.

Notwithstanding the disagreeable features mentioned, I selected this avocation, and on the 10th day of August, 1848, with my first little outfit of six wagons and teams, started in business.

At that time it was considered hazardous to start on a trip of that kind so late in the season; but I made that trip with remarkable success, making the round run in ninety-two days, the quickest on record with ox teams, many of my oxen being in such good condition when I returned as to look as though they had not been on the road. This fact gave me quite a reputation among the freighters and merchants who were engaged in business between the two points above mentioned.

I was by no means the first to engage in the trade between Mexico and the United States, for as early as 1822 Captain Rockwell started in the trade, carrying goods in packs on mules.

The next notable era in the line of this trade was the introduction of wagons in the year 1824. This, of course, was an experiment, as there were no beaten roads, and the sand on some portions of the route was so deep (the worst part being in the valley of the Cimarron) that it was doubted whether wagons could be used with success. But the experiment proved to be so much superior to packing that it did away entirely with the former mode; and wagon-makers at St. Louis and Independence, Mo., commenced to build wagons adapted solely to that trade.

It was not long after the adoption of wagon trains on that route until there was a wide and well-beaten road the entire distance, the country over which it passed being level plains, requiring no bridges; but little work of any kind was necessary to keep the thoroughfare in good traveling condition.

On a large portion of the route there was an abundance of grass and water for the work animals. In those early days a belt of at least 400 miles was covered with herds of buffalo.

This crossing with large and heavy trains so well established the route that, by the year 1846, the people on the west border of Missouri were equipped and prepared in every way for transporting the supplies for Colonel Doniphan's army, when he was ordered to cross from Fort Leavenworth, Kan., to Santa Fé, N. M., at the commencement of the war between the United States and Mexico.

To return to my own operations in the freighting business, it will be seen by the foregoing dates mentioned in this article that two years later I made my first start, and I met on my outward-bound trip many of the troops of Colonel Doniphan returning home, the war being over and peace having been made between the two countries.

I continued in the freighting business continuously from

1848 to 1866, most of the time in the employ of the United States Government, carrying stores to different forts and stations in the Western Territories, New Mexico, Colorado, and Utah. Having freighted on my own account for about seven years, in 1855 I went into partnership with Messrs. Russell & Waddell, residents of Lexington, Lafayette County, Mo., my home being still in Jackson County, Mo. We did business three years under the firm name of Majors & Russell. In 1858, when we obtained a contract from the Government for transporting supplies to Utah, the name of the firm was changed to Russell, Majors & Waddell.

At this time freighting for the Government had increased enormously on account of General Johnston, with an army, having been sent to Utah. All of the supplies for the soldiers and much of the grain for the animals had to be transported in wagons from the Missouri River. However, one of the conditions of the contract the firm made with the Government, through the Quartermaster-General at Washington, was that they should have another starting-point other than Fort Leavenworth, the established depot for supplies going west.

I made this proposition to General Jessup, knowing, from my long experience in handling that kind of business, that it would be next to impossible to handle the supplies from one depot, as there were not herding grounds within a reasonable distance to keep such a vast number of cattle as the business would require when conducted from one point.

My partner, Mr. Russell, remarked to me that if he had to make a station higher up the river I would have to go and attend to it, for he could not. My answer was I would willingly do so, for I knew that loading hundreds of thousands of pounds of supplies daily would create a confusion at one point as would retard the business.

It was then and there agreed between the quartermaster and ourselves that one-half the entire stores should be sent to another point to be selected by his clerk and myself.

Immediately after the contract was signed I went to Fort Leavenworth, and with Lieutenant Dubarry of the Quartermaster's Department set out to locate another point. We traveled up the Missouri River as far as Plattsmouth, when we concluded Nebraska City, Neb., was the most available point upon the river for our business. I at once arranged with the citizens of that town to build warehouses, preparatory to receiving the large quantities of supplies the Government would soon begin to ship to that point.

The supplies sent to Utah in the year 1858 were enormous, being over sixteen million pounds, requiring over three thousand five hundred large wagons and teams to transport them. We found it was as much as we could do to meet the Government requirements with the two points in full operation.

As agreed, I took charge of the new station and moved my family from my farm, nine miles south of Kansas City, Mo., to Nebraska City, where I bought a home for them and commenced to carry out my part of the agreement.

The firm of Russell, Majors & Waddell conducted the business for two years, and in the spring of 1860 I bought out my partners and continued the business in my own name that year.

In Nebraska City I found a very intelligent, enterprising, and clever people, among whom were S. F. Knuckle, J. Sterling Morton, Robert Hawk Dillon, Colonel Tewksberry, McCann, Metcalf, Rhodes, O. P. Mason, Judge Kinney, Rinkers, Seigle, and a great many others of integrity and enterprise. I never did business more pleasantly than with the gentlemen whom I met during my residence of nine years there.

CHAPTER VII.

To ONE who has had to make friends of the brute creation, it is natural for him to claim companionship with those domestic animals with which he is constantly drawn by day and night, such as horses, oxen, mules, and dogs. The dog is most thoroughly the comrade of those who dwell upon the frontier, and a chapter regarding them will not, I feel, be uninteresting to the reader.

I have always been a great admirer of a good dog, but my knowledge of them is a general one, such as you and a great many other Western men have. I have never made him a scientific study, but I think he is the only domestic animal, and I don't know but the only animal that takes a joint ownership in all of his master's property so far as he can comprehend it, whether it be personal, portable, or realistic; in other words, the man owns the dog and his other property, and the dog seems to claim or own the man and all of his other effects, so far as he can comprehend them.

I had a Shepherd dog that would not allow a stranger to take hold of me or my horse, saddle, bridle, rope, spurs, gun, or anything else that he thought belonged to *us*, without making a fuss about it, and he seemed to think stepping upon a rope or blanket, or anything of that kind, was just the same as taking hold with the hands, and yet he was very good-natured with strangers otherwise.

He was very fond of playing with other dogs, especially young ones on the pup order, but if they ever took any freedom with our *joint* property, there was sure to be trouble. He would not allow them to take hold of, or sleep on, or lay down in the shade of a horse, wagon, buggy, or do anything that he thought was taking too much liberty with his peculiar rights. He would go almost any distance to hunt anything that I would lose, and was very quick to pick up anything that I would drop, and give it to me without mussing it, whether I was walking or on horseback.

He was a good retriever, either on land or water, and would cross a river to get a goose or duck if it fell on the opposite side after being shot. He would also take hold of one hind leg of a deer or antelope and help me all he could to drag it home or to where I would leave my horse, but he was more help in driving and handling stock than in any other way. He would also go after a horse that would get away, with a bridle or rope on, and catch him by the rein or rope and bring him back if he could lead him, or if not, he would try and hold on until I would come up. He had a great many other minor tricks to make sport for the boys in camp, such as speaking, jumping, waltzing, etc., and he would also carry in wood to make fires with, and thus save the men trouble.

I have also had experience with the Newfoundland and the Setter dogs, and found them fully as easy to train and as faithful as the Shepherd dog I have written about. A Newfoundland that I brought down from Montana with me would do almost anything that it was possible for a dog to do. When living in Salt Lake City I saw my daughter send him after an apple once when she was sitting in a room up stairs. He went down and found the doors all fastened, so he came back and went out at an upstairs window and onto a lower roof and from there down on a common rung ladder to the ground and out into some one's orchard, got an apple, and returned the same way, and did it quicker than any boy could possibly have performed the same thing. But of course he knew where the ladder was, and had climbed up and down it many times before that. I used to see the children in our neighborhood sending this dog over in the orchards after apples, while they remained at the fence outside, and he would·keep going and returning with the apples until they were satisfied. The people never objected that owned the fruit, as they thought it so smart in the dog to steal for the children that which he did not eat himself.

It came to my knowledge once of a dumb beast that showed the intelligence of a human being.

He was only a dog, but a remarkably clever one. He belonged to the class known as Shepherd dogs, which are noted for their sagacity and fidelity. His master was a little Italian boy called Beppo, who earned his living by selling flowers on the street.

Tony was very fond of Beppo, who had been his master ever since he was a puppy, and Beppo had never failed to share his crust with his good dog. Now, Tony had grown to be a large, strong dog, and took as much care of Beppo as Beppo took of him. Often while standing on the corner with his basket on his arm, waiting for a customer, Beppo would feel inclined to cry from very loneliness; but Tony seemed to know when the "blues" came, and would lick his master's hand, as much as to say: "You've got me for a friend. Cheer up! I'm better than nobody; I'll stand by you."

But one day it happened that when the other boys who shared the dark cellar home with Beppo went out early in the morning as usual, Beppo was so ill that he could hardly lift his head from the straw on which he slept. He felt that he would be unable to sell flowers that day. What to do he did not know. Tony did his best to com-

RIVER SCENE AT NEBRASKA CITY.

fort him, but the tears would gather in his eyes, and it was with the greatest difficulty that he at last forced himself to get up and go to the florist, who lived near by, for the usual supply of buds.

Having filled his basket, the boy went home again and tied it around Tony's neck; then he looked at the dog and said: "Now, Tony, you're the only fellow I've got to depend on. Go and sell my flowers for me, and bring the money home safe; don't let any one steal anything."

Then he kissed the dog and pointed to the door.

Tony trotted out to the street to Beppo's usual corner, where he took his stand. Beppo's customers soon saw how matters stood, and chose their flowers, and put their money into the tin cup in the center of the basket. Now and then, when a rude boy would come along and try to snatch a flower from the basket, Tony would growl fiercely and drive him away.

So that day went safely by, and at nightfall Tony went home to his master, who was waiting anxiously for him, and gave him a hearty welcome. Beppo untied the basket and looked in the cup, and I should not wonder if he found more money in it than ever before. This is how Tony sold the rosebuds, and he did it so well that Beppo never tired of telling me about it.

A farmer's dog who had been found guilty of obtaining goods under false pretenses is worthy of mention. He was extremely fond of sausages, and had been taught by his owner to go after them for him, carrying a written order in his mouth. Day after day he appeared at the butcher-shop, bringing his master's order, and by and by the butcher became careless about reading the document. Finally, when settlement day came, the farmer complained that he was charged with more sausage than he had ordered. The butcher was surprised, and the next time

Lion came in with a slip of paper between his teeth he took the trouble to look at it. The paper was blank, and further investigation showed that whenever the dog felt a craving for sausage, he looked around for a piece of paper, and trotted off to the butcher's. The farmer is something out of pocket, but squares the account by boasting of the dog's intelligence, which enabled him to deliberately steal for him, and deceive the butcher to do so.

While in Edinburgh, Scotland, where my wife and I remained for a year, our apartments were cared for by an English maid, who owned a very fine Scotch terrier. Whenever she would come to our rooms the dog accompanied her, and soon became very much attached to me, and would come into our apartments whenever an opportunity offered, to pay his respects to me. My wife had a great aversion to dogs of all kinds, and particularly objected to having one in the room with her, as she declared she could feel fleas immediately upon the appearance of a canine, no matter how far away they were from her.

One morning, while I was quietly reading, my wife being busy in another part of the room, the dog slipped in and succeeded in establishing himself under my chair, without either of us being aware of his presence; but before many minutes had passed my wife discovered him, and remonstrated with me at once for allowing him to come in, when I knew so well how she detested him. I assured her of my ignorance as to his presence, but said nothing whatever to the dog. He arose with a crest-fallen air, and with his tail tucked between his legs, walked slowly across the room, stopping in the doorway to look once at Mrs. Majors, with the most reproachful, abused expression I have ever seen on any creature's face.

After that he always endeavored to make his calls upon

me when Mrs. Majors was absent, and would often come up and wait in one end of the hall until he would see her go into the adjoining room, when he would come to see me, but immediately upon hearing her opening the door of the other room, he would make a break for the door, making his escape before she would reach the room; and this, too, when she had never been unkind to him except in what she said of him.

One morning while the landlady and her servant were "doing up" our sleeping apartment, the dog as usual accompanying the servant, Mrs. Majors stepped into the room to speak to the landlady, and the servant, knowing the dog's fondness for me, said:

"Prince, ask Mrs. Majors if you can't go in to see Mr. Majors." He turned around, went up to Mrs. Majors and commenced jumping up and down in front of her, asking as plain as dogs can speak for the coveted permission. My wife could not help laughing, and said, "Well, sir, you have won me over this time; you can go," whereupon he made a rush for the other room, leaped upon my lap, and seemed fairly wild with joy. I could not understand his unusual demonstrations until Mrs. Majors came in and explained.

A friend who owned a very fine dog was one morning accosted by a neighbor, who accused the dog of having killed several of his sheep in the night. The owner said he thought it was a mistake, as he had never known the dog to be guilty of such tricks, and after some discussion it was decided to examine the dog's mouth, and if wool was found sticking in his teeth, they would believe him guilty, and the man who had lost the sheep could kill him. They called the dog up while talking about it, and the master opened his mouth, and to his grief, found the evidence of his crime between his teeth. The neighbor knew the man's attachment for the dog, and not wishing to kill him in his presence, said he would defer the execution until a more convenient time. The dog heard the conversation, appeared to understand the situation perfectly, and when the neighbor tried later to find him, he had disappeared, and neither the owner nor the neighbor ever heard of him again. He fled to parts unknown, thus showing his wisdom by putting himself out of harm's way.

It is hardly possible to say enough in the praise of the dog family, especially regarding their services to the pioneers in the settlement of the Mississippi Valley and frontier. At that time, bears, panthers, wolves, and small animals of prey were so thick that without the aid of dogs the stock, such as pigs, lambs, poultry, and such small animals, would have been completely destroyed in one single night. The dogs were constantly on guard, night and day, storm or sunshine, and upon the approach of an enemy, would warn the pioneers, giving them a sense of security against danger. They knew by the smell, often before hearing or seeing an enemy, and would give out the warning long before the pioneers themselves could have known of the proximity of the wild beasts. As a rule those faithful friends and protectors of our race have not been appreciated, more especially, as above stated, in the settlement of the frontier, for without them it would have been impossible for the pioneers to have saved their stock and poultry from the ravages of the wild beasts. I could write a volume upon the sagacity, faithfulness, and intelligence of these remarkable animals, as during my life in the Wild West I learned to fully appreciate them.

CHAPTER VIII.

On the 18th of June, 1846, A. W. Doniphan was elected colonel of the regiment that he commanded in the Mexican War. In his speech at Independence, Jackson County, Mo., on July 29, 1837, he declared he had not been a candidate for office for seven years, and did not expect to be for the next seventy years to come. The passage by the American Congress of the resolutions of annexation, by which the republic of Texas was incorporated into the Union as one of the States, having merged her sovereignty into that of our own Government, was the prime cause which led to the war with Mexico. However, the more immediate cause of the war may be traced to the occupation by the American army of the strip of disputed territory lying between the Nueces and the Rio Grande.

Bigoted and insulting, Mexico was always prompt to manifest her hostility toward this Government, and sought the earliest plausible pretext for declaring war against the United States. This declaration of war by the Mexican government, which bore date in April, 1846, was quickly and spiritedly followed by a manifesto from our Congress at Washington, announcing that a state of war existed between Mexico and the United States. Soon after this counter declaration, the Mexicans crossed the Rio Grande in strong force, headed by the famous generals, Arista and Ampudia. This force, as is well known, was defeated at Palo Alto on the 18th, and at Resaca de la Palma on May 9, 1846, by the troops under command

G

of Major-General Taylor, and repulsed with great slaughter. The whole Union was in a state of intense excitement. General Taylor's recent and glorious victories were the constant theme of universal admiration. The war had actually begun; and that, too, in a manner which demanded immediate action. The United States Congress passed an act about the middle of May, 1846, authorizing President Polk to call into the field 50,000 volunteers designed to operate against Mexico at three distinct points, namely: The southern wing, or the "Army of Occupation," commanded by Major-General Taylor, to penetrate directly into the heart of the country; the column under Brigadier-General Wool, or the "Army of the Center," to operate against the city of Chihuahua; and the expedition under the command of Colonel (afterward Brigadier-General) Kearney, known as the "Army of the West," to direct its march upon the city of Santa Fé. This was the original plan of operations against Mexico, but subsequently the plan was changed. Major-General Scott, with a well-appointed army, was sent to Vera Cruz, General Wool effected a junction with General Taylor at Saltillo, and General Kearney divided his force into three separate commands; the first he led in person to the distant shores of the Pacific. A detachment of nearly eleven hundred Missouri volunteers, under command of Col. A. W. Doniphan, was ordered to make a descent upon the State of Chihuahua, expecting to join General Wool's division at the capital, while the greater part was left as a garrison at Santa Fé, under command of Col. Sterling Price. The greatest eagerness was manifested by the citizens of the United States to engage in the war, to redress our wrongs, to repel an insulting foe, and to vindicate our national honor and the honor of our oft-insulted flag.

The call of the President was promptly responded to,

but of the 50,000 volunteers at first authorized to be raised, the service of about 17,000 only were required. The cruel an inhuman butchery of Colonel Fannin and his men, all Americans, the subsequent and indiscriminate murder of all Texans who unfortunately fell into Mexican hands; the repeated acts of cruelty and injustice perpetrated upon the persons and property of American citizens residing in the northern Mexican provinces; the imprisonment of American merchants without the semblance of a trial by jury, and the forcible seizure and confiscation of their goods; the robbing of American travelers and tourists in the Mexican country of their passports and other means of safety, whereby they were in certain instances deprived of their liberty for a time; the forcible detention of American citizens, sometimes in prison and other times in free custody; the recent blockade of the Mexican ports against the United States trade; the repeated insults offered our national flag; the contemptuous ill treatment of our ministers, some of whom were spurned with their credentials; the supercilious and menacing air uniformly manifested toward the Government, which with characteristic forbearance and courtesy had endeavored to maintain a friendly understanding; Mexico's hasty and unprovoked declaration of war against the United States; the army's unceremonious passage of the Rio Grande in strong force and with hostile intentions; her refusal to pay indemnities, and a complication of lesser evils, all of which had been perpetrated by the Mexican authorities, or by unauthorized Mexican citizens, in a manner which clearly evinced the determination on the part of Mexico to terminate the amicable relations hitherto existing between the two countries, were the causes which justified the war.

On the 18th day of August, 1846, after a tiresome march of nearly 900 miles in less than fifty days, General Kearney with his whole command entered Santa Fé, the capital of the province of New Mexico, and took peaceable possession of the country, without the loss of a single man or shedding a drop of blood, in the name of the United States, and planted the American flag in the public square, where the stars and stripes and eagle streamed above the Palacio Grande, or stately residence of ex-Governor Armigo.

On the 29th of July, 1847, Captain Ruff was dispatched by General Smith with a squadron composed of one company of the Second Dragoons under Lieutenant Hawes and his own company of mounted riflemen, in all eighty-six men, to attack the town of San Juan de los Lianos. In this engagement the Mexicans lost forty-three killed and fifty wounded. Only one American was wounded and none killed. At the battle of San Pascual, on the morning of the 6th of December, General Kearney commanding, with Captains Johnson, Moore, and Hammond as principal aids, drove the enemy from the field. Loss not known. American loss, seventeen killed and fourteen wounded. On the 5th of November, 1846, a small detachment of forty-five volunteers, commanded by Captains Thompson and Burrows, met and totally defeated 200 Californians on the plains of Salinas, near Monterey. American loss, four killed and two wounded. On the 8th of January General Kearney and Commodore Stockton, with 500 men, met the insurgents, 600 strong, to dispute the passage of the river San Gabriel. This action lasted one hour and a half. The next day the Mexicans were again repulsed. Their loss on both days estimated in killed and wounded not less than eighty-five; American, two killed and fifteen wounded. A battle commanded by Doniphan was fought on Christmas day at Brazito, twenty-five miles from El Paso. Mexican loss was seventy-one killed, five prisoners, and 150 wounded, among them their commanding general, Ponce de Leon. The Americans had none killed and eight wounded. On the 27th the city of El Paso was taken possession of without further opposition. On the 13th a battle with the Indians occurred. Americans lost none; Indians had seventeen killed and not less than twenty-five wounded. On the 19th of January, Governor Bent was murdered with his retinue. On the 24th Colonel Rice encountered the enemy. Our loss was two killed and seven wounded. The Mexicans acknowledged a loss of thirty-six killed and forty-five prisoners. On the 3d of February, met the enemy at Pueblo de Taos. The total loss of the Mexicans at the three engagements was 282 killed—wounded unknown. Our total was fifteen killed and forty-seven wounded. On the 24th, in an engagement at Las Vegas, the enemy had twenty-five killed, three wounded; our loss, one killed, three wounded. At Red River Cañon we were vigorously attacked by a large body of Mexicans and Indians; Americans lost one killed and several wounded; Mexicans and Indians, seventeen killed, wounded not known. At Las Vegas Major Edmondson charged the town; there were ten Mexicans slain and fifty prisoners taken. On the 9th of July a detachment of Captain Morin's company was attacked; five of our men killed and nine wounded. On the 26th of June Lieutenant Love was attacked and surrounded by Indians; they cut their way through with a loss of eleven; the Indians lost twenty-five. On the 27th of October Captain Mann's train was attacked; American loss, one killed, four wounded; Indian loss not known.

CHAPTER IX.

On Sunday, the 28th of February, a bright and auspicious day, the American army, under Colonel Doniphan, arrived in sight of the Mexican encampment at Sacramento, which could be distinctly seen at the distance of four miles. His command consisted of the following corps and detachments of troops:

The First Regiment, Colonel Doniphan, numbering about eight hundred men; Lieutenant-Colonel Mitchell's escort, ninety-seven men; artillery battalion, Major Clark and Captain Weightman, 117 men, with light field battery of six pieces of cannon; and two companies of teamsters, under Captains Skillman and Glasgow, forming an extra battalion of about one hundred and fifty men, commanded by Major Owens of Independence, making an aggregate force of 1,164 men, all Missouri volunteers. The march of the day was conducted in the following order: The wagons, near four hundred in all, were thrown in four parallel files, with spaces of thirty feet beween each. In the center space marched the artillery battalion; in the space to the right the First Battalion, and in the space to the left the Second Battalion. Masking these, in front marched the three companies intending to act as cavalry—the Missouri Horse Guards, under Captain Reid, on the right; the Missouri Dragoons, under Captain Parsons, on the left; and the Chihuahua Rangers, under Captain Hudson, in the center. Thus arranged, they approached the scene of action.

The enemy had occupied the brow of a rocky eminence rising upon a plateau between the river Sacramento and the Arroya Seca, and near the Sacramento Fort, eighteen miles from Chihuahua, and fortified its approaches by a line of field-works, consisting ·of twenty-eight strong redoubts and intrenchments. Here, in this apparently secure position, the Mexicans had determined to make a bold stand, for the pass was the key to the capital. So certain of the victory were the Mexicans, that they had prepared strings and handcuffs in which they meant to drive us prisoners to the City of Mexico, as they did the Texans in 1841. Thus fortified and intrenched, the Mexican army, consisting, according to a consolidated report ·of the adjutant-general which came into Colonel Doniphan's possession after the battle, of 4,220 men, commanded by Major-General Jose A. Heredia, aided by Gen. Garcia Conde, former Minister of War in Mexico, as commander of cavalry; General Mauricia Ugarte, commander of infantry; General Justiniani, commander of artillery, and Gov. Angel Trias, brigadier-general, commanding the Chihuahua Volunteers, awaited the approach of the Americans.

When Colonel Doniphan arrived within one mile and a half of the enemy's fortifications (a reconnaissance of his position having been made by Major Clark), leaving the main road, which passed within the range of his batteries, he suddenly deflected to the right, crossed the rocky Arroya, expeditiously gained the plateau beyond, successfully deployed his men into line upon the highland, causing the enemy to change its first position, and made the assault from the west. This was the best point of attack that could possibly have been selected. The event of the day proves how well it was chosen.

In passing the Arroya the caravan and baggage trains followed close upon the rear of the army. Nothing could exceed in point of solemnity and grandeur the rumbling of the artillery, the firm moving of the caravan, the dashing to and fro of horsemen, and the waving of banners and gay fluttering of guidons, as both armies advanced to the attack on the rocky plain; for at this crisis General Conde, with a select body of 1,200 cavalry, rushed down from the fortified heights to commence the engagement. When within 950 yards of our alignment, Major Clark's battery of six-pounders and Weightman's section of howitzers opened upon them a well-directed and most destructive fire, producing fearful execution in their ranks. In some disorder they fell back a short distance, unmasking a battery of cannon, which immediately commenced its fire upon us. A brisk cannonading was now kept up on both sides for the space of fifty minutes, during which time the enemy suffered great loss, our battery discharging twenty-four rounds to the minute. The balls from the enemy's cannon whistled through our ranks in quick succession. Many horses and other animals were killed and the wagons much shattered. Sergeant A. Hughes of the Missouri Dragoons had both his legs broken by a cannon ball. In this action the enemy, who were drawn up in columns four deep, close order, lost about twenty-five killed, besides a great number of horses. The Americans, who stood dismounted in two ranks, open order, suffered but slight injury.

General Conde, with considerable disorder, now fell back and rallied his men behind the intrenchments and redoubts. Colonel Doniphan immediately ordered the buglers to sound the advance. Thereupon the American army moved forward in the following manner, to storm the enemy's breastworks:

The artillery battalion, Major Clark in the center, firing occasionally on the advance; the First Battalion, commanded by Lieutenant-Colonels Jackson and Mitchell, composing the right wing; the two select companies of cavalry under Captains Reid and Parsons, and Captain Hudson's mounted company, immediately on the left of the artillery; and the Second Battalion on the extreme left, commanded by Major Gilpin. The caravan and baggage trains, under command of Major Owens, followed close in the rear. Colonel Doniphan and his aids, Captain Thompson, United States Army, Adjutant De Courcy, and Sergeant-Major Crenshaw acted between the battalions.

At this crisis a body of 300 lancers and lazadors were discovered advancing upon our rear. These were exclusive of Heredia's main force, and were said to be criminals turned loose from the Chihuahua prisons, that by some gallant exploit they might expurgate themselves of crime. To this end they were posted in the rear to cut off stragglers, prevent retreat, and capture and plunder the merchants' wagons. The battalion of teamsters kept these at bay. Besides this force there were a thousand spectators—women, citizens, and rancheros—perched on the summits of adjacent hills and mountains, watching the event of the day.

As we neared the enemy's redoubts, still inclining to the right, a heavy fire was opened upon us from his different batteries, consisting in all of sixteen pieces of cannon. But owing to the facility with which our movements were performed, and to the fact that the Mexicans were compelled to fire plungingly upon our lines (their position being considerably elevated above the plateau, and particularly the battery placed on the brow of the Sacramento Mountain with the design of enfilading our column), we sustained but little damage.

When our column had approached within about 400 yards of the enemy's line of field-works, the three calvary companies, under Captains Reid, Parsons, and Hudson, and

Weightman's section of howitzers, were ordered to carry the main center battery, which had considerably annoyed our lines, and which was protected by a strong bastion. The charge was not made simultaneously, as intended by the colonel; for this troop having spurred forward a little way, was halted for a moment under a heavy cross-fire from the enemy, by the adjutant's misapprehending the order. However, Captain Reid, either not hearing or disregarding the adjutant's order to halt, leading the way, waved his sword, and rising in his stirrups exclaimed: "Will my men follow me?" Hereupon Lieutenants Barnett, Hinton, and Moss, with about twenty-five men, bravely sprang forward, rose the hill with the captain, carried the battery, and for a moment silenced the guns, but were too weak to hold possession of it. By the overwhelming force of the enemy, we were beaten back, and many of us wounded. Here Maj. Samuel C. Owens, who had voluntarily charged upon the redoubt, received a cannon or musket shot, which instantly killed both him and his horse. Captain Reid's horse was shot under him, and a gallant young man of the same name immediately dismounted and generously offered the captain his.

By this time the remainder of Captain Reid's company, under Lieutenant Hocklin, and the section of howitzers under Captain Weightman and Lieutenants Choteau and Evans, rose the hill, and supported Captain Reid. A deadly volley of grape and canister shot, mingled with yager balls, quickly cleared the intrenchments and redoubt. The battery was retaken and held. Almost at the same instant Captains Parsons and Hudson, with the two remaining companies of cavalry, crossed the intrenchments to Reid's left and successfully engaged with the enemy. They resolutely drove him back and held the ground.

All the companies were now pressing forward, and pour-

ing over the intrenchments and into the redoubts, eagerly
vying with each other in the noble struggle for victory.
Each company, as well as each soldier, was ambitious to
excel. Companies A, B, C, and a part of Company D, composing the right wing, all dismounted, respectively under
command of Captains Waldo, Walton, Moss, and Lieutenant Miller, led on by Lieutenant-Colonels Jackson and
Mitchell, stormed a formidable line of redoubts on the
enemy's left, defended by several pieces of cannon and a
great number of well-armed and resolute men. A part of
this wing took possession of the strong battery on Sacramento Hill, which had kept a continued cross-firing upon
our right during the whole engagement. Colonels Jackson
and Mitchell and their captains, lieutenants, non-commis-
sioned officers, and the men generally, behaved with com-
mendable gallantry. Many instances of individual prowess
were exhibited. But it is invidious to distinguish between
men, where all performed their duty so nobly.

Meanwhile the left wing, also dismounted, commanded
by Major Gilpin, a gallant and skillful officer, boldly
scaled the heights, passed the intrenchments, cleared the
redoubts, and, with considerable slaughter, forced the
enemy to retreat from its position on the right. Company
G, under Captain Hughes, and a part of Company F, under
Lieutenant Gordon, stormed the battery of three brass
four-pounders strongly defended by embankments and
ditches filled by resolute and well-armed Mexican infantry.
Some of the artillerists were made prisoners while endeav-
oring to touch off the cannon. Companies H and E, under
Captains Rodgers and Stephenson, and a part of Hudson's
company, under Lieutenant Todd, on the extreme left,
behaved nobly, and fought with great courage. They beat
the Mexicans from their strong places, and chased them

like bloodhounds. Major Gilpin was not behind his men in bravery—he encouraged them to fight by example.

Major Clark, with his six-pounders, and Captain Weightman, with his howitzers, during the whole action rendered the most signal and essential service, and contributed much toward the success of the day. The gallant charge led by Captain Reid, and sustained by Captain Weightman, in point of daring and brilliancy of execution, has not been excelled by any similar exploit during the war.

General Heredia made several unsuccessful attempts to rally his retreating forces, to infuse into their minds new courage, and to close up the breaches already made in his lines. General Conde, with his troop of horse, also vainly endeavored to check the advance of the Missourians. They were dislodged from their strong places, and forced from the hill in confusion.

The rout of the Mexican army now became general, and the slaughter continued until night put an end to the chase. The battle lasted three hours and a half. The men returned to the battle-field after dark, completely worn out and exhausted with fatigue. The Mexicans lost 304 men killed on the field, and a large number wounded, perhaps not less than five hundred, and seventy prisoners, among whom was Brigadier-General Cuilta, together with a vast quantity of provisions, $6,000 in specie, 50,000 head of sheep, 1,500 head of cattle, 100 mules, twenty wagons, twenty-five or thirty caretas, 25,000 pounds of ammunition, ten pieces of cannon of different caliber, varying from four to nine pounders; six culverins, or wall pieces; 100 stand of small colors, seven fine carriages, the general's escritoire, and many other things of less note. Our loss was Major Samuel C. Owens, killed, and eleven wounded, three of whom have subsequently died.

Thus was the army of Central Mexico totally defeated,

and completely disorganized, by a column of Missouri volunteers. The Mexicans retreated precipitately to Durango, and dispersed among the ranchos and villages. Their leaders were never able to rally them.

In this engagement Colonel Doniphan was personally much exposed, and by reason of his stature was a conspicuous mark for the fire of the enemy's guns. He was all the while at the proper place, whether to dispense his orders, encourage his men, or use his saber in thinning the enemy's ranks. His courage and gallant conduct were only equaled by his clear foresight and great judgment. His effective force actually engaged was about nine hundred and fifty men, including a considerable number of amateur fighters, among whom James L. Collins, James Kirker, Messrs. Henderson and Anderson, interpreters, Major Campbell, and James Stewart, deserve to be favorably mentioned. They fought bravely. It was impossible for Captains Skillman and Glasgow to bring their companies of teamsters into the action. They deserve great honor for their gallantry in defending the trains. The soldiers encamped on the battle-field, within the enemy's entrenchments, and feasted sumptuously upon his viands, wines, and pound-cake.

There they rested.

Colonel Doniphan, not like Hannibal loitering on the plains of Italy after the battle of Cannæ when he might have entered Rome in triumph, immediately followed up his success and improved the advantage which his victory gave him. Early the next morning (March 1st) he dispatched Lieutenant-Colonel Mitchell, with 150 men under command of Captains Reid and Weightman, and a section of artillery, to take formal possession of the capital, and occupy it in the name of his Government. This detachment, before arriving in the city, was met by several Ameri-

7

can gentlemen escaping from confinement, who represented that the Mexicans had left the place undefended, and fled with the utmost precipitation to Durango. The Spanish consul, also, came out with the flag of his country to salute and acknowledge the conqueror. This small body of troops entered and took military possession of Chihuahua without the slightest resistance, and the following night occupied the Cuartel, near Hidalgo's monument, which stands on the Alameda.

Meanwhile Colonel Doniphan and his men collected the booty, tended the captured animals, refitted the trains, remounted those who had lost their steeds in the action, arranged the preliminaries of the procession, and having marched a few miles encamped for the night. On the morning of March 2d Colonel Doniphan, with all his military trains, the merchant caravan, gay fluttering colors, and the whole *spolia opima*, triumphantly entered the city to the tunes of "Yankee Doodle" and "Hail Columbia," and fired in the public square a national salute of twenty-eight guns. This was a proud moment for the American troops. The battle of Sacramento gave them the capital, and now the stars and stripes and serpent eagle of the model republic were streaming victoriously over the stronghold of Central Mexico.

CHAPTER X.

IT IS thirteen years since Edward Creighton, the pioneer of frontier telegraphy, died, and that he is so well and honorably remembered in the Omaha of to-day—aye, his memory respected by the thousands who have gone there since he was no more—but illustrates how great was his service to the community, how broad and enduring a mark he made upon his time. No man did so much to sustain Omaha in its early and trying days as Edward Creighton. His career was a notable one in its humble beginning and splendid triumph in the flush of manhood. He was born in Belmont County, Ohio, August 31, 1820, of Irish parentage. His early days were passed upon a farm, but at the age of twenty he took the contract for building part of the national stage road from Wheeling, W. Va., to Springfield, Ohio. He continued in the contracting business, but it was not until 1847 that he entered upon that branch of it in which he achieved his greatest success and laid the foundation of his after fortunes. In that year he received the contract for and constructed a telegraph line between Springfield and Cincinnati. To this business he devoted his time and energies for five years, being successfully engaged in the construction of telegraph lines in all parts of the country, completing the line from Cleveland to Chicago in 1852. In 1856, while engaged in telegraph construction in Missouri, Mr. Creighton visited Omaha, and his brothers, John A., James, and Joseph, and his cousin James, locating there, he returned to Ohio, where he wedded

Mary Lucretia Wareham of Dayton, and in 1857 he also went to Omaha and located. He continued in the telegraph construction business, completing, in 1860, the first line which gave Omaha connection with the outer world via St. Louis.

For years Mr. Creighton entertained a pet project—the building of a line to the Pacific Coast—and in the winter of 1860, after many conferences with the wealthy stockholders of the Western Union Company, a preliminary survey was agreed upon. In those days the stage-coach was the only means of overland travel, and that was beset with great danger from Indians and road agents. In the stage-coach Mr. Creighton made his way to Salt Lake City, where he enlisted the interest and support of Brigham Young, the great head of the Mormon church, in his project. It had been arranged to associate the California State Telegraph Company in the enterprise, and on to Sacramento, in midwinter, Mr. Creighton pressed on horseback. It was a terrible journey, but the man who made it was of stout heart, and he braved the rigors of the mountains and accomplished his mission, and in the spring of 1861 he returned to Omaha to begin his great work. Congress, meanwhile, had granted a subsidy of $40,000 a year for ten years to the company which should build the line. Then a great race was inaugurated, for heavy wagers, between Mr. Creighton's construction force and the California contractors who were building eastward, to see which should reach Salt Lake City first. Mr. Creighton had 1,100 miles to construct and the Californians only 450, but he reached Salt Lake City on the 17th of October, one week ahead of his competitors.

On October 24th, but little more than six months after the enterprise was begun, Mr. Creighton had established telegraphic communication from ocean to ocean. He had taken $100,000 worth of the stock of the new enterprise at about eighteen cents on the dollar, and when the project was completed the company trebled its stock, Mr. Creighton's $100,000 becoming $300,000. The stock rose to 85 cents, and he sold out $100,000 worth for $850,000, still retaining $200,000 of the stock. He continued in the telegraphic construction business until 1867, when his great cattle interests, in which he had embarked in 1864, and his great plains freighting business, established before the building of the Union Pacific and continued even after its completion, to the mining regions of Montana and Idaho, exacted his attention. During all these years of great business success, Mr. Creighton was firm in his allegiance to Omaha. He was the first president of the first national bank in the city, and was ever ready to aid, by his means, and counsel, and enterprise, the furthering of Omaha's interests. He commanded the confidence of all the people, his sterling integrity and unwavering fidelity combining with his generous and charitable nature to make him a very lovable man. No man has an unkind word to say of Edward Creighton, and his memory is revered to this day as an upright, just, and kind man, who, out of his own sterling qualities, had wrought a successful and honorable career. He was stricken with paralysis and died November 5, 1874. To his memory Creighton College was erected and endowed by his widow, in response to his own wish, expressed during his lifetime, to found a free institution for the non-sectarian education of youth—the institution to be under Catholic control

CHAPTER XI.

THE organization of a full-fledged train for crossing the plains consisted of from twenty-five to twenty-six large wagons that would carry from three to three and a half tons each, the merchandise or contents of each wagon being protected by three sheets of thin ducking, such as is used for army tents. The number of cattle necessary to draw each wagon was twelve, making six yokes or pairs, and a prudent freighter would always have from twenty to thirty head of extra oxen, in case of accident to or lameness of some of the animals. In camping or stopping to allow the cattle to graze, a corral or pen of oblong shape is formed by the wagons, the tongues being turned out, and a log chain extended from the hind wheel of each wagon to the fore wheel of the next behind, etc., thus making a solid pen except for a wide gap at each end, through which gaps the cattle are driven when they are to be yoked and made ready for travel, the gaps then being filled by the wagon-master, his assistant, and the extra men, to prevent the cattle from getting out. When the cattle are driven into this corral or pen, each driver yokes his oxen, drives them out to his wagon, and gets ready to start. The entire train of cattle, including extras, generally numbered from 320 to 330 head and usually from four to five mules for riding and herding. The force of men for each train consisted of a wagonmaster, his assistant, the teamsters, a man to look after the extra cattle, and two or three extra men as a reserve to take the places of any men who might be disabled or sick, the latter case being a rare exception, for as a rule there was no sickness. I think perhaps there was never a set of laboring men in the world who enjoyed more uninterrupted good health than the teamsters upon the plains. They walked by the side of their teams, as it was impossible for them to ride and keep them moving with regularity. The average distance traveled with loaded wagons was from twelve to fifteen miles per day, although in some instances, when roads were fine and there was a necessity for rapid movement, I have known them to travel twenty miles. But this was faster traveling than they could keep up for any length of time. Returning with empty wagons they could average twenty miles a day without injury to the animals.

Oxen proved to be the cheapest and most reliable teams for long trips, where they had to live upon the grass. This was invariably the case. They did good daily work, gathered their own living, and if properly driven would travel 2,000 miles in a season, or during the months from April to November; traveling from 1,000 to 1,200 miles with the loaded wagons, and with plenty of good grass and water, would make the return trip with the empty wagons in the same season. However, the distance traveled depended much upon the skill of the wagonmasters who had them in charge. For if the master was not skilled in handling the animals and men, they could not make anything like good headway and success. To make everything work expeditiously, thorough discipline was required, each man performing his duty and being in the place assigned him without confusion or delay. I remember once of timing my teamsters when they commenced to yoke their teams after the cattle had been driven into their corral and a'lowed to stand long enough to become quiet. I gave the word to the men to commence yoking, and held my watch in my hand while they did so, and in sixteen minutes from the time they commenced, each man had yoked six pairs of oxen and had them hitched to their wagons ready to move. I state this that the reader may see how quickly the men who are thoroughly disciplined could be ready to "pop the whip" and move out, when unskilled men were often more than an hour doing the same work. The discipline and rules by which my trains were governed were perfect, and as quick as the men learned each one his place and duty, it became a very pleasant and easy thing for him to do. Good moral conduct was required of them, and no offense from man to man was allowed, thus keeping them good-natured and working together harmoniously. They were formed into what they called "messes," there being from six to eight men in a mess, each mess selecting the man best fitted to serve as cook, and the others carrying the water, fuel, and standing guard, so that the cook's sole business when in camp was to get his utensils ready and cook the meals.

We never left the cattle day or night without a guard of two men, the teamsters taking turns, and arranging it so that each man was on guard two hours out of the twenty-four, and sometimes they were only obliged to go on guard two hours every other night. This matter they arranged among themselves and with the wagonmaster. The duty of the wagonmaster was about the same as that of a captain of a steamboat or ship, his commands being implicitly obeyed, for in the early stages of travel upon the plains the men were at all times liable to be attacked by the Indians; therefore the necessity for a perfect harmony of action throughout the entire band. The assistant wagonmaster's duty was to carry out the wagonmaster's instructions, and he would often be at one end of the train while the master was at the other, as the train was moving. It was arranged, when possible, that no two trains should ever camp together, as there was not grass and water sufficient for the animals of both, and thus all confusion was avoided.

The average salary paid the men was $1 a day and expenses. Most of the traveling in the early days of freighting was done upon what was called the Santa Fé road, starting from Independence, Mo., and unloading at Santa Fé, N. M. The rattlesnakes on that road, in the beginning of the travel, were a great annoyance, often biting the mules and oxen when they were grazing. At first, mules were used altogether for traveling, but they would either die or become useless from the bite of a rattlesnake, and the men would sometimes be sent ahead of the caravan with whips to frighten the snakes out of the pathway, but later on, the ox-teamsters, with their large whips, destroyed them so fast that they ceased to trouble them to any great extent. It has been claimed by men that the snakes and prairie-dogs, who were also found in great numbers upon the plains, lived in the same houses, the dog digging the hole and allowing the snake to inhabit it with him; but I do not think this is correct. Men came to this conclusion from seeing the snakes when frightened run into the dog-holes, but I think they did it to get out of the way of danger, and they lived, too, in the houses that had been abandoned by the dogs. It is a fact that the prairie dogs would only live in one hole for about a year, when they would abandon it and dig a new one, leaving the old ones to be taken possession of by the rattlesnakes and prairie owls. As far as I have been able to find out, there is no creature on earth that will live with a rattlesnake. They are hated and feared by all living animals.

The following are the names of the men who were employed on our trains, in one capacity and another, and a number of them are still alive:

Dr. J. Hobbs,
Jim Lobb,
Alex Lobb,
Aquila Lobb,
Joel Dunn,
Mitchell Wilson,
Hank Bassett,
George W. Marion
N. H. Fitzwater,
George Bryant,
Tom A. Brawley,
Peter Bean,
James L. Davis,
William Hickman,
A. W. Street,
Joel Hedgespeth,
Charles Byers,
Nathan Simpson,
R. D. Simpson,
Ben Tunley,
Hiram Cummings,
John Ewing,
Rev. Ben Baxter,
A. and P. Byram,
Frank McKinney,
John T. Renick,
John D. Clayton,
William Wier,
Frank Hoberg,
Gillis of Pennsylvania,
David Street,
Joel Lyal,
Albert Bangs,
Elijah Majors,

Aquila Davis,
Samuel Poteete,
William Hayes,
George A. Baker,
James Brown,
William Dodd,
Mr. Badger,
Green Davis,
John Scudder,
Jackson Cooper,
Samuel Foster,
Robert Foster,
Chat. Renick,
John Renick,
Mr. Levisy,
Dick Lipscomb,
James Aiken,
Johnson Aiken,
Stephen De Wolfe,
Linville Hayes,
Sam McKinny,
Ben Rice,
Ferd Smith,
Henry Carlisle,
Alexander Carlisle,
Robert Ford,
Joseph Erwin,
Daniel D. White,
Johnny Fry,
Alexander Benham,
Luke Benham,
Benjamin Ficklin,
John Kerr.

CHAPTER XII.

KIT CARSON, as he was familiarly known and called, was born in Madison County, Ky., on the 24th of December, 1809.

During the early days of Carson's childhood his father moved from Kentucky to Missouri, which State was then called Upper Louisiana, where Kit Carson passed a number of years, early becoming accustomed to the stirring dangers with which his whole life was so familiar.

At the age of fifteen years he was apprenticed to a Mr. Workman, a saddler. At the end of two years, when his apprenticeship was ended, young Carson voluntarily abandoned the further pursuit of a trade which had no attractions for him, and from that time on pursued the life of a trapper, hunter, and Indian fighter, distinguishing himself in many ways and rendering invaluable service to the Government of the United States, in whose employ he spent a large part of his life, in which service he had risen to the rank of colonel and was breveted brigadier-general before his death, which occurred at Fort Lyon, Colo., on the 23d of May, 1868, from the effects of the rupture of an artery, or probably an aneurism of an artery in the neck.

Carson as a trapper, hunter, and guide had no superior, and as a soldier was the peer of any man.

The following from the life of Kit Carson will be found most interesting reading regarding this great scout:

"With fresh animals and men well fed and rested, McCoy and Carson and all their party soon started from Fort Hall for the rendezvous again, upon Green River, where they were detained some weeks for the arrival of other parties, enjoying as they best might the occasion, and preparing for future operations.

"A party of a hundred was here organized, with Mr. Fontenelle and Carson for their leaders, to trap upon the Yellowstone and the headwaters of the Missouri. It was known that they would probably meet the Blackfeet, in whose grounds they were going, and it was therefore arranged, that while fifty were to trap and furnish the food for the party, the remainder should be assigned to guard the camp and cook. There was no disinclination on the part of any to another meeting with the Blackfeet, so often had they troubled them, especially Carson, who, while he could be magnanimous toward an enemy, would not turn aside from his course if able to cope with him; and now that he was in a company which justly felt itself strong enough to punish the 'thieving Blackfeet,' as they spoke of them, he was anxious to pay off some old scores.

"They saw nothing, however, of these Indians; but afterward learned that the smallpox had raged terribly among them, and that they had kept themselves retired in mountain valleys, oppressed with fear and severe disease.

"The winter's encampment was made in this region, and a party of Crow Indians which was with them camped at a little distance on the same stream. Here they secured an abundance of meat, and passed the severe weather with a variety of amusements, in which the Indians joined them in their lodges, made of buffalo hides. These lodges, very good substitutes for houses, were made in the form of a cone, spread by means of poles spreading from a common center, where there was a hole at the top for the passage of smoke. These were often twenty feet in height and as many feet in diameter, where they were pinned to the ground with stakes. In a large village the Indians often had one lodge large enough to hold fifty persons, and within were performed their war dances around a fire made in the center. During the palmy days of the British Fur Company, in a lodge like this, only made instead of birch bark, Irving says the Indians of the North held their ' primitive fairs ' outside the city of Montreal, where they disposed of their furs.

"There was one drawback upon conviviality for this party, in the extreme difficulty of getting food for their animals; for the food and fuel so abundant for themselves did not suffice for their horses. Snow covered the ground, and the trappers were obliged to gather willow twigs, and strip the bark from cottonwood trees, in order to keep them alive. The inner bark of the cottonwood is eaten by the Indians when reduced to extreme want. Besides, the cold brought the buffalo down upon them in great herds, to share the nourishment they had provided for their horses.

"Spring at length opened, and gladly they again commenced trapping; first on the Yellowstone and soon on the headwaters of the Missouri, where they learned that the Blackfeet were recovered from the sickness of last year, which had not been so severe as it was reported, and that they were still anxious and in condition for a fight, and were encamped not far from their present trapping grounds.

"Carson and five men went forward in advance ' to reconnoiter,' and found the village preparing to remove, having learned of the presence of the trappers. Hurrying back, a party of forty-three was selected from the whole, and they unanimously selected Carson to lead them, and leaving the rest to move on with the baggage, and aid them if it should be necessary when they should come up with the Indians, they started forward eager for a battle.

"Carson and his command were not long in overtaking the Indians; and dashing among them, at the first fire killed ten of their braves; but the Indians rallied and retreated in good order. The white men were in good spirits, and followed up their first attack with deadly results for three full hours, the Indians making scarce any resistance. Now their firing became less animated, as their ammunition was getting low, and they had to use it with extreme caution. The Indians, suspecting this from the slackness of their fire, rallied, and with a tremendous whoop turned upon their enemies.

"Now Carson and his company could use their small arms, which produced a terrible effect, and which enabled them to again drive back the Indians. They rallied yet again, and charged with so much power and in such numbers, they forced the trappers to retreat.

"During this engagement the horse of one of the mountaineers was killed, and fell with his whole weight upon his rider. Carson saw the condition of the man, with six warriors rushing to take his scalp, and reached the spot in time to save his friend. Leaping from the saddle he placed himself before his fallen companion, shouting at the same time for his men to rally around him, and with deadly aim from his rifle, shot down the foremost warrior.

"The trappers now rallied around Carson and the remaining five warriors retired, without the scalp of their fallen foe. Only two of them reached a place of safety, for the well-aimed fire of the trappers leveled them with the earth.

"Carson's horse was loose, and as his comrade was safe, he mounted behind one of his men and rode back to the ranks, while by general impulse the firing on both sides ceased. His horse was captured and restored to him, but each party, now thoroughly exhausted, seemed to wait for the other to renew the attack.

"While resting in this attitude, the other division of the trappers came in sight, but the Indians, showing no fear, posted themselves among the rocks at some distance from the scene of the last skirmish, and coolly waited for their adversaries. Exhausted ammunition had been the cause of the retreat of Carson and his force, but now, with a renewed supply, and an addition of fresh men to the force, they advanced on foot to drive the Indians from their hiding places. The contest was desperate and severe, but powder and ball eventually conquered, and the Indians, once dislodged, scattered in every direction. The trappers considered this a complete victory over the Blackfeet, for a large number of their warriors were killed, and many more were wounded, while they had but three men killed and a few severely wounded.

"Fontenelle and his party now camped at the scene of the engagement, to recruit their men and here bury their dead. Afterward they trapped through the whole Blackfeet country, and with great success, going where they pleased without fear or molestation. The Indians kept off their route, evidently having acquaintance with Carson and his company enough to last them their lifetime.

"With the smallpox and the white man's rifles the warriors were much reduced, and the tribe, which had formerly numbered 30,000, was already decimated, and a few more blows like the one dealt by this dauntless band would suffice to break its spirit and destroy its power for future and evil.

"During the battle with the trappers the women and children of the Blackfeet village were sent on in advance, and when the engagement was over and the braves returned to them so much reduced in numbers, and without a single scalp, the big lodge that had been erected for the war dance was given up for the wounded, and in hundreds of Indian hearts grew a bitter hatred for the white man.

"An express, dispatched for the purpose, announced the place of the rendezvous to Fontenelle and Carson, who were now on Green River, and with their whole party and a large stock of furs, they at once set out for the place upon Mud River, to find the sales commenced before their arrival, so that in twenty days they were ready to break up camp.

"Carson now organized a party of seven and proceeded to a trading post called Brown's Hole, where he joined a company of traders to go to the Navajo Indians. He found this tribe more assimilated to the white man than any Indians he had yet seen, having many fine horses and large flocks of sheep and cattle. They also possessed the art of weaving, and their blankets were in great demand through Mexico, bringing high prices on account of their great beauty, being woven in flowers with much taste. They were evidently a remnant of the Aztec race.

"They traded here for a large drove of fine mules, which, taken to the fort on the South Platte, realized good prices, when Carson went again to Brown's Hole, a narrow but pretty valley, about sixteen miles long, upon the Colorado River.

"After many offers for his services from other parties, Carson at length engaged himself for the winter to hunt for the men at this fort, and, as the game was abundant in this beautiful valley, and in the cañon country farther down the Colorado, in its deer, elk, and antelope reminding him of his hunts upon the Sacramento, the task was a delightful one to him.

"In the spring Carson trapped with Bridger and Owens, with passable success, and went to the rendezvous upon Wind River, at the head of the Yellowstone, and from thence, with a large party of the trappers at the rendezvous, to the Yellowstone, where they camped in the vicinity for the winter without seeing their old enemy, the Blackfeet

KIT CARSON'S GRAVE.

Indians, until midwinter, when they discovered they were near their stronghold.

"A party of forty was selected to give them battle, with Carson, of course, for their captain. They found the Indians already in the field to the number of several hundred, who made a brave resistance until night and darkness admonished both parties to retire. In the morning, when Carson and his men went to the spot whither the Indians had retired, they were not to be found. They had given them a 'wide berth,' taking their all away with them, even their dead.

"Carson and his command returned to camp, where a council of war decided that, as the Indians would report at the principal encampment the terrible loss they had sustained, and others would be sent to renew the fight, it was wise to prepare to act on the defensive, and use every precaution immediately; and accordingly a sentinel was stationed on a lofty hill near by, who soon reported that the Indians were upon the move.

"Their plans matured, they at once threw up a breastwork, under Carson's directions, and waited the approach of the Indians, who came in slowly, the first parties waiting for those behind. After three days a full thousand had reached the camp about half a mile from the breastwork of the trappers. In their war paint, stripes of red across the forehead and down either cheek, with their bows and arrows, tomahawks and lances, this army of Indians presented a formidable appearance to the small body of trappers who were opposed to them.

"The war dance was enacted in sight and hearing of the trappers, and at early dawn the Indians advanced, having made every preparation for the attack. Carson commanded his men to reserve their fire till the Indians were near enough to have every shot tell; but, seeing the strength of

8

the white men's position, after a few ineffectual shots, the Indians retired, camped a mile from them, and finally separated into two parties, and went away, leaving the trappers to breathe more freely, for, at the best, the encounter must have been of a desperate character.

"They evidently recognized the leader who had before dealt so severely with them, in the skill with which the defense was arranged, and if the name of Kit Carson was on their lips, they knew him for both bravery and magnanimity, and had not the courage to offer him battle.

"Another winter gone, with saddlery, moccasin-making, lodge-building, to complete the repairs of the summer's wars and the winter's fight all completed, Carson, with fifteen men, went past Fort Hall again to the Salmon River, and trapped part of the season there, and upon Big Snake and Goose creeks, and selling his furs at Fort Hall, again joined Bridger in another trapping excursion into the Blackfeet country.

"The Blackfeet had molested the traps of another party who had arrived there before them, and had driven them away. The Indian assailants were still near, and Carson led his party against them, taking care to station himself and men in the edge of a thicket, where they kept the savages at bay all day, taking a man from their number with nearly every shot of their well-directed rifles. In vain the Indians now attempted to fire the thicket; it would not burn, and suddenly they retired, forced again to acknowledge defeat at the hands of Kit Carson, the 'Monarch of the Prairies.'

"Carson's party now joined with the others, but concluding that they could not trap successfully with the annoyance the Indians were likely to give them, as their force was too small to hope to conquer, they left this part of the country for the north fork of the Missouri.

" Now they were with the friendly Flatheads, one of whose chiefs joined them in the hunt, and went into camp near them with a party of his braves. This tribe of Indians, like several other tribes which extend along this latitude of the Pacific, have the custom which gives them their name, thus described by Irving, in speaking of the Indians upon the Lower Columbia, about its mouth:

" ' A most singular custom,' he says, ' prevails not only among the Chinooks, but among most of the tribes about this part of the coast, which is the flattening of the forehead. The process by which this deformity is effected commences immediately after birth. The infant is laid in a wooden trough by way of cradle; the end on which the head reposes is higher than the rest. A padding is placed on the forehead of the infant, with a piece of bark above it, and is pressed down by cords which pass through holes upon the sides of the trough. As the tightening of the padding and the pressure of the head to the board is gradual, the process is said not to be attended with pain. The appearance of the infant, however, while in this state of compression, is whimsically hideous, and its little black eyes, we are told, being forced out by the tightness of the bandages, resemble those of a mouse choked in a trap.

" ' About a year's pressure is sufficient to produce the desired effect, at the end of which time the child emerges from its bandages a complete flathead, and continues so through life. It must be noted, however, that this flattening of the head has something in it of aristocratic significance, like the crippling of the feet among the Chinese ladies of quality. At any rate it is the sign of freedom. No slave is permitted to bestow this deformity upon the head of his children. All the slaves, therefore, are round-heads.' "

In December, 1846, after a severe battle with the Mexi-

I

cans and the condition of General Kearney and his men had become desperate, a council of war was called. After discussing a variety of measures, Carson showed himself "the right man in the right place." He said, "Our case is a desperate one, but there is yet hope. If we stay here we are all dead men; our animals can not last long, and the soldiers and marines at San Diego do not know of our coming, but if they receive information of our condition, they will hasten to our rescue. I will attempt to go through the Mexican lines, then to San Diego, and send relief from Commodore Stockton."

Lieutenant Beale of the United States Navy at once seconded Carson, and volunteered to accompany him. General Kearney immediately accepted the proposal as his only hope, and they started at once, as soon as the cover of darkness hung around them. Their mission was to be one of success or of death to themselves and the whole force. Carson was familiar with the customs of the Mexicans, as well as the Indians, of putting their ears to the ground to detect any sound, and therefore knew the necessity of avoiding the slightest noise. As it was impossible to avoid making some noise wearing their shoes, they removed them, and putting them under their belts crept over bushes and rocks with the greatest caution and silence. They discovered that the Mexicans had three rows of sentinels, whose beats extended past each other, embracing the hill where Kearney and his men were held in siege. They were doubtless satisfied these could not be eluded, but they crept on, often so near a sentinel as to see his figure and equipment in the darkness, and once, when within a few yards of them, discovered one of the sentinels, who had dismounted and lighted his cigarette with his flint and steel. Discovering this sentinel, Kit Carson, as he lay flat on the ground, put his foot back and touched Lieutenant

Beale, as a signal for him to be still, as he was doing. The minutes the Mexican was occupied in this way seemed hours to our heroes, who momentarily feared they would be discovered. Carson asserted they were so still he could hear Lieutenant Beale's heart beat, and, in the agony of the time, he lived a year. But the Mexican finally mounted his horse and rode off in a contrary direction, as if guided by Providence to give safety to these courageous adventurers.

For full two miles Kit Carson and Lieutenant Beale thus worked their way along upon their hands and knees, turning their eyes in every direction to detect anything which might lead to their discovery; and, having passed the last sentinel and left the lines sufficiently far behind, they felt an immeasurable relief in once more gaining their feet. But their shoes were gone. In the excitement of this perilous journey neither had thought of his shoes since he first put them in his belt, but they could speak again and congratulate themselves and each other that the great danger was passed, and thank heaven that they had been aided thus far. But there were still many difficulties in their path, which was rough with bushes, from the necessity of having to avoid the well-trodden trail, lest they be discovered. The prickly pear covered the ground, its thorns penetrated their feet at every step, and their road was lengthened by going out of the direct path, though the latter would have shortened their journey many a weary mile.

All the day following they pursued their journey onward without cessation, and into the night following, for they could not stop until they were assured relief was to be furnished their anxious and perilous conditioned fellow soldiers.

Carson pursued so straight a course and aimed so correctly for his mark that they entered the town by the most direct route, and answering "friends" to the challenge of the sentinel, it was known from whence they came, and they were at once conducted to Commodore Stockton, to whom they related their errand, and the further particulars we have already narrated.

Commodore Stockton immediately detailed a force of nearly two hundred men, and, with his usual promptness, ordered them to go to the relief of their besieged countrymen by forced marches. They took with them a piece of ordnance, which the men were obliged themselves to draw, as there were no animals to be had for this work.

Carson's feet were in a terrible condition, and he did not return with the soldiers; he needed rest and the best of care or he might lose his feet; but he described the position of General Kearney so accurately that the party sent to his relief could find him without difficulty, and yet had the commodore expressed the wish, Carson would have undertaken to guide the relief party upon its march.

Lieutenant Beale was partially deranged for several days from the effects of the severe service, and was sent on board a frigate lying in port for medical attendance, and he did not fully recover his former health for more than two years.

The relief party from Commodore Stockton reached General Kearney without encountering any Mexicans, and very soon all marched to San Diego, where the wounded soldiers received medical assistance.

CHAPTER XIII.

ADVENTURES OF A TRAPPER.

Fifty years ago, when Kansas City consisted of a ware-house and there was not a single private residence of civilized man between the Missouri River and San Francisco, S. E. Ward, a trapper, landed from a steamer at Independence. He was a penniless youth of eighteen years, direct from the parental home in Virginia, filled with eager desire to gain a fortune in the far West. Now, at sixty-eight years of age, Mr. Ward is almost twice a millionaire and one of the most respected citizens of Western Missouri. He is one of the pioneers that are left to speak of the struggles and triumphs of early Western life. The family home is a spacious two-story brick house, $2\frac{1}{2}$ miles south of Westport, on the old Santa Fé trail. The house stands upon a farm of 500 acres at the edge of the great prairie which stretches away through Kansas to the base of the Rocky Mountains. On this very spot where he now lives Mr. Ward camped more than once on his return from trading expeditions, years ago, in the Southwest.

He has had experiences that do not fall to the ordinary lot of man. Thrown by circumstances into a new country in his earlier life, he has traveled thousands of miles alone through the mountains and across the prairies, and often spent weeks without meeting a single human being. Exposed to snow, sleet, and rain, with no shelter but a buffalo robe, and at times with starvation staring him in the face, the chances seemed slight indeed of ever coming out alive. During his experience in the West he met Fremont in his expedition through the mountains, saw Brigham Young on the Platte River as he was on his way to found a Mormon empire, passed through the stormy period of the Mexican War, the California gold excitement, the Civil War, and witnessed the opening of the Pacific Railroad, and the mighty influx of population on the plains of the great West.

The first seven years of his life on the frontier were passed largely in intercourse with Indian tribes, extending from the Red River on the south to the upper waters of the Columbia and Yellowstone on the north. Hunting, trapping, and trading were the only occupations open to white men west of the Missouri River in those days. In little bands of from two to twelve the hunters and trappers roamed through the vast region with but little fear of the redskins. The Indians had not contracted the vices of civilization, and were a different race of people from what they are to-day. The cruelties we read of as practiced by them in later years were unknown. I never knew of a prisoner being burned at the stake, and ordinarily the hunter felt as safe in an Indian country as in his own settlement. The Indians were armed with bows and arrows, not more than one in fifty being the possessor of a gun. When an Indian did use a gun it was usually a light shotgun that proved ineffective at any great distance. An experienced frontiersman considered himself safe against any small number of Indians.

By means of the sign language we were able to talk with the Indians upon all subjects; and as they were very great talkers and inveterate story-tellers, many is the hour I have passed seated by the camp-fire hearing their adventures or the legends of their nations. I have often wondered why the sign language, as recognized and perfected by the

Indians, was not adopted among civilized people instead of the deaf and dumb alphabet. The Indian's method of communicating his ideas is much more impressive and natural. The Cheyennes and Arapahoes were especially noted for their skill in sign language.

In some respects the Indians were superior to the whites as hunters. They knew nothing of trapping beaver until taught by the whites, but they could give valuable points on bagging the large game on the plains. Forty or fifty years ago the plains were swarming with buffalo. I have often seen droves so large that no eye could compass them. Their numbers were countless. The Indian hunter riding bare-backed would guide his horse headlong into the midst of the herd, singling out the fattest and in an instant sending the deadly arrow clean through his victim. In a single day's hunt they sometimes killed 3,000 to 4,000 buffalo. The dead bodies would lie scattered over the prairie for miles. It required the greatest diligence to save the skins and dry the meat for use in winter. They made wholesale slaughter of antelope by forming a "surround." This required the presence of several hundred Indians to make a complete success. Early in the morning the men and boys would form a circle miles in diameter, riding round and round, making the circle smaller at every revolution and growing closer together. All the game within the ranks was gradually collected into a body which was driven to an inclosure formed by weeds piled high up at the sides, behind which were the women and old men. As the game passed the reserve force these bobbed up and set up unearthly shrieks and yells that caused the frightened animals to plunge forward over a precipice to which the inclosure conducted. The slaughter was terrible. Indians stationed below gave the quietus to such game as made the descent with but slight injury. At the close of the day a great feast was held, and nobody enjoys a feast more than an Indian.

I have been asked if marriage was a success among the aborigines. I never heard it hinted that it was otherwise. The Indian had the privilege of taking as many wives as he was able to support, and if he married the oldest sister in a family, all the remaining sisters were considered his property as they became of age. Under favorable circumstances, in some tribes, a warrior took a new wife every two or three years. A separate lodge was provided for each wife, as the women would fall out and scratch each other if kept together. A peculiarity in the Indian family relations was that as soon as a wife found herself to be with child her person was considered sacred, and she lived apart from all the rest of the household until the child had been born and had weaned itself of its own accord. This exclusion extended even to the master of the house, and was never violated. The children were fairly idolized among the more advanced tribes. The parents seemed to live for their children, more particularly when the children were boys.

An Indian's wealth was known by the number of his horses. There were both rich and poor Indians, but the latter were never allowed to want when there was anything to be had. After a great hunt the poor man was granted the privilege of taking the first carcasses nearest the camp.

Some Indians kept their lodges nicely painted and beyond criticism as to cleanliness. The lodges were renewed every year, as frequent moving and exposure to weather made the skins leaky. The Indians' range extended anywhere that game and food for their animals could be found. It was a rare occurrence for them to remain a month in a single vicinity. The monotony of hunting and moving was varied by occasional forays upon an unfriendly tribe, stealing their horses, and carrying off scalps and prisoners. Unless these captives were children they were put to death. The children were usually adopted and treated with the greatest kindness. The older prisoners, both men and women, were dispatched with little ceremony. The killing was usually deferred for several days after the prisoners were brought into camp. A young Pawnee Indian who was killed by a party of Comanches was taken into the open air, his hands were tied to his legs, and he was shot through the heart. He uttered not a word or groan. After the killing, a warrior stepped forward and raised the dead Pawnee's scalp, then the war dance was held. A Crow Indian was dispatched even more expeditiously. Trapper Ward called on the captain in the lodge where he was confined, and they talked together by signs. He said he knew he must die, but felt perfectly resigned to his fate, as he would inflict the same penalty on his enemies if he had the chance. While they were talking, a warrior appeared at the door and made a motion. The Crow stepped forward and was shot within a few feet of the spot he had occupied the moment before. After the scalping and war dance he was tied up in a standing position, with his hands stretched as far apart over his head as possible, making a ghastly spectacle, and left as a warning to all the enemies of his executioners.

The winter of 1838 and 1839, Mr. Ward says, was vividly impressed upon his mind, being his first experience as a trapper. After a journey of 600 miles from Independence, he arrived at Fort Bent, and early in the fall the different hunting and trapping parties started out for a long sojourn in the mountains. He was fortunate in being one of a party of twelve, of which Kit Carson was a member. They made headquarters in Brown's Hole, on the Colorado River, where it enters the mountains. Trapping proved hard work, but he never enjoyed life more, and knew no such thing as sickness. Their clothes were made (by their own hands) of buckskin. Their food was nothing but meat cooked on a stick or on the coals, as they had no cooking utensils. Antelope, dear, elk, bear, beaver, and, in case of necessity, even the wolf, furnished a variety that was always acceptable to eat. At night they gathered round a roaring fire, in comfortable quarters, to listen to the stories which such men as Kit Carson could tell.

At the close of three months a successful trapper was often able to show a pack of 120 beaver skins, weighing about 100 pounds. As he made two trapping expeditions during the year, in the spring and fall, he would show 200 pounds, worth $6 per pound, as his year's work. In addition to this, the musk-stones of the beaver were worth as much as the skins, so that some of them made $3,000 per year as trappers. It was a poor trapper that did not earn half as much. But few of them ever saved any money. The traders from the States charged them enormously for supplies, and Western men were inveterate gamblers. Sugar was $1.50 per pound, coffee the same, tobacco $5 per pound, and a common shirt could not be bought for less than $5, while whisky sold for over $30 a gallon. With flour at $1 per pound, and luxuries in proportion, it was a question of but a few days at the rendezvous before the labor of months was used up. The traders were often called upon to fit out the men upon credit, after a prosperous season.

CHAPTER XIV.

To BE a successful trapper required great caution, as well as a perfect knowledge of the habits of the animals. The residence of the beaver was often discovered by seeing bits of green wood and gnawed branches of the basswood, slippery elm, and sycamore, their favorite food, floating on the water or lodged on the shores of the stream below, as well as by their tracks or foot-marks.

These indications were technically called "beaver signs." They were also sometimes discovered by their dams thrown across creeks and small, sluggish streams, forming a pond in which were erected their habitations.

The hunter, as he proceeded to set his traps, generally approached by water, in his canoe. He selected a steep, abrupt spot in the bank of the creek, in which he excavated a hole with his paddle, as he sat in the canoe, sufficiently large to hold the trap, and so deep as to be about three inches below the surface of the water, when the jaws of the trap were expanded. About two feet above the trap, a stick, three or four inches in length, was stuck in the bank. In the upper end of this stick the trapper cut a small hole with his knife, into which he dropped a small quantity of the essence of perfume, which was used to attract the beaver to the spot. This stick was fastened by a string of horse-hair to the trap, and with it was pulled into the water by the beaver. The reason for this was that it might not remain after the trap was sprung, and attract other beavers to the spot, and thus prevent their seeking other traps ready for them.

This scent, or essence, was made by mingling the fresh castor of the beaver with an extract of the bark of the roots of the spice-bush, and then kept in a bottle for use. The making of this essence was kept a profound secret, and often sold for a considerable sum to the younger trappers by the older proficients in the mysteries of beaver-hunting. Where trappers had no proper bait, they sometimes made use of the fresh roots of the sassafras or spice-bush, of both of which the beaver was very fond.

It is said by old trappers that the beaver will smell the well-prepared essence the distance of a mile, their sense of smell being very acute, or they would not so readily detect the vicinity of man by the scent of his trail. The aroma of the essence, having attracted the beaver to the vicinity of the trap, in his attempt to reach it he has to climb up on the bank where it is sticking. This effort leads him directly over the trap, and he is usually caught by one of his fore legs.

The trap was connected by an iron chain, six feet in length, to a stout line made of the bark of the leather wood, twisted into a neat cord fifteen or twenty feet in length. These cords were usually prepared by the trappers at home, or at their camps, for cords of hemp or flax were scarce in the days of beaver-hunting. The end of the line was secured to a stake driven into the bed of the creek under water, and in the beaver's struggles to escape he was usually drowned before the arrival of the trapper. Sometimes, however, he freed himself by gnawing off his own leg, though this rarely happened.

When setting the trap, if it was raining, or there was a prospect of rain, a leaf, generally of sycamore, was placed over the essence stick to protect it from the rain.

The beaver was a very sagacious and cautious animal, and it required great care in the trapper in his approach to his haunts to set his traps, that no scent of his hands or feet should be left on the earth or bushes that he touched. For this reason the trapper generally approached in a canoe. If he had no canoe it was necessary to enter the stream thirty or forty yards below where he wished to set his trap, and walk up the stream to the place, taking care to return in the same manner, lest the beaver should take alarm and not come near the bait, as his fear of the vicinity of man was greater than his appetite for the essence.

Caution was also required in kindling a fire near the haunts of the beaver, as the smell of smoke alarmed them. The firing of a gun, also, often marred the sport of the trapper.

Thus it will be seen that, to make a successful beaver hunter, required more qualities or natural gifts than fall to the share of most men.

CHAPTER XV.

In the early part of June, 1850, I loaded my train, consisting of ten wagons drawn by 130 oxen, at Kansas City, Mo., with merchandise destined for Santa Fé, N. M., a distance of about eight hundred miles from Kansas City, and started for that point. After being out some eight or ten days and traveling through what was then called Indian Territory, but was not organized until four years later, and was then styled Kansas. Arriving one evening at a stream called One Hundred and Ten, I camped for the night. I unyoked my oxen and turned them upon the grass. Finding the grass so good and the animals weary with the day's work, I thought they would not stroll away, and therefore did not put any guard, as was my custom.

At early dawn on the following morning I arose, saddled my horse, which, by the way, was a good one, and told my assistant to arouse the teamsters, so they could be ready to yoke their teams as soon as I drove them into the corral, which was formed by the wagons. I rode around what I supposed to be all the herd, but in rounding them up before reaching the wagons, I discovered that there were a number of them missing. I then made a circle, leaving the ones I had herded together. I had not traveled very far when I struck the trail of the missing oxen; it being very plain, I could ride my horse on a gallop and keep track of it.

I had not traveled more than a mile when I discovered the tracks of Indian ponies. I then knew the Indians had driven off my oxen. I thought of the fact that I was un-

AN ADVENTURE WITH INDIANS.

armed, not thinking it necessary to take my gun when I left the wagons, as I only expected to go a few hundred yards. We had not yet reached the portion of the territory where we would expect to meet hostile Indians, so I went ahead on the trail, thinking it was some half-friendly ones that had driven my oxen away, as they sometimes did, in order to get a fee for finding and bringing them back again.

I expected to overtake them at any moment, for the trail looked very fresh, as though they were only a short distance ahead of me. So on and on I went, galloping my horse most of the time, until I had gone about twelve miles from my camp. I passed through a skirt of timber that divided one portion of the open prairie from the other, and there overtook thirty-four head of my oxen resting from their travel.

About sixty yards to the east of the cattle were six painted Indian braves, who had dismounted from their horses, each one leaning against his horse, with his right hand resting upon his saddle, their guns being in their left. I came upon them suddenly, the timber preventing them from seeing me until I was within a few rods of them. I threw up my hand, went in a lope around my oxen, giving some hideous yells, and told the cattle they could go back to the wagons on the trail they had come. They at once heeded me and started. I never saw six meaner or more surprised looking men than those six braves were, for I think they thought I had an armed party just behind me, or I would not have acted so courageously as I did. So I followed my cattle, who were ready to take their way back, and left the six savages standing in dismay. The oxen and myself were soon out of sight in the forest, and that is the last I saw of the six braves who had been sent out by their chief the night before to steal the oxen.

J

Very soon after I got through the timber and into the prairie again I met, from time to time, one or two Indians trotting along on their ponies, following the trail that the cattle made when their comrades drove them off. When within a short distance of the herd they would leave the trail and leave plenty of space to the cattle, fall in behind me, and trot on toward the six braves I had left. I will say here that I began to feel very much elated over my success in capturing my cattle from six armed savages, and being given the right-of-way by other parties also armed. But I did not have to travel very far under the pleasant reflection that I was a hero; when I was about half-way back to the wagons I looked ahead about half-a-mile and saw a large body of Indians, comprising some twenty-five warriors, who proved to be under the command of their chief, armed and coming toward me. I then began to feel a little smaller than I had a few minutes previous, for I was entirely unarmed, and even had I been armed what could I have done with twenty-five armed savages?

My fears were very soon realized, for when they arrived within a few hundred yards of me and the chief saw me returning with the cattle he had sent his braves to drive off, he commanded his men to make a descent upon me, and he undertook the job of leading them. They raised a hideous yell and started toward me at the top of their horses' speed. If my oxen had not been driven so far and become to some extent tired, I would have had a royal stampede. The animals only ran a few hundred yards until I succeeded in holding them up. By this time the Indians had reached me and my cattle. The braves surrounded the cattle, and the chief came at the top of his horse's speed directly toward me, with his gun drawn up in striking attitude. Of course I did not allow him to get in reaching distance. I turned my horse and put spurs to him; he was a splendid animal and

it was a comparatively easy matter for me to keep out of
the reach of the vicious chief, who did not want to kill me,
but desired to scare me, or cause me to run away and leave
my herd, or disable me so I could not follow him and his
band if they attempted to take the cattle.

This chasing me off for some distance was repeated three
times, I returning in close proximity to where his braves
surrounded the cattle on every side, some on foot holding
their ponies, others on horseback. Those who had alighted
were dancing and yelling at the tops of their voices. The
third time I returned to where the chief and one of his
braves, armed with bow and arrows, were sitting on their
horses, some distance from the cattle and in line between
me and the group of braves. When I got within thirty or
forty yards of him he beckoned me to come to him, for
all the communication we had was carried on by means of
signs; I did not speak their language nor they mine. I rode
cautiously up side by side, a short distance from the chief,
with our horses' heads in the same direction. When I had
fairly stopped to see what he was going to do, his brave
who was on the opposite side from me slid off his horse,
ran under the neck of the chief's, and made a lunge to
catch the bridle of my horse. His sudden appearance
caused the animal to jump so quick and far that he had
just missed getting hold of the rein. Had he succeeded in
the attempt they would have taken my horse and oxen and
cleared out, leaving me standing on the prairie. When he
found he had failed in his attempt, he returned to his horse,
mounted, and he and the chief rode slowly toward me, for
I had reined up my horse when I found I was out of reach.
I sat still to see what their next maneuver would be. The
brave changed from the left of the chief to the right as
they came slowly toward me. When they got within a few
feet of me, with the heads of our horses in the same direc-

tion, they reined up their ponies and the brave suddenly drew his bow at full bend, with a sharp-pointed steel in the end of the arrow. He aimed at my heart with the most murderous, vindictive, and devilish look on his face and from his eyes that I ever saw portrayed on any living face before or since. Of course there was no time for doing anything but to keep my eye steadfast on his. To show the influence of the mind over the body, while he was pointing the arrow at me I felt a place as large as the palm of my hand cramping where the arrow would have struck me had he shot. While in this position he pronounced the word " say " with all the force he could summon. I did not at that time understand what he meant. The chief relieved my suspense by holding up his ten fingers and pointing to the oxen. I then understood that if I gave him ten of my animals he would not put the dart through me. I felt that I could not spare that number and move on with my train to its destination, and in a country where I had not the opportunity of obtaining others, so I refused. He then threw up five fingers and motioned to the cattle. Again I shook my head. He then motioned me to say how many I would give, and I held up one finger. The moment I did so he gave the word of command to his braves, who were still dancing and screaming round the cattle, and they, whirling into line, selected one of the animals so quickly that one had hardly time to think, and left thirty-three of the oxen and myself standing in the prairie. I had held them there so long, refusing to let them go without following them, I think they were afraid some of my party would overtake me. There was no danger of that had they only known it, for on my return I found all my men at the wagons wondering what had become of me. I had left the camp at daylight and it was after noon when I returned.

In conclusion, I will say that never at any time in my

life, and I have encountered a great many dangers, have I
felt so small and helpless as upon this occasion, being surrounded by twenty-five or thirty armed savages and with
whom I could communicate only by signs. To surrender
the animals to them was financial ruin, and to stay with
them was hazarding my life and receiving the grossest
abuse and insults. The effect of passing through this
ordeal, on my mind, was that I became so reduced in stature, I felt as if I was no larger than my thumb, a humming-
bird or a mouse; all three passed through my mind, and I
actually looked at myself to see if it was possible I was so
small.

No one can tell, until he has been overpowered by hostile savages, how small he will become in his own estima-
tion. However, when they left me, I at once came back
to my natural size and felt as if a great weight had been
lifted from me.

Although the Indians were nothing more nor less than
specimens of nature's sons, without any education whatever of a literary nature, they were very shrewd and quick
to see and take up an insult. They were remarkable for
reading faces, and although they were not able to understand one word of English, they could tell when looking
at a white man and his comrades when in conversation
about them, almost precisely what they were saying by the
shadows that would pass over their faces, and by the nod-
ding of heads and movement of hands or shoulders, for the
reason that they talked with each other and the different
tribes that they would meet by signs, and it was done generally by the movement of the hands.

They had but few vices, in fact might say almost none
outside of their religious teachings, which allowed them to
steal horses and fur skins, and sometimes take the lives of
enemies or opposing tribes. Persons who were not thor-

oughly acquainted with Indian character and life might wonder why there were so many different tribes—or bands, as they were sometimes called—and if it could be there were so many nationalities among them. This is accounted for solely and truly upon the fact that when a tribe grew to a certain number it became a necessity in nature for them to divide, which would form two bands or tribes and at that point of time and condition it became necessary for the one leaving the main tribe to have a name to designate themselves from the family that they had of necessity parted from, for as soon as a tribe reached such a proportion in numbers that it was inconvenient for them to rendezvous at some given point easy of access, their necessities in such cases demanded a new deal or different arrangements; hence the different names by which tribes were called.

These tribes differed in their methods of living according to the conditions with which they were surrounded. Indians who lived along the Atlantic Coast and made their living from fishing, as well as from hunting, were very different from the Indians of the plains and Rocky Mountain regions, who live almost solely upon buffalo and other varieties of game that they were able to secure.

The Indians from the Atlantic and Mississippi valleys were more dangerous, as a rule, when they came into a combat with white soldiers, than were the Indians of the plains and Rockies. The Shawnee and Delaware Indian braves a hundred years ago, when my grandfather was an Indian fighter in Kentucky, were considered equal to any white soldiers and proved themselves in battle to be so. Their mode of warfare, however, was not on horseback, as was the mode of warfare with the Indians of the plains. They were "still" hunters, as they might be called, and when they met with white men in battle array, would get behind trees, if possible, as a protection, and remain and fight to the bitter end. When these tribes became overpowered, it was easy, compared with the Indians of the plains, to bring them under some of the conditions of civilization; therefore the Cherokees, Seminoles, Chickasaws, Choctaws, Shawnees, Delawares, Wyandottes, Kickapoos, Sacs, Foxes, the Creeks, and many others whose names I can not now recall, have become somewhat civilized, and many of them semi-civilized tribes, but the Indians of the plains and Rocky Mountain regions have been very slow to accept what we term civilization. They seem somewhat like the buffalo and other wild animals that we have never been able to domesticate. It looks to one like myself that has known them for so many years, that before they are civilized they will become almost exterminated; that is to say that civil-ized life does not agree with them, and they die from causes and conditions that such life compels them to exist under, and in my opinion the day will come when there will be few, if any, in the near future, left of the tribes that were known to belong to the territory west of the Missis-sippi River and extending to the Pacific Coast. There was often among the wildest tribes of America many good traits. If they found you hungry and alone and in distress, as a rule they would take care of you, giving you the very best they had, and never with a view of charging you for their kindness. If they had a grudge against the white race for some misdemeanor some white man may have com-mitted, they might kill you in retaliation. For this reason white men always felt, when they were among them, that their safety depended largely upon how the tribe had been treated by some other white man, or party of white men. As far as I know, throughout the entire savage tribes retal-iation is one of the laws by which they are governed. The women, as a rule, were very generous and kind-hearted,

and I know of one case where a friend of mine, Judge
Brown of Pettis County, Mo., had his life saved and his
property restored to him through the instrumentality of an
Indian woman. The Indians were at that time quite hostile toward the whites, and had held council and determined
to kill him, as they had him a prisoner and at their mercy.
This woman seemed to be one of great influence in the
tribe, and when the braves held their council and decided
to take his life and property, she rose to her feet and
plead for the life of my friend. Of course he could not
understand a word she said, but he saw in her face a
benevolence and kindness that gave him heart, for he had
about despaired of ever living another hour. From the
way in which she looked, talked, and gestured, he felt certain that she was assuming his cause, and he in relating
the circumstances to me and others said he never saw a
greater heroine in the appearance and conduct of any
woman in his life. Of course this he had to judge largely
of from appearances, as the Indians judge of the white
people that I before alluded to.

CHAPTER XVI.

EVERYTHING worked along smoothly on my westward way, after my adventure with the Indians, until I reached Walnut Creek, at the Big Bend of the Arkansas River. At that point the buffalo, running past my herd of oxen in the night, scattered them, part running with the buffalo and crossing the river where it was very high, it being the season of the year when the channel was full of water, from the melting of the snow in the mountains from which it received its waters. The next morning, as before, at the One Hundred and Ten, I found a portion of my herd missing, but not so many this time as to prevent me from traveling. I had the teams hitched up, some of them being a yoke of oxen minus, but sufficient remained to move the wagons, and I started my assistant, Mr. Samuel Poteet, one of the most faithful of my men, on the road with the teams, and I took my extra man to hunt for the missing oxen. We crossed the river where it was almost at swimming point and at the place where the buffalo had crossed the night before, for we had followed their trail for several miles. After losing the trail, for they had so scattered we could not tell which trail to take, we wandered around for a time in the open prairie, expecting Indians to appear at any moment; but in that we were happily disappointed. I finally found my cattle all standing in a huddle near a pond. We soon surrounded them and started driving them to the river, crossed them and reached the road, following the train, until we overtook it a little before sundown that evening. From that point there was nothing to trouble or disturb our movements until we reached the Wagon Mounds, beyond the borders of New Mexico, now a station upon the Atchison, Topeka & Santa Fé Railroad. There we came upon the ruins of a stage-coach which had been burned; the bones and skeletons of some of the horses that drew it, as well as the bones of the party of ten men who were murdered outright by the Indians. Not one escaped to tell the story, and they were, I think, a party of ten as brave men as could be found anywhere. Whether there were any Indians killed while they were massacring this party is not known, for it was some few days before the news of the affair was known, as there was little travel over the road at that season of the year.

This party had passed me on the road some weeks before, and being able to travel three times as far per day as I could, had reached the point of their fate several weeks before, so we could see nothing but the bones the wolves had scratched out of the ground where they had been buried. In fact there was nothing to bury when we found them. The wolves would not even let them lie at rest. It seemed there was no flesh the wolves could get hold of they were so fond of as the flesh of an American or white man, and, strange to say, they would not eat a Mexican at all. It frequently happened that when the Indians killed a party on the Santa Fé Road there were both Mexicans and Americans left dead upon the same spot. When found the bodies of the Americans would invariably be eaten, and the bodies of the Mexicans lying intact without any interference at all.

There were various speculations with travelers along that road as to why this was so. Some thought it was because the Mexicans were so saturated with red pepper, they making that a part of their diet. Others thought it was because they were such inveterate smokers and were always smoking cigarettes. I have no suggestions to make on the subject any further than to say such was a fact, and there are many American boys to-day who would not be eaten by wolves, so impregnated are they with nicotine.

After passing this gloomy spot at the Wagon Mounds, which almost struck terror to our hearts to see the bones of our fellow-men who had been swept away by the hand of the savages, without a moment's warning, we pursued our way to Santa Fé, N. M., and delivered my freight to the merchants. They paid me the cash, $13,000 in silver—Mexican dollars—for freighting their goods to that point, a distance of 800 miles from the place of loading at Kansas City, Mo. I returned home without any further drawbacks or molestations on that trip.

On arriving home I found that Maj. E. A. Ogden of Fort Leavenworth desired to send a load of Government freight to Fort Mann, 400 miles west on the same road I had just traveled over, at about the point on the Arkansas River where Fort Dodge now stands. I agreed with him on terms at once, and loaded my wagons for that point. Lieutenant Heath of the United States Army was in command of the litttle post at Fort Mann. I arrived in good time, with everything in good order, and when the Government freights were unloaded he expressed a desire that I should take my entire train and go south about twenty-five miles, where there was some large timber growing near a stream called Cottonwood, for the purpose of bringing him a lot of saw-logs to make lumber for the building of his post. A more gentlemanly or clever man I never met in the United States Army or out of it—thoroughly correct in his dealings, and kind and courteous as could be. I made the trip and brought him a fine lot of cottonwood and walnut saw-logs, for these were the only kinds of timber that grew along the stream, unloaded them at his camp and returned home without losing any men or animals. The men were all in fine health and good spirits, as men generally are when everything moves successfully in their business, and particularly a business which hangs upon so many contingencies as our trips across the plains did.

In the year 1851 I again crossed the plains with a full outfit of twenty-five wagons and teams. This trip was a complete success; we met with no molestations, and returned home without the loss of any animals, but, owing to the cholera prevailing to some extent among the men who were on the plains, I lost two men by that disease. Several would have died, perhaps, but for the fact that I had provided myself with the proper remedies before leaving Kansas City. In 1852 I corraled my wagons, sold my oxen to California emigrants, and did no more work upon the plains that year. In 1853 I bought a new supply of work-cattle and again loaded my wagons at Kansas City for Santa Fé, N. M., as I had previously been doing. ·I was very successful in my operations that year, meeting with no loss of men and no animals worth mentioning. I also made a second trip that year from Fort Leavenworth to Fort Union, in New Mexico, returning to my home near Westport, Mo., late in November. During the year 1854 I also went upon the plains as a freighter, changing my business from freighting for the merchants in New Mexico to carrying United States Government freights. At this time I added to my transportation, making 100 wagons and teams for that year, divided into four trains. Everything moved along this year in a most prosperous way, without loss of life among my men, but I lost a great many of my work-cattle on account of the Texas fever. The loss was not so great, however, as to impede my traveling. The Government officers with whom I came in contact at either end of the route were well pleased with my way of doing business as a freighter, for everything was done in the most prompt and business-like manner.

In 1855 W. H. Russell of Lexington, Mo., and I formed a partnership under the name and style of Majors & Russell. That year we carried all the Government freight that had to be sent from Fort Leavenworth to the different posts or forts. The cholera prevailed among our men that year. Not more than two or three died, however, but quite a delay and additional expense were caused on account of this dire disease among our teamsters, with a train load of freight for Fort Riley. This was in June, and the train was almost deserted. Another train was entirely deserted, the sick men being taken to some of the farmers in the neighborhood, the well ones leaving for their homes, our oxen scattering and going toward almost every point of the compass. It was not long, however, until we got straightened again, and the train started for its destination.

Not long after this Maj. A. E. Ogden, the United States quartermaster at Fort Leavenworth, was taken with the cholera, and died at Fort Riley. A more honest, straightforward, and Christian gentleman could not be found in any army, or out of it. He had more excellent qualities than are generally allotted to man, and his death was much mourned by all who had the pleasure of his acquaintance. He left a very estimable wife and several children to mourn his death.

After the cholera disappeared that year, the freighting business moved along nicely and resulted in a prosperous year's work, after all the drawbacks in the early part of the season.

We also did a large business in freighting in 1856. I think that year we had about three hundred to three hundred and fifty wagons and teams at work, and our profits for 1855 and 1856 footed up about three hundred thousand dollars. This sum included our wagons, oxen, and other freighting and transportation outfits, valuing them at what we thought they would bring the beginning of the freighting season the next year.

In 1857 the Government extended the contract to Majors & Russell for one year longer, and it was during this year the United States Government determined to send an army to Utah to curtail the power that Brigham Young was extending over the destiny of that country; many complaints having reached Washington through the Government officials who had been sent to the Territory to preside as judges in the United States Courts. This resulted in a very great increase of transportation that year, and great difficulties were encountered, to begin with, which required quite an increase in the facilities for transportation, which had to be very hurriedly brought together. Before all the Government freight reached Fort Leavenworth, it became too late for trains to reach the headquarters of the army before cold weather set in, in the high altitude of Fort Bridger and that portion of the country where the army was in winter quarters; therefore many of the animals perished on account of having to be kept, under army orders, where grass and water were sometimes scarce, and they suffered more or less from severe cold weather. The result was great loss of the work-animals and an entire loss of the previous two years' profits.

A party of Mormons, under command of Col. Lott Smith, had been sent out by the Mormon authorities in the rear of Johnston's army to cut off his supplies. They captured and burned three of our trains, two on the Sandy, just east of Green River, and one on the west bank of Green River. They gave the captain of each train the privilege of taking

one of his best wagons and teams and loading it with supplies, to return home or back to the starting point. They
committed no outrage whatever toward the men, and, as soon
as the captain of each train told them he had all the food
necessary to supply him to get back to the starting point,
they told him to abandon the train, and they were set on
fire and everything burned that was consumable. The captains of the trains, with their teamsters, returned to the
States in safety. The cattle were driven off by the Mormons, and those that were not used for beef by the hungry
men were returned in the summer to the company after
peace had been made between the Mormons and the Government. The loss to the army was about five hundred
thousand pounds of Government supplies. This loss put
the army upon short rations for that winter and spring,
until they could be reached with supplies in the spring of
1858.

That spring, our firm, under the name of Russell,
Majors & Waddell, obtained a new contract from the
United States Government to carry Government freight to
Utah for the years 1858–59. That year the Government
ordered an immense lot of freight, aggregating 16,000,000
pounds, most of which had to be taken to Utah. We had
to increase the transportation from three or four hundred
wagons and teams we had previously owned to 3,500 wagons
and teams, and it required more than forty thousand oxen to
draw the supplies; we also employed over four thousand
men and about one thousand mules.

Our greatest drawback that year was occasioned by floods
and heavy rains upon the plains, which made our trains
move tardily in the outset. We succeeded admirably, however, considering the vast amount of material we had to
get together and organize, which we could not have done
had we not had so many years' experience, previous to this

great event, in the freighting enterprise; and especially was this so with me, for I had had, previous to this, a great many years' experience in handling men and teams, even before I crossed the plains ten years before. We succeeded this year in carrying everything to the army in Utah, fifty miles south of Salt Lake City, to Camp Floyd, the head-quarters of Sidney Johnston's command, a distance of 1,250 miles.

After unloading the wagons at Camp Floyd, they were taken to Salt Lake City and placed as near as they could stand to each other in the suburbs of the city, and covered many acres of ground, where they remained for one year or more, when our agent sold them to the Mormon author-ities for $10 apiece, they having cost us at the manufacturers' $150 to $175 apiece. The Mormons used the iron about them for the manufacture of nails. The oxen we sent to Skull Valley and other valleys near Camp Floyd, known to be good winter quarters for cattle and mules. During the year 1859, while our teams were at Camp Floyd we selected 3,500 head as suitable to drive to California and put on the market, and they were driven to Ruby Valley, in Nevada, where it was intended they should remain, that being con-sidered a favorable winter locality; and in the spring of 1860 they were to be driven to California, the intention being to let them graze on the wild oats and clover in the valleys of the Sacramento, and convert them into beef-cattle when fully ready for the market. A very few days after the herders reached the valley with them, which was late in November, a snow-storm set in and continued more or less severe, at intervals, until it covered the ground to such a depth that it was impossible for the cattle to get a particle of subsistence, and in less than forty days after the animals were turned out in the valley they were lying in great heaps frozen and starved to death. Only 200

A ROUGH TRAIL

out of the 3,500 survived the storm. They were worth at the time they were turned into the valley about $150,000, as they were a very superior and select lot of oxen. This was the largest disaster we met with during the years 1858 and 1859.

In 1857 the Indians attacked the herders who had charge of about one thousand head on the Platte River, west of Fort Kearney, which is now called Kearney City, in Nebraska, killing one of the herders and scattering the cattle to the four winds. These were also a complete loss.

We had very little trouble with the Indians in 1857, 1858, and 1859 in any way, owing to the fact that Johnston's army, consisting of about five thousand regulars, besides the teamsters, making in all about seven thousand well-armed men, had passed through the country in 1857, and they had seen such a vast army, with their artillery, that they were completely intimidated, and stayed at a very respectful distance from the road on which this vast number of wagons and teams traveled. Each one of our wagons was drawn by six yoke, or twelve oxen, and contained from five to six thousand pounds of freight, and there was but one wagon to each team. The time had not yet come when, what was afterward adopted, trail wagons were in use. This means two or three wagons lashed together and drawn by one team. Twenty-five of our wagons and teams formed what was called a train, and these trains were scattered along the road at intervals of anywhere from two to three miles, and sometimes eight to ten miles, and even greater distances, so as to keep out of the way of each other.

The road, until we reached the South Pass, was over the finest line of level country for traveling by wagons, with plenty of water and grass at almost every step of the way. Crossing the South Platte at what was then called Julesburg, and going across the divide to North Platte, at Ash

10

Hollow, we continued in the valley of the North Platte to the mouth of the Sweetwater, and up that stream until we passed through the South Pass. After passing that point it was somewhat more difficult to find grass and water, but we were fortunate enough all along the road to get sufficient subsistence out of nature for the sustenance of our animals, and were not obliged to feed our oxen. They did the work allotted to them, and gathered their own living at nights and noon-times.

In the fall of 1857 a report was sent by the engineers who were with General Johnston's army at Fort Bridger, and who had crossed the plains that year, to the Quartermaster's Department at Washington, stating it was impossible to find subsistence along the road for the number of animals it would require to transport the freight necessary for the support of the army. General Jessup, who was then Quartermaster of the United States Army at Washington, and as fine a gentleman as I ever met, gave me this information, and asked me if it would deter me from undertaking the transportation. I told him it would not, and that I would be willing to give him my head for a foot-ball to have kicked in Pennsylvania Avenue if I did not supply the army with every pound that was necessary for its subsistence, provided the Government would pay me to do it. We satisfied him after the first year's work had been done that we could do even more than I assured him could be done.

There is no other road in the United States, nor in my opinion elsewhere, of the same length, where such numbers of men and animals could travel during the summer season as could over the thoroughfare from the Missouri River up the Platte and its tributaries to the Rocky Mountains. In fact, had it been necessary to go east from the Missouri River, instead of west, it would have been impossible in

the nature of things to have done so, owing to the uneven
surface of the country, the water being in little deep ravines
and, as a rule, in small quantities, often muddy creeks to
cross, at other times underbrush and timber that the animals could have roamed into and disappeared, all of which
would have prevented progress had we started with such
an enterprise east instead of west. But the country west of
the Missouri River for hundreds of miles, so far as making
roads for travel of large numbers of animals is concerned, is
as different from the east as it is possible for two landscapes
to be. The whole country from the west border of the
Missouri, Iowa, and Arkansas was thoroughly practical,
before inhabited by farmers, for carrying the very largest
herds and organizations of people on what one might term
perfectly natural ground, often being able to travel hundreds of miles toward the sunset without a man having to
do one hour's work in order to prepare the road for the
heaviest wagons and teams.

The road from Missouri to Santa Fé, N. M., up the
Arkansas River, a distance of 800 miles, was very much
like the one up the Platte River, and over which millions
of pounds of merchandise were carried, and where oxen
almost invariably, but sometimes mules, did the work and
subsisted without a bite of any other food than that obtained from the grasses that grew by the roadside.

The roads all running west from the Missouri River came
up the valleys of the Platte, Kansas, or Arkansas rivers,
running directly from the mountains to the Missouri River.
These rivers had wide channels, low banks, and sandy bottoms, into which a thousand animals could go at one time,
if necessary, for drink, and spread over the surface, so as
not to be in each other's way, and whatever disturbance
they made in the water, in the way of offal or anything of
that kind, was soon overcome by the filtering of the water

through the sand, which kept it pure, and thousands of men and animals could find purer water on account of these conditions.

Then again the first expedient in the way of fuel was what was called buffalo chips, which was the offal from the buffalo after lying and being dried by the sun; and, strange to say, the economy of nature was such, in this particular, that the large number of work-animals left at every camping-place fuel sufficient, after being dried by the sun, to supply the necessities of the next caravan or party that traveled along. In this way the fuel supply was inexhaustible while animals traveled and fed upon the grasses.

This, however, did not apply to travel east of the Missouri River, as the offal from the animals there soon became decomposed and was entirely worthless for fuel purposes. This was altogether owing to the difference in the grasses that grew west of the Missouri River on the plains and in the Rocky Mountains and that which grew in the States east of the Missouri. Thus the fuel supply was sufficient for the largest organizations of people who, in those days, were traveling on the plains. Armies, small and great, that found it necessary to cross the plains, found sufficient supply of this fuel, and it seemed to be a necessity supplied by nature on the vast open and untimbered plains lying between the Missouri River and the Rocky Mountains, far beyond the Canadian line to the north, without which it would have been practically impossible to have crossed the plains with any degree of comfort, and in cold weather would have been absolutely impossible.

The small groups of timber growing along the streams would soon have been exhausted if used for fuel, and there would have been nothing to supply those who came later.

History records no other instance of like nature, where an immense area of country had the same necessity and where that necessity was supplied in such a manner as on the vast plains west of the Missouri River. These chips would lay for several years in perfect condition for fuel.

CHAPTER XVII.

"THE JAYHAWKERS OF 1849."

IN THIS year a number of gentlemen made up a party and started for the far West. During that fearful journey they were lost for three months in the "Great American Desert," the region marked on the map as the "unexplored region." General Fremont, with all the patronage of the Government at his command, tried to cross this desert at several points, but failed in every attempt. This desert is bounded by the Rocky Mountains and Wasatch range on the east and the Sierra Nevada on the west. From either side running streams sink near the base of the mountains, and no water exists except alkali and the hot springs impregnated with nitre.

The party arrived at Salt Lake late in the season of '49. It was thought by the older members of the company to be too late to cross the Sierra Nevada by the northern routes. No wagon had ever made the trip to the Pacific Coast by way of the Spanish Trail from Santa Fé to the Pacific, but it was determined to undertake this perilous journey. Captain Hunt, commander of the Mormon Battalion in the Mexican War, agreed to pilot the train through to Pueblo de los Angeles for the sum of $1,200. The weather south being too warm for comfortable travel, the party remained in Salt Lake City two months, leaving that place October 3, 1849. Upon their arrival at Little Salt Lake, a few restless comrades, angry that the party did not go through by the northern route, formed a band and determined to cross the desert at all hazards, and thus save hundreds of miles' travel via Los Angeles route. The sufferings they endured can not be described.

The survivors have since been scattered through the country, and have never come together since they separated at Santa Barbara, on the Pacific, February 4, 1850, until the twenty-third anniversary of their arrival was celebrated at the residence of Col. John B. Colton. The following letter will explain:

GALESBURG, ILL., January 12, 1872.

DEAR SIR: You are invited to attend a reunion of the " Jayhawkers of '49," on the 5th day of February next at 10 o'clock in the forenoon, at my house, to talk over old times and compare notes, after the lapse of twenty-three years from the time when the " Jayhawkers" crossed the " Great American Desert."

In the event that you can not be present, will you write a letter immediately on receipt of this, to be read on that occasion, giving all the news and reminiscences that will be of interest to the old crowd?

Yours fraternally,

JOHN B. COLTON.

A short sketch of the party's wanderings may not be amiss. On the 5th of April, 1849, a large party of men, with oxen and wagons, started from Galesburg, Ill., and vicinity for the then newly discovered gold-fields of California. To distinguish their party from other parties who went the same year, they jestingly took the name of " Jayhawkers," and that name has clung to them through all the years that have come and gone.

They encountered no trouble until after leaving Little Salt Lake, when taking the directions given them by Indian Walker and Ward—old mountaineers, who gave them a diagram and told them they could save 500 miles to the mines in California by taking the route directed—the Jayhawkers branched off from the main body. They found nothing as represented, and became lost on the desert, wandering for months, traversing the whole length of the Great American Desert, which Fremont, with all the aid of the Government at his call, could not cross the shortest way, and laid it down on the map as the "unexplored region."

They cut up their wagons on Silver Mountain and made of them pack-saddles for their cattle. Here thirteen of their number branched off, on New Year's day, taking what jerked beef they could carry, and started due west over the mountains, which the main party could not do on account of their cattle, but when they came to a mountain they took a southerly course around it. Of these thirteen, but two lived to get through, and they were found by ranch Indians in a helpless condition, and brought in and cared for. They had cast lots and lived on each other until but two remained. When questioned afterward in regard to their trip, they burst into tears and could not talk of it.

The main body of Jayhawkers kept their cattle, for they were their only hope; on these they lived, and the cattle lived on the bitter sage-brush and grease-wood, except when they occasionally found an oasis with water and a little grass upon it. The feet of the cattle were worn down until the blood marked their every step. Then the boys wrapped their feet in raw hides, as they did their own. Many died from exposure, hunger, and thirst, and were buried in the drifting sands where they fell, while those who were left moved on, weak and tottering, not knowing whose turn would be next. But for their cattle, not a man could have lived through that awful journey. They ate the hide, the blood, the refuse, and picked the bones in camp, making jerked beef of the balance to take along with them. People who are well fed, who have an abundance of the

ALEXANDER MAJORS.

R. H. HASLAM ("Pony Bob").   PRENTISS INGRAHAM.
JOHN B. COLTON.   W. F. CODY ("Buffalo Bill").

good things of life, say: "I would not eat this; I would not eat that; I'd starve first." They are not in a position to judge. Hunger swallows up every other feeling, and man in a starving condition is as savage as a wild beast.

After many desert wanderings and untold suffering, they at last struck a low pass in the Sierra Nevada Mountains, and emerged suddenly into the Santa Clara Valley, which was covered with grass and wild oats and flowers, with thousands of fat cattle feeding, a perfect paradise to those famished skeletons of men. There were thirty-four of the party who lived to reach that valley, and every one shed tears of joy at the sight of the glorious vision spread before them and the suddenness of their deliverance.

The boys shot five head of the cattle, and were eating the raw flesh and fat when the ranch Indians, hearing the firing, came down with all the shooting irons they could muster, but seeing the helpless condition of the party, they rode back to headquarters and reported to Francisco, the Spaniard who owned the ranch and cattle. He came down and invited them to camp in a grove near his home, bade them welcome, and furnished the party with meat, milk, grain, and everything they needed, and kept them until they were recruited and able to go on their way. Verily, he was a good Samaritan. They were strangers, and he took them in; hungry, and he fed them; thirsty, and he gave them drink. In the grand summing up of all things, may the noble Francisco be rewarded a thousand-fold.

They reached the Santa Clara Valley the 4th of February, 1850, and on that day each year they celebrate their deliverance by a reunion, where in pleasant companionship and around the festive board they recount reminiscences of the past, and live over again those scenes, when young and hopeful, they lived and suffered together.

There are but eleven of the survivors of that party alive to-day, and these are widely scattered east of the Rocky Mountains and on the Pacific Slope. Some are old men, too feeble to travel, and can only be present in spirit and by letter at the annual reunions. Gladly would every Jay-hawker welcome one and all of that band, bound together by ties of suffering in a bond of brotherhood which naught but death can sever.

The names and residences of the original party are as follows:

John B. Colton, Kansas City, Mo.

Alonzo C. Clay, Galesburg, Ill.

Capt. Asa Haines, Delong, Knox County, Ill., died March 29, 1889.

Luther A. Richards, Beaver City, Neb.

Charles B. Mecum, Perry, Greene County, Iowa.

John W. Plummer, Toulon, Ill., died June 22, 1892.

Sidney P. Edgerton, Blair, Neb., died January 31, 1880.

Edward F. Bartholomew, Pueblo, Colo., died February 13, 1891.

Urban P. Davidson, Derby P. O., Fremont County, Wyo.

John Groscup, Cahto, Mendocino County, Cal.

Thomas McGrew, died in 1866, in Willamette Valley, Ore.

John Cole, died in Sonora, Cal., in 1852.

John L. West, Coloma, Cal., since died.

William B. Rude, drowned in the Colorado River, New Mexico, in 1862.

L. Dow Stevens, San José, Cal.

William Robinson, Maquon, Ill., died in the desert.

——— Harrison, unknown.

Alexander Palmer, Knoxville, Ill., died at Slate Creek, Sierra County, Cal., in 1853.

Aaron Larkin, Knoxville, Ill., died at Humboldt, Cal., in 1853.

Marshall G. Edgerton, Galesburg, Ill., died in Montana Territory in 1855.

William Isham, Rochester, N. Y., died in the desert.

—— Fish, Oscaloosa, Iowa, died in the desert.

—— Carter, Wisconsin, unknown.

Harrison Frans, Baker City, Baker County, Ore.

Capt. Edwin Doty, Naples, Santa Barbara County, Cal., died June 14, 1891.

Bruin Byram, Knoxville, Ill., died in 1863.

Thomas Shannon, Los Gatos, Santa Clara County, Cal.

Rev. J. W. Brier, wife, and three small children, Lodi City, San Joaquin County, Cal.

George Allen, Chico, Cal., died in 1876.

Leander Woolsey, Oakland, Cal., died in 1884.

Man from Oscaloosa, Iowa, name not remembered, died in California.

Charles Clark, Henderson, Ill., died in 1863.

—— Gretzinger, Oscaloosa, Iowa, unknown.

A Frenchman, name unknown, became insane from starvation, wandered from camp near the Sierra Nevada Mountains, captured by the Digger Indians, and was rescued by a United States surveying party fifteen years after.

The following are to-day the sole survivors of the Jayhawk party of 1849:

John B. Colton, Kansas City, Mo.

Alonzo G. Clay, Galesburg, Ill.

Luther A. Richards, Beaver City, Neb.

Charles B. Mecum, Perry, Iowa.

Urban P. Davidson, Derby, Wyo.

John Groscup, Cahto, Cal.

L. Dow Stevens, San Jose, Cal.

Rev. J. W. Brier and Mrs. J. W. Brier, Lodi City, Cal.

Harrison Frans, Baker City, Ore.

Thomas Shannon, Los Gatos, Cal.

The last reunion of the Jayhawkers was held at the home of Col. John B. Colton of Kansas City, Mo., just forty-four years after the arrival of the party upon the Pacific Slope.

Of the eleven survivors there were but four able to be present, but the absent ones responded to their invitations with their photographs and letters of good will.

Among the invited guests to meet these old heroes were Col. W. F. Cody (Buffalo Bill), Col. Frank Hatton of the Washington *Post*, General Van Vliet, Capt. E. D. Millet (an old ranger), and the writer, who wishes the remnant of the little hero band may yet live to enjoy a score more of such delightful meetings.

CHAPTER XVIII.

MIRAGES.

About September 1, 1848, on my way from Independence, Mo., to Santa Fé, N. M., I met some of the soldiers of General Donaldson's regiment returning from the Mexican War on the Hornather or dry route, lying between the crossing of the Arkansas and Cimarron. It was about noon when we met. I saw them a considerable distance away. They were on horseback, and when they first appeared, the horses' legs looked to be from fifteen to eighteen feet long, and the body of the horses and the riders upon them presented a remarkable picture, apparently extending into the air, rider and horse, forty-five to sixty feet high. This was my first experience with mirage, and it was a marvel to me.

At the same time I could see beautiful clear lakes of water, apparently not more than a mile away, with all the surroundings in the way of bulrushes and other water vegetation common to the margin of lakes. I would have been willing, at that time, to have staked almost anything upon the fact that I was looking upon lakes of pure water. This was my last experience of the kind until I was returning later on in the season, when one forenoon, as my train was on the march, I beheld just ahead the largest buffalo bull that I ever saw. I stopped the train to keep from frightening the animal away, took the gun out of my wagon, which was in front, and started off to get a shot at the immense fellow, but when I had walked about eighty yards in his direction, I discovered that it was nothing more nor

L

less than a little coyote, which would not have weighed more than thirty pounds upon the scales.

The person who imagines for a minute that there is nothing in the great desert wastes of the Southwest but sand, cacti, and villainous reptiles is deluded. It is one of the most common fallacies to write down these barren places as devoid of beauty and usefulness. The rhymester who made Robinson Crusoe exclaim, "Oh, solitude, where are the charms that sages have seen in thy face?" never stood on a sand-dune or a pile of volcanic rock in this Southwestern country just at the break of day or as the sun went down, else the rhyme would never have been made to jingle.

To one who has never seen the famous mirages which Dame Nature paints with a lavish hand upon the horizon that bounds an Arizona desert, it is difficult to convey an intelligent portrait of these magnificent phenomena. And one who has looked upon these incomparable transformation scenes, the Titanic paintings formed by nature's curious slight-of-hand, can never forget them. They form the memories of a lifetime.

Arizona is rich in mirage phenomena, which, owing to the peculiar dryness of the atmosphere, are more vivid and of longer duration than in other parts. The variety of subjects which from time to time have been presented likewise gives them an unusual interest. Almost every one who has lived in the Territory any length of time, and one who has merely passed through, especially on the Southern Pacific Route, is familiar with the common water mirage which appears at divers places along the railroad. The most common section in which this phenomenon may be seen is between Tucson and Red Rock, and through the entire stretch of the Salton Basin from Ogilby to Indio.

Here in the early morning or in the late afternoon, if the atmospheric conditions be right, lakes, river, and lagoons of water can be seen from the train windows. Ofttimes the shimmering surface is dotted with tiny islands, and the shadows of umbrageous foliage are plainly seen reflected in the supposed water; yet an investigation shows nothing but long rods of sand-drifts or saline deposits.

Animals as well as men are deceived by these freaks of the atmosphere. Many instances are recorded where whole bands of cattle have rushed from the grazing grounds across the hot parched plains in pursuit of the constantly retreating water phantom, until they perish from exhaustion, still in sight of running brooks and surging springs. Prior to the advent of the railroad through this region, when overland passengers passed by on the old Yuma road to San Diego, scores of adventurous spirits perished in chasing this illusive phantom. It is said that one entire company of soldiers was thus inveigled from the highway and perished to a man.

One of the most interesting sights of this class is to be seen almost any time of the year in Mohave County, down in the region of the Big Sandy. Here for leagues upon leagues the ground is strewn with volcanic matter and basalt. It is one of the hottest portions of the continent, and except in the winter months it is almost unendurable by man or beast

At a point were the main road from the settlements on the Colorado to Kingman turns toward the east, there are a number of volcanic buttes. At these buttes just before sunrise the famous cantilever bridge which spans the Colorado River near the Needles, seventy miles distant, is plainly visible, together with the moving trains and crew. The train has the appearance of being perhaps an eighth of a mile distant, and every motion on board, the smoke, the escaping steam, are as natural and vivid as though not a hundred yards away.

At this same point huge mountains are seen to lift themselves up bodily and squat down again in the highway. Near these buttes, which are known as the Evil Ones, away back in the sixties a small force of cavalry was making its way from Fort Yuma to Fort Whipple. Owing to the extreme heat during the day, and as a further precaution against the hostile Indians, they were obliged to march at night, finding shelter in some mountain cañon during the day.

Shortly after daybreak, as they were preparing to go into camp, a whole legion of painted devils appeared on their front and hardly a quarter of a mile distant. The troops were thrown into confusion, and an order was immediately given to break ranks, and every man concealed himself behind the rocks, awaiting the attack which all felt must necessarily end in massacre.

For some minutes the Indians were seen to parley and gesticulate with each other, but they gave no signs of having noticed their hereditary foe. The unhappy troopers, however, were not kept in suspense long. As the great red disk of the day began to mount slowly up over the adjoining mountains, the redskins vanished as noiselessly and as suddenly as they had appeared.

Used as they were to treachery, and fearing some uncanny trick, the soldiers maintained their position throughout the long hot day, nor did they attempt to move until late in the night. Some weeks later it was learned from captives that on that very morning a band of nearly one thousand Chinhuevas and Wallapais were lying in wait for this same command but ninety miles up the river, expecting the soldiers by that route.

The most remarkable of all the mirages which have been witnessed in Arizona, at least by white man's eyes, was seen some years ago by an entire train-load of passengers on the Southern Pacific Railroad, near the small eating station of Maricopa, thirty-five miles below Phœnix. The train was due at the eating station at 6.30 A. M.

At 6.15 o'clock it stopped at a small water-tank a few miles east. During this stop the trainmen and such of the passengers as were awake were amazed to see spring out of the ground on the sky a magnificent city. The buildings were of the old Spanish and Morisco architecture, and were mostly adobe. Spacious court-yards lay before the astonished lookers-on, filled with all varieties of tropical fruits and vegetation.

Men and women clothed in the picturesque garbs of Old Spain were seen hurrying along the narrow, irregular streets to the principal edifice, which had the appearance of a church. Had the astonished spectators been picked up bodily and landed in one of the provincial towns of Seville or Andalusia, they would not have seen a more dazzling array of stately senoras and laughing black-eyed *muchachas* of the land of forever *manana*.

But the vision lasted much less time than it takes to write of the strange occurrence. It vanished as mysteriously as it came. Of course all of the hysterical women fainted. That is one of woman's prerogatives, in lieu of an explanation.

This phenomenon remained unsolved for two or three years. About that time, after the mirage was seen, a young civil engineer who was among the witnesses was engaged on the Gulf coast survey from the headwaters below Yuma to Guaymas. In the course of his labors he found himself at the old Mexican pueblo of Altar, and there he saw the original of the picture in the sky seen three years before near Maricopa Station. The distance, as a buzzard flies, from Maricopa to Altar is more than a hundred miles.

The native tribes are very superstitious concerning the
11

mirage, and when one is once observed, that locality receives a wide berth in the future.

In the secluded Jim-Jam Valley of the San Bernardino Mountains there are the most marvelous mirages known to the world. The wonderful mirages of the Mojave Desert have been talked about a great deal, and they are entitled to all the prominence they have had. But those of the Jim-Jam Valley are far more wonderful than these.

It is called Jim-Jam Valley because of the strange things seen there, and I defy any man, however sound of mind he may be, to go in there and not think he has "got 'em" before he gets out.

This valley is about twenty-five miles long by fifteen miles wide. It is uninhabited. It is bordered by the main San Bernardino range on the east, and by a spur of the Sierra Magdalenas on the west. There is no well-defined trail through the heart of it. The valley is a desert. The surrounding mountains are terribly serrated and cut up. The peaks are jagged. Altogether the surroundings are weird and forbidding.

Leaving Fisk's ranch on the trail at the foot of the Sierra Magdalenas, you climb an easy grade to Dead Man's Pass, the entrance to the valley.

Go in, and pretty soon you see lakes, and running rivers, and green borders, and flying water-fowl. Willows spring up here and there, and in the distance you see water-lilies.

What you behold contrasts finely with the rugged mountains, and you are charmed with it, and go on thinking you have struck an earthly paradise. Indian camps appear in view, and little oarsmen propel fantastic crafts upon the waters. Advancing still farther, dimly outlined forms may be seen, and the pantomime reminds you of a strange hobgoblin dance.

Sometimes a storm brews in the valley, and then the scene is all the more terrible. Forked lightning blazes about, and strange, uncouth animals, differing from any you have ever read about, are to be seen there.

These phenomena are seen for a stretch of about fifteen miles, up and down the middle of the valley principally, and they have been viewed by a great many people. They can not understand why the forms of the mirage, if such it may be called, are so much more strange there than on the Mojave Desert.

Everybody is in awe of the valley, and there are mighty few men, however nervy they may be ordinarily, who care to go there a second time.

CHAPTER XIX.

IN THE winter of 1858, while my partner, Mr. W. H. Russell, John S. Jones, a citizen of Pettis County, Mo., and myself were all in Washington, D. C., which was about the time that the Pike's Peak excitement was at its highest pitch, Messrs. Jones and Russell conceived the idea (I do not know from which one it emanated), and concluded to put a line of daily coaches in operation between the Missouri River and Denver City, when Denver was but a few months old. They came to me with the proposition to take hold of the enterprise with them.

I told them I could not consent to do so, for it would be impossible to make such a venture, at such an early period of development of this country, a paying institution, and urgently advised them to let the enterprise alone, for the above stated reasons. They, however, paid no attention to my protest, and went forward with their plans, bought 1,000 fine Kentucky mules and a sufficient number of Concord coaches to supply a daily coach each way between the Missouri River and Denver. At that time Leavenworth was the starting point on the Missouri. A few months later, however, they made Atchison the eastern terminus of the line and Denver the western.

They bought their mules and coaches on credit, giving their notes, payable in ninety days; sent men out to establish a station every ten to fifteen miles from Leavenworth due west, going up the Smoky Hill fork of the Kansas River, through the Territory of Kansas, and direct to Denver. The line was organized, stations built and put in running shape in remarkably quick time.

They made their daily trips in six days, traveling about one hundred miles every twenty-four hours. The first stage ran into Denver on May 17, 1859. It was looked upon as a great success, so far as putting the enterprise in good shape was concerned, but when the ninety days expired and the notes fell due they were unable to meet them. And in spite of my protests in the commencement of the organization as against having anything to do with it, it became necessary for Russell, Majors & Waddell to meet the obligation that Jones & Russell had entered into in organizing and putting the stock on the line. To save our partner we had to pay the debts of the concern and take the mules and coaches, or, in other words, all the paraphernalia of the line, to secure us for the money we had advanced.

The institution then having become the property of Russell, Majors & Waddell, we continued to run it daily. A few months after that, we bought out the semi-monthly line of Hockaday & Liggett, that was running from St. Joseph, Mo., to Salt Lake City, thinking that by blending the two lines we might bring the business up to where it would pay expenses, if nothing more.

This we failed in, for the lines, even after being blended, did not nearly meet expenses. Messrs. Hockaday & Liggett had a few stages, light, cheap vehicles, and but a few mules, and no stations along the route. They traveled the same team for several hundreds of miles before changing, stopping every few hours and turning them loose to graze, and then hitching them up again and going along.

I made a trip in the fall of 1858 from St. Joseph, Mo., to Salt Lake City in their coaches. It was twenty-one days from the time I left St. Joseph until I reached Salt Lake, traveling at short intervals day and night. As soon as we bought them out we built good stations and stables every ten to fifteen miles all the way from Missouri to Salt Lake, and supplied them with hay and grain for the horses and provisions for the men, so they would only have to drive a team from one station to the next, changing at every station.

Instead of our schedule time being twenty-two days, as it was with Hockaday & Liggett, and running two per month, we ran a stage each way every day and made the schedule time ten days, a distance of 1,200 miles. We continued running this line from the summer of 1859 until March, 1862, when it fell into the hands of Ben Holliday. From the summer of 1859 to 1862 the line was run from Atchison to Fort Kearney and from Fort Kearney to Fort Laramie, up the Sweet Water route and South Pass, and on to Salt Lake City.

This is the route also run by the Pony Express, each pony starting from St. Joseph instead of Atchison, Kan., from which the stages started. We had on this line about one thousand Kentucky mules and 300 smaller-sized mules to run on through the mountain portion of the line, and a large number of Concord coaches. It was as fine a line, considering the mules, coaches, drivers, and general outfitting, perhaps, as was ever organized in this or any other country, from the beginning.

And it was very fortunate for the Government and the people that such a line was organized and in perfect running condition on the middle route when the late war commenced, as it would have been impossible to carry mails on the route previously patronized by the Government, which ran from San Francisco via Los Angeles, El Paso, Fort Smith, and St. Louis, for the Southern people would have interfered with it, and would not have allowed it to run through that portion of the country during the war.

It turned out that Senator Gwin's original idea with reference to running a pony express from the Missouri River to Sacramento to prove the practicability of that route at all seasons of the year was well taken, and the stage line as well as the pony proved to be of vital importance in carrying the mails and Government dispatches.

It so transpired that the firm of Russell, Majors & Waddell had to pay the fiddler, or the entire expense of organizing both the stage line and the pony express, at a loss, as it turned out, of hundreds of thousands of dollars. After the United States mail was given to this line it became a paying institution, but it went into the hands of Holliday just before the first quarterly payment of $100,000 was made. The Government paid $800,000 a year for carrying the mails from San Francisco to Missouri, made in quarterly payments.

The part of the line that Russell, Majors & Waddell handled received $400,000, and Butterfield & Co. received $400,000 for carrying the mails from Salt Lake to California. During the war there was a vast amount of business, both in express and passenger traveling, and it was the only available practicable line of communication between California and the States east of the Rocky Mountains.

CHAPTER XX.

THE GOLD FEVER.

DURING the winter of 1858–59 the public generally, throughout the United States, began to give publicity to a great gold discovery reported to have been made in the Pike's Peak region of the Rocky Mountains.

From week to week, as time passed, more extended accounts were given, until the reports became fabulous.

The discovery was reported to have been made in Cherry Creek, at or near its junction with the South Platte River, and one of the newspapers at the time, published in Cleveland, Ohio, came out, giving a cut which was claimed to be a map of the country. Pike's Peak was given as the central figure. The South Fork of the Platte River was represented as flowing out from the mountain near its base, and Cherry Creek as coming out of a gorge in the mountain's side, and forming a junction with the Platte in the low lands, at which point Denver was designated.

Reports went so far as to state that gold was visible in the sands of the creek-bed, and that the banks would pay from grass roots to bed rock.

People became wild with excitement, and a stampede to Pike's Peak appeared inevitable.

The great question with the excited people was as to the shortest, cheapest, and quickest way to get to the country, with little thought of personal safety or comfort, or as to how they should get back in the event of failure. But the problem was soon believed to have been solved to the satisfaction of all concerned.

A brilliant idea took possession of the fertile brain of an energetic Buckeye citizen, and a plan was conceived and to an extent put in execution. A canal-boat which had been converted into a steam tug was secured, not only for the purpose of transporting the multitudes from Cleveland to Denver, but to transport the millions of treasures back to civilization, or, as it was then put, "to God's country." Passengers were advertised for at $100 per head; the route given as follows: From Cleveland, Ohio, via the lake to Chicago, thence via Illinois Canal and River to the Mississippi River, then to the mouth of the Missouri River and up the Missouri to the mouth of the Platte River, and, thence up the Platte to Denver, and it was with pride that this boat was advertised as the first to form a line of steamers to regularly navigate the last named stream.

Of course this trip was never made, for in fact, at certain seasons of the year, it would be difficult to float a two-inch plank down the river from Denver to the Missouri, and yet this is but illustrative of the hundreds of visionary, crude and novel plans conceived and adopted by the thousands of so-called Pike's Peakers who swarmed the plains between Denver and the border during the early part of 1859.

Having caught the fever, and there being no remedy for the disease equal to the gold hunter's experience, horses and wagon were secured and, with traveling companions, the trip was made by land. Many novel experiences to the participants occurred during that trip.

At Leavenworth one of my companions concluded to economize, which he did by piloting six yoke of oxen across the plains for me. He drove into Denver in the morning and drove out of it in the evening of the same day, fully convinced (as he himself stated) that all reports of the country were either humbugs or greatly exaggerated, and that he had seen and knew all that was worth seeing and knowing of that land. I suggested the advisability of further investigation before moving on, but not being favorable to delay, and suiting himself to his means, he secured an ox and cart that had been brought in from the Red River of the North, and loading it with all necessary supplies headed for Denver, with a determination so aptly and forcibly expressed in the usual motto, " Pike's Peak or bust." All went well until he reached the Little Blue River in Kansas, when he "busted," or at least the cart did, and the result was the location of a ranch on that stream and an end to his westward career.

Thus Kansas is largely indebted for her early and rapid settlement to the discovery of gold in Colorado, and to the misfortunes of many of the Pike's Peakers who, for some cause, failed to reach the end desired, and who were thus compelled to stop and become settlers of that now great State.

Shortly before the time of which I write, June, 1859, Horace Greeley passed through Leavenworth en route for Denver, and thousands of people were to be found in every principal town and city, from St. Louis to Council Bluffs (there was no Omaha at that time), who were awaiting his report, which was daily expected, and for once, at least, the New York *Tribune* was in demand on the borders. I may say here that Horace Greeley was *dead-headed* through to California.

In the early part of July came a favorable report in the *Tribune*, and at that time a shipment of gold was made from Denver and put on exhibition in one of the banks at Leavenworth.

Thus new life was given to the immigration movement, and soon the towns along the border were largely relieved of their floating population, and the plains at once became alive with a moving, struggling mass of humanity, moving westward in the mad rush for the gold-fields of Pike's Peak.

Among my friends an association was formed and the following party organized, viz.: Alfred H. Miles and his wife, their son George T., and two daughters, Fannie D. and Emma C. Miles, with William McLelland and P. A. Simmons.

They outfitted with two wagons, four yoke of oxen, two saddle-mules, one cow, and all supplies presumed to be sufficient for at least one year. On the first day of August, 1859, they moved out from Leavenworth, happy and full of "great expectations" for the future. Forty-nine days were spent in making the drive, and then they landed in Denver on the eighteenth day of the following month. And here let me say, that I believe this party of seven proved an exception to the rule, in this, that every member of it became a permanent settler, and for the last thirty-three years they have been actively connected with, and identified in, the various departments of life and business, both public and private.

All are yet living and residents of the State, except Mrs. Miles, who recently passed to a higher life, respected and loved by all who knew her; and I here venture the opinion that no other party of emigrants in this country, of equal number, can show a better record.

Many novel events occurred on this trip also, but to mention all the new and novel experiences incident to an expedition of that kind would require more than the allotted space for a chapter. I will, therefore, confine the account to one incident alone which will make manifest the radical changes that are sometimes wrought in the individual lives of people, in a sometimes radically short space of time. Two of the ladies of the party before mentioned arrived in Leavenworth about one month previous to their departure on this trip. They were just graduated from a three years' course of study in a female seminary, and in thirty days from that time they were transported from their boarding-school surroundings to the wilds of the Great American Desert, and after passing into the timberless portion of the great desert, the great query with them was as to how and where they were to secure fuel necessary for culinary purposes; and when informed that it would be necessary to gather and use buffalo chips for that purpose, their incredulity became manifest, and their curiosity was rather increased than satisfied. When called upon to go, gunny-sack in hand, out from the line of travel to gather the necessary fuel, it was difficult to persuade them they were not being made the victims of a joke; but when finally led into the field of " chips," and the discovery made of their character, the expression upon the face of each would have been a delight to an artist and amusing to the beholder; and to say that the distance between the chip-field and the camp was covered by them in the time rarely, if ever, covered by the native antelope, is to speak without exaggeration.

As before stated, all of the seven members of this party, on their arrival in Denver, became residents and actively identified in the various departments of life and business, and to each and every one there is no spot on the face of this globe that is quite so good, so grand, and so dear as the Centennial State, of which Denver is the center of their love.

CHAPTER XXI.

THE OVERLAND MAIL.

OVER thirty-two years ago, when a bachelor occupied the President's mansion at Washington, and there was no Pacific Railroad and no transcontinental telegraph line in operation over the Great American Desert of the old school-books, and the wild Indian was lord of the manor—a true native American sovereign—St. Joseph, Mo., was the western terminus of railway transportation. Beyond that point the traveler bound for the regions of the occident had his choice of a stage-coach, an ox-team, a pack-mule, or some equally stirring method of reaching San Francisco.

Just at that interesting period in our history—when the gold and silver excitement, and other local advantages of the Pacific Coast, had concentrated an enterprising population and business at San Francisco and the adjacent districts—the difficulty of communication with the East was greatly deplored, and the rapid overland mail service became an object of general solicitude. In the year 1859 several magnates in Wall Street formed a formidable lobby at Washington in the interests of an overland mail route to California, and asked Congress for a subsidy for carrying the mails overland for one year between New York and San Francisco.

The distance was 1,950 miles. Mr. Russell proposed to cover this distance with a mail line between St. Joseph, Mo., and San Francisco, that would deliver letters at either end of the route within ten days.

Five hundred of the fleetest horses to be procured were

M

immediately purchased, and the services of over two hundred competent men were secured. Eighty of these men were selected for express riders. Light-weights were deemed the most eligible for the purpose; the lighter the man the better for the horse, as some portions of the route had to be traversed at a speed of twenty miles an hour. Relays were established at stations, the distance between which was, in each instance, determined by the character of the country.

These stations dotted a wild, uninhabited expanse of country 2,000 miles wide, infested with road-agents and warlike Indians, who roamed in formidable hunting parties, ready to sacrifice human life with as little unconcern as they would slaughter a buffalo. The Pony Express, therefore, was not only an important, but a daring and romantic enterprise. At each station a sufficient number of horses were kept, and at every third station the thin, wiry, and hardy pony-riders held themselves in readiness to press forward with the mails. These were filled with important business letters and press dispatches from Eastern cities and San Francisco, printed upon tissue paper, and thus especially adapted by their weight for this mode of transportation.

The schedule time for the trip was fixed at ten days. In this manner they supplied the place of the electric telegraph and the lightning express train of the gigantic railway enterprise that subsequently superseded it.

The men were faithful, daring fellows, and their service was full of novelty and adventure. The facility and energy with which they journeyed was a marvel. The news of Abraham Lincoln's election was carried through from St. Joseph to Denver, Colo., 665 miles, in two days and twenty-one hours, the last ten miles having been covered in thirty-one minutes. The last route on the occasion was traversed by Robert H. Haslam, better known as " Pony Bob," who carried the news 120 miles in eight hours and ten minutes, riding from Smith's Creek to Fort Churchill, on the Carson River, Nevada, the first telegraph station on the Pacific Coast.

On another occasion, it is recorded, one of these riders journeyed a single stretch of 300 miles—the other men who should have relieved him being either disabled or indisposed—and reached the terminal station on schedule time.

The distance between relay riders' stations varied from sixty-five to one hundred miles, and often more. The weight to be carried by each was fixed at ten pounds or under, and the charge for transportation was $5 in gold for each half of an ounce. The entire distance between New York City and San Francisco occupied but fourteen days. The riders received from $120 to $125 per month for their arduous services. The pony express enterprise continued for about two years, at the end of which time telegraph service between the Atlantic and Pacific oceans was established. Few men remember those days of excitement and interest. The danger surrounding the riders can not be told. Not only were they remarkable for lightness of weight and energy, but their service required continual vigilance, bravery, and agility. Among their number were skillful guides, scouts, and couriers, accustomed to adventures and hardships on the plains—men of strong wills and wonderful powers of endurance. The horses were mostly half-breed California mustangs, as alert and energetic as their riders, and their part in the service—sure-footed and fleet—was invaluable. Only two minutes were allowed at stations for changing mails and horses. Everybody was on the *qui vive*. The adventures with which the service was rife are numerous and exciting.

The day of THE FIRST START, the 3d of April, 1860, at noon, Harry Roff, mounted on a spirited half-breed broncho, started from Sacramento on his perilous ride, and covered the first twenty miles, including one change, in fifty-nine minutes. On reaching Folson, he changed again and started for Placerville, at the foot of the Sierra Nevada Mountain, fifty-five miles distant. There he connected with " Boston," who took the route to Friday's Station, crossing the eastern summit of the Sierra Nevada. Sam Hamilton next fell into line, and pursued his way to Genoa, Carson City, Dayton, Reed's Station, and Fort Churchill—seventy-five miles. The entire run, 185 miles, was made in fifteen hours and twenty minutes, and included the crossing of the western summits of the Sierras, through thirty feet of snow. This seems almost impossible, and would have been, had not pack trains of mules and horses kept the trail open. Here "Pony Bob"—Robert H. Haslam—took the road from Fort Churchill to Smith's Creek, 120 miles distant, through a hostile Indian country. From this point Jay G. Kelley rode from Smith's Creek to Ruby Valley, Utah, 116 miles; from Ruby Valley to Deep Creek, H. Richardson, 105 miles; from Deep Creek to Rush Valley, old Camp Floyd, eighty miles; from Camp Floyd to Salt Lake City, fifty miles; George Thacher the last end. This ended the Western Division, under the management of Bolivar Roberts, now in Salt Lake City.

Among the most noted and daring riders of the Pony Express was Hon. William F. Cody, better known as Buffalo Bill, whose reputation is now established the world over. While engaged in the express service, his route lay between Red Buttes and Three Crossings, a distance of 116 miles. It was a most dangerous, long, and lonely trail, including the perilous crossing of the North Platte River, one-half mile wide, and though generally shallow, in some

A FRONTIER VILLAGE.

places twelve feet deep, often much swollen and turbulent. An average of fifteen miles an hour had to be made, including changes of horses, detours for safety, and time for meals. Once, upon reaching Three Crossings, he found that the rider on the next division, who had a route of seventy-six miles, had been killed during the night before, and he was called on to make the extra trip until another rider could be employed. This was a request the compliance with which would involve the most taxing labors and an endurance few persons are capable of; nevertheless, young Cody was promptly on hand for the additional journey, and reached Rocky Ridge, the limit of the second route, on time. This round trip of 384 miles was made without a stop, except for meals and to change horses, and every station on the route was entered on time. This is one of the longest and best ridden pony express journeys ever made.

Pony Bob also had a series of stirring adventures while performing his great equestrian feat, which he thus describes:

"About eight months after the Pony Express commenced operations, the Piute war began in Nevada, and as no regular troops were then at hand, a volunteer corps, raised in California, with Col. Jack Hayes and Henry Meredith—the latter being killed in the first battle at Plymouth Lake—in command, came over the mountains to defend the whites. Virginia City, Nev., then the principal point of interest, and hourly expecting an attack from the hostile Indians, was only in its infancy. A stone hotel on C Street was in course of erection, and had reached an elevation of two stories. This was hastily transformed into a fort for the protection of the women and children.

"From the city the signal fires of the Indians could be seen on every mountain peak, and all available men and

12

horses were pressed into service to repel the impending assault of the savages. When I reached Reed's Station, on the Carson River, I found no change of horses, as all those at the station had been seized by the whites to take part in the approaching battle. I fed the animal that I rode, and started for the next station, called Buckland's, afterward known as Fort Churchill, fifteen miles farther down the river. This point was to have been the termination of my journey (as I had been changed from my old route to this

"PONY BOB."

one, in which I had had many narrow escapes and been twice wounded by Indians), as I had ridden seventy-five miles, but to my great astonishment, the other rider refused to go on. The superintendent, W. C. Marley, was at the station, but all his persuasion could not prevail on the rider, Johnnie Richardson, to take the road. Turning then to me, Marley said:

"'Bob, I will give you $50 if you make this ride.'

"I replied:

"'I will go you once.'

"Within ten minutes, when I had adjusted my Spencer rifle—a seven-shooter—and my Colt's revolver, with two cylinders ready for use in case of an emergency, I started. From the station onward was a lonely and dangerous ride of thirty-five miles, without a change, to the Sink of the Carson. I arrived there all right, however, and pushed on to Sand's Spring, through an alkali bottom and sand-hills, thirty miles farther, without a drop of water all along the route. At Sand's Springs I changed horses, and continued on to Cold Springs, a distance of thirty-seven miles. Another change, and a ride of thirty miles more, brought me to Smith's Creek. Here I was relieved by J. G. Kelley. I had ridden 185 miles, stopping only to eat and change horses.

"After remaining at Smith's Creek about nine hours, I started to retrace my journey with the return express. When I arrived at Cold Springs, to my horror I found that the station had been attacked by Indians, and the keeper killed and all the horses taken away. What course to pursue I decided in a moment—I would go on. I watered my horse—having ridden him thirty miles on time, he was pretty tired—and started for Sand Springs, thirty-seven miles away. It was growing dark, and my road lay through heavy sage-brush, high enough in some places to conceal a horse. I kept a bright lookout, and closely watched every motion of my poor horse's ears, which is a signal for danger in an Indian country. I was prepared for a fight, but the stillness of the night and the howling of the wolves and coyotes made cold chills run through me at times, but I reached Sand Springs in safety and reported what had happened. Before leaving I advised the station-keeper to come with me to the Sink of the Carson, for I was sure the Indians would be upon him the next day. He took my advice, and so probably saved his life, for the following morning Smith's Creek was attacked.   The whites, however, were well protected in the shelter of a stone house, from which they fought the Indians for four days.   At the end of that time they were relieved by the appearance of about fifty volunteers from Cold Springs.   These men reported that they had buried John Williams, the brave station-keeper of that station, but not before he had been nearly devoured by wolves.

"When I arrived at the Sink of the Carson, I found the station men badly frightened, for they had seen some fifty warriors, decked out in their war-paint and reconnoitering the station.   There were fifteen white men. here, well armed and ready for a fight.   The station was built of adobe, and was large enough for the men and ten or fifteen horses, with a fine spring of water within ten feet of it.   I rested here an hour, and after dark started for Buckland's, where I arrived without a mishap and only three and a half hours behind the schedule time.   I found Mr. Marley at Buckland's, and when I related to him the story of the Cold Springs trag-edy and my success, he raised his previous offer of $50 for my ride to $100.   I was rather tired, but the excitement of the trip had braced me up to withstand the fatigue of the journey.   After the rest of one and one-half hours, I pro-ceeded over my own route, from Buckland's to Friday's Station, crossing the western summit of the Sierra Nevada. I had traveled 380 miles within a few hours of schedule time, and surrounded by perils on every hand."

After the "Overland Pony Express" was discontinued, "Pony Bob" was employed by Wells, Fargo & Co., as a pony express rider, in the prosecution of their transporta-tion business.   His route was between Virginia City, Nev., and Friday's Station, and return, about one hundred miles, every twenty-four hours, schedule time ten hours.   This engagement continued for more than a year; but as the

Union Pacific Railway gradually extended its line and operations, the pony express business as gradually diminished. Finally the track was completed to Reno, Nev., twenty-three miles from Virginia City, and over this route "Pony Bob" rode for over six months, making the run every day, with fifteen horses, inside of one hour. When the telegraph line was completed, the pony express over this route was withdrawn, and "Pony Bob" was sent to Idaho, to ride the company's express route of 100 miles, with one horse, from Queen's River to the Owhyee River. He was at the former station when Major McDermott was killed, at the breaking out of the Modoc war. On one of his rides he passed the remains of ninety Chinamen who had been killed by the Indians, only one escaping to tell the tale, and whose bodies lay bleaching in the sun for a distance of more than ten miles from the mouth of Ive's Cañon to Crooked Creek. This was "Pony Bob's" last experience as a pony express rider. His successor, Sye Macaulas, was killed the first trip he tried to make. Bob bought a Flathead Indian pony at Boisé City, Idaho, and started for Salt Lake City, 400 miles away, where his brother-in-law, Joshua Hosmer, was United States Marshal. Here "Pony Bob" was appointed a deputy, but not liking the business, was again employed by Theodore Tracy—Wells-Fargo's agent—as first messenger from that city to Denver after Ben Holliday had sold out to Wells, Fargo & Co.—a distance of 720 miles by stage—which position Bob filled a long time.

"Pony Bob" is now a resident of Chicago, where he is engaged in business.

CHAPTER XXII.

DURING the winter of 1859, Mr. W. H. Russell, of our firm, while in Washington, D. C., met and became acquainted with Senator Gwin of California. The Senator was very anxious to establish a line of communication between California and the States east of the Rocky Mountains, which would be more direct than that known as the Butterfield route, running at that time from San Francisco via Los Angeles, Cal.; thence across the Colorado River and up the valley of the Gila; thence via El Paso and through Texas, crossing the Arkansas River at Fort Gibson, and thence to St. Louis, Mo.

This route, the Senator claimed, was entirely too long; that the requirements of California demanded a more direct route, which would make quicker passage than could be made on such a circuitous route as the Butterfield line.

Knowing that Russell, Majors & Waddell were running a daily stage between the Missouri River and Salt Lake City, and that they were also heavily engaged in the transportation of Government stores on the same line, he asked Mr. Russell if his company could not be induced to start a pony express, to run over its stage line to Salt Lake City, and from thence to Sacramento; his object being to test the practicability of crossing the Sierra Nevadas, as well as the Rocky Mountains, with a daily line of communication.

After various consultations between these gentlemen, from time to time, the Senator urging the great necessity

of such an experiment, Mr. Russell consented to take hold
of the enterprise, provided he could get his partners, Mr.
Waddell and myself, to join him.

With this understanding, he left Washington and came
west to Fort Leavenworth, Kan., to consult us. After he
explained the object of the enterprise, and we had well
considered it, we both decided that it could not be made to
pay expenses. This decision threw quite a damper upon
the ardor of Mr. Russell, and he strenuously insisted we
should stand by him, as he had committed himself to Senator Gwin before leaving Washington, assuring him he
could get his partners to join him, and that he might rely
on the project being carried through, and saying it would
be very humiliating to his pride to return to Washington
and be compelled to say the scheme had fallen through
from lack of his partners' confidence.

He urged us to reconsider, stating the importance
attached to such an undertaking, and relating the facts
Senator Gwin had laid before him, which were that all his
attempts to get a direct thoroughfare opened between the
State of California and the Eastern States had proved
abortive, for the reason that when the question of establishing a permanent central route came up, his colleagues,
or fellow senators, raised the question of the impassability
of the mountains on such a route during the winter
months; that the members from the Northern States were
opposed to giving the whole prestige of such a thoroughfare to the extreme southern route; that this being the
case, it had actually become a necessity to demonstrate, if
it were possible to do so, that a central or middle route
could be made practicable during the winter as well as
summer months. That as soon as we demonstrated the
feasibility of such a scheme he (Senator Gwin) would use
all his influence with Congress to get a subsidy to help pay

the expenses of such a line on the thirty-ninth to forty-first parallel of latitude, which would be central between the extreme north and south; that he could not ask for the subsidy at the start with any hope of success, as the public mind had already accepted the idea that such a route open at all seasons of the year was an impossibility; that as soon as we proved to the contrary, he would come to our aid with a subsidy.

After listening to all Mr. Russell had to say upon the subject, we concluded to sustain him in the undertaking, and immediately went to work to organize what has since been known as "The Pony Express."

As above stated, we were already running a daily stage between the Missouri River and Salt Lake City, and along this line stations were located every ten or twelve miles, which we utilized for the Pony Express, but were obliged to build stations between Salt Lake City and Sacramento, Cal.

Within sixty days or thereabouts from the time we agreed to undertake the enterprise, we were ready to start ponies, one from St. Joseph, Mo., and the other from Sacramento, Cal., on the same day. At that time there was telegraphic communication between the East and St. Joseph, Mo., and between San Francisco and Sacramento, Cal.

The quickest time that had ever been made with any message between San Francisco and New York, over the Butterfield line, which was the southern route, was twenty-one days. Our Pony Express shortened the time to ten days, which was our schedule time, without a single failure, being a difference of eleven days.

To do the work of the Pony Express required between four hundred and five hundred horses, about one hundred and ninety stations, two hundred men for station-keepers, and eighty riders; riders made an average ride of thirty-three and one-third miles.   In doing this each man rode three ponies on his part of the route; some of the riders, however, rode much greater distances in times of emergency.

The Pony Express carried messages written on tissue paper, weighing one-half ounce, a charge of $5 being made for each dispatch carried.

As anticipated, the amount of business transacted over this line was not sufficient to pay one-tenth of the expenses, to say nothing about the amount of capital invested.   In this, however, we were not disappointed, for we knew, as stated in the outset, that it could not be made a paying institution, and was undertaken solely to prove that the route over which it ran could be made a permanent thoroughfare for travel at all seasons of the year, proving, as far as the paramount object was concerned, a complete success.

Two important events transpired during the term of the Pony's existence; one was the carrying of President Buchanan's last message to Congress, in December, 1860, from the Missouri River to Sacramento, a distance of two thousand miles, in eight days and some hours.   The other was the carrying of President Lincoln's inaugural address of March 4, 1861, over the same route in seven days and, I think, seventeen hours, being the quickest time, taking the distance into consideration, on record in this or any other country, as far as I know.

One of the most remarkable feats ever accomplished was made by F. X. Aubery, who traveled the distance of 800 miles, between Santa Fé, N. M., and Independence, Mo., in five days and thirteen hours.   This ride, in my opinion, in one respect was the most remarkable one ever made by any man.   The entire distance was ridden without stopping to rest, and having a change of horses only

once in every one hundred or two hundred miles. He kept
a lead horse by his side most of the time, so that when the
one he was riding gave out entirely, he changed the saddle
to the extra horse, left the horse he had been riding and
went on again at full speed.

At the time he made this ride, in much of the territory
he passed through he was liable to meet hostile Indians,
so that his adventure was daring in more ways than one.
In the first place, the man who attempted to ride 800
miles in the time he did took his life in his hands. There
is perhaps not one man in a million who could have lived
to finish such a journey.

Mr. Aubery was a Canadian Frenchman, of low stature,
short limbs, built, to use a homely simile, like a jack-screw,
and was in the very zenith of his manhood, full of pluck
and daring.

It was said he made this ride upon a bet of $1,000 that
he could cover the distance in eight days.

One year previous to this, in 1852, he made a bet he
could do the same distance in ten days. The result was
he traveled it in a little over eight days, hence his bet he
could make the ride in 1853 in eight days, the result of that
trip showing he consumed little more than half that time.

I was well acquainted with and did considerable business
with Aubery during his years of freighting. I met him
when he was making his famous ride, at a point on the
Santa Fé Road called Rabbit Ear. He passed my train
at a full gallop without asking a single question as to the
danger of Indians ahead of him.

After his business between St. Louis and Santa Fé
ceased, his love for adventure and his daring enterprise
prompted him to make a trip from New Mexico to California with sheep, which he disposed of at good prices, and
returned to New Mexico.

Immediately upon his return he met a friend, a Major Weightman of the United States Army, who was a great admirer of his pluck and daring. Weightman was at that time editor of a small paper called the Santa Fé *Herald*. At their meeting, as was the custom of the time, they called for drinks. Their glasses were filled and they were ready to drink, when Aubery asked Weightman why he had published a damned lie about his trip to California. Instead of taking his drink, Weightman tossed the contents of his glass in Aubery's face. Aubery made a motion to draw his pistol and shoot, when Weightman, knowing the danger, drew his knife and stabbed Aubery through the heart, from which blow he dropped dead upon the floor.

The whole affair was enacted in one or two seconds. From the time they started to take a friendly drink till Aubery was lying dead on the floor less time elapsed than it takes to tell the story.

This tragedy was the result of rash words hastily spoken, and proves that friends, as well as enemies, should be careful and considerate in the language they use toward others.

In the spring of 1860 Bolivar Roberts, superintendent of the Western Division of the Pony Express, came to Carson City, Nev., which was then in St. Mary's County, Utah, to engage riders and station men for a pony express route about to be established across the great plains by Russell, Majors & Waddell. In a few days fifty or sixty men were engaged, and started out across the Great American Desert to establish stations, etc. Among that number the writer can recall to memory the following: Bob Haslam ("Pony Bob"), Jay G. Kelley, Sam Gilson, Jim Gilson, Jim McNaughton, Bill McNaughton, Jose Zowgaltz, Mike Kelley, Jimmy Buckton, and "Irish Tom." At present "Pony Bob" is living on "the fat of the land" in Chicago. Sam and Jim Gilson are mining in Utah, and all the old

N

"Pony" boys will rejoice to know they are now millionaires. The new mineral, gilsonite, was discovered by Sam Gilson. Mike Kelley is mining in Austin, Nev.; Jimmy Bucklin, "Black Sam," and the McNaughton boys are dead. William Carr was hanged in Carson City, for the murder of Bernard Cherry, his unfortunate death being the culmination of a quarrel begun months before, at Smith Creek Station. His was the first legal hanging in the Territory, the sentence being passed by Judge Cradlebaugh.

J. G. Kelley has had a varied experience, and is now fifty-four years of age, an eminent mining engineer and mineralogist, residing in Denver, Colo. In recalling many reminiscences of the plains in the early days, I will let him tell the story in his own language:

"Yes," he said, "I was a pony express rider in 1860, and went out with Bol Roberts (one of the best men that ever lived), and I tell you it was no picnic. No amount of money could tempt me to repeat my experience of those days. To begin with, we had to build willow roads (corduroy fashion) across many places along the Carson River, carrying bundles of willows two and three hundred yards in our arms, while the mosquitoes were so thick it was difficult to discern whether the man was white or black, so thickly were they piled on his neck, face, and hands.

" Arriving at the Sink of the Carson River, we began the erection of a fort to protect us from the Indians. As there were no rocks or logs in that vicinity, the fort was built of adobes, made from the mud on the shores of the lake. To mix this mud and get it the proper consistency to mold into adobes (dried brick), we tramped around all day in it in our bare feet. This we did for a week or more, and the mud being strongly impregnated with alkali (carbonate of soda), you can imagine the condition of our feet. They were much swollen, and resembled hams. Before that time

I wore No. 6 boots, but ever since then No. 9s fit me snugly.

"This may, in a measure, account for Bob Haslam's selection of a residence in Chicago, as he helped us make the adobes, and the size of his feet would thereafter be less noticeable there than elsewhere.

"We next built a fort of stone at Sand Springs, twenty-five miles from Carson Lake, and another at Cold Springs, thirty-seven miles east of Sand Springs.

"At the latter station I was assigned to duty as assistant station-keeper, under Jim McNaughton. The war against the Piute Indians was then at its height, and we were in the middle of the Piute country, which made it necessary for us to keep a standing guard night and day. The Indians were often seen skulking around, but none of them ever came near enough for us to get a shot at them, till one dark night, when I was on guard, I noticed one of our horses prick up his ears and stare. I looked in the direction indicated and saw an Indian's head projecting above the wall.

"My instructions were to shoot if I saw an Indian within shooting distance, as that would wake the boys quicker than anything else; so I fired and missed my man.

"Later on we saw the Indian camp-fires on the mountain, and in the morning saw many tracks. They evidently intended to stampede our horses, and if necessary kill us. The next day one of our riders, a Mexican, rode into camp with a bullet hole through him from the left to the right side, having been shot by Indians while coming down Edwards Creek, in the Quakenasp bottom. This he told us as we assisted him off his horse. He was tenderly cared for, but died before surgical aid could reach him.

"As I was the lightest man at the station, I was ordered to take the Mexican's place on the route. My weight was then 100 pounds, while now I weigh 230. Two days after taking the route, on my return trip, I had to ride through the forest of quakenasp trees where the Mexican had been shot. A trail had been cut through these little trees, just wide enough to allow horse and rider to pass. As the road was crooked and the branches came together from either side, just above my head when mounted, it was impossible to see ahead more than ten or fifteen yards, and it was two miles through the forest.

"I expected to have trouble, and prepared for it by dropping my bridle reins on the neck of the horse, put my Sharp's rifle at full cock, kept both spurs into the flanks, and he went through that forest like a 'streak of greased lightning.'

"At the top of the hill I dismounted to rest my horse, and looking back, saw the bushes moving in several places. As there were no cattle or game in that vicinity, I knew the movements must be caused by Indians, and was more positive of it when, after firing several shots at the spot where I saw the bushes moving, all agitation ceased. Several days after that, two United States soldiers, who were on their way to their command, were shot and killed from the ambush of those bushes, and stripped of their clothing, by the red devils.

"One of my rides was the longest on the route. I refer to the road between Cold Springs and Sand Springs, thirty-seven miles, and not a drop of water. It was on this ride that I made a trip which possibly gave to our company the contract for carrying the mail by stage-coach across the plains, a contract that was largely subsidized by Congress.

"One day I trotted into Sand Springs covered with dust and perspiration. Before reaching the station I saw a number of men running toward me, all carrying rifles, and as I supposed they took me for an Indian, I stopped and threw up my hands. It seemed they had a spy-glass in camp, and recognizing me had come to the conclusion I was being run in by Piutes and were coming to my rescue.

"Bob Haslam was at the station, and in less than one minute relieved me of my mail-pouch and was flying westward over the plains. Some of the boys had several fights with Indians, but they did not trouble us as much as we expected; personally I only met them once face to face. I was rounding a bend in the mountains, and before I knew it, was in a camp of Piute Indians. Buffalo Jim, the chief, came toward me alone. He spoke good English, and when within ten yards of me I told him to stop, which he did, and told me he wanted 'tobac' (tobacco). I gave him half I had, but the old fellow wanted it all, and I finally refused to give him any more; he then made another step toward me, saying that he wanted to look at my gun. I pulled the gun out of the saddle-hock and again told him to stop. He evidently saw that I meant business, for, with a wave of his hand, he said: 'All right, you pooty good boy;' you go.' I did not need a second order, and quickly as possible rode out of their presence, looking back, however, as long as they were in sight, and keeping my rifle handy.

"As I look back on those times I often wonder that we were not all killed. A short time before, Major Ormsby of Carson City, in command of seventy-five or eighty men, went to Pyramid Lake to give battle to the Piutes, who had been killing emigrants and prospectors by the wholesale. Nearly all the command were killed in a running fight of sixteen miles. In the fight Major Ormsby and the lamented Harry Meredith were killed. Another regiment of about seven hundred men, under the command of Col. Daniel E. Hungerford and Jack Hayes, the noted Texas ranger, was raised. Hungerford was the beau ideal of a soldier, the hero of three wars, and one of the best tacticians of his time. This command drove the Indians pell-mell for three miles to Mud Lake, killing and wounding them at every jump. Colonel Hungerford and Jack Hayes received, and were entitled to, great praise, for at the close of the war terms were made which have kept the Indians peaceable ever since. Jack Hayes died several years since in Alameda, Cal. Colonel Hungerford, at the ripe age of seventy years, is hale and hearty, enjoying life and resting on his laurels in Italy, where he resides with his granddaughter, the Princess Colona.

"As previously stated, it is marvelous that the pony boys were not all killed. There were only four men at each station, and the Indians, who were then hostile, roamed all over the country in bands of 30 to 100.

"What I consider my most narrow escape from death was being shot at one night by a lot of fool emigrants, who, when I took them to task about it on my return trip, excused themselves by saying, 'We thought you was an Indian.'

"I want to say one good word for our bosses, Messrs. Russell, Majors & Waddell. The boys had the greatest veneration for them because of their general good treatment at their hands. They were different in many respects from all other freighters on the plains, who, as a class, were boisterous, blasphemous, and good patrons of the bottle, while Russell, Majors & Waddell were God-fearing, religious, and temperate themselves, and were careful to engage none in their employ who did not come up to their standard of morality.

"Calf-bound Bibles were distributed by them to every employe. The one given to me was kept till 1881, and was then presented to Ionic Lodge No. 35, A. F. & A. M., at Leadville, Colo.

"The Pony Express was a great undertaking at the time, and was the foundation of the mail-coach and railroad that quickly followed."

During the war J. G. Kelley was commissioned by Gov. James W. Nye as captain of Company C, Nevada Infantry, and served till the end of the war, after which he resumed his old business of mining, and is still engaged in it.

CHAPTER XXIII.

THE BATTLE OF THE BUFFALOES.

IT WAS the afternoon of a day in early summer, along in 1859, when we found ourselves drifting in a boat down the Missouri. The morning broke with a drizzling rain, out of a night that had been tempestuous, with a fierce gale, heavy thunder, and unusually terrific lightning. Gradually the rain stopped, and we had gone but a short distance when the clouds broke away, the sun shone forth, and the earth appeared glistening with a new beauty. Ahead of us appeared, high up on the bluffs, a clump of trees and bushes.

As we drew near, a sudden caprice seized us, and shooting our boat up on the shelving bank, we secured it, and then climbed the steep embankment. We intended to knock around in the brush a little while, and then resume our trip. A fine specimen of an eagle caught our eye, perched high up on the dead bough of a tree.

Moving around to get a good position to pick him off with my rifle, so that his body would not be torn, I caught sight through an opening of the trees of an immense herd of buffaloes, browsing and moving slowly in our direction. We moved forward a little to get a better view of the herd, when the eagle, unaware to us, spread his pinions, and when we looked again for him he was soaring at a safe distance from our rifles.

We were on the leeward side of the herd, and so safe from discovery, if we took ordinary precaution, among the trees. It was a fine spectacle which they presented, and,

(194)

what was more, we were in just the mood to watch them.
The land undulated, but was covered for many acres with
minute undulations of dark-brown shoulders slowly drifting toward us. We could hear the rasping sound which
innumerable mouths made chopping the crisp grass. As
we looked, our ears caught a low, faint, rhythmical sound,
borne to us from afar.

We listened intently. The sound grew more distinct,
until we could recognize the tread of another herd of
buffaloes coming from an opposite direction.

We skulked low through the undergrowth, and came to
the edge of the wooded patch just in time to see the van of
this new herd surmounting a hill. The herd was evidently
spending its force, having already run for miles. It came
with a lessening speed, until it settled down to a comfortable walk.

About the same time the two herds discovered each
other. Our herd was at first a little startled, but after a
brief inspection of the approaching mass, the work of
clipping the grass of the prairies was resumed. The fresh
arrivals came to a standstill, and gazed at the thousands of
their fellows, who evidently had preëmpted their grazing
grounds. Apparently they reached the conclusion that
that region was common property, for they soon lowered
their heads and began to shave the face of the earth of its
green growths.

The space separating the herds slowly lessened. The
outermost fringes touched but a short distance from our
point of observation. It was not like the fringes of a
lady's dress coming in contact with the lace drapery of a
window, I can assure you. Nothing so soft and sibilant as
that. It was more like the fringes of freight engines coming in contact with each other when they approach with
some momentum on the same track.

The powerful bulls had unwittingly found themselves in close proximity to each other, coming from either herd. Suddenly shooting up from the sides of the one whose herd was on the ground first, flumes of dirt made graceful curves in the air. They were the signals for hostilities to commence. The hoofs of the powerful beast were assisted by his small horns, which dug the sod and tossed bunches that settled out of the air in his shaggy mane.

These belligerent demonstrations were responded to in quite as defiant a fashion by the late arrival. He, too, was an enormous affair. We noticed his unusual proportions of head. But his shoulders, with their great manes, were worth displaying to excite admiration and awe at their possibilities, if they could do nothing more.

Unquestionably the two fellows regarded themselves as representative of their different herds, the one first on the ground viewing the other as an interloper, and he in his turn looking upon the former as reigning, because no one had the spirit to contest his supremacy and show him where he belonged. They sidled up near each other, their heads all the while kept low to the ground, and their eyes red with anger and rolling in fiery fury. This display of the preliminaries of battle drew the attention of an increasing number from either herd. At first they would look up, then recommence their eating, and then direct their attention more intensely as the combatants began to measure their strength more closely. And when the fight was on they became quite absorbed in the varying fortunes of the struggle.

At last the two huge fellows, after a good deal of circumlocution, made the grand rush. I reckon it would be your everlasting fortune if one of you college fellows who play football had the force to make the great rush which either one of these animals presented. The collision was straight and square.   A crash of horns, a heavy, dull thud of heads.   We thought surely the skull of one or the other, or possibly both, was crushed in.   But evidently they were not even hurt.

Didn't they push then?   Well, I guess they did.   The force would have shoved an old-fashioned barn from its foundations.   The muscles swelled up on the thighs, the hoofs sank into the earth, but they were evenly matched.

For a moment there was a mutual cessation of hostilities to get breath.   Then they came together with a more resounding crash than before.   Instantly we perceived that the meeting of the heads was not square.   The new champion had the best position.   Like a flash he recognized it and redoubled his efforts to take its full advantage. The other appeared to quadruple his efforts to maintain himself in position, and his muscles bulged out, but his antagonist made a sudden move which wrenched his head still farther off the line, when he went down on his knees. That settled the contest, for his enemy was upon him before he could recover.   He was thrown aside and his flank raked by several ugly upward thrusts of his foe, which left him torn and bruised, all in a heap.   As quick as he could get on his feet he limped, crestfallen, away.

The victorious fellow lashed his small tail, tossed his head, and moved in all the pride of his contest up and down through the ranks of his adversary's herd.   How exultant he was!   We took it to be rank impudence, and though he had exhibited some heroic qualities of strength and daring, it displeased us to see him take on so many airs on account of his victory.

But his conquest of the field was not yet entirely complete.   As he strode proudly along his progress was stopped by a loud snort, and, looking aside, he saw a fresh challenge. There, standing out in full view, was another bull, a monster of a fellow belonging to his late enemy's herd. He pawed the earth with great strokes and sent rockets of turf curving high in air, some of which sifted its fine soil down upon the nose of the victor.

As we looked at this new challenger and took in his immense form, we chuckled with the assurance that the haughty fellow would now have some decent humility imposed upon him. The conqueror himself must have been impressed with the formidableness of his new antagonist, for there was a change in his demeanor at once. Of course, according to a well-established buffalo code, he could do nothing but accept the challenge.

Space was cleared as the two monsters went through their gyrations, their tossings of earth, their lashings of tail, their snorts and their low bellows. This appeared to them a more serious contest than the former, if we could judge from the length of the introductory part. They took more time before they settled down to business. We were of the opinion that the delay was caused by the champion, who resorted to small arts to prolong the preliminaries. We watched it all with the most excited interest. It had all the thrilling features of a Spanish bull-fight without the latter's degradation of man. Here was the level of nature. Here the true buffalo instincts with their native temper were exhibiting themselves in the most emphatic and vigorous fashion. It was the buffalo's trial of nerve, strength, and skill. Numberless as must have been these tournaments, in which the champions of different herds met to decide which was superior, in the long ages during which the buffalo kingdom reigned supreme over the vast western prairies of the United States, yet few had ever been witnessed by man. We were looking upon a spectacle rare to human eyes, and I confess that I was never more excited than when this last trial reached its climax. It was a question now whether the champion should still hold his position. It stimulates one more when he thinks of losing what he has seized than when he thinks of failing to grasp that which he has never possessed. Undoubtedly both of these animals had this same feeling, for as we looked at this latest arrival, we about concluded that he was the real leader, and not the other that limped away vanquished.

While these and other thoughts were passing through our minds, the two mighty contestants squared and made a tremendous plunge for each other. What a shock was that! What a report rolled on the. air! The earth fairly shook with the terrific concussion of buffalo brains, and both burly fellows went down on their knees. Both, too, were on their feet the same instant, and locked horns with the same swiftness and skill, and each bore down on the other with all the power he could summon. The cords stood out like great ropes on their necks; the muscles on thighs and hips rose like huge welts. We were quite near these fellows and could see the roll of their blood-red fiery eyes. They braced and shoved with perfectly terrible force. The froth began to drip in long strings from their mouths. The erstwhile victor slipped with one hind foot slightly. His antagonist felt it and instantly swung a couple of inches forward, which raised the unfortunate buffalo's back, and we expected every instant that he would go down. But he had a firm hold and he swung his antagonist back to his former position, where they were both held panting, their tongues lolling out.

There was a slight relaxation for breath, then the contest was renewed. Deep into the new sod their hoofs sunk, neither getting the advantage of the other. Like a crack of a tree broken asunder came a report on the air, and one of the legs of the first fighter sank into the earth. The other buffalo thought he saw his chance, and made a furious lunge toward his opponent. The earth trembled beneath us. The monsters there fighting began to reel. We beheld an awful rent in the sod. For an instant the ground swayed, then nearly an acre dropped out of sight.

We started back with horror, then becoming reassured, we slowly approached the brink of the new precipice and looked over. This battle of the buffaloes had been fought near the edge of this high bluff. Their great weight—each one was over a ton—and their tremendous struggles had loosened the fibers which kept the upper part of the bluff together, and the foundations having been undermined by the current, all were precipitated far below.

As we gazed downward we detected two moving masses quite a distance apart, and soon the shaggy fronts of these buffaloes were seen. One got into the current of the river and was swept down stream. The other soon was caught by the tides and swept onward toward his foe. Probably they resumed the contest when, after gaining a good footing farther down the banks of the Missouri, they were fully rested.

But more probably, if they were sensible animals, and in some respects buffaloes have good sense, they concluded after such a providential interference in their terrific fight that they should live together in fraternal amity. So, no doubt, on the lower waters of the Missouri two splendid buffaloes have been seen by later hunters paying each other mutual respect, and standing on a perfect equality as chief leaders of a great herd.

CHAPTER XXIV.

My father, being one of the very first pioneers of Jackson County, Missouri, abundant opportunity was afforded me to become acquainted with the habits of wild animals of every description which at that time roamed in that unsettled portion of the country, such as elk, deer, bear, and panther.

Among these animals the most peculiar was the black bear, which was found in considerable numbers. Bears, in many respects, differ from all other animals; they are very small when born, and when grown the females, in their best state of fatness, will weigh from two hundred and fifty to three hundred and fifty pounds. The male bears weigh at their best much more; from four hundred to five hundred pounds. They are remarkably intelligent animals, and are very wild, wanting but little to do with civilization, for as soon as white people made their appearance in the regions of country inhabited by them, it was not long before they migrated to other portions of the country. To the early settlers of the new country bear meat proved of great value, being very fat, and on account of this great fatness particularly useful to them in the seasoning of leaner meats, such as wild turkey, venison, etc., which constituted much of the living of the early settlers or pioneers of the Mississippi and Missouri valleys.

The bear's life each year is divided into three distinct periods. From the first of April to the middle of September they live upon vegetables, such as they can find in the wild woods, fruits of every description, and meats of every kind, from the insect to the largest animal that lives; periwinkles, frogs, and fish of all kinds; all living things in the water as well as on the land. From the middle of September they cease to eat of the various things they have lived on during the summer, and take entirely to eating mast, that is, acorns, beech-nuts, pecans, chestnuts, and chincapins. On commencing to eat mast, they begin to fatten very rapidly. I should have remarked that during the summer months, the season in which they live on insects and meats of every variety, they lose every particle of the fat they had accumulated while eating mast. On account of his abstemious habits the prohibitionists should value the bear as emblematical of their order. Coming out of their long sleep the first of April, or when the vegetation has grown sufficient for them to feed upon, they commence to eat herbs, meats, and fruits of every kind. They are remarkably fond of swine at this period, and unlike the wolf, who seeks to catch the *young* pigs, the bear picks up the mother and walks off with her. She affords him a splendid opportunity for so doing, it being a trait of the mother hog, as it is of the mother bear, to fight ferociously for her young. The strength of the bear is phenomenal. They can take up in their mouths and carry off with perfect ease an ordinary sized hog, calf, or sheep. During this season they frequent corn fields, devouring the corn when it comes to the size of roasting ears. Indeed there is little to be found that is edible by man or beast that the bear at some period of his life does not eat. When they commence eating mast, which is about the middle of September or the first of October, as stated, they eat nothing else until about the 15th to the 20th of December, by which time most of them become exceedingly fat; so much so, indeed, that in some cases it is difficult for them to run very fast, not half as fast as they could before becoming so fat. All of the very fat ones, about the middle of December, cease to eat or drink anything, make themselves beds and lie down in them, preparatory to going into their caves or dens for their long sleep. They lie in these beds, which may be several miles from the caves in which they intend to take their winter sleep, several days, or sometimes a week, and by this temporary stay in the open air, nature is given time to dispose of every particle of water and food in the body. After this time has elapsed, they leave these temporary beds and go as straight as the crow flies to their intended quarters, which are generally caves in the rocks, if such can be found in the regions they inhabit. This sleep is taken when the animals are the very fattest. None but the very fat ones go through the period of hibernating. They do not lose one pound's weight during this sleep, unless it be in respiration, which is a very small quantity compared with the entire mass, for no excretions are made during that period. Entering the caves they remain there from three to four months, this being their dormant or hibernating period, and for this reason they are known among hunters as one of the family of seven sleepers. Each makes his bed in the bottom of the cave by scratching out a large, round, basin-shaped place in the dirt; these beds after being once made remain intact, as the caves are invariably dry, and are used by the same bear year after year if he is not disturbed; and after his demise will be adopted by another of his kind. Some of these caves have been perhaps for ages during the winter time the abode of a number of these " seven sleepers."

In my opinion there is no animal in the world that is so healthy, and the meat of which is more beneficial to mankind, than is the meat of the black bear. The doctors invariably recommend it for patients who are troubled with

O

indigestion or chest diseases. Bear's oil (for that is what
.it really is) is considered a better curative and much preferable on account of its pleasant taste, to cod-liver oil,
which is very disagreeable.

In settling the Mississippi Valley, when bear's meat was
such a factor in the way of food, each of the frontiersmen
kept a pack of dogs—all the way from three to half-a-
dozen—partly for bear hunting, which was a very exciting
sport, in fact the most of any other game hunting.   I have
been long and well acquainted with the courage shown by
dogs in hunting and fighting game, and there is nothing I
ever saw a dog undertake that arouses his courage so much
as a contest with a bear.   The dog seems to think a fight
with a bear the climax of his existence.   One familiar with,
and accustomed to, bear hunting can tell at long distances
whether the dogs are having a combat with a bear or some
other animal, by the energy they put into their yelping.
When fighting a bear the dogs continually snap and bite at
his hind legs, as this is the only way they have of exasper-
ating and irritating him, as they dare not approach him in
front.

The full-grown bear is able to stand off any number of
dogs that can get around him.   So strong are they that if
they can get hold of a dog in their fore arms or mouth, he
is very likely to be killed.   The large she-bear can take an
ordinary sized dog in her fore paws and crush him to death,
and they can strike with such force as to send.the sharp
nails of their paws fairly through the dog.   On account of
the adeptness with which bears use their fore paws, the dogs
try constantly to be in their rear, and the bears are always
trying to confront them.   The bear in moving his paws to
strike never draws them back, but invariably makes a forward movement, which is a surprise to the dogs, as it gives

them no warning, hence the aim of the former to confront the enemy, and of the latter not to be confronted.

I have stood several times, when a boy, upon the door-step of my father's log-cabin and watched the men and dogs in their chase after a bear, only a few hundred yards away. This was, of course, only a few months after the first settlers came into the country, for it was the habit of these bears to leave as soon as they knew the white people had come to stay.

Bears roam in the very thickest woods and roughest portions of the country, and it is difficult to find one so far away from the rough woods that he can not reach such locality in a very few moments after he is attacked; and unlike other game that was found on the frontier, instead of trying to get into the open prairie, where they can run, they make at once after being disturbed for the cliffs of the rivers and creeks and the canebrakes; in fact into the very roughest places they can find, and take the shortest cut to get to them.

Bears do not depend on the senses of sight and hearing for their protection as much as upon the sense of smell, by which they can distinguish perfectly their friends or enemies. The scent of man would strike terror to their hearts as much as the sight of him, and they scent him much farther than they can see him, especially when they are in the thick woods or canebrakes, where they often feed.

Frequently instead of fighting dogs on the ground, when tired, the bear climbs a tree, sometimes going up fifty feet, and there rests, lodged in a fork or upon a limb, surveying with complacency the howling pack of dogs, and they in turn, becoming more bold as the distance between their victim and themselves increases, defiantly extend their necks toward their black antagonist in the tree. Notwithstanding the bear's dread of the howling pack of dogs in waiting for their prey, if he sees a *man* he loses his hold and drops, falling among the dogs, sometimes falling on one or more and killing them.

I have known the hunter to be so cautious in showing himself that before he came near enough to shoot he would select the trunks of large trees, hiding behind them as he approached, until being near enough, and concealed from the bear by one of these trunks, he moved his head a little to one side to take aim; the moment he moved his head sufficient to do so, if the bear chanced to be looking that way, he would let go his hold and drop, showing that, after all, he knew where the real danger was.

It is very desirable in bear hunting that the bear should climb a tree and give his pursuer an opportunity to fire at him there, for while he is in the fight with the dogs it would be almost impossible for the hunter to shoot the bear without taking the chance of injuring or killing one or more of the dogs. The dogs are also in great danger when a bear weighing from three to five hundred pounds falls a distance of forty or fifty feet, be the bear dead or alive. No other animal that I know of could fall such a distance and not be more or less hurt, but bears are not injured in the least, being protected by their immense covering of fat, which forms a complete shield, or cushion, around the body.

The bear can stand on his hind legs just as easily as a man can stand on his feet, and in their fights with dogs they shield themselves by standing up against large trees, cliffs, or rocks, so that the dogs have no chance at them except in front. In this position they can stand off any number of dogs, and the dogs well know the danger of approaching from the front. No body of drilled men could act their part better than the dogs do, without any training whatever, which is a great proof of their intelligence.

The moment a bear shows that he is about to climb a tree in order to get out of the ground scuffle with his opponents, the dogs, and attempts to do so, the dogs with one accord pitch at him, until there are so many hanging to his hind legs that often he can not climb, and falls on his back to rid himself of and to fight them. He can fight when on his back as well as in any other position, for he embraces them in his arms, by no means gently.

He may try climbing a tree three or four times before he can sufficiently rid himself of the dogs; even then, perhaps, he may have one or two hanging to his legs, which he carries with him maybe ten or twelve feet up the tree, and the dogs, under the greatest excitement, keep perfect consciousness of the distance, and they are able to fall without being injured.

Let us now turn our attention to the mothers, or she-bears. They become mothers during the period of their hibernation, going into the caves at the time already mentioned when the other fat bears hibernate, and lie dormant until the time their cubs are born, which is about the middle of February. These require a great deal of the mother's attention, and she is faithful and follows her motherly instincts to her own death, if need be. After the cubs are born she goes once every day for water, which, with her accumulated fat, produces milk for the sustenance of her young, she having selected her cave near a stream of running or living water.

She does not eat a particle of any food from the first of December to the middle of April. By the time she leaves her bed, where she has been for four months in solitude, the cubs are sufficiently large to follow the mother, and should any danger threaten them, to climb a tree, which they are very quick to do, and if they do not do so at the bidding of the mother at once, she catches them up in her fore paws and throws them up against the tree, giving them to understand they must climb for their protection. The male bear is the greatest enemy the mother and the cubs have to look out for; for unless protected by the mother, he will seize and eat the cubs, during the season of the year when bears eat meat, but he is not disposed to hurt the mother bear, unless in a scuffle in trying to get hold of the young; therefore it is necessary for her to have her little ones with her every moment after they come out of the cave where they are born, and where they stay for more than two months before they are brought out into the sunlight.

Should danger threaten, and there is a small tree near, she will invariably make her cubs climb it, where they are safe, because the large male bear can not climb very small trees. If she is compelled to send her cubs up a large tree, she stands ready and willing to sacrifice her life for the protection of her young, and not in the annals of natural history can there be found a mother which shows such desperation in the protection of her young as does the mother bear.

Nothing daunts her when her cubs are imperiled, and neither man nor dogs in any number will avail in driving her from them. I have seen mother bears stand at the roots of trees up which their cubs had climbed, cracking their teeth and striking their paws, which sounded like the knocking of two hammers together, as warning to their enemies they would fight till they dropped dead, or killed their antagonist.

They all fast during the entire period of hibernation. Bears bring forth their young but once in two years, and nature has wisely designed it so. In order to protect

ALEXANDER MAJORS' FIRST BEAR HUNT.

the cubs from the male bear, and other enemies, the mother's constant presence and care are necessary until they'are old and large enough to protect themselves. On this account she keeps them with her until they are over a year old, and they generally hibernate the first year with her, after which they leave her, to roam where they will.

As my knowledge of the bear was obtained by being brought up and living in the portion of the State of Missouri they inhabited, it was natural when I grew up that I became a bear-hunter. I have killed them at all times of the year; when in their caves, shortly after they have come out in the spring, and while in their beds, before going to their caves. I have traced them by their tracks in the snow from their temporary beds to their winter caves. On account of my own experience, and my association with the best and oldest bear-hunters, I have had good opportunities to learn the nature and habits of black bear. Although I have seen a great many bears of the Rocky Mountains, and have had some little experience with the cinnamon, the brown, and the silver-gray bear, I am not as familiar with their modes of life as I am with those of the black bear that were found in such numbers in the Mississippi Valley when the white people first emigrated to that country. Bears of the Rocky Mountains, and especially grizzly bears, are very much larger than black bears, and, as far as I have been able to learn from those who have hunted them, their meat, as food, does not compare with that of the black bear.

One of my personal experiences in bear hunting occurred about the 15th of December, 1839, in Taney County, Missouri, where I then lived. After a deep snow had fallen, I had provided myself with some bread, a piece of fat bear meat, and a little salt, and some corn for my horse, and unaccompanied, except by my horse and four dogs, I

14

started out to try and kill a bear. On reaching that part
of the mountains where I expected to find them, I came
across a number of trails, and soon found one which I
knew must have been by a very fat bear. Hunters know
by the trail whether the bear is fat, for if fat he makes two
rows of tracks about a foot apart, while a lean bear makes
only one row of tracks, similar to that of a dog. I
spent part of one day in tracking this animal, which I was
sure would be well worth my pains. While on this trail I
was led to the deserted bed of one of the largest bears I
ever saw, for I afterward had ample opportunity of judg-
ing of its size and weight. He had lain in his temporary
bed during the falling of the snow, after which he had
gone in a bee-line to the cave for his intended hibernation.
Feeling sure he was such a large animal, I followed the
trail four or five miles, going as straight as if I had followed the bearings of a compass. On a very high peak
at the mouth of one of those caves, of which there are so
many in that country, his trail disappeared. The openings
of many of these caves are so small that it is often with
great difficulty a large bear effects an entrance. However,
though the openings are so small, the caves are broad and
spacious. In these caves bears hibernate. This particular cave had a very small and irregular opening, so that I
could not enter it with my gun; but, as is the custom with
bear-hunters, I cut a pole ten or twelve feet long, sharpened
one end, and to this tied a piece of fat bear meat, set fire
to it, and made another attempt to enter the cave. Finding I could not do this, on account of the opening being
so irregular, I abandoned the idea of shooting him in his
cave, and proceeded to kindle a fire at the mouth, and putting a pole across the opening, hung my saddle-blanket
and a green buckskin that I procured the day before, when
getting meat for my dogs, upon it. This covering drove

the smoke from the fire into the cave, which soon disturbed the animal, so that he came and put the fire out by striking it with his paws. Instead of coming out of the cave as I supposed he would, after putting out the fire, he went back to his bed. He had gotten such draughts of the suffocating smoke that he made no other attempts to get to the mouth of the cave, where my four dogs were standing, ready, nervous, and trembling, watching for him, and I was standing on one side of the mouth of the cave, prepared to put a whole charge into him if he made his appearance. I waited a few moments after I heard him box the fire for him to return, but as he did not, I took the covering from the mouth of the cave and found the fire was entirely out. I then rekindled it and replaced the coverings, and it was not long after until I heard him groaning, like some strong-chested old man in pain. I listened eagerly for his moanings to cease, knowing that he must die of suffocation. It was not, however, very long until all was still. I then uncovered the mouth of the cave to let the smoke out. It was some time before I could venture in; before I did so I relit my light, and going in I found my victim not twenty feet from the mouth of the cave, lying on his back, dead; and, as before stated, he was the largest animal of the kind I ever saw or killed. It took me seven or eight hours to slaughter him and carry the meat out of the cave, as I could not carry more than fifty pounds at a time and crawl out and in.

When I opened the chest of this big bear, I found two bullets. These were entirely disconnected with any solid matter. They had been shot into him by some hunter who knew precisely the location of a bear's heart, which is different from what it is in other animals. His heart lies much farther back in his body, being precisely in the center of the same, while the heart of all other quadrupeds, and

I think I have known all those of North America, lies just back of their shoulders; in other words, in the front part of the chest.

These bullets, from the necessity of the case, must have been shot into the animal when he was the very fattest, and when he was ready for hibernation, because they were not lodged in the flesh, but entirely loose in the chest, each one covered with a white film, and tied with a little ligament, about the size of a rye straw, to the sack that contained the heart. When the bear lay down, these bullets could not have been more than half or three-quarters of an inch from each other, for each one was covered separately, and had a separate ligament attaching it to the sack above alluded to; and the two ligaments, where they had grown to the sack, were not more than a quarter of an inch apart. I cut out the piece containing both the bullets, and taking it in my fingers reminded me of two large cherries with the stems almost touching at the point where they were broken from the limb. What I have just described would indeed have been an interesting study to the medical fraternity, as perhaps there has never been anything like it. It could not have occurred in this particular way, except where the bear had gone through the preparation peculiar to him before hibernating, and after leaving his temporary bed he could lie dormant and give nature ample opportunity to restore the injury to the system which the bullet had caused. The above facts proved that it was just at the season of the year when the bear was ready to hibernate.

In this article at the outset, I mentioned the fact that the bear is a peculiar animal. Indeed he is the most peculiar of any quadruped with which I am familiar. He has many marked characteristics. He assumes in twelve months three different modes of life, each one thoroughly distinct from the other. He hibernates, during which time he abstains entirely from food and water. On coming out of this dormant condition he commences to eat food of every kind, peculiar to that season of the year. After living for months on anything and everything he can get, he ceases to eat any of these various things, and begins a totally different kind of diet, eating only mast—acorns and nuts of every kind. Another of their peculiarities is the cubs are not permitted to see the light for sixty days after being born, as they are in the dark solitude of a cave in the ground. Still another characteristic is the mother bear takes care of her young until they are fourteen months old, they hibernating with her the second winter of their lives.

The bear differs from other quadrupeds in being able to stand or walk on his two hind feet as well as on all-fours, and in this position he can make telling efforts at protecting himself. He climbs trees, and thus gets the mast by breaking the branches and picking off the acorns. He is also so constituted that he can fall great distances, even from the top of a tree, without injuring himself in the least. The mother bear has, as far as I know, generally two, never more than three, cubs at a time; when young these cubs can be easily tamed, and become in time very devoted to their owner. They are very intelligent, so that with proper training they will learn the tricks any animal has been known to learn. When small they are great playmates for boys, and will wrestle with them and enter into sports with great intelligence. They are never dangerous until grown, and not then unless crossed or abused. Wild bears are not considered dangerous unless they are attacked and are unable to make their escape. Under no circumstances, as already stated, does the mother bear forsake her young when they are in danger. In teaching bears tricks, one lesson is sufficient, as they seem never to forget. A friend of mine owned a pet bear which became so familiar about the place and so attached to all, that he could be turned loose with a chain several feet long dragging after him. He conceived the idea of scratching a hole beside the wall, where he could go and hide himself to take his naps. One day his owner wanted to show him to some one while he was asleep in his hole, and took hold of the chain, which was lying extended for some distance, and pulled the little bear out. This gentleman stated to me that this never occurred but once. After this, whenever the bear went to take his nap, the first thing he did after getting into the hole was to pull the chain in after him. His owner had a post set in the yard fifteen or twenty feet high, with a broad board nailed on the top. The bear would climb this post and lie down on the board. The first thing he did after lying down was to pull that chain up and put it in a coil at his side. His owner told me that one lesson sufficed to teach him anything. I have repeated many of these facts in order to bring them more clearly and forcibly to the mird of the reader.

CHAPTER XXV.

In the settlement of the Western States and Territories one of the sources of income, and the only industry which commanded cash for the efforts involved, was that of beaver trapping, the skin of the beaver selling as high as fifteen or twenty dollars. The weight of the beaver is from thirty to sixty pounds, and it is an animal possessed of great intelligence, as the amount and kind of work accomplished by it shows. It is a natural-born engineer, as connected with water; it can build dams across small streams that defy the freshets, and that hold the water equal, if not superior, to the very best dams that can be constructed by skilled engineers.

In making their dams the sticks and poles which they use in the construction of the same are cut with their teeth, of which they have four, two in the upper part of the mouth and two in the lower.

These poles they place across each other in all directions. They build their dams during the fall usually, and should they need repair, the work is done before the very cold weather commences, working only at night if danger is near.

In the month of October they generally collect their food, which consists largely of the cottonwood; this is cut in lengths of from two to six feet, the diameter being some-times six inches, and carry it into their ponds made by the dams, and sunk in the deepest portion of the same. I should have stated that the higher up the stream they go, their dams are built correspondingly higher; hence a dam built at an altitude of 1,000 feet would not be built as high as one built at an altitude of 3,000 feet, in order to overcome the deeper freezing at that point, for in constructing these dams they must be of sufficient height to give plenty of room to get at their food in the water under the ice. The beaver does not eat a particle of meat of any kind. The popular idea is that as they are animals that live in and about the water, that they live upon fish, but this is not so; for, as above stated, their principal food is the bark and the tender-wood of the cottonwood, and they also eat of other barks.

They are one of the most cleanly animals that lives. They live in the purest water that can be found, generally selecting streams that take their rise in the mountains, and where they can have an abundance of water the year round to live in. They dam up the streams in order to make ponds of sufficient depth to swim in under the ice to obtain their food, for the bottom of this pond is their store-room during the winter months.

Beavers are exceedingly wild, seldom showing themselves, and from the bottom of their pond they make a tunnel leading to the house where they sleep, so that they can pass to the same unobserved by man or beast. When they make their ponds where the banks are low, they make their house upon the top of the ground, sometimes a rod or more from the edge of the pond, cutting timber of the size of a finger to two or three inches in diameter, placing the sticks in very much the same way as they do in building their dams, crossing and recrossing them so that it is quite a job to tear one of their houses to pieces; in fact no one but a man would undertake the task, and one that has never had any experience would find it very difficult to accomplish. If one does it in the hope of catching the animal, he toils in vain, for he is soon scented, and the beaver takes refuge in the pond, passing through the underground tunnel. Where they find high banks, they start a tunnel several feet below the surface of the water and run it ascending, so as to reach a point in the bank six or eight or may be ten feet above the surface of the water underground, stopping before reaching the top of the ground, and at which point they take out dirt until they have a place sufficiently large for their bed. This kind of a house they much prefer to one made with sticks on the surface of the ground, as they are completely hidden from observation or the possibility of interruption from any one.

The beaver's feet are webbed for the purpose of swim-ming, and there are nails on his feet, so that he can scratch the earth almost equal to a badger. He has a paddle-formed tail, which on a large full-grown beaver is from ten to twelve inches long and from six to seven inches broad, and without any hair on it. These are tough and sinewy, and when cooked they make a very fine food, the flavor reminding one of pig's feet or calf's head. They make considerable use of their tail in performing their work as well as in swimming.

The beaver reproduces itself each year. The offspring are generally two in number, and these can be easily tamed.

The trappers in trapping for the beaver have to use great precaution in approaching the place where they intend to set the traps, often getting into the stream above or below and wading for some distance. If they walked upon the bank the beaver would scent them from the footprints. Beavers, like all other wild animals, dread the sight or scent of man more than anything else. In setting the traps the trappers invariably choose as deep water as they can find, so that when a beaver is caught he will drown himself in

P

his struggles to get free from the trap; for if this does not occur, he has often been known to cut off, with the sharp chisel used in cutting timber, the foot that is caught in the trap, so that it is not infrequent when the trapper comes in the morning to find a foot of the beaver instead of the beaver himself, and often he catches a beaver with only three feet.

The beaver, considered as an engineer, is a remarkable animal. He can run a tunnel as direct as the best engineer could do with his instruments to guide him. I have seen where they have built a dam across a stream, and not having a sufficient head of water to keep their pond full, they would cross to a stream higher up the side of the mountain, and cut a ditch from the upper stream and connect it with the pond of the lower, and do it as neatly as an engineer with his tools could possibly do it. I have often said that the buck beaver in the Rocky Mountains had more engineering skill than the entire corps of engineers who were connected with General Grant's army when he besieged Vicksburg on the banks of the Mississippi. The beaver would never have attempted to turn the Mississippi into a canal to change its channel without first making a dam across the channel below the point of starting the canal. The beaver, as I have said, rivals and sometimes even excels the ingenuity of man.

Another of the peculiarities of the beaver is the great sharpness of its teeth, remaining for many years as sharp as the best edged tool. The mechanic with the finest steel can not make a tool that will not in a short time become so blunt and so dulled as to require renewed sharpening, and this, with the beaver, would have to be repeated hundreds of times in order to do service with it during the whole of its lifetime, which is from ten to fifteen years if it is permitted to live the allotted years of a beaver.

In one of my trips on a steamer of the Upper Missouri, one
day while the boat's crew were getting their supply of wood, I
took my gun and started along the river-bank in the hope of
seeing an elk or deer that I might shoot. I came to a place
on the river where the banks were very high, and I observed
that a lot of cottonwood saplings from six to eight inches in
diameter had been felled and cut into sections. I saw that
it had been recently done, and I at first supposed that it
had been done by some one with an ax, but when I
reached the spot, I saw that it was the work of the beavers
and that some of the wood had been dragged away. I followed the trail for a few steps, when I came to the mouth
of a tunnel, and discovered that the timber had been
dragged through it. The tunnel had an incline of about
thirty-five degrees, and was as straight as if it had been
made with an auger. This was in the month of October, at
the time when it was their custom to stow away their food
for the winter. They had no dam at this point, as the
water was deep, and they were drawing the timbers down
through the tunnel and sinking them in the deep water, so that
they could have access to it during the period when the river
would be frozen over. The reason for the tunnel, of which
I have spoken, was that the river-bank for some distance
was high and almost perpendicular, and the beaver, being a
very clumsy animal with short legs, his only alternative
was to make a tunnel in order to get his winter food. They
have a way of sinking the cottonwood and keeping it down
in their pond or simply in the deep water when they do not
make dams. This family of beavers evidently had their
house far under the surface of the ground, for the place
was admirably adapted for them to make such a home, the
banks being so high above the water. One could see no
trace whatever of the beaver, or have a knowledge of where
he was, more than the opening of the tunnel and where the

timber had been cut; indeed, one might pass hundreds of times and not be conscious that beavers were living right under one's feet. I picked up one of the chips which the beaver had cut, measuring about seven inches in length, and carried it home with me as a curiosity.

CHAPTER XXVI.

REMEMBERING my own love of adventure as a boy, I can not refrain from giving here a chapter contributed by my son, Green Majors, which will be found both instructive and interesting. He says: " At the inexperienced age of twelve years I was seized with a strong desire to go overland to Montana. For a number of years I had lived at Nebraska City, on the Missouri River, a starting point in those days for west-bound freight and emigrant wagon trains; and having so long seen the stage-coaches go bounding over the hills and rolling prairies, headed for the golden West, it was with a feeling of great satisfaction that on the morning of April 26, 1866, I was seated on top of one of those same coaches, as a fellow passenger with my father, Alexander Majors, bound for the Rocky Mountains, and Helena, Mont., in particular. To my boyish fancy the never-ceasing rocking to and fro of the overland coach of early days was a constant delight. Denver we reached in six days and nights of incessant travel. Rain nor shine, floods nor deserts, stopped us. If a passenger became too sleepy or exhausted to hold on and sleep at the same time on the outside, he could get inside by submitting to the 'sardining' process. But inside, the clouds of dust and the cramped position necessary to assume made one at times feel like the coach were spinning round like a top in the dark. At Denver we laid in a big supply of luncheon material, for the next continuous ride, without a town, was for 600 miles, to Salt Lake City. However, before we reached

Zion, our troubles were many, one of which was being caught in a violent snow-storm one dark night while bowling along over Laramie Plains. Our driver and his mules both lost the road. He so notified us, and we got out to wade through the innumerable drifts to see if we could feel the hard-beaten trail with our feet. But it was of no use. So for fear we might wander away from the emigrant road too far, or that he might drive over some precipice or into some hole or other in the blinding storm, we unhitched his four mules and tied each one with its head to a wheel, so there could be no runaway, and then all hands got back into the coach, tucked our wraps about us as best we could, and there we sat, like Patience on a monument, smiling at grief, with the wind whistling in all its many sad cadences through the flapping wings of that desolate coach, until the longest night I ever saw went by. Next morning we found two and a half feet of 'the beautiful' on the level, and the struggle to gain another station began. We tramped snow and broke trails for that coach to get through the drifts for about ten or fifteen miles, before we got to a lower altitude, out of the path of the storm, for all of which distance we of course paid the stage company 25 cents a mile fare, with no baggage allowance to speak of.

"Not a great ways farther on, we struck the famous Bitter Creek country, a section that was the terror of travelers, because of poor grass, water that was foul and bitter, and alkali plains that were terrific on man and beast. At one place along Bitter Creek its water was as red as blood, at another as yellow as an orange; but generally its color was a dark muddy drab, and highly impregnated with vegetable and earthy matter. I suppose Bitter Creek is the only place on earth where highwaymen had the cold-blooded nerve to charge travelers $1.50 for nothing but fat bacon, poorly cooked, and an inferior quality of mustard, as a meal's victuals, but the stage station-keepers had it there. By the time we finished our Bitter Creek experience we were proof against peril, so that subsequent floods in the cañons from melting snows in the mountains, sitting bolt upright with three on a seat to sleep over the rough mountain roads at night, and passing over long stretches of country with no water fit to drink, were trivial circumstances.

"After a thirty-day siege of this sort of experience, we alighted on the gravelly streets of Helena, Mont., then a town of canvas houses and tents, and log huts. Helena at that time was the liveliest town I have ever seen in my life, either in America or Europe, over the whole of both of which I have since traveled. At that time her business houses were largely propped up on stilts, while underneath the red-shirted placer miner was washing the blue gravel soil for gold-dust. Her streets, in many places, were bridged over, to allow of the same thing. Sunday was the liveliest day in the week for business. The plainest meal at a restaurant cost $1.50, and bakery pies, with brown paper used for a crust, cost 75 cents each. Everybody had money, and nobody appeared to want to keep what he had. Gold-dust was the money of the country, no greenbacks nor coin being used. A pennyweight of the yellow dust passed for a dollar, but expert cashiers, at the gaming places and stores, were said to know how to weigh the article so deftly that $100 of it in value would only go $50 in distance. However, wages were very high, and so was everything else, so that if a man were robbed pretty badly, he could soon recuperate his lost fortunes. There were no churches in Helena then, if, indeed, there were any in the Territory. The first Sunday after arriving there, I remember attending divine service in a muslin building, but the blacksmith's hammer next door and the lusty auctioneer's voice in the street made so much noise the congregation could not understand the divine's injunctions, so that church-going there, at that time, was attended with considerable annoyance. Everything was crude and primitive, everybody was cordial, generous, and open-hearted, and anything or anybody justly appealing to those roughly appareled yeomanry for aid or sympathy invariably opened the floodgates of their plenty and fired the great, deep, warm heart-throbs of their noble natures.

"But they were as prompt in meting out retributive justice to the wrong-doer as in loosing their purse-strings to a worthy applicant, and many were the wayward souls jerked into eternity through the deadly and inexorable noose of the ubiquitous vigilante, whose will was law, and the objects of whose adverse edicts were soon plainly told to recite their last prayers in the body.

"Cattle-raising on the rich, nutritious bunch-grass of the broad valleys of the Territory also soon grew to be a very lucrative business, to supply the numerous placer-mining towns of Montana, a number of which were quite important and thrifty camps at that time. Farming was also followed to a limited extent. Inasmuch as potatoes, cabbage, and other vegetables were largely imported from Salt Lake, about five hundred miles, all sorts of soil products yielded handsome returns.

"Montana has had her periods of depression as well as of prosperity. For after her then-discovered and easily accessible placer ground became washed out, which took several years, times there grew very dull, but not until something like $200,000,000 worth of gold had been washed from her auriferous gulches and hillsides. Quartz mining was rare in those days, because freight and everything else was 'so high that few had the means to engage in that kind of mining. From a State of such prosperous activity in the sixties, with a large and well-to-do population, in 1874-75

SUNRISE IN CAMP.

it grew so dull and so many had left the Territory that those remaining wished they could get away too. In the Centennial year of 1876, however, Montana's true era of prosperity dawned, when rich silver quartz was discovered at the now famous city of Butte, styled 'the greatest mining camp on earth.' The Territory's business in every avenue soon rose from its low ebb to an affluent flood, all kinds and lines almost immediately feeling its vitalizing, stimulating influence. From an isolated mountain fastness it forthwith again became the theater of activity and thrift, and the stream of precious metals that it again poured into the world's commercial channels not long after required the capacity of a line of railroad to handle its vast volume. Chicago, New York, Boston, and other Eastern centers recognized Montana merchants as among their heaviest and best-paying customers, again demonstrating that mining for the precious metals is the great vanguard of a rapid and substantial civilization. The Utah & Northern was the pioneer railroad into her confines, but its business soon grew to such enormous proportions that the Northern Pacific followed in three or four years, and then Jim Hill swooped in with his Great Northern Road. So that that apparently isolated section has three transcontinentals now running east and west through her entire length, with the Chicago, Burlington & Quincy on her eastern border, impatient to share her immense traffic, and the Butte, Boise & San Francisco soon to give her a direct outlet to San Francisco Bay.

" But to return to the early days of Montana, certainly one of the grandest and richest sections of the Union. It is in this State that the muddy Missouri River has its source, although in the mountainous part of its course its water is as clear as crystal. Here, also, the broad and majestic Columbia has its inception, the heads of these two noble

15

streams bubbling up out of her lofty mountains quite close together. And it is a striking coincidence that the same section that sends these two noble streams down through fertile fields to the sea, bearing on their mighty bosoms the wealth and water supply of empires, should also possess the largest and richest deposits of the precious metals that the world has ever known. But such is the case. Speaking of precious metals recalls some of the ' stampedes ' to newly discovered mining camps in early days. A 'stampede ' is a panic reversed, usually instigated by the wild and rainbow-colored statements of over-enthusiastic persons, and often those statements had utterly no foundation in fact. Men would rise from their beds in the middle of the night, if thought necessary, and with insufficient food, clothing, or implements, afoot or horseback, climb dark mountains or cañons, swim floods, tramp over alkali plains, or submit to any and all kinds of hardships, all for the sake of being among the first on the ground of newly discovered ' diggins.' ' First come, first served,' was the rule, and each man was determined, as nearly as possible, to be first served. In the famous Sun River stampede, in the winter of 1866–67, with the mercury coquetting with the 30-degree-below-zero point, it was said men actually started out in their shirt sleeves to make a hundred-mile journey through the deep snow to the reputed new camp without food supplies to carry them through. And as it often proved in other cases, there wasn't a particle of truth in the reputed rich fields. Dame Rumor, that ever versatile and fertile-brained jade, had had an inning, and she batted hard, firing her hot balls of deception to all quarters of the field. In those days buffalo were plentiful on the plains of Eastern Montana. I think I have seen from twenty to fifty thousand in a single herd there. They blackened the hills and plains with their shaggy coats, they swarmed the rivers in their peregrinations, and raised clouds of dust like a simoon in their journeys across the country. I have seen hundreds of them in a group mired down in the quicksands along the Upper Missouri River. Hunters walked on their backs and shot the fattest of them as trophies of the chase, and the ever ubiquitous, keen-scented wolves came and gnawed their vitals while they were yet alive, but helpless, in their inextricable positions. At that time bands of stately elk also abounded there. Deer were plentiful, and the fleet-footed antelope bounded over every plain. Mountain sheep, whose tender meat was fat and juicy, climbed the terraced rocky cliffs in great numbers, while ducks, geese, pheasants, fool hens, and many other table fowl were to be had for a little effort on the part of the hunter. A fool hen is a species of bird weighing about two pounds, that is so foolish as to allow the gunner to lay aside his fire-arms and kill the whole flock with sticks and stones, so closely can it be approached without taking flight. Its meat is delicious.

" Many volumes could be written on Montana's early reminiscences, her vast resources, her brilliant past, and her glorious prospective future. But the brief space allotted me precludes the possibility of detailed mention of people, places, or things, and I reluctantly stop sharpening my pencil. Montana has been great in the past, but her future will be much grander and greater still."

CHAPTER XXVII.

HENRY ALLEN was the first postmaster of Denver, so called, and charged 50 cents for bringing a letter from Fort Laramie. The first Leavenworth and Pike's express coach arrived there on May 17, 1859, having made the trip in nineteen days. This company reduced the postage rates on letters to 25 cents. The first postmaster of this concern was Mr. Fields, who was succeeded by Judge Amos Steck in the fall of 1859.

On June 6, 1866, Horace Greeley, of the New York *Tribune*, arrived in Denver by express coach en route to California, and addressed the citizens that same Monday evening. The next day he straddled a mule for the Gregory mines in company with A. D. Richardson, then a Western correspondent of the *Tribune*. On the 11th, they returned from Gilpin County mines, and published under Greeley's signature in a *News* extra his views concerning the extent and richness of the gold diggings which he had just witnessed with his own eyes. The circulation of this extra along the routes to the States soon caused another immense immigration to return there that fall.

On October 3d the first election for county officers was held under provisional government. B. D. Williams was then elected to represent the new Territory of Jefferson in Congress.

The first marriage took place in Aurora (West Denver) October 16, 1859, Miss Lydia R. Allen to Mr. John B. Atkins, Rev. G. W. Fisher officiating. The first school ever started in Denver was by O. J. Goldrick, October 3, 1859, in a little cabin with a mud roof, minus windows and doors; and the first Sunday-school was organized October 6, 1859, by Messrs. Tappen, Collier, Adrian, Fisher, and Goldrick, in the preacher's cabin on the west bank of Cherry Creek.

The first theater, called Apollo, was opened in Denver October 3, 1859, by D. R. Thorn's troupe from Leavenworth, with Sam D. Hunter for leading man and Miss Rose Wakely for leading lady. Old-timers will remember her well. She was considered the most beautiful lady that had graced Denver City in the first years of its existence.

The first election for territorial officers and legislative. assembly occurred October 24, 1859, when R. W. Steele, a miner, was made first governor. Over 2,000 votes were cast in the twenty-seven precincts of the Territory at that election.

The first legislature assembled in Denver November 7, 1859, comprising eight councilmen and nineteen representatives. On New Year's, 1860, Denver had about 200 houses and Aurora (now West Denver) nearly 400, with a total combined city census of over 1,000 people, representing all classes, creeds, and nationalities; hence its cosmopolitan style from that day to this. Many brick and frame buildings, stores, hotels, shops, and dwellings were put up in both towns during 1860. One was the banking house of Streeter & Hobbs, corner of Eleventh and Laramie streets. The rate of interest charged by them at that time was from 10 to 25 per cent per month, according to the collateral security, and from 10 to 25 cents per hundred pounds was the rate from the Missouri River for freight by ox or mule train.

On the 8th of December, the day of the adjournment of the first legislature, an election was held by those in favor of remaining under the Kansas regime, and Capt. Richard Sopris was sent as representative in the Kansas legislature.

John C. Moore was elected the first mayor of Denver, December 19, 1859, under a city charter granted by the first provisional legislature. In the fall of '59 there were no particular politics there. The great question of the day was: "Are you a Denver man or an Aurorian?" Rivalry ran high between the two towns until the consolidation of Denver, Aurora, and Highlands, April 3, 1860. The first officers of the Aurora town company were W. A. McFadding, president, and Dr. L. J. Russell, secretary. Those of the Denver town company were E. P. Stout, president, and H. P. A. Smith, secretary. Strange to say, not a single one of these property holders is now living there, or is now the owner of a single lot in this large city.

I must not forget an event that happened in Denver then. A family arrived there from the East, consisting of father, mother, two daughters, and a son. One of the young Denverites took a fancy to one of the young ladies, but parents and son were opposed to the young man; yet he was not to be got rid of. One evening he took advantage of the absence of the parents and married the girl, and on the return of the parents in the evening the mother and son started to look for them, and threatened to kill the young man if they could find him. They found them at the Platte House, on Blake Street. The mother of the girl went to break in the door, but finally concluded not to do so, and left for her home. The parties are still living in Denver, and are well off and greatly respected.

On November 10, 1859, a lager-beer brewery was established by Solomon, Tascher & Co. It was said that the beer was drinkable. It was as innocent of malt and hops as our early whisky was of wheat or rye.

Thirty-three years ago next July the patriotic pioneers celebrated the Fourth of July in this city. It took place in a grove near the mouth of Cherry Creek. One Doctor Fox read the Declaration, and James K. Shaffer delivered an oration. There was music by the Council Bluffs band.

July 12, 1860, a series of murders and violence began there by desperadoes who had infested Denver during the summer. They tried to muzzle the mouth of the press, which bravely condemned their dastardly outrages, and as a consequence they raided the *Rocky Mountain News* and tried to kill its proprietor.

The first regular United States mail arrived there on August 10, 1860; P. W. McClure, postmaster. The first Odd Fellows lodge was instituted there on Christmas Eve, 1860.

The close of the year 1860 saw 60,000 people in the Territory, 4,000 of whom were in and around Denver.

At this juncture of time Denver was tolerably well favored with the three great engines of civilization, to-wit, schools, churches, and newspapers. There were three day schools, two or three newspapers, and the following church denominations, each with a place for holding services: Methodist Episcopal, Methodist Episcopal South, Roman Catholic, Presbyterian, and Protestant Episcopal. The latter denomination was well and truly cared for by the Rev. J. H. Kehler, who established St. John's Church in the wilderness, as he then called it. Therefore, to the praise of our pioneers let it be recorded that though then remiss in many of the modern enterprises, their liberality encouraged religion, morality, and popular education. They claimed that Whittier's apostrophe to Massachusetts might and should apply equally to Colorado in these regards:

> The riches of our commonwealth
> Are free, strong minds and hearts of health;
> And more to her than gold or grain
> The cunning hand and cultured brain.
> Nor heeds the sceptic's puny hands,
> While near the school the church-spire stands;
> Nor fears the blinded bigot's rule,
> While near the church-spire stands the school.

Q

CHAPTER XXVIII.

THE DENVER OF TO-DAY AND ITS ENVIRONS.

The Denver of to-day, the capital of Colorado, has a population of 160,000, and it stands at an elevation of 5,196 feet.

In 1858 the Pike's Peak gold excitement caused a rush from the East to Colorado, and a camp was pitched at the junction of Cherry Creek and the Platte. From this small beginning sprang Denver, the "Queen City of the Plains." Beautiful in situation, with the great range of the Rocky Mountains towering in the west, and the illimitable plains stretching 600 miles to the Missouri River on the east, Denver is worthy of the attention and admiration of all who behold it. It is one of the greatest railroad points in the West, twelve railroads centering here and radiating to all parts of the United States, thus giving Denver almost unsurpassed facilities for transcontinental traffic. The foot-hills of the Rocky Mountains are only fourteen miles distant, and Long's Peak, James' Peak, Gray's Peak, and Pike's Peak are in plain view, connected by the gleaming serrated line of the Snowy Range. Parks, boulevards, opera houses, and costly and elegant public buildings and private residences are a few of the most obvious signs of wealth, cultivation, and luxury which are to be found in Colorado's capital. Among the principal places of interest may be mentioned the Tabor Grand Opera House, erected at a cost of $850,000, and which is the finest building of its kind in America, having but one rival in the world, the Grand Opera House in Paris; the United States

Mint; the County Court House, a most elegant and costly structure occupying an entire block with the buildings and grounds; the City Hall, University of Denver, St. Mary's Academy, Wolfe Hall, Trinity M. E. Church, St. John's Cathedral, College of the Sacred Heart, Jarvis Hall, Baptist Female College, Brown's Palace Hotel, and hotels and business blocks, any of which would do credit to any of the metropolitan cities of the East. The city has extensive systems of street cars, motor lines and cables, is lighted by gas and electricity, has excellent waterworks, a well-disciplined and effective paid fire department, good police force, and telephone communication in the city and with suburban towns to the distance of 120 miles. The discovery that artesian wells can be sunk successfully has added much to the attractiveness of the city. The water is almost chemically pure, and is forced to a great height by hydrostatic pressure. Denver is the objective point for a large tourist travel, and it is estimated that the arrivals during the year will average 1,000 daily. The climate is heathful and invigorating, and invalids find this an excellent place to regain their health. There is always some pleasing attraction to divert the mind. The theaters are open the year round, and the best companies and stars from the East appear upon their boards. The churches are presided over by clergymen of talent and culture. The newspapers are metropolitan in size and management. In a word, Denver is one of the most pleasant residence cities in the world. Rapid as has been the growth of this wonderful city, it is evident that it is but on the threshold of its prosperity, and that the future holds for it much more and greater success than has been vouchsafed it in the past.

Thirty-three miles south of Denver, on the Denver & Rio Grande Railroad, is Castle Rock. It is a picturesque little village, and derives its name from a bold and remarkable promontory which springs directly from the plain and under whose shadow the village stands. This promontory always attracts the attention of tourists, and is therefore worthy of special mention.

Perry Park is situated within half an hour's drive of Larkspur Station, and in natural attractions has few if any superiors in the State. Bountifully supplied with pure and sparkling water, and protected on the west by the Front Range of mountains, it forms a quiet and romantic resting-place for those who wish a pleasant summer's outing free from the annoyances of business. The park is filled with many remarkable rock formations equal in unique grandeur to those of the better known but not more attractive Garden of the Gods.

Palmer Lake is situated on the Denver & Rio Grande Railroad, about midway between Denver and Pueblo, the two principal towns of Colorado. It was formerly called "Divide," a very significant and appropriate title, as on the crest of this summit the waters divide, flowing northward into the Platte, which empties into the Missouri, and southward into the Arkansas as it wends its way to the Mississippi.

The traveler will enjoy a most delightful variety of scenery. On either side are rolling plains dotted with numerous herds of sheep and cattle, agricultural settlements with cultivated ranches, giving evidence of enterprise and thrift. Now and then we catch a glimpse of the river threading its way amid valleys and glens, while stretching away in the distance the cliffs and towering peaks of the Snowy Range, in their dazzling whiteness, appear like fleecy clouds upon the horizon, and form a striking contrast with the blue-tinted foot-hills, which, as we near them, appear covered with oak shrubbery, bright flowers, castled rocks, scattered pines, and quaking aspen glimmering in the sunshine. Gradually ascending the mountain pathway we reach the summit (2,000 feet higher than either Denver or Pueblo), and entering a gap in the mountains, before us lies Palmer Lake. Nestled here in this mountain scenery, sparkling like a diamond in its emerald setting, this lake is a delightful surprise to the tourist—a rare and unlooked-for feature in the landscape.

Glen Park, the Colorado Chautauqua, is within half a mile of Palmer Lake, in a charming park-like expanse between two mountain streamlets, and at the mouth of a beautiful cañon, fifty-three miles from Denver. One hundred and fifty acres are comprised in the town site. The park is at the foot of the Rocky Mountain range, and is sheltered at the rear by a towering cliff, 2,000 feet high, and on two sides by small spurs of the range. A noble growth of large pines is scattered over the park. A skillful landscape engineer has taken advantage of every natural beauty, and studied the best topographical effect in laying out the streets, parks, reservoirs, drives, walks, trails, and lookout points. It is a spot that must be seen to be appreciated, and every visitor whose opinion has been learned has come away captivated. There are building sites for all tastes. Some have a grand outlook, taking in a sweep of the valley for a distance of fifty miles.

Colorado Springs is the county seat of El Paso County, has a population of 12,000, and stands at an elevation of 5,982 feet. This delightful little city is essentially one of homes, where the families of many of the most influential business men of the State reside. It is a temperance town, with charming society, and an elegant opera house, built as a place of enjoyment rather than as an investment, by some of the most successful citizens. There are many points of scenic interest within an hour's ride of the city. Among them may be mentioned Cheyenne Cañons, Austin's Glen,

Blair Athol, Queen's Cañon, and Glen Eyrie. No more delightful places can be found in which to enjoy the beautiful in nature and to breathe the health-giving and exhilarating air than these mountains and Pike's Peak. There are a number of smaller hotels and a good supply of comfortable and home-like boarding houses, in different parts of the town; also fine livery stables, where riding and driving horses and carriages of the best are furnished at reasonable rates.

Colorado City, the first Territorial capital of Colorado, and at present a thriving railroad town, is situated on the Denver & Rio Grande Railroad, midway between Colorado Springs and Manitou Springs, seventy-eight miles from Denver.

Manitou Springs. Of all nature's lovely spots few equal, and none surpass, in beauty of location, grandeur of surroundings, and sublimity of scenery this veritable "Gem of the Rockies." As a pleasure resort it presents to the tourist more objects of scenic interest than any resort of a like character in the Old or New World; while its wonderful effervescent and mineral springs, soda and iron, make it the favorite resting-place for invalids. The great superiority of Manitou's climate is found in its dryness and the even temperature the year round. In summer the cool breezes from the mountains temper the heat, the nights always being cool enough to allow that refreshing sleep so grateful to all and most needed by the invalid.

There are more points of interest near Manitou than any other watering place in the world. The following is a partial list, with the distances in miles from town attached:

	MILES.
Ruxton Creek to Iron Springs and Hotel	1
Ute Pass to Rainbow Falls and Grand Cavern	1½
Red Cañon	3

MILES.

Crystal Park	3
Garden of the Gods	3
Glen Eyrie	5
Monument Park by trail	7½
Monument Park by carriage	9
Seven Lakes by horse trail	9
Seven Lakes by carriage road	12
North Cheyenne Cañon	8½
South Cheyenne Cañon	9
Summit of Pike's Peak	12

In addition to these well-known localities there are scores of cañons, caves, waterfalls, and charming nooks which the sojourner for health or pleasure can seek out for himself.

The Garden of the Gods has been described and photographed more than any other place of scenic interest in Colorado, but words or pictures fail to give even the faintest idea of its wealth of gorgeous color, or of the noble view which its gateway frames. The portals of the gateway spring from the level plain to a height of 330 feet, and glow with the most brilliant coloring of red. There is an outer parapet of pure white, and there are inner columns of varied hues, the whole suggesting the ruins of a vast temple, once the receptacle of the sacred shrine of the long-buried gods. Within the garden the rocks assume strange mimetic forms, and the imagination of the spectator is kept busy discovering resemblances to beasts or birds, of men and women, and of strange freaks in architecture.

Glen Eyrie is situated at the entrance to Queen's Cañon, and is a wild and romantic retreat, in which is built the summer residence of a gentleman of wealth, whose permanent home is now in the East. Within the glen, which is made sylvan by thickly growing native shrubbery, covered with wild clematis, are a great confusion of enormous pillars of exquisite tinted pink sandstone.

Cathedral Rock and the Major Domo, which have gained a world-wide fame through pictures and descriptions, are to be found in Glen Eyrie, as are also " The Sisters," "Vulcan's Anvil," and "Melrose Abbey." These are all grand and impressive shapes of stone glowing with the most brilliant hues of red and pink, and cream and white, and umber.

Blair Athol is about a mile north of Glen Eyrie, and resembles the latter, with the exception of shrubbery and water. No residence has been erected here, as the difficulty of obtaining water has been too great to be successfully overcome. The quaint forms of rock and their brilliant color, together with the frequent shade of evergreen trees, make this an interesting and attractive spot.

Bear Creek Cañon is reached by taking the road to Colorado Springs and turning to the right just before reaching Colorado City. This is a beautiful drive of five miles, at the end of which the Government trail to Pike's Peak carries the horseman and footman to the summit. The cañon is a picturesque wooded glen, with a dashing torrent and abounding in wild flowers. Bears are still frequently seen here, but they shrink modestly from forcing their attention upon strangers, and retire precipitately when made aware of the vicinity of callers.

The Cheyenne Cañons are favorite resorts for picnic and pleasure parties. Both these cañons give one a good idea of the gorges which abound in the fastnesses of the Rocky Mountains. They are deep gashes in the heart of Cheyenne Mountain, and display grand faces of magnificent red granite hundreds of feet in height. The Douglas spruce, the Rocky Mountain pine, the white spruce, and that most lovely tree of all, the *Picea grandis*, grow in great numbers in both cañons, while the Virginia creeper, two species of clematis (mauve and white), and other climbers add grace and charm to the scene. A stairway at the Seven Falls in South Cañon leads to the last resting place of "H. H." (Helen Hunt Jackson), who selected this spot for her grave. The stream in North Cheyenne Cañon is larger than that in the southern gorge, but the latter forms a magnificent cascade, descending 500 feet in seven leaps.

Seven Falls is the name given to the cascade referred to above, and it is well worthy the admiration its beauty always excites.

The Cheyenne Mountain toll-road is well worth seeing. It ascends the mountains about one-half mile south of the entrance to South Cheyenne Cañon, winding, with easy grades, through very fine scenery, and at times affording glimpses down in the cañon below.

The Seven Lakes are reached by means of the last described road. The lakes are picturesque, and such sheets of water usually are among the mountains, and there is a hotel for the accommodation of visitors.

"My Garden" is a very favorite resort, discovered by "H. H.," the authoress and poet. Take the Cheyenne road one and one-half miles from Colorado Springs, then follow due south past Broad Moor Dairy Farm half a mile, then through a gate across the "Big Hollow," and "My Garden" is reached, a lovely pine grove crowning the plateau, with an exquisite view of the range behind it.

Monument Park, Edgerton Station, sixty-seven miles south from Denver and eight miles northward from Colorado Springs and Manitou, is a pleasant day's excursion. "The Pines" is a comfortable hotel, situated in the center of the park, one-half mile from the depot, commanding a fine view of Pike's Peak and Cheyenne Mountain Range; is open at all times for the accommodation of guests, and can furnish saddle-horses and carriages on premises. This park is chiefly remarkable for its very fantastic forms, in which time and the action of air and water have worn the cream-colored sandstone rocks which the valleys have exposed, forming grotesque groups of figures, some of them resembling human beings, viz.: Dutch Wedding, Quaker Meeting, Lone Sentinel, Dutch Parliament, Vulcan's Anvil and Workshop, Romeo and Juliet, Necropolis, or Silent City, The Duchess, Mother Judy, and Colonnade. All of these, and many others too numerous to mention, are within easy walking distance of " The Pines."

A very pleasant drive can be taken to Templeton's Gap, which is situated just north of Austin's Bluffs, and is a sharp depression in the surrounding hills, characterized by quaint monumental forms of rock.

Ute Pass leads westward from Manitou over the range into South Park. It is now a wagon road cut in many places from the face of the cliff, the rocks towering thousands of feet above it on one side and on the other presenting a sheer descent of nearly as many feet down to where the fountain brawls along over its rugged channel. The pass was formerly used as a pony trail by the Ute Indians in their descent to the plains and in their visits to the " Big Medicine " of the healing springs—the name given Manitou by the aborigines. No pleasanter ride or drive can be taken than up Ute Pass. The scenery is grand and the view one of great loveliness.

Rainbow Falls are only a mile and a half from Manitou up the Pass, and are well worthy of a visit. They are the most accessible and the most beautiful on the eastern slope of the Rocky Mountains, and are visited by thousands of tourists every season.

The Great Manitou Caverns have added an attractive feature to the diversified wonders of nature surrounding Manitou Springs.   The caverns are located one and a half miles from Manitou Springs.   They were discovered by their present owner, Mr. George W. Snider, in the year 1881, but were only opened to the public in 1885.

The cog-wheel railroad to the summit of Pike's Peak, which was completed and put in operation in July, 1891, is the most novel railway in the world.   When it reaches its objective point above the clouds, at a height of 14,147 feet above sea-level, it renders almost insignificant by comparison the famous cog-way up Mount Washington and the incline railway up the Rhigi in Switzerland.   From its station in Manitou, just above the Iron Springs, to the station on the summit of Pike's Peak, the Manitou & Pike's Peak Railway is just eight and three-quarters miles in length.   The cost of construction of the road was a half million dollars.   While it could have been built for many thousands of dollars less by putting in wooden bridges and trestles, light ties and light rails, those in charge of the building of the road would not consent to the use of any flimsy material for the sake of saving any sum of money— a substantial road that would insure absolute safety being economical, as well as a guarantee for putting the road from the start on a paying basis.   The road-bed is solid and from fifteen to twenty feet wide, leaving fully five feet on each side of the cars.   The culverts are solid masonry; the four short bridges are of iron girders resting on first-class masonry.   There are an extra number of ties, which are extra heavy and extra long.   The rails are standard " T " rails, with a double cog rail in the center.   This cog rail weighs 110 tons to the mile, which is unusually heavy. The rail is built in sections, each being put into a lathe and the teeth cut.   The contract requires that each tooth

16

shall be within the fifteenth part of an inch of the size
specified.   At intervals of every 200 feet the track is
anchored to solid masonry to prevent any possibility of the
track slipping from its bed.   The cars are designed to
hang low, within eighteen inches of the rails.   Each
engine built by the Baldwin Locomotive Works has three
cog and pinion appliances, which can be worked together
or independently.   In each cog appliance is a double set
of pinion brakes that work in the cog, either one of which
when used can stop the engine in ten inches, going either
way, on any grade and at the maximum speed, eight miles
an hour.   The cars are not tilted, but the seats are arranged
so as to give the passenger a level sitting.   The engine
pushes the cars instead of drawing them, which is of great
advantage.   And such is Denver to-day, and its attractive
surroundings, changed from a border wilderness to civilization and grandeur within thirty years.

CHAPTER XXIX.

It may not be amiss just here, while writing of this "Land of the Setting Sun," its changes from savagery to civilization, to refer to one who has done so much to aid those who followed the Star of Empire toward the Rocky Mountains.

I refer to Col. W. F. Cody, known in almost every hamlet of the world as Buffalo Bill, one upon whom the seal of manhood has been set as upon few others, who has risen by the force of his own gigantic will, his undaunted courage, ambition, and genius, to be honored among the rulers of kingdoms, as well as by his own people.

Nearly forty years ago, in Kansas, a handsome, wiry little lad came to me, accompanied by his good mother, and said that he had her permission to take a position under me as a messenger boy.

I gave him the place, though it was one of peril, carrying dispatches between our wagon-trains upon the march across the plains, and little did I then suspect that I was just starting out in life one who was destined to win fame and fortune.

Then it was simply "Little Billy Cody," the messenger, and from his first year in my service he began to make his mark, and lay the foundation of his future greatness.

Next it became "Wild Will," the pony express rider of the overland, and as such he faced many dangers, and overcame many obstacles which would have crushed a less strong nature and brave heart.

Then it became "Bill Cody, the Wagonmaster," then overland stage driver, and from that to guide across the plains, until he drifted into his natural calling as a Government scout.

"Buffalo Bill, the Scout and Indian Fighter," was known from north to south, from east to west, for his skill, energy, and daring as a ranger of mountain and plain.

With the inborn gift of a perfect borderman, Buffalo Bill led armies across trackless mountains and plains, through deserts of death, and to the farthest retreats of the cruel redskins who were making war upon the settlers.

Buffalo Bill has never sought the reputation of being a "man killer."

He has shunned difficulties of a personal nature, yet never backed down in the face of death in the discharge of duty.

Brought face to face with the worst elements of the frontier, he never sought the title of hero at the expense of other lives and suffering.

An Indian fighter, he was yet the friend of the redskin in many ways, and to-day there is not a man more respected among all the fighting tribes than Buffalo Bill, though he is feared as well.

In his delineation of Wild West life before the vast audiences he has appeared to in this country and Europe, he has been instrumental in educating the Indians to feel that it would be madness for them to continue the struggle against the innumerable whites, and to teach them that peace and happiness could come to them if they would give up the war-path and the barbarism of the past, and seek for themselves homes amid civilized scenes and associations.

Buffalo Bill is therefore a great teacher among his red friends, and he has done more good than any man I know who has lived among them.

Courtly by nature, generous to a fault, big-hearted and brainy, full of gratitude to those whom he feels indebted to, he has won his way in the world and stands to-day as truly one of Nature's noblemen.

One of the strongest characteristics of Buffalo Bill, to my mind, was his love for his mother—a mother most worthy the devotion of such a son. His love and devotion to his sisters has also been marked throughout his lifetime.

When he first came to me he had to sign the pay-roll each month by making the sign of a cross, his mark. He drew a man's pay, and earned every dollar of it.

He always had his mother come to get his pay, and when one day he was told by the paymaster to come and " make his mark and get his money," his face flushed as he saw tears come into his mother's eyes and heard her low uttered words:

"Oh, Willie! if you would only learn to write, how happy I would be."

Educational advantages in those early days were crude in the extreme, and Little Billy's chances to acquire knowledge were few, but from that day, when he saw the tears in his mother's eyes at his inability to write his name, he began to study hard and to learn to write; in fact his acquiring the art of penmanship got him into heaps of trouble, as " Will Cody," " Little Billy," " Billy the Boy Messenger," and " William Frederic Cody" were written with the burnt end of a stick upon tents, wagon-covers, and all tempting places, while he carved upon wagon-body, ox-yoke, and where he could find suitable wood for his pen-knife to cut into, the name he would one day make famous.

With such energy as this on his part, Billy Cody was not very long in learning to write his name upon the pay-roll instead of making his mark, though ever since, I may add, he has made his mark in the pages of history.

All through his life he was ever the devoted son and brother, and true as steel to his friends, for he has not been spoiled by the fame he has won, while to-day his firmest friends are the officers of the army with whom he has served through dangers and hardships untold, as proof of which he was freely given the indorsements of such men as Sherman, Sheridan, Gen. Nelson A. Miles, Generals Carr, Merritt, Royal, and a host of others.

CHAPTER XXX.

From the dawn of history to the present time, civilization has followed the valleys. From the Garden of Eden
which was in the valley of the Euphrates to modern times
the water courses have been the highways of civilization,
and made the Tiber and the Thames, the Rhine and the
Rhone famous in the annals of the world's progress. In
our own country this fact has been especially illustrated.
The valley of the Rio Grande del Norte was the pathway
of the Spaniard in his march to the northward, and it is
one of the curious facts of history that, before the Pilgrims
had landed on Plymouth Rock, the adventurous cavaliers
of Spain had penetrated the center of the continent and
discovered the sources of the great river in the Sangre de
Cristo Mountains of Colorado.

It was along the Connecticut and the Hudson, the Delaware and the Susquehanna, the Ohio and the Mississippi,
that the pioneers of the republic pushed their way westward and planted the civilization which has enjoyed so
substantial and prosperous a growth. And when the pioneer resumed his westward march to the Rocky Mountains,
his trains lay along the Missouri, the Arkansas, and the
Platte, thus giving to the valley of the Platte an historic
place in the records of the nation's advancement.

The Louisiana Purchase, within whose boundaries lay
the great valley of the Platte and its tributaries, was completed in 1804, by President Thomas Jefferson. It was an
act of statesmanship worthy of the man who had drafted

R

the Declaration of Independence, and assured the young republic a future little dreamed of by the men of that day, but which we have lived to realize. Two years later, in 1806, Lieut. Zebulon Pike received an order to explore the newly acquired national possessions, and to find the headwaters of the Platte River. In pursuance of the order, Lieutenant Pike marched up the Arkansas to the Fountaine Qui Bouille, discovered and ascended the great peak which bears his name, entering the South Park from the present site of Cañon City by the Current Creek route. Aside from his discovery of the headwaters of the Platte, Lieutenant Pike's expedition was more largely devoted to the Arkansas and the Rio Grande than to this valley.

The second expedition up the Platte Valley was ordered in 1819 by John C. Calhoun, Secretary of War for President James Monroe, and was under the command of Major Stephen S. Long, of the corps of topographical engineers. Leaving Pittsburg, Pa., in April, 1819, Major Long proceeded westward and established his camp near the present site of Council Bluffs, Iowa, to which was given the name of Engineer Cantonment. Thence on June 6, 1820, with a number of scientists and a small detail of regular troops, he marched toward the mountains. On June 30th the party sighted the magnificent range of the Rocky Mountains, a view of which burst upon them in the full glory of the morning light. On July 3d they passed, as Long's annals read, "the mouth of three large creeks, heading in the mountains and entering the Platte from the northwest." These were undoubtedly the Cache la Poudre, the Thompson, and the St. Vrain. On July 5th they camped on the present site of Fort Lupton, and on July 6th on the present site of Denver, at the mouth of Cherry Creek. Thence the party followed the valley to the Platte Cañon, and, proceeding southward along the base of the mountains, returned eastward along the Arkansas.

Twenty-two years later, in 1842, came Lieut. John C. Fremont, the famous pathfinder, who traversed the Blue toward the Platte, reaching the valley at Grand Island, a portion of the party going up the North Fork toward Fort Laramie, and the larger part marching up the South Fork to Fort St. Vrain, which had then been established a number of years, and had become a noted rendezvous for trappers, hunters, and plainsmen. The following year the intrepid explorer left St. Louis on his second expedition, traveling the valleys of the Kaw and the Republican, reaching the Platte at the mouth of Beaver Creek, and arriving at Fort St. Vrain on July 4, 1843. I quote the words of Lieutenant Fremont as prophetic of the future of the valley. "This post," he says, "was beginning to assume the appearance of a comfortable farm. Stock, hogs and cattle, were ranging about the prairie. There were different kinds of poultry and there was the wreck of a promising garden in which a considerable variety of vegetables had been in a flourishing condition, but had been almost entirely ruined by recent high water."

Between the dates of the expeditions of Long and Fremont three noted trading posts had been established along the Platte in the immediate vicinity of the spot on which we are now assembled. The first of these was Fort Vanquez, built by Louis Vanquez in 1832, at the mouth of Clear Creek, then known as Vanquez Fork of the Platte. The next was Fort Lupton, a portion of whose walls are still standing, and the third was Fort St. Vrain, built in 1840. These forts, as they were called, were trading posts at which a large traffic in skins and furs was conducted, and which became the headquarters of such famous frontiersmen as Kit Carson, Jim Bridger, Jim Baker, Jim Beckwouth, and others, who in those days constituted the vedettes of the civilization of the country. I have not time to dwell upon their exploits, but I note their names as indicating that we stand upon historic ground, and that here in this valley were planted the first germs of the prosperous growth which to-day enfolds it in every department of its social, industrial, and commercial life.

In 1847 the Platte Valley became the highway of the Mormons in their exodus from Illinois to Utah. Two years later its trails were broadened by the California pioneers en route to the shores of the Pacific to share in the golden discoveries of Sutter and his companions.

In 1857 came the expedition of Col. Albert Sidney Johnston marching to Utah to sustain the laws and authority of the United States.

But a greater movement was now organizing to traverse and possess the valley of the Platte. In the fullness of time the crisis of its destiny had arrived. The year of 1859 dawned upon a nation fast drifting into the vortex of a civil war. The irrepressible conflict which for half a century had been going on between free and slave labor was nearing the arbitrament of arms, and absorbed all men's minds to the exclusion of events which were happening on the distant frontier. In the summer of 1858 Green Russell and a party of adventurous prospectors had discovered gold in Cherry Creek, a tributary of the Platte. The news spread, and grew as it spread, until the people living along the Missouri, which was then the frontier of the Republic, became excited over the richness of the discoveries.

They were ripe for adventure, desperate almost in their determination to reëstablish the fortunes that had been wrecked by the financial panic of 1857, which had swept with disastrous effect along the entire borderland of the entire nation. In the spring of 1859 the march of the pioneers began. The Platte Valley was their grand pathway to the mountains, whose summits they greeted with exultant joy, and beneath whose protecting shadows they camped; here to make their homes, here to lay the foundations of the future State.

Thus in a little over half a century from the date of its purchase by the Federal Government, the Platte Valley had become the home of civilized man, and the work of its development begun. As gold was first discovered in this valley, so was quartz mining first begun on one of the tributaries in Gilpin County.

The first pioneer's cabin was erected in Denver; the first school-house was built at Boulder; the first church was consecrated at Denver; the first colony located at Greeley, and the first irrigating ditches taken out, all within the Platte Valley. As the valley had been the route of Major Long and other of the early explorers, so, following in the train of the pioneer, came first the pony express, then the stage-coach, then the locomotive and the Pullman car. And it is a fact which I believe has never yet been published, that the last stage-coach of the great overland line was dispatched from the town of Brighton to Denver, thus associating its name with an act, insignificant in itself, but far-reaching in its importance, when it is remembered that that act marked the end of our pioneer period and ushered in the new growth of the railroad era.

We stand to-day at the distance of three-fourths of a century from the date when the foot of the white man first trod the valley of the Platte. The names of Pike and Long are perpetuated by the two magnificent peaks which raise their summits to the clouds and stand as guardians of the plains below. Fremont lived to see his wildest dreams realized in the progress of the West, but whatever fame he may have achieved as a soldier and a statesman, his name will longest be remembered as the pathfinder of the Rocky Mountains. Wheat-fields now flourish where once stood the trading-posts of Vanquez and St. Vrain. The trails of the early explorers and of the pioneers of 1859 are almost obliterated, and grass is growing upon their once broad and beaten pathways. A happy, contented, prosperous people possess the land. A great line of railway now rolls the traffic of a continent along the valley where once the stage-coach and ox-trains of Russell, Majors & Waddell wended their slow and weary way. Thriving towns and villages and cities dot the plain, and reflect in the activity of their commercial life the industrial development by which they are surrounded.

CHAPTER XXXI.

KANSAS CITY BEFORE THE WAR.

In August, 1838, there appeared in the far West a newspaper published at Liberty, in Clay County, Missouri, the only newspaper within many miles, a notice which read as follows: "Circuit Court of Jackson County, Missouri, at Independence, August term, 1838." Then followed a description of lands now included in what is known as the "old town" of Kansas City. Then continues: "The above mentioned lands are situated in the county of Jackson, one and one-half miles below the mouth of the Kansas River, and five miles from the flourishing town of Westport. The situation is admirably calculated for a ferry across the Missouri River, and also one of the best steamboat landings on the river, and an excellent situation for a warehouse or town site. The terms of sale will be a credit of twelve months, the purchaser giving bond and approved security, with interest at the rate of 10 per cent from day of sale. All those wishing to invest capital advantageously in landed estate will do well to call upon Justice H. McGee, who is guardian for the heirs.

"James B. Davenport,
"Peter Booth,
"Elliott Johnson,
"Commissioners."

The purchasers were William L. Sublette, John C. McCoy, William Gillis, Robert Campbell, and others, and the price paid for the entire tract, extending along the Missouri River from Broadway to Troost Avenue, containing 156 acres, was $4,220.

(253)

These gentlemen put their purchase into lots and blocks and called it "Kansas," but very little was done toward founding a city until some eight years later, when a new company was organized by H. M. Northup, who is still living; John C. McCoy, who died within the past few months; Fry P. McGee, Jacob Ragan, William Gillis, Robert Campbell, who have been dead but a few years respectively; Henry Jobe, W. B. Evans, and W. M. Chick, who have been dead much longer.

The first sale of lots was had in April, 1848, at which sale 150 lots were sold at an average price of $55.65 per lot.

The business of the city was confined almost entirely, for a number of years, to the levee, and was of the general character of that done in all river towns in their early history, pretty rough, pretty miscellaneous, and not altogether unmixed with "wet goods." Prohibition was an unknown element in social science, and the proportion of whisky consumed in the retail trade, compared with that of tea or coffee, was very like that described by Shakespeare in referring to Falstaff's "intolerable deal of sack to the half penny worth of bread." But very few men of those days remain nowadays; yet, as I have said, H. M. Northup still lives, vigorous and active. Dr. I. M. Ridge still continues to practice his profession, although less extensively than forty years ago. John Campbell traverses our streets, but has long since turned his well-known and faithful old sorrel mule out to grass. William Mulkey looks hale and hearty, but has discarded his former buckskin suit, though he still maintains a portion of his farm in the center of the city. Once in a long while one of the old French settlers of those early days, or even an old plainsman, ventures into the busy city and looks about him in a bewildered sort of way for a day or two, and then disappears again into the nearest wilderness or prairie, as being far more congenial to his tastes and habits of life.   Not all of them, however, are of this character and disposition.   It is but a few weeks since I met one of our most noted pioneer plainsmen and freighters across the prairies of Kansas, Colorado, and New Mexico, in the earliest of the days I have been speaking of.   In those times no name was better or more widely known than that of Seth E. Ward, the post trader at Laramie.

The descendants of most of the original owners of the "Town of Kansas," as it was first called, or "Westport Landing," as it was nicknamed later, still remain there, and are among its most prominent and respected citizens to-day.

Ten years later the "western fever" struck Ohio, and hundreds of young men of my acquaintance left there for Kansas and Nebraska. Omaha was a favorite objective point, and a town named Columbus was founded still farther west than Omaha, which was almost entirely colonized by people from Franklin County, Ohio.   One of my friends, Dr. Theodore S. Case, also holding the rank of colonel, was studying medicine at the time in Columbus, Ohio, and resisted the fever until the following year, 1857, when, with a few books and a sheepskin authorizing him to write M. D. after his name, and to commit manslaughter without being called to account for it, started for the West.   He knew nothing of the West, but had a general idea that he would go to St. Louis, or Keokuk, or Des Moines, or Omaha, or Council Bluffs, or possibly to "Carson City," Kan.; for a sharper, originally from Columbus, had been out West and came back with a lithographic map of a city by that name, fixed up very attractively, and with all the modern improvements of court house, city hall, depots, churches, colleges, steamboats, etc., and he bought some $15 worth of lots on one of the principal thoroughfares of the city not far from the depot. However, before he got as far west as St. Louis, he had learned the manners and tricks of such gentry, and did not go to "Carson City." By some accidental circumstance his attention was called particularly to the geographical location of Kansas City, and he at once determined to give it a look anyhow. There being no railroad nearer than Jefferson City at that time, he took the steamer Minnehaha at St. Louis, along with some other 299 fellows who were going "out west to grow up with the country," and four days afterward landed at Kansas City, May 1, 1857, almost thirty-five years ago.

The first view of Kansas City was by no means prepossessing, as it consisted principally of a line of shabby looking brick and frame warehouses, dry-goods stores, groceries, saloons, restaurants, etc., strung along the levee from Wyandotte Street to a little east of Walnut Street, the whole backed up and surmounted by a rugged and precipitous bluff, from 100 to 150 feet high, covered with old dead trees, brush, dog fennel and jimson weeds, with an occasional frame or log house scattered between and among them, and a few women and children, principally darkies, looking down at the boats.

To a young man, however, the levee, with its three or four steamers, huge piles of Mexican freight, prairie schooners, mules, greasers, Indians, negroes, mud clerks, roustabouts, Frenchmen, consignees, emigrants, old settlers, tenderfeet, hotel drummers, brass bands, omnibuses, etc., presented attractions not easily resisted. Notwithstanding all the tooting for hotels, there were really but two in the place, one on the levee, then known as the American Hotel, now remembered more familiarly as the "Gillis House," and the other the "Farmers' Hotel," on Grand Avenue, between Sixteenth and Seventeenth streets. The first was

LEE'S FERRY, ON THE COLORADO.

technically known as the " Free State Hotel," having been built by the New England Aid Emigrant Society, and the other as the " Pro-Slavery," or " Border Ruffian House," as it was or had been the headquarters of the pro-slavery party in the border war of 1854 and 1856 between the free state and pro-slavery contestants for the possession of political control of the Territory of Kansas.

All travelers, however, who knew the ropes dodged both these hotels and took the omnibus for Westport, where two really good hotels were kept. To show the amount of travel toward Kansas at that time I may say that at the American Hotel alone there were 27,000 arrivals in the year 1856–57.

Such was Kansas City in early days and the experience there of a tenderfoot, but now an honored citizen of what is really to-day a great city.

17

CHAPTER XXXII.

MANY an Eastern city has more dead people than living. Instead of the West being young, the East is growing old. The antiquities of the Eastern cemetery are often more interesting to the Westerner than the life and energy of the living city. How the old names of Concurrence, Patience, Charity, Eunice, Virtue, Experience, Prudence, Jerusha, Electra, Thankful, Narcissa, Mercy, Wealthy, Joanna, Mehitable, on the tombstones of the old Puritan grandmothers have been supplanted by the new names of these modern times! And the old-time grandfathers—well, their names suggest a scriptural chapter on genealogy. These old-time names, with quaint and queer epitaphs, on less pretentious monuments than the costly ones now erected, make an interesting study, for the ancient dates and names show that the cemetery has a history from the earliest settlement. The ancestral bones from the Mayflower down to the present have been saved. It is true that the great Western cities now have costly, beautiful, and often magnificent monuments for the dead, for the modern cemetery is becoming aristocratic.

But for the reason it might be considered almost a sacrilege, the model of a typical New England graveyard, with its odd names and quaint epitaphs, would be an interesting historical study at the World's Fair. In fact it would be as much of a curiosity to millions of people in the West as Buffalo Bill's Wild West Show was in the East.

In all the cities of the West there are more live people

than dead ones, which is not always true of the East, where the cemetery population is often larger. With the exception of some of the old Spanish mission cemeteries, those of the West are all new, unless one would wish to explore the ancient homes of the mound-builders and cliff-dwellers. A white man's graveyard is a new thing for the West. There are many thousands among the 17,000,-000 people west of the Mississippi River who can tell of the days when Kansas City, Omaha, St. Paul, Minneapolis, Denver, Salt Lake, Galveston, Dallas, Helena, San Francisco, Portland, and Seattle hardly had a cemetery. Even St. Louis and New Orleans have been American cities less than a century.

But during all this time many millions have been added to the silent cities of the dead in the East, and the older the cemetery the more there is to it that is new to a Western tourist. One born in the West, on making his first trip to the East, finds almost as much of interest in a New England burial-ground, and often views it with as little reverence as does the Bostonian in gazing upon the mummies and antiquities of Egypt.

It is interesting to contrast the frontier funeral and burial-ground in the West with that of the East. The cemetery, the necessary but last adjunct to the organization of a civilized community, follows in the wake of immigration and empire. No monuments mark the last resting-place of those buried in the first five great cemeteries in the far West. They are in the region of nameless and unknown graves.

Those five historic cemeteries, where thousands from the East and South died and fill unknown graves, are the Missouri River, and the Santa Fé, Oregon, California, and Pike's Peak trails. The trans-Alleghany, and later the trans-Mississippi pioneers, followed, in the main, the water-courses. There was no prairie-farming, and hence the term, "backwoodsman." It was a kind of a Yankee trick in the West, in later years, to leave the forests and begin plowing the prairies, and save the time that had been hitherto used in log-rolling and clearing the river-bottoms for agriculture. The early trappers, hunters, and fur dealers followed up the Missouri River and its tributaries. Only with great difficulty could a corpse be concealed from wolves and coyotes, the latter animal always having been known as the hyena of the plains country. Hence many an old hunter, when far from the borderland of civilization, has buried his "pard" in the Missouri River! Landsmen and plainsmen with a seaman's burial—a watery grave! The body wrapped in a blanket—when the blanket could be spared—and tied to rocks and boulders, was lowered from the drifting canoe into the "Big Muddy," as that river is commonly known in the West. Many an old hunter and trapper has been buried in the mighty rushing waters of the great Western river, even as the faithful followers of De Soto lowered his remains into the bosom of the Mississippi. When it was necessary or convenient to bury the dead on land, the greatest precaution was taken to protect the body from wolves and coyotes, which were especially dangerous and ravenous when off of the trail of the buffalo. Rocks and large pieces of timber were placed on the newly made grave, but often these hyenas of the plains could be seen scratching and growling at this debris before the comrades of the dead man were out of sight. With these facts so well known, it is not strange that many in those early days preferred a burial in the rivers to that of the land. It seems almost paradoxical to thus find in the old trapper some of the instincts and traditions of the sailor. Far out on the plains cactus was often put in the grave, just over the corpse, as a protection against the wolves and coyotes.

The earlier expeditions starting from St. Louis went up the Mississippi a few miles, to the mouth of the Missouri River, and then followed the latter stream. For some time the old Boone's Lick country, now known as Howard County, Mo., and Old Franklin, was the frontier commercial head.

The town of Old Franklin, where was the original terminus of the old Santa Fé trail, when Kit Carson was only an apprentice to a saddler and harness-maker, is now the bottom of the Missouri River, for there a current of seven miles an hour has cut away the old town site.

But the pioneers became bolder. Instead of following the river they began to venture out from St. Louis overland, about the time of the old Boone's Lick settlement. It was considered a brave and hazardous journey to start from St. Louis overland in those days, for it was a village town, and all of the country to the west was a wilderness. It was about the year 1808 that the Workman and Spencer party started from St. Louis, and far out on the plains, before reaching the Rocky Mountains, one of the party sickened and died.

The Indians rendered what assistance they could in bringing herbs and such crude medicines as they used for fevers. The poor fellow died, and they dug for him a grave, which was among the first, if not the first, burial of a white man on the great plains of the West.

It was a novel sight for the Indians to see the hunters and trappers wrap up their dead comrade in a blanket, and put the body into a deep hole they had dug. They piled up brush and what heavy things they could find, and placed on the grave, carved his name in rude letters, and went on their way. But they had hardly resumed their journey before the wolves began to dig at the grave.

Were it not foreign to the purpose of this article, it would be interesting to relate at some length the fate of this expedition. The most of the party were slain in battles with the Indians, and Workman and Spencer are reported to have gone through the grand cañons of the Colorado River to California in 1809, but that remarkable feat is discredited by some, leaving honors easier with Major Powell, whose expedition through these cañons was in more modern times.

This lonely and desolate grave dug by the Workman and Spencer party is supposed to have been somewhere in what is now Kansas or Nebraska. It was the beginning of making graves on the plains and in the mountains, but time, wind, rain, and sand made them unknown.

Many thousands perished on the old-time trails to Santa Fé, the Rocky Mountains, and the Pacific Coast. Exposure, sickness, thirst, starvation, and massacre were the dangers the immigrants had to face. Many of their graves were marked with slabs, but the inscription was soon effaced. These graves are as unknown in the great ocean of plain, prairie, and mountain as though the pioneer dead had been buried at sea.

The most fatal days was when the cholera raged on the Western trails. Sometimes an entire train would be stricken and the captain would be compelled to corral the wagons until aid could be obtained from other caravans on the desert, then so called, or the teamsters recovered to continue the journey. Women sometimes helped to dig the graves and assisted in burying the dead, and have then taken the dead teamster's place at the wagon, driving the oxen until men could be employed.

With the opening of the Western trails for wagons, a larger number were buried in boxes made from rude pieces of lumber, or sometimes a part of the sideboard of the wagon was utilized for that purpose. The earlier expeditions were on horseback, and hence at that time the best that could be done would be to roll the body in a blanket. Only those in the East who have seen a burial at sea, although they may never have been on the plains, can realize the sadness and desolation of those who left their friends in the nameless graves of the old-time American desert. Many of the babies lived that were born on the California and Oregon trails, but the saddest of all was when the pioneer mother and babe were added to the thousands of nameless graves. The death-couch was a pile of straw and a few blankets in an old freight wagon. If the angels ever hover over the dying, there never would have been a more appropriate place for their ministrations. Nameless graves! Unknown! Only the drifting sands and the ceaseless flow of the mighty Western rivers know the place of their nameless dead. These are the famous cemeteries of the far West. There are no granite shafts or beautiful emblems carved in marble. Heroic men and women! They died unknown to fame and honor, but they gave their lives that a new civilization and a new empire might be born in the far West. The brave men, North and South, who fell in battle, have their graves marked "unknown" when they could not be identified, but no one knows where sleep the thousands who died on these trails. Even a slab to the "unknown" could not be placed, for who knows the grave? Farm-houses, fertile fields, cities and towns, and the rushing railway car now mark the spot. The path of civilization and the rapid building of empire in the West is their only living monument.

During the cholera days there was a heavy loss of life on the Western steamboats. On the Missouri River some of the old boats had a burial crew. At night-time, when the passengers were hardly aware of what was going on, the boat would stop near a sand-bar. The bodies of those who had died during the day were taken to the sand-bar, where they were quickly buried. What would have been the use of putting up even a pine board, for the rising waters would soon have washed it away?

But this is not simply Western history. It is a part of the history of the North and the South, for those who came never to return were from those sections. In many an Eastern and Southern home it is as unknown to them as to the people of the West where sleep their dead on those old trails of the Western empire.

The emigrants and gold-seekers were population in transit. Their burial-places were as fleeting. With the building of new towns and cities were established cemeteries, but there still continued to be the thousands of unknown graves. A father, brother, husband, or son dies away from home. His name may not have been known, or if it was, the pencil-marks on the pine board soon lost their tracing in the weather-beaten changes that time brings. How often in my own experience in the mining camps I have seen men die far away from the tender and loving care of mother, wife, and sister. How terrible then is the struggle with death! The desire to live and to see the old home-faces again becomes a passion. In their delirium the passion becomes a reality. In their feverish dreams I have seen the dying miner in his cabin fancy he was home again. He talks to his wife, and with words of endearment tells her that he has found a fortune in the mines. I never knew of a miner who, in the delirium of death, when he was talking of the mines, but what he was rich. He had struck the precious metal. He tells his people at home about it, and many a poor fellow has seemingly died content, founded on the fancy that he had a mine and that his wife and family would always have plenty. Out of many instances I will relate but one.

A young man from Galena, Ill., eleven years ago, was taken sick and soon the fever was upon him. He grew rapidly worse, but bravely fought the pale reaper, for he wanted to see home again. But courage was not equal to the task. The poor fellow had to die, and when the fever was at its height, he imagined that he was with his wife and baby. How tenderly he spoke to his young wife. He thought he had a rich mine, and told her where it was located. Then he imagined that his pillow was his baby, and that he was running his fingers through the child's curly hair, and would fondle the child up to his bosom. As I gazed on the bronze and weather-beaten faces of those present in the cabin, I saw tears come into the eyes of some when the dying man was murmuring child-love talk to the baby.

At the time of the great Leadville rush, many came who never returned. Unknown, many of them sleep in their last resting place—in the gulches, on the mountain sides, and under the shadows of the pine trees and granite peaks. Exposure and not being prepared to guard against the sudden changes of climate caused many to die of pneumonia and fevers. The writer went through a hard attack of typhoid pneumonia in one of the mining camps. After the worst was over and I was conscious again, one of the boys said to me, "Hello, pard, when you were in the fever you thought you had found enough gold mines to have bought out the Astors and Vanderbilts."

The greatest number of deaths for a while seemed to come from what was known as the "sawdust gang." In the wild excitement of a new mining camp boom, people rush in by the hundreds and thousands. Many have only enough money to get there, and are compelled to sleep on the sawdust floor of the saloons. Thus they caught cold, which turning into pneumonia often proved fatal. And the cowboys—how often on the long Texas-Montana drives they have dug a hasty grave and with the lassos lowered their dead pard into it.

The sporting and theatrical element always have a swell

funeral in the booming mining camps. The musicians from the dance-halls turn out, play dirges, and with due pomp and ceremony the funeral is conducted. The band returns from the new cemetery usually playing some lively air. The deceased has had a fine funeral and a good send-off, and now to business. The dance-halls are crowded again, the music goes on, and men and women gamble, dance, and drink, unmindful of what has occurred.

Those were days of death, hell, and the grave. But what will not men undergo and dare for gold? They have braved anything for it in the past, and will in the future. Friendships and home ties are broken, and in the wild, mad rush for fortune, thousands of gold hunters have lost their lives, and fill nameless and unknown graves in the far West. There is something of romance in the death of a humble prospector searching for wealth on the mountain side. Whether rich or poor the old gold hunter often sees wealth ahead in his last hours. And, perchance, through the fading light on the mountain peaks, may he not see a trail leading to a city where the streets are golden? Who knows?

In 1849 and 1850, all along the trail of the overland freighters' route, were scattered unknown graves, clear into California, my dear father being one of the pioneers who died and filled an unknown grave. In the fall of 1850. on the east bank of the San Joaquin River, he died of cholera, and was buried, and his grave is unknown.

Another instance that I recall was of the death of one of the women of the party. She was buried at the South Pass, and they built a pen of cottonwood poles over the grave, placing her rocking chair to mark the spot, and which had her name carved on it.

CHAPTER XXXIII

SILVER MINING.

My son Benjamin and I worked as contractors almost a year in 1868, upon the building of the Union Pacific Railroad, and we were present at the Promontory when the Union and Central Pacific roads met, and saw the gold and silver spikes driven into the California mahogany tie. It was regarded at that time as the greatest feat in railroad enterprise that had ever been accomplished in this or any other country, and it was a day that will be remembered during the lifetime of all that were present to witness this great iron link between the two oceans, Atlantic and Pacific. My calling as a freighter and overland stager having been deposed by the building of telegraph lines and the completion of a continental railway, I was compelled to look after a new industry, and as the silver mining at that time was just beginning to develop in Utah, I chose that as my next occupation, and my first experience in prospecting for silver mines was in Black Pine District north of Kelton some twenty-five miles, and I believe in the northwest corner of Utah. The district proved to be a failure, but leaving it, I met with Mr. R. C. Chambers, who, upon acquaintance, I found to be a very pleasant gentleman. I left the camp and went to Salt Lake City, and wrote Mr. Chambers that I thought mines in the mountains were a better show for prospectors than the Black Pine District, and in a few days he came to Salt Lake City, and we then engaged in prospecting in the American Fork and Cottonwood districts, which lay in the Wasatch Mountains, twenty-five or thirty miles southeast of Salt Lake City. We had some success, but were not able to find anything in the way of bonanzas. We were connected with each other more or less until 1872, when a gentleman came to me one day in July of that year and told me that he had a bond upon McHenry mine, in Park District, and that the mine was a remarkably rich one. He desired me to telegraph to Mr. George Hearst of San Francisco to come to Salt Lake City and go and see the mine. He said that he wanted me to send the message because he knew Mr. Hearst, with whom I had become acquainted through Mr. Chambers, would come for my telegram, when he would perhaps pay no attention to his. I sent the message, and received a reply forthwith that he would start at once for Salt Lake City. He arrived in due time, and we together went to the McHenry mine. Upon arrival we found it was not what was represented. We were thoroughly disappointed in our expectations. But while sitting, resting on a large boulder, a man by the name of Harmon Budden (who a day or two before had discovered and located the Ontario mine) approached us and spoke to Mr. Hearst. Mr. H. said he did not remember him, but Mr. Budden said he had previously met him in some mining camp in Nevada, and remarked that he had a prospect that he would like us to look at, only a short distance away. We went with him to the location. His shaft was then only about three feet deep, and when Mr. Hearst jumped down into the hole that he had dug, the surface of the ground was about as high as his waist, and he could jump in and out by putting his hands on the earth. I saw that he was very much interested in the appearance of the ore, which at that depth and at that time did not show more than a streak of eight or ten inches of mineral. I was at that time what they called a "tenderfoot," and had not been in the mining business long enough to be an expert, and to my inexperienced eye there was nothing unusual in the appearance of the ore, but Mr. Hearst did see something, and he determined then and there to purchase the Ontario prospect, and arranged when we returned to Salt Lake City with Mr. Chambers to keep a watch over its development, and purchase it when he saw an opportunity to do so. Mr. Budden and his associates asked $5,000 for the prospect when we were there, but Mr. Hearst thought it might be bought for less, as it was nothing but a prospect. But as the development of the mine progressed they raised their price for it $5,000 every time they were asked the terms, until at last it was up to $30,000, when Mr. Chambers purchased it for Mr. Hearst and his associates in San Francisco, Messrs. Tebis and Haggin. Mr. R. C. Chambers was made superintendent of the mine, and has remained its manager from that period until the present, he being one of the stockholders, as well as the superintendent. The mine has grown and developed until it is one of the great mines of the Rocky Mountain region, and under Mr. Chamber's supervision has been extremely successful and profitable to its owners. Its output, up to 1892, has been over $26,000,000, over $12,000,000 of which has been paid in dividends to the stockholders. This showed that Mr. Hearst was an expert, for he was really one of the best judges of minerals I ever met.

Utah has furnished the mining industry with some very remarkably rich silver mines, among them the Eureka, in Tintick District; the Eureka Centennial; the Chrisman Mammoth, a large gold and silver mine, and the Beck and Hornsilver, in the Frisco District; the Crescent; the Daly, in Park City District; and Ontario, as well as a great many smaller mines in the various parts of Utah. In Montana we have one of the greatest copper mines in America, called the Anaconda. It is the leading mine in Butte City, though they have many other remarkable mines in that district. Then there is the Granite Mountain, the Drumlummen, in Marysville District, also in Montana. But the greatest output from any mine yet discovered was the Comstock, in Virginia City, Nev. It has produced more millions of dollars than any other silver mine in the United States, its output being about one-third gold. The mining industry of the Rocky Mountain States and Territories is only in a fair way for development. The State of Colorado furnishes some very rich mining camps; also New Mexico and Arizona.

In Colorado there is the Central City and Black Hawk, and the adjacent mining district, from which there has been millions of dollars in gold extracted; also the Leadville, which has produced its millions in silver and lead; the Aspen District, with its Molly Gibson and other immensely rich mines. Then there is the Crede District, with its Amethyst and others, now producing large amounts of silver and some gold; the Silverton, where there are a great many rich mines being opened; the Ouray District and Cripple Creek, a newly discovered gold camp, with various others in that State too numerous to mention. Nearly all of the entire mining camps of the State produce both gold and silver in greater or less proportions, and with more or less galena or lead contained in the ores with the precious metals, and this great mining industry, when it is allowed to go on as it did before the demonetization of silver, will prove to be among the greatest and best paying industries in the whole Rocky Mountain region.

The Black Hills mining district of South Dakota is a very large mining camp, where millions and millions of dollars in gold and silver have been taken out, and where, no doubt, hundreds of millions more will be produced.

Idaho has also proven to be a very rich State in mineral

wealth, both gold and silver, with many places where gold is washed out of the sands and gravel of the valleys.

Silver City, in New Mexico, has produced a great many millions in gold and silver, and at present seems to be a mining camp of great merit.

The mining industry of the mountains has, of course, been the means of influencing the building of numerous railroads through and into some of the most difficult mountain ranges; in fact wherever there has been a flourishing mining district the railway people have found a way, with capital behind them, to build a road to it, and it has now become apparent that a rich mining camp will have a railway connection sooner or later, no matter how difficult of access it may be. I think the men and the companies who have had the building of roads through and into the Rocky Mountains, and the interests of the country at heart, are deserving of great praise. No doubt, as many camps are discovered, it will be necessary to build many more roads than are now in existence, without which the mining industry could not be conducted with profit.

I may, in concluding this chapter on mining, speak of the great future there is for both Washington and Oregon as mineral States.

CHAPTER XXXIV.

IT IS still within the memory of boys when it was almost universally agreed that nothing was more impossible than successful fruit raising in Colorado, with the exception of certain varieties of small fruits. It is easy to see how such a belief grew up, for even now in many places it requires ocular demonstrations to convince that, in parched valleys where frequently even cactus and sage-brush are but sparsely represented, fruit can be grown that in lustrous bloom and richness of flavor can not be surpassed in any country or climate. That such is the case, however, has already been so thoroughly proven, and the proof is being so persistently repeated year after year, and in widely separated localities, that to longer disbelieve or cavil is sufficient evidence either of ignorance or determination not to believe.

When travelers first crossed the prairies and followed the sandy or adobe river bottoms they could hardly be expected to think of the barren tracts as covered with orchards and gardens within a few years. Yet there were indices even then, and had not every mind been wholly absorbed in the search for gold, some one might have drawn a lesson from the laden plum and cherry trees that lined every foot-hill, cañon, and ravine, sometimes following the stream far out on the prairie. In the mountains, too, were raspberry patches, sometimes covering thousands of acres and yielding almost incalculable quantities of luscious fruit that, having no more appreciative pickers than bears and birds, annually decayed among the rocks and fallen logs.

There were, and still are, countless numbers of huckleberries, and in every part of the mountains grow more or
less wild strawberries, raspberries, currants, gooseberries,
thimbleberries, huckleberries, and numerous varieties of
cherries, plums, and nuts. Considering these things it
would not have required a great stretch of imagination of
some old fruit man from the East to have foreseen something of the possibilities now beginning to be almost
phenomenally realized in every part of the State.

A history of horticulture in the Centennial State has not
yet been written, and it is impossible to say when and
where the first domestic fruit was grown, or to whom is
due the honor of having taken the initial step in the
industry that from its rapid development and the enthusiasm
already enlisted bids fair to outstrip all other pursuits in
the State. In rapidity the growth has been much like
that of our magic capital city, and as fruit is one of the
things with which a luxury-loving people will not dispense,
it may fairly be predicted that the infant industry, without
any protection or coddling, will keep pace with the State
and city.

It is not difficult to find good reasons for believing that
its progress will not only exceed that of any other industry
in the State, but that it will be out of proportion to that of
the State itself. Irrigating is an expensive process, and
whatever crop will bring the greatest return for the least
outlay in that direction is the one to which the energy of
the Colorado people should logically be directed. Not only
can fruit be raised with much less water than any other crop,
but a good yield in a single year after the trees are fairly
well developed will reimburse the purchase price of the land
and the other expenses, besides leaving a handsome profit.

If any one argues that only the southern half of the
State can be relied upon for fruit, a visit to Larimer County

18

will promptly and effectually convince him of his error. If he believes only in the western slope, let him follow the Arkansas River from several miles above Salida to where it enters Kansas, or the Platte from the foot-hills to Nebraska, examining the embryo orchards that enrich nearly every farm on his journey.

It is readily conceded that certain locations are, by nature, better adapted than others to certain kinds of fruits. To fit the varieties to the localities most suitable to their respective natures requires years of experiment. The fruit industry of Colorado is now in that experimental stage. To conduct the experiment so as to secure the best results, men of skill, long experience, and indomitable energy are necessary. Such men do not at present average one to the county. This fact does not reflect discredit on the men who are growing fruit. No one could realize the truth more fully than they do themselves. Hundreds of them who are succeeding with orchards scarcely knew one tree from another until they began putting them out on their farms.

The fact that so much has been accomplished without the experience and skill so essential to success in every country is the strongest possible evidence that the natural elements are here in the right combination and ready to do their part, and more, to win for the Centennial State a greater distinction as a fruit producer than has for years been hers as the silver queen. Just as sure as the conditions of climate and soil remain as they are, will this new industry eventually hold first place in every respect. In the immediate vicinity of the capital city, where only a few years ago was nothing but barren prairie, there are now hundreds of acres in orchards and vineyards. Apples, pears, plums, cherries, and numerous varieties of grapes are grown in abundance, and with such success that the fruit acreage is annually increasing. Up and down the Platte, on Cherry Creek and Clear Creek, on the prairie wherever water can be had for irrigating, farmers are putting out more and more in standard and small fruits. The never-failing demand for good fruit, to fill which California annually ships thousands of car-loads, is encouragement enough, for it insures good prices without the trouble and expense of shipment.

Westward the same conditions are manifest, and the limited area of tillable land shows a yearly increasing number of fruit trees. Here close to the foot-hills a single acre, mostly in cherry trees, has yielded a cash return of $1,000 from one year's crop just harvested. It is but a matter of a few years until many another acre will yield as much or more, either English Morello cherry trees, as in this case, or from other varieties of standard fruits.

Boulder County has long been known as the home of small fruits. Last year the county furnished 184,300 pounds of grapes and 304,810 quarts of berries. In a walk through the streets of Boulder more grapes of the finer varieties, such as Delaware, can be seen than in the market of any other city in the State, without excepting even Denver in the present year. Nor is the county's output confined to small fruits, for in last year's report were 25,622 bushels of apples, 102 of peaches, and 143 of pears, besides 4,745 quarts of plums and 1,905 of cherries.

The same condition prevails in all the counties in the northwest part of the State, though, with the exception of the Greeley neighborhood and the Platte Valley, the country is too recently settled to have made much progress in the culture of fruit. In the last few years the blight has been causing considerable discouragement in the Platte Valley and up the tributary streams in Larimer and Boulder counties. Like other diseases, it has struck hard in a few spe-

T

cially valuable places, and in the riot of its march has caused
more annoyance through fear than through actual ravages.
It may thin out a few susceptible varieties of trees, but
when it shall have run its course, the orchards that remain
and those that will grow up in the future will be practically impregnable to its attacks.   There are many varieties of fruits that will flourish just as well as apples and
pears, and which the blight never touches.   Men who are
ready to drop the business when the fruit pest appears are
not the ones who will win success.   Many of the trees
from which the finest apples are picked this year were
badly blighted last year or the year before.

CHAPTER XXXV

THERE are thousands, if not millions, of people in the United States who, if asked how they accounted for the fact that there are so many millionaires in the United States, could not give us a satisfactory explanation of the phenomenon.

It is a fact that there are hundreds who have amassed fortunes ranging from $1,000,000 to $100,000,000 each, within the last thirty years, and but very few people have any idea how they have made such immense fortunes in so short a time.

Not only our own people have made these vast fortunes, but hundreds of foreigners have accumulated immense wealth in this country, and now hold it. To give an idea of the immensity of these fortunes, I will call the attention of the reader to some well-known facts. First, to the fact, as is shown by Poor's Railroad Manual, that there is now about $5,500,000,000 of railroad bonds and floating debt, and there is about $4,500,000,000 of railroad stock, making a total of about $10,000,000,000, and this vast wealth is in the hands of comparatively few people.

Then there are national bonds to the amount of about $600,000,000. In addition to these are the bonds that have been issued by the States, counties, cities, towns, and school districts, amounting in the aggregate to probably $3,000,000,000. Then there are, according to the last census, about 9,000,000 of mortgages upon the farms, homes, and property of the people. The aggregate of these 9,000,000 of mortgages is probably not less than $5,000,-000,000, and all of this vast amount of bonds, stocks, and mortgages draw interest, requiring about $1,000,000,000 each year to pay interest.

All of this wealth is in the hands of but a small percentage of the people, and what is incomprehensible to the masses is the fact that a very large per cent of it is in the hands of foreign capitalists. Of the $10,000,000,000 of railroad bonds and stocks, it is a conservative estimate to say that one-half of it belongs to foreign, principally English, capitalists. The question is often asked, How did they acquire this property? What did they give us in exchange for it? Was it gold, silver, or merchandise? If neither of these, what did we get? To prove that they did not send us either gold, silver, or merchandise in payment for at least $5,000,000,000 of our railroad bonds, we have only to refer to the report of the Secretary of the United States Treasury for 1891, and we find that since the close of the war, in 1865, our exports of gold, silver, and merchandise have exceeded our imports in the sum of $872,000,000; so that it is very clear that we have been sending them an enormous amount of money and merchandise over and above the amount we have imported from them, and whatever may have been received from the railroad bonds is still to be accounted for. To understand how they have acquired this hold upon the resources of the country, imposing a burden on the people that is surely and certainly reducing them to the condition of paupers and serfs, we shall have to go back to the days of the war, and review the financial policy of the Government, and point out how the laws have been framed exclusively in the interest of capital.

During the war the Government issued many kinds of paper money, such as greenbacks, seven-thirty notes, one-year notes, compound-interest notes, and one, two, and three year notes, all amounting to nearly \$2,000,000,000. This money was put in circulation by paying it out at its full face value to the soldiers, sailors, and creditors of the United States, but the Government would not receive it back in payment of duties upon imports, but would receive it from any one who wished to purchase five-twenty Government bonds, taking it at its face value.

The interest on these bonds was 6 per cent, payable in coin. This continued until February, 1863, when the laws were enacted that provided that after July 1, 1863, the paper money should not be received in exchange for bonds having interest payable in coin. The result of this was that shortly after the law went into effect the paper issued by the Government rapidly depreciated, and very soon it was worth only about 40 cents on the dollar, but our soldiers were still compelled to take it at its full face value, that is, 100 cents on the dollar.

At the close of the war, in 1865, our Government issued many hundreds of millions of their depreciated paper and paid it out to the soldiers, sailors, and other creditors of the Government at its full face value, 100 cents on the dollar.

After the soldiers had been paid off in the depreciated currency of the Government, and it had gone into general circulation, one of the most gigantic schemes ever concocted by the money-power was then devised.

The object was to destroy the money of the country, and issue in its place many hundreds of millions of dollars of Government bonds drawing 6 per cent interest in coin, payable semi-annually.

During the winter of 1865–66, an agent of the Rothschilds went to Washington and secured the enactment of a law providing that any person might take any of the depreciated paper that had been issued by the Government for the purpose of paying off the soldiers and the other expenses of the war, and exchange it at its full face value for bonds of the United States drawing 6 per cent interest in coin, payable semi-annually, and that the money paid for such bonds should be destroyed within three years after the close of the war. By this means nearly $1,000,000,000 of the currency of the country was withdrawn from circulation and destroyed, and an equal amount of 6 per cent coin bonds were issued in place of the currency that was so destroyed.

No laws that were ever enacted, and no decrees that were ever promulgated by any tyrant that ever sat upon a throne, ever enabled a few to amass wealth as rapidly as they were enabled to do under the provisions of these laws.

Under the provisions of the laws of 1863 the currency was depreciated to less than 50 cents on the dollar, and under the law of 1866 hundreds of millions of dollars were bought up by the Rothschilds and other English and European bankers, at from 40 to 60 cents on the dollar, and were converted into five-twenty United States bonds drawing 6 per cent interest in coin, the interest to be paid semi-annually. This was equivalent to 12 per cent upon the actual cash paid for the depreciated paper with which they bought the bonds.

But this was only a part of the profit they were enabled to make. The interest was paid every six months in gold. The interest on $1,500,000,000 every six months was $45,000,000, and as the law that required the duties on imports to be paid in coin had never been repealed, gold was for many years at a high premium. The bondholders could take their $45,000,000 every six months to the gold-room in Wall Street and sell it for 50 per cent premium.

This was equivalent to 9 per cent on the face value of the bonds and 18 per cent on the coin they had paid for the currency with which they had bought the bonds.

But this was not all the profit they were enabled to make, for still other laws had been framed in the interests of capital and speculators.

Congress had assumed all the power that was claimed by the kings of old who claimed to rule by divine right; that is to give away the land of the nation to whomsoever they saw proper, and exempt it from all taxation for a term of years.   In the exercise of this right they had given to individuals and corporations more land than there is in Great Britain; more land, in fact, than any king of England ever claimed to own.   This land was given for the purpose of enabling these favored corporations to build railroads for themselves (not for the people); the people had no interest in the roads, and could only use them on such terms as the railroad companies might dictate.

Railroad companies could not build railroads with land; it took money to build them; but the English bondholders had $50,000,000 or $60,000,000 coming in every six months for interest on their United States bonds, and they were willing to lend it to the railroad companies and take railroad bonds, secured by mortgage upon the railroad and their lands.   Now, as there were a great many railroad companies that wanted to borrow money, they began to offer extra inducements to secure loans; they offered their bonds at 10, 15, and often 20 per cent discount.   These railroad bonds usually drew 6, 7, and even 8 per cent interest, which was paid semi-annually.   The profits made by these English capitalists were immense.   Never in the world's history had such profits been made.   The wildest dreams of John Law and the South Sea schemers were more than realized.

To fully understand this, let us take the actual results of one year's operations. The English capitalists, we will say, in 1867, invested $500,000,000 in the purchase of $1,000,-000,000 of our depreciated currency. They took it to the United States Treasurer and exchanged it for United States bonds drawing 6 per cent interest in coin. At the end of six months they drew $30,000,000 in gold coin, and took it to the gold-room and sold it for $45,000,000 in greenbacks. Then they exchanged their greenbacks for railroad bonds at 20 per cent discount. They would thus receive about $54,000,000 of railroad bonds drawing 7 per cent interest. At the end of the next six months they would draw another $30,000,000 in coin and sell it for $45,000,000 in greenbacks, and exchange them for another $54,000,000 in railroad bonds. They would also draw 7 per cent interest on the first $54,000,000 of railroad bonds, which, for six months, would be $1,840,000. The account of the first year would stand as follows: $500,000,000 in gold brought $1,000,000,000 of depreciated currency, and was exchanged for $1,000,000,000 of United States bonds; one year's interest on $1,000,000,000 amounted to $60,000,-000. This was sold in the gold-room for $90,000,000 in greenbacks. Then the greenbacks were exchanged for railroad bonds at 20 per cent discount on the bonds. In this way at the end of the first year, for their investment of $500,000,000, they found themselves in possession of $1,000,000,000 of United States bonds, and $108,000,000 of railroad bonds, and $1,840,000 in cash for the first six months' interest on the first $54,000,000 of railroad bonds. Nor was this all the profit of the English capitalists, for in 1869 they secured the passage of a law by Congress pledging the Government to pay not only the interest but the principal of the United States bonds in coin. This rapidly increased the value of the bonds, and in a few years they were eagerly sought for by English capitalists, and they rose to a premium of 25 per cent in gold on their full face value.

Within five years after the passage of the law of 1866, the bonded debt of the United States reached the sum of over $1,800,000,000. The interest was paid in coin, and was sold in the gold-room in Wall Street at a premium until 1878, and the profits realized upon the sale of this gold were simply enormous. These profits were promptly invested in railroad bonds at a discount of from 5 to 25 per cent.

In 1866 the bonded indebtedness of the railroads had got up to $2,165,000,000, and was in the hands principally of English capitalists, who had paid for them with the prof-its they had made on the United States bonds they had bought at a discount of from 40 to 60 per cent.

Not only the British capitalists made enormous profits, but our railroad corporations and speculators made still greater profits. For every dollar of the bonds they sold to the English capitalists they issued a dollar or more of the railroad stocks, so that in 1876 the amount of railroad stock reached the sum of $2,248,000,000.

From 1876 to 1890 the English and European capitalists continued to invest the interest they drew upon their Government and railroad bonds in the new issues of railroad bonds, so that, in 1890, they had secured the enormous sum of $4,828,000,000 of railroad bonds, and it took $219,877,000 to pay the interest annually. During the same time the railroads had increased the amount of railroad stock to $4,495,000,000 and it took $80,000,000 to pay the dividends.

The railroad people not only made vast fortunes out of the $4,495,000,000 of watered stock (for it was in reality nothing but water, for the actual cost of building the roads was no more than was received from the sale of their bonds to the English capitalists), but they made hundreds of millions of dollars from the sale of the lands that had been given to them by the Government, and had not cost them one cent, not even for taxes. They ran their roads through their lands for thousands of miles, and wherever they thought proper they would lay out towns and cities and sell the lots at fabulous prices.

They also induced towns, counties, and cities to issue millions of dollars of bonds and give to the companies, as a bonus, to run their roads through such towns and cities.

When we look at these facts, that are matters of history and can not be gainsaid, is it not plain to every man of common sense, that the policy of the Government for the last quarter of a century has been in the interest of capitalists and speculators, and against the interest of the producing classes, who, either directly or indirectly, must pay the interest annually on this vast accumulation of wealth that is in the hands of the favored few?

And to pay this vast amount of interest in gold, as these capitalists insist upon, and are trying to compel the people to do by using every means in their power to prevent the free and unlimited coinage of silver, will, in the near future, reduce the producing classes to the condition of serfs.

CHAPTER XXXVI.

The " Bonanza " State, young as she is to-day, has more towns and cities than such old and well developed States as Wisconsin, Illinois, or Minnesota had at a period in their history at which they might easily have expected to be far better developed, as regards population, than Montana could reasonably expect.

A half-century marks the time when the great Chicago of to-day was Fort Dearborn, planted, as it were, on a boundless prairie to watch a few blanketed Indians and traders at the mouth of the Chicago River. This was the nucleus of the great city—the second in rank of the many wonderful cities of the United States. Fifty years ago the pioneers of the Badger and Prairie States were doing what the old-timers and pioneers of Montana are doing to-day, building towns and founding cities. In the Eastern pioneer States where a few straggling hamlets were first fashioned by the efforts of the early emigrants, there are thousands of towns and cities, where the unpretentious log cabins and town sites were no more inviting than those of the early settlers of Montana.

Dating the first settlement of our State at twenty-eight years ago, it may be said, without contradiction, that no Eastern State from its foundation to the twenty-eighth year of its age was half so marked or half so prosperous as Montana, with her hundred towns and cities at no greater age. If the State of Illinois has produced a Chicago at fifty years of growth, and Wisconsin a Milwaukee at a less number of years, and Minnesota the dual cities of St. Paul and Minneapolis in a much shorter time, what may not be expected of Montana, whose boundaries embrace probably the richest country in the world, and whose area equals that of the New England States and New York combined?

We see with open eyes what a half-century of American genius and Western enterprise has wrought; may we not see by a prophetic vision a grander half-century's work as the future of Montana? As certain as history repeats itself, the prospector's wickie-up will become the mining camp, the corral of the round-ups will furnish the location for rustic villages, the villages will become towns, and scores of towns will become cities, each one of which must be larger than the other, and one of which must be the great metropolis of the Northwest.

Following is a list of the towns and cities of the State, arranged in counties, together with the assessed valuation of those counties:

BEAVERHEAD COUNTY.—Assessed valuation for 1890, $3,175,949. County seat, Dillon; Bannack, Glendale, Red-rock, Spring Hill, Barratts.

CASCADE COUNTY.—Assessed valuation, $12,383,864. County seat, Great Falls; Sun River, Cascade, Sand Coulee.

CHOTEAU COUNTY.—Assessed valuation, $5,364,264. County seat, Fort Benton; Chinook, Choteau, Harlem, Shonkin.

CUSTER COUNTY.—Assessed valuation, $6,350,915. County seat, Miles City; Rosebud, Forsyth.

DAWSON COUNTY.—Assessed valuation, $3,025,332. County seat, Glendive; Glasgow.

DEER LODGE COUNTY.—Assessed valuation, $7,359,589. County seat, Deer Lodge; Anaconda, Beartown, Blackfoot, Drummond, Phillipsburg, Elliston, Granite, Helmville, New Chicago, Pioneer, Warm Springs, Stuart.

FERGUS COUNTY.—Assessed valuation, $4,186,555. County seat, Lewiston; Cottonwood, Utica, Maiden, Neihart.

GALLATIN COUNTY.—Assessed valuation, $6,170,381. County seat, Bozeman; Three Forks, Gallatin, Galesville, Madison.

JEFFERSON COUNTY.—Assessed valuation, $4,917,382. County seat, Boulder; Jefferson City, Radersburg, Basin, Placer, Elkhorn, Whitehall, Alhambra, Clancy.

LEWIS AND CLARKE COUNTY.—Assessed valuation, $31,081,030. County seat, Helena; Marysville, Unionville, Rimini, Cartersville, Augusta, Dearborn, Harlow.

MADISON COUNTY.—Assessed valuation, $2,948,046. County seat, Virginia City; Fullers Springs, Sheridan, Twin Bridges, Laurin, Silver Star, Pony, Red Bluff, Meadow Creek.

MEAGHER COUNTY.—Assessed valuation, $5,239,882. County seat, White Sulphur Springs; Neihart, Castle, Martinsdale, Townsend, Clendennin, York.

MISSOULA COUNTY.—Assessed valuation $8,815,854. County seat, Missoula; Demersville, Kalispel, Stevensville, Columbia Falls, Ashley, Grantsdale, Corvallis, Horse Plains, Thompson Falls, Camas Prairie.

PARK COUNTY.—Assessed valuation, $4,936,451. County seat, Livingston; Red Lodge, Cook City, Cokedale, Big Timber, Melville.

SILVER BOW COUNTY.—Assessed valuation, $32,426,794. County seat, Butte City; Melrose, Silver Bow, Divide.

YELLOWSTONE COUNTY.—Assessed valuation, $3,823,140. County seat, Billings; Park City, Stillwater.

WEALTH OF MONTANA.—Nothing speaks louder for the future of Montana than the figures that tell of her wealth and of the rapid increases which the last few years, as they rolled along one by one, have shown.

The increase during the last year has been no exception to this rule.

From a total assessable valuation of $116,767,204 in 1890, her wealth has increased to a total of $142,205,428 for 1891, a gain of over twenty-five millions. The valuation of the State, given by counties, is as follows:

County of	Beaverhead	$ 3,175,949
"	" Cascade	12,383,864
"	" Choteau	5,364,264
"	" Custer	6,350,915
"	" Dawson	3,025,332
"	" Deer Lodge	7,359,589
"	" Fergus	4,186,555
"	" Gallatin	6,170,381
"	" Jefferson	4,917,382
"	" Lewis and Clarke	31,081,030
"	" Madison	2,948,046
"	" Meagher	5,239,882
"	" Missoula	8,815,854
"	" Park	4,936,451
"	" Silver Bow	32,426,794
"	" Yellowstone	3,823,140
	Total	$142,205,428

But even this vast sum does not tell the whole story, for Montana's additional real wealth is not included in the assessable property of the State, as the vast millions of the intrinsic value of the silver, gold, copper, coal, and lead mines, and their precious output, are not assessable for taxation—only the improvements. So if the value of all of Montana's mines were put in the calculation of her wealth, what a vast amount of money-value would be placed to her credit. Of the hundreds of her gold and silver mines, two are valued at $25,000,000 each.

The above assessment value of $142,205,428 is made up of real estate, acre property, town lots, railroad rolling stock, road-bed and improvements, and personal property.

Montana's present ratio of population is not quite one person to the square mile, so with an assessment of over $142,000,000 with a population (according to the census of 1892) at 140,000, what will be the value of the State when its population shall have increased to ten persons to the square mile? The calculation is easily made—so within the next decade Montana's population may reach 1,440,000, and if the assessed value then is equal to the present wealth per capita of her citizens, the assessed value will reach the prodigious volume of $1,203,000,000—a calculation not unreasonable, since Montana's population in the last ten years increased 235 per cent.

CHAPTER XXXVII.

NOT only is California the land of gold, the garden of fruit, and the home of the vine, but its rich soil is the footing for the greatest trees in the world. The redwoods of California are known all over the earth, and their fame is deserved, for they are the loftiest, the grandest trees that ever raised their crests to heaven, swayed in the breeze, and defied the storm. Though usually spoken of as the redwoods, these big trees are of two varieties. The redwood proper is the *Sequoia sempervirens* of the botanist, and the sister tree is the great Washington *Sequoia*, Wellington *Sequoia*, or *Sequoia gigantea*, being known by all three names, the last being the most correct. Another forest giant of a different nature to either, and yet commanding attention, on account of its giant size and age, is the *Pinus lambertiana*, the great sugar-pine of California. These three are the greatest trees on earth.

To single out the largest individual tree, it is probable that the *Sequoia sempervirens* would have to be awarded the palm; while to the greatest number of very large trees, the palm would have to be awarded to the *Sequoia gigantea*. Redwood trees (*Sequoia sempervirens*) are found only on the Coast Range, and *Sequoia giganteas* only in the Sierra Nevada Mountains. There are no redwoods south of Monterey County or north of Trinity County. The trees are different in foliage, and in their cones the *Sequoia gigantea* has a larger, more compact, firm cone than the *Sequoia sempervirens*, the cone of which is small and split open, though the similarity in form of the cones is noticeable. It is not generally known that "*sequoia*" is the name of the *genus*, just like oak, cypress, maple, and hence that the *gigantea* and *sempervirens* are species of the same *genus*. The name *sequoia* comes from *Sequoyah*, a Cherokee Indian chief of mixed blood, whose wisdom raised him as much above his fellows as the redwoods tower above other trees.

As to the age of the trees, it is conceded by botanists that the concentric rings interpret their annual growth. Objection has been taken to this on the ground that the distance between the rings varies very much in different trees of the same species. This fact has, however, no weight. The closer the rings the thriftier the tree, and their distance apart has no more to do with their age than a man's height or weight have to do with his age. Differences in soil and location account for the closeness of the rings, but, unquestionably, every added ring represents an added year of growth. In some cases there are but six or eight rings to the inch, in others thirty to forty. The ages of the big trees in the Calaveras and Mariposa groves range from 1,000 to 4,320 years of age. One can scarcely conceive what this means; and the historic incidents of the days when these trees were already old may help to convey an idea of their age. When Carthage was founded some of these trees were centuries old; before Solomon built his temple, or David founded Judea, some of these forest giants fell crashing to earth, and have lain prone there ever since. All through the ages of Christianity the changing winds have shaken their tapering tops, and have swayed their crests in the gentle zephyrs, or rocked them to and fro in the gale, and now man, the pigmy, with his piece of jagged steel, his span of life three score years and ten, comes along, cuts through the forest giant, and the growth

U

of thousands of years, that has defied storm and tempest, falls a victim to the pigmy.

The largest stump extant is in Mill Valley, Marin County, half an hour's ride north of San Francisco. This remnant of a great tree belongs to the redwood family; is, in fact, a genuine *Sequoia sempervirens.* How high it may have been it is impossible to say. Its circumference now is 135 feet, and measures across, on an average, 43 feet 6 inches. The saplings which stand round the ruin measure from 3 to 10 feet in diameter. The largest standing tree is the "Mother of the Forest," in the Calaveras grove. It now measures, without the bark, at the base 84 feet, and the full circumference, with the bark, which was stripped off in 1854 for exhibition purposes, was 90 feet. Its height is 321 feet, and the tree is estimated to contain 537,000 feet of inch lumber, allowing for saw cuts. Close to it, prone upon mother earth, lies the "Father of the Forest." When standing, it is accredited with having been 400 feet high, with a circumference at the base of 110 feet, and he unquestionably was once king of the grove. "The living and representative trees of the Calaveras groves," says J. M. Hutchings, in "The Heart of the Sierras," "consist of ten that are each 30 feet in diameter, and over seventy that measure from 15 to 30 feet at the ground." About six miles to the southeast of the Calaveras grove (in Calaveras County, Cal.) is the South grove. It contains 1,380 *Sequoias,* ranging from 1 foot to 34 feet in diameter.

In the Mariposa grove, in Mariposa County, Cal., there are many large trees, among them the "Grizzly Giant," measuring 91 feet at the ground, and 74 feet 6 inches three feet six inches above the ground, and is 275 feet high. Many very large trees and many interesting facts might be mentioned relative to them.

The *Sequoia gigantea* in the Sierras, in addition to the differences in cone and flower from the *Sequoia sempervirens*, has this one that, while the former grows only from seeds, the latter grows from both seeds and suckers, though mainly from the latter. The *Sequoias* of the Sierras rise to a height of 275 or even 350 feet, and are from 20 to 30, or even in rare cases 40 feet in diameter.

CHAPTER XXXVIII.

For centuries the rose—the queen of flowers—has been a never ceasing inspiration to poets and writers. Every bard has sung his lay to the majesty of this peerless flower.

Every ancient country has its rose traditions. Fashions do not assail the rose, only in specialty and variety.

The unanimity characterizing its nomenclature is but another feature in the unvarying and universal popularity of the rose.

All research fails to reveal the white rose as known to the ancients; the Greek word "rodon," ruddy, being used synonymously by all countries.

It was the flower dedicated to love—to Cupid and Venus. Cupid bestowed it as an emblem upon Harpocrates, the god of silence, to bind him not to betray the evil of his mother, Venus. In consequence the rose became symbolical of silence, and was gracefully distributed on the guest-table as a delicate reminder that all confidences should be respected. Comus, deity of the table, Hebe and Ganymede, nectar-bearers to the gods, were crowned with roses. The rose is typical of youth as well as beauty.

During the greatest opulency of the ancient empires its purity was often sullied by effeminacy and sensuality.

Who has not heard of the roses of the valley of Cashmere? Who has not longed to behold their exquisite perfection? Who, in contemplating the forms and colors, the lights and shadows of Flora's choicest blooms, has not found language failing in fineness to express the delicate eloquence of the rose? Who, in cultivating it, has not felt solicitude and affection for these creatures of the garden? Who has not had his anger excited in beholding a bud ruthlessly torn by sacrilegious hands and has not looked upon the broken stem as he would upon a bleeding artery? Who, in cultivating roses, has not spiritually felt the better for it? The subtlety of its fragrance, the grace of its form, the perfect harmony of its tones appeal to the imagination like music to the soul. In the whole range of nature's variety and completeness nothing so satisfies the idea of perfection as the rose. 'Tis grace idealized and the quintessence of beauty in its flowing lines and curves.

The relative position of the rose to its stem suggests majesty; its color in contrast to its leaves, completeness; the unfolding of its petals, grace; its tintings fulfill that esthetic delight, harmony; its fragrance, the sublimated breath of a fairer existence. In all candor, does it not more than satisfy the degree superlative?

Nature has richly endowed the earth with roses. Every country can offer its wild-rose tributes on Flora's shrine, with but one single exception, and that Australia. There are over eighty varieties of the wild rose known, the greater number being indigenous to Asia.

With experimenting and cultivating, varieties of roses have multiplied by hundreds; and rose culture, like everything else in this nineteenth century, has become a science.

Roses are like children, requiring warmth and affection. In a mild climate, where the seasons do not vary greatly in regard to temperature, the rose outvies tradition itself, and unfolds and matures with a regularity quite astonishing.

California climate is nature's elected home for roses. In almost any portion of the State removed from the immediate harsh influences of the coast, roses revel, from the tiniest boutonniere rose, with its pert little face, to that great lusty fellow, big as a large saucer and as hardy as a cabbage.

To the old residents, no rose in California appeals more to the poetical sense than the old Castilian, one of the oldest varieties in the State, and one now greatly despised by its more fortunate and voluptuous sisters. The fragrance of this rose is incomparable, its color an intense glowing old pink, its foliage painfully disappointing. Having such a vigorous and healthy trunk and lusty system of roots, the Castilian is employed largely to graft other stock upon.

An ideal climate should produce nothing but ideal forms. This natural and just hypothesis is amply proven in presenting the full array of California roses as evidence. What better class of evidence could be desired?

There are several general groups into which California roses are usually divided: Tea roses, Bourbon roses, hybrid perpetual roses, China or Bengal roses, moss and climbing roses.

Of these classes, but several can be mentioned. Roses, as a theme, are practically inexhaustible, and the few kinds that appeal most strongly to the writer's sympathies will receive a passing word.

A rose-covered cottage, the material expression of peace, lowliness, beauty, and picturesqueness; a picture that most of us mirror in our minds in youth as connected with great and simple happiness. Many of the old Spanish houses of California are overrun with climbing roses. These old houses, simple in style of architecture, broad and square in appearance, are inviting abodes for the clinging loveliness of California's climbers.

Some fine April morning take a little trip to San Rafael, one of San Francisco's suburban villages. In this hill-girth town blooms the fairest rose of all the climbers. Some call it the "San Rafael Rose," others the "Beauty of Blazenwood."

The trunk rises bare and sturdily from the ground; as it approaches the top of a porch it spreads and bursts forth into a cloud of tawny yellow loveliness. Each rose presses hard upon its neighbor until special fancy is lost in the bewildering mass of bloom.

In this rose, the palest cream tint to the richest glowing apricot tones are observable. Frequently here a dash of color almost vermilion is discovered; there a long slender-necked bud thrusts forth its head, as in derision to its closely-packed companions.

These roses are not very double, and a mass of their bloom presents features of ragged, wild grace; the vivid colors enthrall, hasty steps are slackened to gaze at this golden corona of smiling April.

The brilliant William Allen Richardson, the mellow-toned and sweet-breathed Salina Forrester, the lusty-growing and superb bearing Reve d'Or, the daintily flowering and enameled-leaved single white Cherokee, the prolific blooming and tiny-flowered Lady Banksia, and California's old stand-by, the Lamarque, a profusely bearing, many petaled white rose, perfect in all stages of development, and very handsome foliage.

In many of the old towns of California may be seen rose trees of really enormous size.

The writer saw a Duchesse de Brabant rose tree in Colusa County at least nine feet high and thirty feet or more in circumference. It was covered with hundreds of silvery pink roses; the trunk looked scraggy, and was probably twelve inches in circumference. Such a case is rare, however.

The Loretta is a rose of exquisite texture, of a creamy

tone, and petals as clear-cut and dainty as a cameo. Too much praise can not be showered upon this long-stemmed vigorous grower. Such a galaxy of beautiful roses, each clamoring for recognition, that the only way to render justice is to stop right short and write nothing more.

The La France roses, Perle de Gardin, Marie Van Houtte, Archduc, Charles Catharine Mermet, Homer, Papa Gontier, Jacqueminot, and hundreds of others that nothing short of a book can satisfy their vanity and express their many graces.

The western coast of Europe and the western coast of America have about the same annual mean temperature—50° Fahrenheit, with a limit of 51° 30″ of north latitude.

The Pacific Coast has greatly the advantage over western Europe, in that the extremes of heat and cold are nearer together, a characteristic that is attributable to two paramount causes: Firstly, the Japanese current emanating from the Indian Ocean. The main body of this heated water sweeps toward the west coast of America, turns easterly and southerly, helping to produce a delightful insular climate along the coast of Oregon and California. Secondly, the mountain barriers upon the east and north; the sheltering influences of the Sierra Nevadas and Cascade mountains as they reach the coast of Alaska encircling its southern and western coasts, thus cutting off the polar winds that would otherwise flow over Oregon and California.

The State possesses three distinct climates, that of the coast, valleys, and mountains, similar in the matter of seasons, but otherwise totally dissimilar.

Degrees of latitude have no bearing upon fruit culture in California, for it is an ascertained fact that fruits ripen earlier in the north than in the south of the State.

Horticulture and geographical situations have nothing

in common. In other regions one is quite dependent upon the other, but in California horticulture laughs at geographical boundaries.

These surprising conditions depend wholly upon topography, and consist not in parallels of latitude, but by topographical curves varying in direction and governed by deposit and natural formation, altitude, rainfall, and temperature.

What is known as the Citrus Belt of California is a great valley lying between the Coast Range on the west and the Sierra Nevadas on the east, and runs in a direction northwest to southeast, and extends from Red Bluff on the north to the Tejon Mountains on the south. The total area is about 17,200 square miles. This great valley contains about one-half of all the fruit trees and a third of all the vines in the State. Within the limits of this belt to the northernmost boundaries, in favored spots the orange flourishes side by side with the apple.

Immense tracts of this great valley are used for agricultural and pasturage purposes, and, as yet, orchards occupy but an insignificant area of this immense valley.

Several characteristics of the California climate and soil conjoin not only to produce glorious flowers, both wild and cultivated, but the greatest possible variety of fruits and berries. The abundant heat, almost perennial sunshine, and dry atmosphere, together with the fine adaptability of the soil and the great length of the growing season, join forces to produce fruits of superior size and excellence. The trees are amazingly prolific bearers, and also produce mammoth fruit.

All conscientious horticulturists resort to the "thinning out" process in order to preserve the quality and size of what they allow to remain on the trees.

The fruit industry in California, in spite of the immense

crops matured every year, is but in its infancy. Millions of trees and vines are not yet in bearing, or only yielding third, fourth, and fifth year crops.

Since the formation of the Fruit Growers' Union in 1881, when the first law was enacted to protect California horticulturists, there has been steady progress and practical expenditure of brains and money to further the interests, in every way possible, of the fruit growers of California.

Horticulture has been reduced to a science by disseminating knowledge and a hearty coöperation of fruit growers to extend the interests of the State in every way possible.

The history of horticulture in the State of California almost up to the present time has been one of experimenting, ascertaining the adaptability of the soil to certain kinds of fruits, and testing what European and Eastern trees do well in this climate, for many varieties make utter failures, while others are improved beyond recognition.

Californians have had to learn also that a horticultural precedent has been established here, independent of what obtains in other countries. Although ideas and methods have been gleaned from abroad, application to local and special needs have metamorphosed them to a great extent. Hap-hazard planting in California is humbug unless wedded to Yankee shrewdness.

Know your soil and its elements, the atmosphere, heat, and moisture and exposure; then ascertain what fruits do well under those limitations.

Clear your land, plow and sow a crop of something to mellow up the soil, the next year plant your young trees. Climate will be your fellow-worker and steadfast friend. Nine-twelfths of the year a man can sit down and watch nature work. The man who complains of climate in California should be banished from this paradise, for even the golden fruit of Hesperides would be but clay to one whose birthright is discontent.

What will constitute California's future glory will be the division of the lands into small holdings of from twenty acres up to about two hundred acres; where owners give their personal supervision; where the excellence of the fruits should be the consideration, over and above the profits; where men who resort to practices in the business that cheapen the standard of fruits should be forced out of the market; where every man works for the good of the whole; where the pride of the horticulturist, and not the greed of the speculator, obtains, and where the specialist and student flourish. If these conditions will not make California the greatest fruit-producing country on earth, then human ingenuity is at fault, and not climate.

Many a tourist in coming to San Francisco, and it might be said it is the exception when it is not so, has wondered if California fruits can make no better showing than the sour, half-ripened fruit he partakes of; last, but not least, the prices he pays for this fruit are so incredulously high that he wonders if it can be possible he can be eating imported fruit, and not the production of the California soil. Then he compares his experience here with that abroad; at the forts along the Mediterranean for a cent or two he can entirely satisfy a robust appetite with luscious fruit.

California fruit growers are so busy at present over their export trade that home consumption is relegated to the leavings, under the same principle a cobbler's children have no shoes.

Great things are expected of the olive industry of this State. Although the last returns showed but little over eleven thousand gallons of oil from the last crop, there are thousands upon thousands of young trees not yet in bearing. The oil produced is of a superior quality, and leads the sanguine to believe that the olive crown will yet rest upon our brows.

Fruit curing is, and will continue to be, one of the first industries of the State. The figures for the season just passed will aggregate 48,700,000 pounds of dried fruit, nearly four-fifths of which will represent French prunes; this is but a mere bagatelle to what the crop will be several years hence.

The prune industry is centered in Santa Clara County; the biggest prune orchard in the State is now in the Salinas Valley, San Luis Obispo County. In this orchard there are 300 acres of prune trees planted in a body, representing 324,000 trees. Prune trees make such quick returns, four-year-old trees bear heavily.

All temperate zone and semi-tropical fruits are raised with equal facility. Berries do superbly; strawberries, however, are too often forced.

Fruits in California, where irrigation methods are too much employed, depreciate in quality; the fine flavor is sacrificed for the early ripening—a too frequent method of producers, that should be cried down. Flavor is what makes fine fruit. Size and beauty do much in their way, but flavor is the nectar of the gods. Size and beauty constitute the shell, flavor is the subtle spirit that animates it.

In many localities the orchards are merely cultivated, that is, plowed and harrowed three or four times a year, but never irrigated artificially. In portions of the State where midsummer irrigation is required, and where the country presents a level surface, as in Yolo County, whole orchards are flooded with an abundant supply of water.

The raisin of late years has received a greater impetus than any other fruit in the State. The ease with which raisin vines are propagated, the early profits, immense crops, and excellent prices induce hundreds to engage in the industry.

About a thousand acres are set to raisin vines. Fresno County is the center of this industry. Over 50,000,000 pounds were produced this year, and one-third only of the vines are in bearing.

The orange crop was enormous; lemons, figs, apricots, nuts, pears, peaches, and cherries each and all have made excellent records for themselves.

The shipping record for the year 1890 was 16,191 car-loads, which would make a continuous train of cars 123 miles long.

The report of the State Board of Horticulture says: "It is a significant fact that while our wheat output has not materially increased from 1880 to 1890, our fruit output has increased more than thirty times, and is growing with great rapidity. While the showing here made still keeps California in the front rank of wheat-growing States, being third in the rank, it demonstrates the great advantages of the State as a fruit-producing country.

"In 1880 our exports of fruit brought us probably about $700,000, while they now amount to about $20,000,000. This wonderful result has brought with it what is above all computation, to wit: the demonstration that fruit-growing in this State is very profitable, and is almost absolutely safe from frosts and other drawbacks, and has practically no limit."

CHAPTER XXXIX.

It is a mistake to believe that, because Colorado has a high elevation, the mercury in the thermometer drops down below zero in the winter season and stops there, and that the snow mounts up with the altitude. The fact is that the average precipitation of moisture at Denver during the entire year is only 14.77 inches. With such a slight precipitation there is practically no danger of snow blockades on the railroads, save at a few points exposed to drifts, and these points have been amply protected. This is especially true of the through line of the Denver & Rio Grande Railroad from Denver to Salt Lake City and Ogden.

Facts speak louder than words, and the fact is that travel over " the Scenic Line of the World " has gone on with less interruption from snow during the last five winters than it has on the plains lines, which are popularly supposed to be more free from such delays than the mountain systems.

A winter's residence in Colorado will banish forever the false impression that this is a boreal region, given over to inclemency and snow-drifts. There is more sunshine in Colorado than in Florida; there is less snow than in any State east of the Missouri River. A single trip over the Denver & Rio Grande Railroad from Denver to Ogden, in midwinter, will disabuse the mind of the tourist or transcontinental traveler of the erroneous notion that mountain railroads suffer from delays by snow to any greater extent than do the trains upon the less attractive, and by far more bleak, plains.

The glories and pleasures of a summer trip by rail through the Rocky Mountains have been lauded *ad infinitum*, and, indeed, too much can not be said in this direction; but winter adds new grandeur to the scene, lends a new charm to the massive bulwarks of the gigantic ranges, and introduces a new element of variety and beauty to these unsurpassed and unsurpassable wonders of nature. These sights can be enjoyed, these wonders witnessed, with no dangers of delay and no anticipation of vexatious detentions. There are those, however, who, knowing that the Denver & Rio Grande Railroad climbs great passes over the mountains, are apprehensive of snow blockades at these points. Here facts come to the rescue. The trains are not delayed, for the exposed places of this character have been amply protected, and the experiences of years prove that delay of trains from snow is a rarer event on this mountain-climbing system than on the level, and in fact more exposed, lines of the East.

For the benefit of those who are unacquainted with the peculiarity of the mountain-base climate, it may be well to mention some of its characteristics. In summer the days are seldom hot, and it is rare to see the thermometer reach 90° at Manitou. The farther one moves eastward from the foot-hills, the greater are to be found the extremes of temperature. Omaha, although much lower in elevation, experiences far greater extremes of heat and cold.

In the dry air of the Colorado plateau the feeling of heat and cold is much less marked. One is not oppressed at all by a temperature of 90°, nor does almost any amount of cold produce the chilliness in the open air, which is really the distressing and objectionable feature of a low temperature. The nights in summer are always cool and refreshing.

It must not be supposed that the climate of Colorado is an equable one, or that there is a distinct dry and rainy

20

season, as in California and on the Pacific Coast. The contrary is true. The diurnal range of temperature, as in all high countries, is great; and there are rains throughout the warm parts of the year and snows in winter, but both are moderate in quantity.

A glance at the reports compiled by the United States Signal Service shows the remarkable fact that 340 out of 365 were " sunny days " in Colorado.

It is not necessary to add an elaborate argument. The conclusion is self-evident and inevitable. The winter climate of Colorado, on the whole, presents advantages for the invalid and the pleasure-seeker that can not fail to command attention. The Denver & Rio Grande is not alone a summer road. Its trains run on schedule time all the year round, and give to the traveling public all the comforts, conveniences, elegancies, and luxuries to be found on any line, with the added attraction of scenery the grandest in the world.

Climate and health go together so closely associated that they have become almost synonymous terms. So beneficial have been found the climatic influences of Colorado that her fame as a sanitarium has become world-wide, and this reputation has been so well-founded in recent years that thousands of people from all parts of America and Europe— from many parts of the world, in fact—are now coming annually to Colorado for recuperation or permanent residence. The dryness and lightness of the air, and its invigorating character, together with the almost constant prevalence of sunshine, impart new energy to the well and a fresh lease of life to those whose constitutions are impaired. All the conditions of life to the newcomer in Colorado are fresh and inspiring, and even wasted and shattered constitutions are restored to vigor. This is illustrated daily by the experiences of thousands who have sought the benign influences of Colorado climate with scarcely a hope, in the beginning, of recovery. These climatic influences are especially beneficial to persons suffering from all kinds of lung diseases, except to those in the last stage of consumption. That the climate itself is a preventative of consumption is evidenced in the fact that phthisis does not originate here. The places of peculiar advantage in seeking health are the towns and cities on the plains, and parks and pleasure resorts on the mountains. The plains in some instances are the most beneficial for a permanent residence, while in other cases the mountains are preferable. There are not exceeding an average of sixty-five cloudy days per year in Colorado, while there are scarcely twenty days that the sun is all the day invisible at any given point. Summer weather usually continues till October, and the autumn till January. Usually the winters are mild, followed by an early spring. In summer the temperature rarely reaches 90° and is normal at 70°. Colorado climate is beneficial not to consumptives alone, but persons of kidney and liver and kindred diseases are benefited both by climate and the mineral waters which everywhere abound in the State, and are especially numerous and available on the Denver & Rio Grande Railroad lines.

The supply of coal in Colorado is inexhaustible, the lignite or brown coal area extending from St. Vrains on the north to the Raton Mountains on the south, about 220 miles in length and varying from twenty to twenty-five miles in breadth, along the eastern base of the mountains. Large portions of this field have been swept away by floods resulting from melting glaciers. The principal developments of this vast field have been made in the vicinity of Trinidad and Walsenburg, Cañon City, Coal Creek, Colorado Springs, Golden, Loveland, Erie, and Boulder. Lignite also exists in North Park and at various points on

V

the divide between North and Middle parks. Jet, or the black variety of coal, occurs in seams from one-half to six inches in width in the shale about Cañon City and Little Fountain Creek. The most important mines of bituminous coal are the Trinidad group and the mines at Crested Butte. Anthracite coal appears to be confined mainly to the coal basins in the Elk Mountain. Native coke is found near Crested Butte, where a dyke of lava has intruded the coal strata. Official geological surveys give a coal-bearing strata of 40,000 square miles, or one-third of the entire area of the State. In 1873, when coal-mining began to take shape as an industry, the output was 69,977 tons; to-day the output is 2,373,954 tons, which comparison gives the reader some idea of the rapidity of its growth.

It has been said, with a great deal of truth, that all of Colorado is a health resort. With its gorgeous peaks and lovely valleys, its beautiful cities on the plains, its forests and its streams, its broad green parks and charming crystal lakes amid the mountains, with its sunshine and pure air, it is certainly a land for man's health and pleasure. The most desirable resorts in the world are upon the lines of the Denver & Rio Grande Railroad. Only eighty miles from Denver, or five miles from Colorado Springs, and nestling at the foot of Pike's Peak, is situated Manitou, that delightful resort for health and pleasure seekers, as popular to-day as Newport or Saratoga, attracting tourists from all parts of the United States and Europe. It has wonderful effervescent and medicinal springs, and is surrounded by more objects of attraction than any other spot in the world, including the Garden of the Gods, Glen Eyrie, Red Rock Cañon, Crystal Park, Engleman's Cañon, Williams Cañon, Manitou Grand Caverns, Cave of the Winds, Ute Pass, Rainbow Falls, and Bear Creek Cañon, all places of great attraction to the visitor. Palmer Lake is a local pleasure resort. Poncha Springs, five miles from Salida, are the noted hot springs—altitude, 7,480 feet—a great health resort. Wagon Wheel Gap, in the picturesque San Luis Valley; hot springs of great curative qualities. It is a favorite health and pleasure resort; the best place in the West for trout fishing. Glenwood Springs is a fine town and a watering place and health resort, having extensive hot springs of great curative properties. Formerly the Mecca of the Indians. Elevation 5,200 feet. Twin Lakes, a beautiful body of crystal water, a pleasure resort and place of entertainment; fine boating and fishing; near Leadville, and reached by the Denver & Rio Grande. Trimble Hot Springs, nine miles from Durango; hot springs noted for remedial qualities. Ouray, hot and cold mineral springs; summer resort. The Great Salt Lake, the famous hot springs of Albuquerque, and numerous other attractions are reached by the Denver & Rio Grande.

The number of irrigable acres in Colorado is placed at 35,000,000 in round numbers, an area fully one-seventh larger than the State of New York. Ten years ago there were but 600 miles of irrigating ditches; now, including canals and laterals, there are 34,000 miles, and $9,500,000 have been expended in their construction. With these figures one can not but be impressed with the possibilities of the future, and believe with the most enthusiastic in the ultimate reclamation of the so-called arid land. It has been by the aid of irrigation that agriculture has been made to vie with mining as the chief industry of the State, and in the future, through its agency, the waters of the mountains will be more generally distributed by reservoir systems. The first of these reservoirs is now being constructed on the line of the Denver & Rio Grande Railroad, between Castle Rock and Palmer Lake. It will irrigate a large portion of the divide country. Of so vast an extent

is this reservoir that the projectors contemplate the
erection of a hotel and the various appurtenances of a
mountain resort. When the Government puts into execution its vast plan of irrigation the seed so modestly planted
ten years ago will have its fruition. The number of square
miles and the acreage under irrigation are found in the
following table:

	Sq. Miles.	Acres.
San Luis Valley	3.096	1,981,440
Southwestern Colorado	1,080	691,200
Grand River Valley	360	230,400
Gunnison and Uncompahgre Valleys	720	460,800
Northwestern Colorado	1,980	1,267,200
North Central Colorado	720	460,800
Small areas	3,600	2,304,000
Eastern Colorado	41,868	26,795,520
	54,000	34,560,000

In addition to these irrigated lands may be placed the
Arkansas Valley, from Pueblo to the Kansas State line, and
the country between Cherry Creek and the foot-hills, and
from Cherry Creek Cañon to Denver. During the past
twelve months there has been an increased activity in this
sort of construction. It is a record unprecedented in irrigation, and taken in connection with the organization of
new companies, this fact indicates no limit to this species
of development.

Even the people of Colorado do not comprehend that in
this State may be grown fruit of a superior quality to that
raised in the orchards of California. The pears and
peaches are more luscious, and all the boasted varieties of
California grapes are here grown successfully. The truth
of these statements was satisfactorily demonstrated at the

recent State fair in Pueblo, and by the fruit exhibit made by the Bureau of Immigration and Statistics at Chicago last fall. The apple, for luxurious growth and flavor, is without a superior in any State, and the orchards of this fruit alone aggregate half a million trees. The success with which grape culture has been conducted indicates for the future a great vintage industry. Fruit-tree planting is progressing at an enormous rate. It is profitable. In 1891 the number of trees planted was 200,000, the yield of apples was 60,000 bushels, and the largest yield from a single orchard of 2,000 trees was 15,000 bushels. The yield last year almost doubled that of the year previous. Strawberries, raspberries, blackberries, gooseberries, and currants are prolific, and for size and flavor are unsurpassed. They grow on the highest mountain and in the lowest valley, and the yield is from 3,000 to 6,000 quarts per acre. One of the most profitable of the recent plantings, in the direction of fruit-plants, is that of the watermelon. In the Arkansas Valley they grow in great abundance, and are of superior merit to the Georgia melon. In fact most varieties of fruit indigenous to the temperate zone are successfully grown in Colorado. Fruit culture is no longer an experiment; it is a great success, and in the future will take its place as a distinctive and most profitable industry.

Colorado's future as a great manufacturing State is assured. In her hills, upon her mountain sides, on the plains, and in the valleys, her deposits of raw material abound, both in variety and richness, second to no other State in the Union. In fact she stands alone in this respect. At present these resources are undeveloped; the surface has been merely touched, and yet this superficial view reveals to the observer possibilities beyond conception. As this empire, of which Colorado is the geographical center, becomes settled more thickly, the demand upon these resources will increase, and with this increasing demand manufactures will multiply, and soon every article known to the trade will be furnished direct from her vast deposits. Not only will she supply the wants of her own and contiguous territories, but in time markets remote will come to Colorado for supplies. The abundance of the raw material and the economy in manufacturing will level competition, and the high quality of the product will place her supreme in the world's commercial marts. The results of last year, aggregating $50,000,000 in the reported values of the manufacturing product in eighteen cities, give some conception of Colorado's manufacturing future; and it has only been a very short time since, in the whole breadth of the State, when not a single article was manufactured, and everything used was shipped from eastern cities at enormous prices. Within the past year the following manufactories have been added: A paper-mill, a match factory, a cotton-mill, a woolen-mill, a boot and shoe factory, an overall factory, and a knit-underwear establishment. The manufactured product of 1892 will not fall below $75,-000,000.

Colorado continues to be the paradise of the sportsman. Its myriads of streams teem with mountain-trout; the forests are, as ever, the domain of the elk, deer, and other game; and its many lakes, while abounding in fish, are the haunts for the wild feathery tribe, and offer great attraction for both rod and gun. Everywhere on the various lines of the Denver & Rio Grande the tourist and the pleasure-seeker at home may find a field of sport to his liking. Should he choose a day of recreation after small game, he may stop off in the valleys among the farms, and a bag of birds and rabbits will be his trophy. For elk and deer he may follow the valley of the Upper Arkansas, deploying to the near-by hills, or go to the valleys and

mountains of Southern Colorado, or follow the line of the
Denver & Rio Grande down to Gunnison, or cross the
range to Glenwood, and search the wooded hills and the
glens and valleys of the Yampa and the Grand; thence
southward, via Ouray, he may follow the Dolores from the
San Miguel to the San Juan and Muncos, following the
footsteps of the Indians, now departed, upon their favorite hunting-grounds. For the angler, as has been stated,
fish are abundant in all the streams and lakes reached by the
Denver & Rio Grande; but for the best sport and most enjoy-
able entertainment Wagon Wheel Gap, on the Rio Grande del
Norte, in Rio Grande County, is conceded to be the choice
of all places. This is both a pleasure and a health resort,
affording at the same time rest and recreation for the sick
and weary, and rare amusement for the invalid and the
tourist alike. At this point the finest of mountain-trout
are always abundant, and the angler may enjoy himself
with the speckled beauties to his heart's content. The
Gunnison River likewise abounds in fine trout, and there
are many points of advantage on this as many other streams
along the line of the Denver & Rio Grande.

Ores are found under all conceivable conditions in Colorado, and, as a rule, in sufficient quantities to admit of
their profitable extraction. In the metamorphosed granite
mountains of the main range the typical fissure veins, with
well-defined and nearly perpendicular walls, are found
often aggregated in great numbers, and universally min-
eralized to a profitable degree. In the trachytic and por-
phyric districts rich fissures also prevail, running very high
in silver as a rule, while occasionally the precious metals
are associated with such quantities of lead or copper ore
that the base metals more than pay all cost of mining and
treating the ore. In other sections, again, where there
have been large overflows of prophyry upon the carbon-

iferous or silurian limestone, great deposits of silver lead ore are found, often covering many acres of ground like vast coal-beds. To this latter class belong the mines of Leadville, which in the past ten years have yielded over $100,000,000. Also the mines about Aspen, Robinson, Red Cliff, Monarch, White Pine, and Rico. Wherever the deposits, however, and whatever the character of the mineral, the result is the same—an increase in the wealth of the State where developed. A number of valuable and important discoveries of gold and silver have been made this year (1892). The enormous deposits of silver at Crede promise to make it a rival of Leadville, while the immense gold-fields at Cripple Creek, near the line of this road, will add millions of dollars to the yellow metal wealth of the country. Rico, in the San Juan country, will produce millions of dollars more this year than ever before in its history. The quantity of the precious metal and the prosperity of the mining sections are only measured by the energy of the communities themselves and the extent of the capital employed. The record of the mining industry last year can be gleaned in the subjoined table:

	1889.	1890.
Silver, ounces	21,119,613	25,788,819
Gold, "	194,908	4,016,229
Lead, tons	3,166,970	3,932,814
Copper, pounds	3,127,739	2,422,000

The estimate for 1889 does not include the metals contained in the ore shipped out of the State, while that for 1890 does include them.

Colorado has exceeded every other section in the growth of her farming industry. This growth has been phenomenal. In 1880 the State imported 500,000 bushels of wheat, 2,000,000 bushels of corn, 500,000 bushels of potatoes,

1,000,000 bushels of oats, and 100,000 tons of hay. Last year there were produced in the State about 10,000,000 bushels of cereals, and instead of importing, the State exports; and in eastern markets Colorado wheat and oats command a premium. So great has been the development that authorities on agriculture assert that the agricultural output exceeds that of mining, which assertion is contradicted by mining people. But be this as it may, no other section presents a parallel to the rapid advance of agriculture in this State. One-half of the 66,880,000 acres of land in Colorado is estimated as agricultural land, of which 12,000,000 acres can be turned to the plow. There are now 2,000,000 acres under cultivation. The remarkable feature of this progress is the success attained by the " rain belt," which only a few years since was considered irreclaimable land. All over the State farming has been profitable, and by the contiguity of markets prompt returns for the products are the rule. This has induced immigration, and is one of the contributory causes of the influx of settlers into every section where cheap lands may be obtained.

IRON.—The largest deposit of iron in Colorado is in Gunnison County, and when taken in connection with the fact that in this locality cheap fuel abounds, it is a deposit of magnitude unequaled anywhere in this country. By this fortuitous combination of deposits, No. 1 Bessemer pig iron can be produced at Gunnison for a cost not exceeding $12 per ton, or 50 per cent less than the price at Pittsburg. The deposit is near Sargent, on the Denver & Rio Grande Railroad. With an outcrop that is enormous and high in grade, it extends at intervals for a mile on the mountain side. A number of openings have been made, one of which is a tunnel run across the vein ninety-seven feet and an open cut exposing a face of forty feet all in solid iron. There are about fifty acres in the five iron claims which compose the White Pine deposit. There are iron beds on Gold Hill and Cebolla rivers. At the latter place the iron lies in an immense ledge of unknown depth. Iron abounds in other portions of the State, especially in Chaffee County, where the Colorado Coal & Iron Company of Pueblo have been drawing material for the manufacture of railroad iron, merchant bar, and steel. Iron and steel can be manufactured as cheaply in Colorado as in any other section of the United States, and the advantages that contribute to the State's superiority in this respect are the increasing demands, which can not be affected by the overproduction of the East and South; no rival point west of the Rocky Mountains claiming competitive facilities and an advantageous position as the geographical center of a vast territory; an intelligent class of labor; an abundance of building material and the most extensive fields of coking and fuel coal, and the only anthracite found west of Pennsylvania.

The annual production of 1,000,000 tons of crude pig iron, representing a value of say $14,000,000, the evolution of that 1,000,000 tons of pig iron into its higher products of bar iron, and steel, and sheets, and plates, and machinery, and cars, and locomotives, and pipes, and plows, and other farm implements, and all the long list of appliances and commodities of iron and steel, aggregating in value, at a lower estimation than can be legitimately placed, more than $50,000,000, means more for Colorado than many of her most sanguine advocates have anticipated.

CHAPTER XL.

WHILE dwelling upon the scenes and incidents of my life upon the frontier, and speaking of those with whom I came in contact, I wish to refer to one whose meeting with me toward the latter days of overland travel began with a sincere friendship that has lasted until this day, and will continue to the end of our lives.

The person to whom I refer is Dr. D. Frank Powell, an army surgeon in those days, and whose gallant services as an officer and scout, as well as his striking appearance, gained for him the border cognomens of "White Beaver" (by which he is as frequently called to-day as by his own name) and "The Surgeon Scout," "Mighty Medicine Man," and "Fancy Frank."

Doctor Powell was the firm friend of Buffalo Bill, and his valuable services, rendered as a scout, guide, and Indian-fighter, made him famous as the Surgeon Scout.

His dash and handsome style of dress also gained for him the name of "Fancy Frank," while the other two appellations by which he was known were gained by his skill and service as a surgeon and physician.

When the Indians were stricken with an epidemic of small-pox, although at the time at war with the whites, Surgeon Powell conceived the idea of boldly entering their village and checking the dread disease.

Leaving the fort upon his perilous mission, Surgeon Powell made his way alone to the Indian country, and rode forward at sight of them, making signs of peace.

The astonished red-skins received him with amazement, but, assured that he was in their power, they listened to the bold proposition he had to make them, and which was that

he would check the epidemic then raging or forfeit his own life.

Struck with the boldness of the man, whom they knew so well as the comrade of Buffalo Bill, and who spoke their language fluently, the chiefs listened to all he had to say and then put him to the test.

Then it was that the strange circumstance occurred of a pale-face foe and medicine man *vaccinating* the Indians, young and old, all except the medicine men of the tribe, who would have nothing to do with him.

The result of Doctor Powell's work was that the dread disease was soon checked, and under his care many desperate cases of sickness were cured, and he became the ideal of his friends, who held a grand pow-wow, and presented him with a robe of sixteen white beaver-skins—the white beaver being a sacred animal among them.

Nor was this all, for they made him a mighty medicine man, or chief of their tribe, and bestowed upon him the name of "White Beaver," which he uses to-day in connection with his own name.

A resident now of La Crosse, Wis., Doctor Powell has a large practice there, resides in an elegant home, and is for the fourth time mayor of that beautiful city, and one of the most popular men in the State, socially and politically.

The doctor has been a most extensive traveler, in this country and abroad, and yet each year, for a couple of weeks, entertains as his guests the tribe of Winnebago Indians, of whom he is still the medicine chief, and who make a pilgrimage to see him, consult him as to the affairs of their people, and show him devoted respect during the time they are encamped upon his grounds, where he has a place set apart for them.

A handsome man, of splendid physique, one who has known a strange life of adventure, he is yet as gentle as a woman, and ever generous to those with whom he comes in contact; and this tribute to his worth as a man and skill as physician and surgeon he most justly deserves.

CONCLUSION.

There was but little occurred of very great note west of the Mississippi during the twenties. The State of Missouri was admitted into the sisterhood of the States in the beginning of the twenties; after that there was very little of note that transpired during the twenties, with the exception of a few Indian scares on the frontier of Missouri, which, as a rule, were brought about without any real cause, and some trapping expeditions going west to the Rocky Mountains to trap for beaver fur, and also trading expeditions to Santa Fé, in New Mexico. With those exceptions, everything went along as quiet and almost as calm as a summer morning. In those days the entire community west of the Mississippi River, as well as the States east of it, were self-sustaining, producing all that they consumed in clothing and food, in their own homes, and I might say that this state of things also existed during the term of the thirties. Very little of note occurred outside the regular course of events save the Blackhawk war upon the Upper Mississippi and the appearance of steamboats in the Missouri River, as far west as the west border of the State of Missouri, which commenced in the early thirties, and became a very large source of transportation and passenger travel, and there was also, in the commencement of the thirties, some Mormon elders that came to the county of Jackson, in Missouri, bringing with them the revelations of their

prophet Joseph Smith, and claimed that they had been sent to that county by the direction of the Lord to their prophet to establish the Zion of the Lord, or a " New Jerusalem," and, of course, a new church, which has since kept its existence until the present time, with its head-quarters now in Salt Lake City, Utah. With the arrival of steamboats in the Upper Missouri, farmers commenced to raise hemp and other commodities that they could ship to St. Louis and New Orleans upon the steamers, which was the commencement of the people in that State to market the surplus that they could produce upon their farms; but the advantage of this trade or business only applied to the farmers and producers living in the river counties (I mean the counties located on the river), as it was too costly to haul their products upon wagons and with teams for any great distance; so the steamboat transportation could only be very beneficial to the counties, as above stated, the interior portions of the State having to plod along very much as was the case before steamboats came into use. There was no finer passenger travel ever inaugurated than the accommodations that travelers enjoyed as passengers upon those floating palaces, and I have lived to see them come and go, so far as their operations upon the Missouri is concerned. The Missouri afforded nearly 3,000 miles of water navigation, measured by the windings of the river. I have traveled on steamboats from its mouth, or St. Louis, to the head of navigation at Fort Benton, in Montana.

Now, commencing with the forties, there was nothing of great moment happened until the great freshet of '44, which was the largest flood that has been known in the Missouri, about the mouth of the Caw, in the last seventy-five years, and I think that there never has been in the history of the country as great a flood in the Missouri at

W

that point. In '46 the Mexican War came up, and produced quite a stir among the business men upon the west border of the Missouri, as at that time there was no Kansas and Nebraska, the whole country being called "the Indian Territory" west of the State of Missouri. The Santa Fé trade, by this time, had become a regular annual business, and men had learned how to outfit wagons and teams so as to carry large amounts of merchandise and Government stores from the Missouri River to Santa Fé, N. M. and when General Donathan organized his regiment of troops, by the authority of the Governor of the State of Missouri, to march to Santa Fé, N. M., he found no trouble, neither did the Government, in securing all the transportation necessary to meet any emergency that might arise, with a plain and well-beaten road the entire route that they had to travel, this road having been opened by the merchant-trains in previous years.

In '47 the Mormon leader, Brigham Young, with a company of his elders and members of the church, left the Missouri River in the early spring and traveled 1,000 miles into the interior of the country, and formed a colony in that year in Salt Lake Valley, and named the city that they found Salt City, which proved to be a half-way house, as we might call it, between the Missouri River and the Pacific Coast, which proved of great advantage to the emigrants who left the Missouri in the spring of '49 to reach the gold-fields of California; for it was in '49, or rather the winter of '48, when the placer-gold in California was discovered, and it was on this account that '49 became one of the most eventful years of the forties, the Mexican War having closed, and peace negotiations established in '48, which gave the United States the entire domain of the Pacific Coast lying north of the line now dividing Old Mexico from the United States. There were vast numbers of

brave and daring citizens from almost every State in the
Mississippi Valley who attempted to reach California by
the overland route, and at no time, not even during the
Mexican War, up to '49, had there ever been any overland
travel to compare with that of '49. Tens of thousands of
emigrants or gold-hunters left the west border at that time,
outfitting themselves, some with ox-teams and some with
mules and the best wagons that could be found in the
market, loaded to the guards with supplies of food and
clothing to make the trip and return, for at that time none
of them expected to remain or make their homes in California; if so, it must have been a very small percentage of
the number. Many of them died with cholera on the way;
the large majority, however, reached their destination, but
many of them through great suffering and privation from
one cause or another. One of the misfortunes that attended the majority of them was want of experience in
traveling their animals; they started off in too big a hurry,
and pressed their teams too much at the outset, the result
of which was, many of their animals died from fatigue,
caused by overtraveling, long before they reached the Pacific Coast, the result of which was to leave on the road,
or rather in the road, often the valuables that they had
secured in the outset for their comfort and preservation
when they reached the land of gold.

The year '50 was also a very fatal year to emigration,
for it did not cease with '49, but the success of the " forty-
niners " in gathering gold proved to be a great inducement
to the country to continue the movements of '49 in the way
of outfitting and emigrating to the Pacific Coast; in fact, it
continued in a greater or smaller degree during the entire
fifties; but in the year '50, as in '49, there were great numbers died with cholera. It was fatal among the emigrants
from their starting point from Missouri till they would

reach the Rocky Mountains, after which time the cases of death from cholera were very few compared with what they suffered upon the plains before reaching the mountains. There were but few cases that occurred after they reached the Sacramento Valley in California. Instead of returning, as the most of the gold-seekers intended to do on leaving their homes, they found California a delightful climate, with rich and fertile valleys, and many, very many of them concluded, after having a year's experience in the country, to become citizens, and a little later in the fifties, there were a great many people in the Western States who sold their homes and started with their families for the golden shores of the Pacific—in other words, for California—in view of adopting that State for their future homes. I was acquainted with numbers who did so, and who I have since met at their homes in California, who were delighted with the change that they made, and it is a very common thing now, after the country has been settled so many years, to find numbers of people there who think that California is the only country fit to live in.

Returning to the fifties, there was nothing of great note happened until the admission of Kansas and Nebraska in 1854, when floods of emigrants, mostly from the Northern States, passed into those Territories. A number, however, were from the Southern States, and held pro-slavery views.

In '56 what is known as the Kansas war occurred, from the invasion of men from Missouri and other States.

In '57 and '58 the Mormon war occurred, when Gen. Albert Sidney Johnston was sent to Utah with an army of 5,000 regulars.

In 1859 the great Comstock mine was developed, and it added to the currency of the world between one and two hundred millions of dollars in gold and silver. Also in '58 began the Pike's Peak excitement, which resulted in the settlement of Denver.

In 1860 the election of Abraham Lincoln was followed, in '61, by the breaking out of the Civil War.

In '62 the initial steps for the establishment of the Union and Central Pacific railroads were taken, and the idea was fulfilled in '69. Daily stages were put on in 1859 from the Missouri River to Denver and Salt Lake.

It was during the sixties that the telegraph was established across the continent, following in the track of the Pony Express.

Gold was discovered in Montana in the sixties, resulting in the settlement of that Territory.

During the seventies and eighties, the most important happenings in our country were the remarkable growth of the railroad interests.

THE END.